North Somerset, 1205ad

It was just a hollow in the ground, a bowl shaped depression in a meadow that looked as if a tree had been ripped from the earth, roots and all. The limestone bedrock was exposed on one side and a gnarled old thorn tree created a patch of shade at the base of the waist high rock face. Sheep and cattle often congregated there to shelter from the heat of the summer sun or the chill of winter winds. They had worn away the grass and topsoil to make dusty scoops to lie in. In the heat of summer, the place stank of urine and cow shit and, although no-one had ever noticed, the hollow was peculiar in that it never flooded, even after the heaviest rain.

The meadow with the mysterious hollow at its centre lay below a wooded escarpment that formed the northern boundary of a broad and fertile river valley. The river, known back then simply as the bourne – the river – flowed from east to west on its gently meandering journey to the sea. Between the hollow and the bourne, the meadow sloped gently down to within a stone's throw of the water's edge where it steepened finally to end in a reedy bank.

A young man by the name of Thomas Howk farmed the area between the escarpment and the river. He didn't own the land, the King did, but his tenancy allowed him to graze his small herd of scraggy sheep and his twelve dairy cows. The year 1205 was a very dry year. Little rain had fallen during the preceding winter and both spring and summer proved hotter and drier than anyone could remember.

A Well Kept Secret

A novel by David Hermelin

Copyright © David Hermelin, 2016

For my wonderful wife, Sam

Contents

As Lulius – July – gave way to Augustus, life became ever more tough for the inhabitants of the valley and their animals. As the dewponds, pools and wells dried up on the plateau above the scarp, more and more farmers moved their livestock down to the river valley. There were confrontations as grazing became ever more scarce. Thomas Howk fought hard for his land and his short stretch of bourne bank where his cattle and sheep could drink from the little muddy water that remained in the almost dried up bed.

Then came just another desperate day when the sky was as blue as ever and the sun beat down so that it seemed as if the whole world would shrivel in the heat. That afternoon, when Thomas started to round up his sheep to take them down to the river, a bunch of three old ewes had taken shelter under the thorn tree in the hollow. Thomas noticed that they were pawing at the ground, panting in the heat, desperate for something, but what? Surely there could be no water there. He thought that maybe they were after roots.

Thomas walked across to hurry them out and away down the field and at that very instant, when he was barely three paces from them, two of his sheep vanished.

One moment all three were there, pale shapes in the shade of the tree, scraping and scuffing at the dust, then, an eye blink later there was just one, scrambling in panic away from a gaping black hole in the earth.

Thomas dropped to his knees, terrified, his hands clasped in front of his face, his heart pounding in his chest with superstitious dread. He muttered all the prayers he could remember as he knelt, waiting for something else to happen – an explosion, a burst of flame maybe. Anything would have been better than the dreadfully normal silence that lay across the baking landscape. It must have been God, Thomas thought, or the Devil Himself. Much more likely the Devil, dragging them down below like that. That was not God's style, surely.

Just as he dared to open his eyes again, a slither of dry soil disappeared into the darkness, leaving a feathery trail of dust in the still air. When nothing more happened and five long minutes had passed, Thomas climbed slowly to his feet and moved a little closer to the edge of the hollow, close enough so that he could see into the terrible hole at its centre. Nervously, he picked up a small stone and tossed it into the darkness, hoping to gauge the depth of the pit. He heard nothing. Then, with his feet and legs tensed and ready to run for his life, and careful not to get too close to the top of the slope, he picked up a much larger rock, something nearer the size of his own head, and heaved it over and into the centre of the hole. Three heartbeats later, he heard the sound of a distant booming splash.

Chapter 1

North Somerset, April 1979

The woman soon to become Britain's first ever female Prime Minister stared straight ahead, her face ashen beneath the brim of a severe black hat, her familiar politician's smile replaced for once with a truly honest emotion, grief.

The caption beneath the photograph read: In the presence of his grieving family, wartime comrades and fellow members of parliament, Airey Neave, victim of an IRA bomb, was laid to rest in the parish church of St Mary's in the village of Longworth, Oxfordshire yesterday.

The accompanying text explained how, right from her earliest days in Parliament, the man had been her trusted mentor and closest friend. Surely there was little wonder she looked the way she did.

The folded newspaper lay on top of a mess of maps, paperwork and the remains of a takeaway breakfast on the passenger seat of the stationary car.

Kate picked it up and read the article for what felt like the hundredth time that morning. By then she knew the piece backwards, but a single word stood out with stark simplicity from all the rest – bomb.

Hadn't she had enough of bombs to last more than one lifetime?

Hadn't everyone?

Having fled her Irish homeland to escape the Troubles, she had effectively abandoned twenty-seven precious years of family and friends. But even after such a sacrifice, it seemed she hadn't run far enough.

So the man was a bloody Tory, she thought, and a bloody Englishman, but he didn't deserve an end like that. Hadn't he escaped from Colditz or some such place back in the war? The man was a hero and no mistake, yet those bastards had still blown him to fragments without even the courage to look him in the eye.

Ever since she had snatched the newspaper from the rack in the filling station, she had hardly been able to tear her eyes away from the inset picture of the man's gutted car, with part of what looked like its gearbox lying in the road beside the torn and gaping hole where the passenger door had been.

God knows what state the poor man would have been in.

It brought back too many painful and distressing memories – the stench of blood, dust and acrid smoke, the sirens and the breathless screams.

She shook her head in angry despair.

Was there no end to it?

And, as a further insult, it seemed that even the English press couldn't get their facts right. Didn't everyone know that it wasn't the IRA that planted the bomb under the man's car, but the Irish National Liberation Army as they so grandly called themselves?

God knows they'd no right to call themselves human let alone Irish.

Enough!

She screwed the newspaper into a rough and angry bundle and stuffed it behind her seat out of sight and, at least temporarily, out of mind.

To ease the accumulated stiffness of the long drive and to give herself a few moments to think, Kate stretched her back, pushing herself back into her seat and wincing at the familiar stab of pain from her leg as it straightened.

After two long, calming breaths, she sifted through the remaining mess on the passenger seat and pulled out the solicitor's letter detailing her appointment that morning.

No mistake then.

Dear God, so this must be it.

This was what she got for dragging herself out of bed at five in the morning and driving for three and a half hours through murderous traffic and pouring rain – a prospect that would have made an east London slum look attractive.

The advertisement had read well enough: 'Self-contained furnished flat in one wing of a Manor House, best suited to a single, professional person. No pets, no children, ample parking and use of grounds'.

It had sounded like the answer to her prayers.

At least the directions had been good – after finding the estate's brick built boundary wall, all she'd had to do was follow it for half a mile until she got to the entrance gateway.

A small, sun blistered sign screwed to the wall read HAWKSWELL HOUSE in white capital letters on a black background with, underneath, No trespassers, vagrants or uninvited tradespeople.

So welcoming.

The boundary wall curved inwards on either side of the open space where she'd pulled up, each wing terminating in a crumbling brick pillar topped with a badly eroded guardian lion. A pair of massive but decrepit wrought iron gates hung wide open and, judging from the build-up of soil and debris, looked as if they hadn't moved in decades. To the left of the gateway, a fly tipped fridge lay alongside some rotting rolls of old carpet and a pile of fox ripped bin bags.

As if the entrance itself wasn't off-putting enough, what lay beyond almost caused her to turn around and head straight back to London. Impenetrable banks of long untended greenery reared up and over a potholed driveway creating a dark and forbidding tunnel.

A lorry roared past, rocking Kate's Mini on its suspension and hurling filthy water against the back window.

She leaned back against the headrest for a moment and closed her eyes. Right then, the entire exhausting journey was beginning to look like a complete waste of time.

It had all started two weeks earlier with a message on her answerphone.

"Is that Kate O'Donnell? Oh, hi. Er, my name is Andy Travis at GreenGauge, you may have heard of us. We ran with that article you wrote for the Guardian about developers building on floodplains, you know the one? We spoke briefly on the phone back in August I think it was. Anyway, as you're not there right now, I wonder if you could maybe give me a call as soon as you get this message. You should already have the number, but just in case, it's…"

Kate picked up the message when she got back to her basement flat at one in the morning after a horrendous day chasing a pollution story in Huddersfield. She recognised Andy Travis's Californian drawl from when they'd spoken before.

Not only did she remember the man, she also remembered that particular article very well. GreenGauge was a small circulation but passionate environmental magazine, and they had taken her Guardian piece and plunged their teeth right into the maggoty meat at its heart. They'd given planners, developers, local politicians and a whole raft of government departments a really bad time for a few months until something even more offensive came along.

She'd hoped at the time that the piece might have led to a closer link with the magazine but after she hadn't heard anything for six weeks, she'd put that dream to bed and carried on, as she put it, prostituting herself to the lowest bidder.

She thought about phoning back right away, knowing that magazine editors, especially those of the smaller magazines, seldom slept. But then she thought better of it.

Whatever it was could wait until the morning.

When she did phone the GreenGauge offices the next day, she was put straight through to the boss.

"Kate. Thanks for calling back. Look, can we meet up sometime soon?"

"Wow. Er, yes. Whenever you want."

"How about tomorrow?"

She thought for a moment and decided to be a little more proactive.

"I could do something today if it's that important."

She heard a slight chuckle.

"Do you reckon you could get to Bath by lunchtime?"

What?

"Did you say Bath, as in City of?"

"I sure did."

"But I thought you were based in London."

Andy really laughed then.

"Have you seen the cost of renting office space in the city, Kate? It's outrageous. We couldn't have lasted a month at those rates. We've done some jiggery pokery with the mail and the phones so most people think we're based there, although I'm not sure it matters much anymore. So what do you reckon, think you can make it?"

Kate looked at her watch. It was nine thirty.

She reckoned it was about two hours to Bath once she was clear of London traffic. She'd need to wash her hair and change into something suitably impressive, but she reckoned she could get there.

"One o'clock, OK?"

"That'll be great. There's a pub called the Royal Oak, it's on the A36 just before you get into Bath. It'll save you the hassle of parking and it does great food. See you there as near one as you can make it."

She got there at twelve thirty and decided to wait in her car, while running over all the reasons she could think of why Andy Travis would want to drag her all the way down to the West Country for lunch. Fifteen minutes after she arrived, a beat up Volkswagen camper pulled into the car park with GreenGauge graphics on its door panels. The guy that uncurled himself from the driver's seat must have been well over six feet tall and, with his long grey hair tied back in a ponytail, faded Levis and a beaten up leather jacket, looked a lot more like a country and western singer than a magazine editor.

He glanced around the car park before catching sight of Kate, who gave him a nervous wave.

He even sounded like a bluegrass boy as he gripped her hand in both of his.

"Hey, Kate. Really glad you could make it. Hope you've not been waiting too long. Come on in out of the wind, I've got us a table. Guess you're wondering what this is all about huh? Well, don't you worry, I'll put you out of your misery just as soon as we've gotten ourselves a drink."

Putting her out of her misery didn't even come close.

Talking like a machine gun, Andy Travis blew her away by offering her the post of Assistant Editor of GreenGauge magazine at a salary that was, although modest, a hell of a lot preferable to the hand-to-mouth existence of freelancing.

"Of course, it's primarily a journalistic role, but you'll get to edit your own work which can't be bad. It'll mean relocating of course, but we can help with expenses at least. We ain't very big yet and it'll be a while before we can compete with the big boys, but we carry some serious clout and we're building a hell of a reputation for digging the dirt. So, what do you think?"

What did she think? Jesus.

"I've only got the obvious question for now, Andy. Why me?"His face split into a broad grin.

"Because of your work, Kate, simple as that. To be honest, I would have offered you the job right after we ran that piece on flood plains, but we didn't have the funds right then. Amazingly, it was as a direct result of that little shit storm that brought us to the notice of one of our biggest sponsors yet. So in a way you were pretty much responsible for creating this opportunity for yourself. If, that is, you reckon it's the sort of opportunity you might think about taking on."

"Think? I don't need to think. I might be crazy in a lot of ways, but I'm certainly not stupid. This is the opportunity of a lifetime and we both know it. I sure hope I can justify your faith in me and not let you down."

"OK then. So you won't mind moving down here?"

"Andy, the sooner I get out of London, the better. I've just about coped with it for the last three years, but I can't face the idea of another three. I live in a hideous basement in Lewisham, working all the hours God sends just to put food in my belly. When do you want me to start?"

"How about next month, or as soon as you can find somewhere to live."

They shook on the deal and, if Kate hadn't got to drive back to London, they would probably have sunk a bottle or two. As it was, they each had coffee, agreeing to defer the celebration until later.

It was only later, when trawling through the local property papers that Andy had mailed her, that she discovered a problem. Domestic property rents in Bath were astronomical, way more than she could afford.

Then, just as she was about to revise her plans down to a bedsit, her mother suggested that she contact her cousin Michael, a lawyer in Bristol, to see if he knew of anywhere suitable in the area. When she received a letter the very next day containing an advertisement for a pair of self-contained flats that were about to come onto the market in a village only twelve miles south of Bath, it looked as if the advice had paid off. The rent was apparently negotiable and, if Kate got her skates on, she might just get lucky.

Within hours of receiving the letter, she had called the agent and arranged an appointment to view. That had been three days ago and now here she was, wondering if the place could possibly be worth trashing her car's suspension.

The dashboard clock told her she'd got a little under fifteen minutes to make up her mind. She forced a smile. Welcome to Wuthering Heights, Cathy. Then, almost but not quite laughing, she started the car and eased forwards through the gateway.

The festoons of overhanging foliage brushed wetly against the roof and sides of the car as she crept forwards into the gloom, headlights on and wipers sweeping away the cascade of heavy drips. While the going was not quite as bad as she had feared, even at walking pace it threatened to shake her Mini back into its component parts.

Luckily, barely fifty metres from the entrance, the track took a sharp left and plunged her back into daylight at the moment the rain stopped and a watery spring sun burst free from the hurrying clouds.

Kate stopped, shielded her eyes against the sudden glare and stared in astonishment.

Just like a Victorian landscape painting, a broad expanse of freshly mown meadow sloped gently downhill to a magnificent old manor house placed almost as if to complete the view. The scene was so bucolic and unexpected that she had to glance in her mirror to check that the vegetated tunnel was still there and she hadn't inadvertently slipped through some Narnian portal.

Turning off the engine, she opened her window, the quick wash of chilly air bringing the rich green scent of grass clippings. What little traffic noise that still filtered through from the road was so muffled by the high brick wall and the dense banks of foliage that she could ignore it. Otherwise, all she could hear was bird song and the gentle murmur of wind in the trees.

Now this is a bit more like it.

Directly in front of the house, surrounded by the faint geometric outlines of what might once have been a formal garden, an ornamental lake gleamed like a silver disk in the sunlight while to her left, the lawns continued down to a line of willows bordering a wide meandering river. Beyond, a patchwork of fields sloped upwards again to a distant wooded horizon. To her right the lawns were bordered by the boundary wall that curved away downhill towards a dense conifer plantation that filled the valley from side to side.

After taking in the view and just daring to hope that her journey might not have been in vain after all, Kate continued slowly down the gently sloping drive to eventually pull up in the centre of a threadbare expanse of mossy gravel fronting the house.

And there all her misgivings returned in a chilling rush.

Up close the house looked as neglected as its entrance gateway.

Crumbling stonework was streaked with dark green water stains from cracked downpipes while tufts of grass and Buddleia poked from the sagging guttering. Twin clusters of chimneys wore crow's nests like untidy hats, while sun blistered shutters blinded most of the windows like cataracts. The few that weren't blanked off stared balefully across the forecourt providing the only evidence that the place was occupied at all.

If the house is in such a state, God knows what the flat'll be like.

But before she could give in to her overwhelming instinct to drive away, a movement at one of the staring windows suggested that she had been seen.

Ad so, not wishing to appear rude, she braced herself, reckoning that as she'd come this far she might as well go the last few yards.

She flipped down the sun visor and took a quick look in the vanity mirror. The thin strip of scar tissue that ran in front of her ear to her jaw line would inevitably invite a question. Maybe one day, she thought, but not today. She quickly reached behind her head and released the elastic band holding her hair. A quick shake and the disfigurement was hidden behind a mass of rebellious copper locks.

She grinned at her reflection.

Hey there, Queenie mad hair. Time for battle.

A flight of worn stone steps led up to a covered portico and an imposing nail studded door with a huge bronze lion's head knocker at its centre. A modern plastic bell push to one side looked incongruous but a lot less daunting than the lion.

Kate pressed the button and heard a faint chime from inside the house.

She straightened her jacket, held her breath and crossed her fingers.

Although a little disappointed when the heavy door failed to creak, her faith in the overall illusion was restored when she came face-to-face with the man who opened it.

Dressed in an ancient wax jacket, baggy corduroy trousers, heavy leather boots and a tweed cap, the old boy who squinted out into the brightness of the day looked every inch an elderly version of Bronte's Heathcliff. His weather-beaten face and hands could have been made from the same material as his jacket.

When he spoke, it was with a soup rich Somerset accent.

"Good morning my dear. You must be Miss O'Donnell come to take a look at the flat, then."

"Ms O'Donnell," she corrected instinctively.

Without so much as a blink, the old man looked her up and down in her gunmetal grey business suit and nodded slowly before continuing, "Would you be so kind as to drive your car around to the rear of the house... Miss?" He gestured to his right.

"Just follow the drive round to the carriage gate and go on through into the yard. I'll meet you there in a moment or two."

He stepped back into the deeply shadowed hallway and closed the door softly.

So I'm not grand enough for the front door then. Kate thumped into her seat, slammed the car door and started up.

Arrogant bloody English, they're all the same.

The track, now mercifully free of potholes, ran below a stone balustraded terrace before turning sharp right around to the rear of the house where a carriage gateway provided access to a cobbled courtyard. Bordered at its far end by the rear elevation of the main house, a pair of three storey wings bracketed the square.

Piles of farmyard junk, nettle and bramble shrouded, littered the periphery, although the central area had been kept clear, presumably to provide the 'ample parking' detailed in the advertisement.

As Kate climbed out of her car, the old boy appeared from a doorway to her right and beckoned her over. But as she approached, lips buttoned tight on her annoyance, he stepped forward with an outstretched hand and a disarming smile.

"Ms O'Donnell. I'm really sorry about the Miss. Can't say as how I quite know what the difference is, but I get the feeling that it matters. Won't happen again, I promise. I'm Tom Gerrard. I look after the gardens here, along with just about everything else. I been asked to show you around the flat."

Kate shook his warm, hard hand, unable to contain an answering grin.

Afterwards, she reckoned it was his eyes that did for her. They were as clear and bright as raindrops, and looked as if they were more used to laughing than frowning. Whatever the reason, the fuse was snuffed out and the incendiary put away for later.

Hopefully she wouldn't need it at all.

"No apology necessary, really, Mr Gerrard. Tell you what, if I can call you Tom and you call me Kate, we won't have to worry about the Miss, Ms or Mister again."

The man grinned, his features almost disappearing into a web of wrinkles.

"That's very kind of you Kate. Tom'll be fine. Now then, if you'd like to follow me."

Once inside, they climbed a set of steep stairs to the first floor and, a few yards along a corridor, came to freshly painted door, which Tom unlocked before holding it open and ushering her through.

She hardly noticed the acrid tang of fresh gloss paint as she stood on the threshold, frozen in place as if she'd been nailed to the newly polished floorboards. Confronting her was a spacious, high ceilinged room with three tall sash windows, their wooden shutters clipped back, which looked out across the grounds to the horizon beyond the river. It was one of the lightest, brightest rooms Kate had ever been in, the low spring sunlight laid in wide golden stripes across the floor. A trendy looking breakfast bar separated a kitchenette from the rest of the room, which was sparsely but elegantly furnished with pieces quite obviously culled from other parts of the house.

Everything looked unbelievably bright and clean and… dry.

Tom touched her arm and pointed to a doorway to her left.

"The bedroom is through there."

A massive brass bedstead set against one wall dominated the bedroom, which was only marginally smaller than the sitting room. An enormous armoire and equally huge dressing table and chest of drawers completed the furnishings. Kate couldn't hide her wide-eyed, delighted grin.

"Dear God, Tom. I've never seen anything like it in my life. It's amazing. The whole place is so… I mean it's just unbelievable."

Tom smiled.

"So you like it then?"

"Like it? Jesus, you should see the place I'm in now, a grotty little basement in the middle of London. It's no bigger than a boot box, with damp running down the walls and dark even with all the lights on. This is totally bloody amazing, excuse my Irish."

Tom laughed, "I'll take that as a yes. I'm pleased. I think you and Hawkswell will suit one another nicely." He paused a moment. "If you'll excuse me saying so, your manner of speaking sounds very familiar. Would I be right in thinking that you come from the southern part of Ireland?"

"The Republic you mean? Well, you were nearly right. Not the north for certain, but the west. I was born and raised in County Clare, in a little place called Clonkerry, on the Shannon. I'm one hundred per cent made in Ireland and proud of it."

"Well now, that's nice to hear… especially after recent goings on. There's not a lot to be proud of on either side, if you know what I mean."

He left a silence which Kate chose not to fill and, after a brief pause stepped across to indicate another door leading off the bedroom.

"I'm afraid this part of the flat might not come up to some folks' expectations, since it's not been modernised hardly at all."

That part of the flat turned out to be a classic Victorian bathroom with a cast iron roll top bath that would have graced a palace, with toilet and hand basin to match. The single concession to modern living was an electric shower on the wall above the bath.

Kate laughed, "Well it might not be to anyone else's taste, Tom, but it surely is to mine. This is proper plumbing and no mistake. I'll bet it'd take an hour to fill that thing!" She pointed at the bath.

"That's why there's a shower, Miss… er sorry, Kate."

After a closer look at the bedroom and a cursory peek into the wardrobe and chest of drawers, Kate stood in numbed amazement as Tom talked her through the kitchen facilities, the wood burning stove, the night storage heaters and explained about how the hot water and the cooker worked. Still listening with half an ear, she wandered over to the windows.

The view was quite simply irresistible.

Directly below the windows lay a wide, flag-stoned terrace with the low ornamental balustrade she'd driven alongside when she first arrived. Beyond, the prairie of mown grass stretched a hundred yards down to the slow moving river and the lichen blotched roof tiles of what looked like an old boathouse.

Against all her best intentions, she dared to imagine for a second or two what it might be like to wake up to a view like that every morning, with the mist rising on the river and the sound of rooks in the trees.

Tom's voice broke into her reverie.

"Is there anything else you'd like to know, Miss?"

She realised she hadn't been listening properly, that he'd been nattering away and she hadn't heard a word.

"Er, sorry Tom. I was miles away. So is this where you break the bad news?"

He looked puzzled.

"Bad news?"

"The cost. The rent, I mean."

"Ah, no. Not me. That's for the mistress to talk through with you."

Kate couldn't help smile at 'the mistress'.

"Er, I'm sorry but who exactly would the mistress be?"

"Miss Penelope Townshend. Her what owns this place, always has done. She deals with all that sort of thing."

"OK. So when can I see her and get the bad news over?"

He smiled. "Right after I've shown you around the rest of the place. Don't worry, it won't take long." He lowered his voice, a habit Kate would come to recognise. "And don't you fret too much about the rent neither. I'm sure you'll be able to sort something out. Don't tell her I said so, but her's much more concerned about getting the nicest possible people in here than she is about the money."

As they closed the door on the flat and its fabulous view, Kate wondered what the chances were of her ever setting eyes on the place again.

As stated in the advertisement, there were only to be two flats at Hawkswell, both on the first floor of the west wing, the second not due to be finished for another few weeks. The floor above, once servants' quarters, was out of bounds because of its unsafe floorboards, while the ground floor rooms were also empty, stripped bare, their doors tightly closed.

Kate's leg began to give her trouble during the descent down the steep stairs, and as soon as Tom noticed that she was struggling, he slowed his pace to match hers without comment.

She felt his discretion deserved an explanation, no matter how untrue.

"Car crash four years ago. Totalled my left leg and ankle so now I'm full of rusty old scaffolding. On the flat or going uphill is fine, it's coming down that's the bugger."

Tom instinctively glanced down at Kate's trouser clad leg.

"I would never have noticed until just then on the stairs, my dear. Is it very painful?"

"Only when it rains." Kate laughed. "I know it's what everyone says, but it really is true. When the weather turns damp or wet, I know long before anyone else." Anxious to change the subject, she asked, "Is Miss Townshend thinking about letting any more of the house?"

"No," Tom replied, "Just the two flats. It's the plumbing you see. Too expensive to put in more bathrooms. This wing used to be guest apartments, so it was quite easy to convert."

At the bottom of the stairs, heading back towards the courtyard, Kate passed what looked like a strong room door. If it wasn't solid iron or steel, it was certainly heavily reinforced and hung on massively strong hinges, its single keyhole covered with a metal flap. On the point of mentioning it, she saw that Tom was already five or six paces ahead, so her question went unasked.

Maybe if she'd known what lay beyond that door and the massive impact it would have on her life and the lives of everyone at Hawkswell, she might have behaved differently.

She followed Tom out through the carriage gate, past what looked like an abandoned stable block, to an arched stone gateway where he stepped aside to usher her through. The sight brought Kate to a standstill for the second time that morning.

There, spread out in all its glory was what she reckoned to be a third of an acre of walled kitchen garden complete with white painted greenhouses ranged along one side and trellised fruit trees along the other. The beds were all freshly turned and dotted with bright green shoots in ruler straight lines against the deep brown soil.

One look at Tom's face told Kate that she was looking at his pride and joy.

"The mistress likes her home grown vegetables and fruit, always has done. Won't have nothing frozen nor messed about. We sell quite a lot of the produce now, can't eat it all ourselves, just the three of us. Are you a gardener then, Kate?"

"I... wow. Sorry Tom, but this is all so unexpected. I mean, yes, I used to love gardening back home in Ireland, helping my pa, but I haven't had the chance since being over here. Not much you can do in a cellar flat in London. Is this all you, Tom?"

He shook his head. "Not quite, no. There's a lad comes up from the village a couple of days a week to help with the heavy work. I'm not so young as I was, more's the pity. Perhaps you might care to lend a hand, if you take the flat, like."

Kate had to take a deep breath and swallow hard before she answered.

"I'd like that Tom. I'd like that very much indeed."

After showing her around the garden, Tom then gave her a brief tour of the areas immediately adjacent to the house, most of which had fallen into the same degree of neglect as the house itself. There were orchards and paddocks, a stand of massive elms, carriage houses, potting sheds, even an ice house and all the other buildings and facilities that must have once made up a thriving farmstead.

As they walked, Kate felt she could almost hear echoes of the many voices that must have once cried out greetings, instructions, warnings and even laughter as they went about their daily lives. The whole place felt saturated with its own history, as if the people had not long left. Occasional tools and items of farming or gardening equipment looked as if they had just been dropped, their users walking away, never to return.

Kate had to suppress a shiver more than once, but whether it was the chilly east wind, or something else entirely, she couldn't be sure.

Eventually, Tom looked at his watch.

"Right Kate, now's as good a time as any. I expect Miss Townshend's good and ready for us by now."

With that, he led the way back into the main part of the house.

Where the flat had been airy and light, the heart of the house couldn't have been more different. In place of bright white walls were heavy Victorian wallpapers, dark framed paintings and faded photographs. Heavy furniture crowded even the hallway, while all the windows were either shuttered or obscured by dusty velvet drapes, what few slices of light that managed to penetrate soon absorbed by the dusty gloom. The place smelled overwhelmingly of damp, cigarette smoke and yesterday's evening meal.

Arriving at a pair of tightly closed panel doors, Tom fiddled for a moment with his shirt collar before knocking, quietly and deferentially. A muffled but peremptory voice answered his knock.

"Come."

He opened the doors with a creaking flourish and stepped forward, Kate following at his heels, feeling like some kind of an acolyte, half expecting to see the old man give a flourishing bow as he stepped over the threshold.

The room was a shock.

Her first thought was that someone was preparing for a jumble sale.

Dozens of bookcases and glass-fronted cabinets were ranged around the walls, all crammed with hundreds of books of every shape, size and binding, from lowly broken spined paperbacks to sets of expensively leather bound volumes. Some were placed neatly in ordered rows on specific shelves, while others were piled haphazardly in the cabinets, or on the floor. It felt and looked like the worst kind of second hand bookshop. The room was hot and stuffy, the stench of cigarette smoke almost unbearable.

A hideous 1960s brown and orange three-piece suite was clustered around the fireplace in which sat the source of the warmth, an ancient electric fire, all three of its elements glowing brightly.

Just like the rest of the house, the shutters were tightly closed, the only light coming from randomly scattered standard and table lamps.

To the right of the fireplace and directly beneath one of the largest standard lamps stood a rickety looking card table, its surface covered with the dismembered remains of a broadsheet newspaper. In a winged armchair pulled up tight to the table sat a frail old lady, her dark green woollen suit so bagged and misshapen that she might well have been wearing it for a month. The collar gaped where a button had been missed, or was missing, and a simple string of discoloured pearls draped themselves around a scrawny neck.

The old lady's face was in deep shadow and all Kate could see from where she was standing was an untidy froth of yellowish white hair. Quite suddenly the old lady looked up, her eyes squinting against a curl of cigarette smoke spiralling up from an overflowing ashtray at her elbow.

"So what do you think of the place, then?" adding in the same abrupt manner, "Thank you, Tom."

Kate held her breath while nice Tom Gerrard shuffled away and closed the door behind him. Dismissed, just like that.

Without waiting for an answer, the woman, whom Kate presumed was Penelope Townshend, continued, squinting at a piece of paper she had picked up from the table.

"So you must be... let me see... Good heavens, C-a-t-r-a-o-i-n-e," she spelled the name out one letter at a time, "Catra... How in God's name do you pronounce that? Irish is it?"

Kate thought about the flat and wondered if she was making a huge mistake by even speaking to this dreadful woman. She took a deep breath and nailed on a smile.

"It's pronounced Catharine in English. And yes, I am Irish... for my sins."

Her voice must have sounded cooler than she intended because the old lady pulled herself upright and peered at Kate over the top of her reading glasses.

"Hair doesn't come much redder than yours I'll be bound, and you've certainly got the green eyes and complexion that goes with it. So how come a fine looking lass like you isn't married already with half a dozen children? You must be what, late twenties?"

Kate took another long, slow breath. OK, if you want a fight, I'm in the mood, she thought.

"I'm very proud of my hair, thank you. I inherited it from my grandmother. I am twenty-seven years old and I have not yet found a man, or woman for that matter, that I felt like spending the next three weeks with, let alone the rest of my life. And before you ask, I am a lapsed Catholic and a pacifist even though I believe firmly in a united Ireland. I have no criminal convictions even though the police keep stopping my car to look for bombs. Now, is there anything else you would like to know?"

"Yes. Why do they keep stopping your car?"

Kate bit her lip hard before answering. "Because it's got an Irish number plate. It's got a Z in it. So the police obviously think I must belong to an IRA terror cell, which of course I do not. Now, if you don't mind, please can we talk about the flat?"

What followed was a long ten seconds of charged silence during which the interview could have been legitimately terminated by either party.

Eventually it was the old lady's shoulders that slumped as she breathed a long, life weary sigh.

When she spoke again, her voice was quite different from before; softer, almost gentle.

"I am so sorry, my dear. Please can we start again? I ask too many questions and I know I must seem very rude. I don't mean to be, please believe me. The trouble is that I hardly see anyone these days, apart from the Gerrards, and I have lost any social skills I might once have had. Catharine is a lovely name and I am delighted that you are Irish. I have only been to the emerald isle once, and then only for a flying visit. But I liked what I saw and the people I met. I still think it is a shame that you haven't met anyone special yet. Just take my advice and don't leave it too late or else you'll end up a sad old spinster like me. Now, please sit down and tell me whether you think the flat might suit you."

Mollified by the old lady's apology and its obvious sincerity, Kate did as instructed, glad to take the weight off her now quite painful leg. She tried to sound off-hand, still convinced that the rent would prove to be prohibitive and that she was wasting hers and Miss Townshend's time.

"The truth is I think it's a beautiful flat and it will suit me very well, assuming of course I can afford the rent…"

She left the statement hanging, hoping to bring the negotiations to a speedy conclusion. The old lady, however, seemed determined not to be hurried.

"Would you mind very much my dear, if I ask you another question, that is what you do for a living?"

"Not at all. I'm a journalist. I have just accepted a position with an environmental magazine based in Bath. That's why I'm moving down here from London."

"A journalist, eh, and you say it's an environmental magazine, yes? I'm sorry to say that I've never heard of anything like it, but then I only ever take the damned Telegraph these days. I'm addicted to the crossword you see." She flapped a hand at the scattered newspaper in front of her and, as she did so, picked up a half empty pack of cigarettes and wafted it in Kate's direction.

"Er, no thank you," said Kate, "I don't."

"Good girl. Filthy habit. It'll be the death of me that's for certain." The old lady reached across to the wall at her side and hauled on an ancient bell pull. "Tea, that's what we need". She cleared her throat noisily. "While we wait, do you mind if I ask you one or two further questions?"

In the few minutes it took for the tea to arrive, Kate confirmed that both her parents were still living, that she had two sisters, both of whom were married and still living in Ireland, and that she had only lived in England for the last three years.

A genteel clatter and a light tap on the double doors signalled the arrival of the tea trolley, which was wheeled in by a dumpy little lady whom Kate assumed to be Tom Gerrard's wife.

They were not introduced.

The bone china tea service had plainly seen better days, its crop of brown stained chips, a poor repair to the pot lid and an ill matching sugar bowl speaking of years of hard use. But the tea was good and the delicate little cakes ranged on an ornate silver stand were deliciously fresh and obviously home baked.

As soon as the tea was poured, Mrs Gerrard departed to some distant domain, her mission accomplished. Strangely, Miss Townshend seemed relieved to see her go, as if then, and only then, could she really relax.

"I must apologise once again for the inquisition my dear, but at my age there's little time left for finesse. I am embarking on a course of action I have always sworn I would never take – sharing this house with strangers. Letting off rooms or flats has often been suggested but I have always resisted fiercely. Now, at last, circumstances have forced my hand. This place costs a small fortune to run and maintain and I have to generate what little income I can. So I am sure you will understand why I need to be certain that anyone who moves into my house does not remain a stranger for too long. To that end, will you please call me Penelope?"

Kate said she would and, while sipping her tea, braced herself for the financial bombshell she was sure was imminent.

But as Tom had predicted, she needn't have worried.

The brief negotiations that followed left her in a state of stunned euphoria. Penelope Townshend was asking less than the rent Kate was currently paying for her hideous cellar. Even with the additional travelling and parking costs, she would still be better off than she had been in London.

The improvement in her quality of life would be beyond price.

With no deposit to pay, and only a nominal contribution towards heating and electricity, the only serious proviso was that Kate was to commit herself to a twelve month let. It seemed that continuity of tenancy was of particular importance.

"I am sure you will be able to come to an amicable agreement with Tom Gerrard regarding produce from the garden and there are excellent tradesmen, including a particularly obliging butcher, who deliver every week."

Kate laughed, more out of relief and excitement than anything else.

"Don't worry about that, Penelope, I won't be needing the butcher. I'm a vegetarian. But I am looking forward to sampling Tom's vegetables though."

Penelope looked horrified. "Goodness, and how long have you been, er… like that?"

Kate laughed again. "You mean a veggie? I always have been, ever since I can remember. It's only meat I don't touch, I eat loads of fish and cheese."

"Hah! Thank goodness for that. Although looking at you, avoiding meat doesn't appear to have done you any harm."

They both laughed until Penelope started coughing. It took a slug of lukewarm tea and a long drag on another cigarette before she was able to speak again. But by then it seemed that there wasn't much else left to be said and, quite suddenly, the audience was at an end.

"Tom will give you all the details of my solicitor, Catharine, and I shall look forward to your moving in as soon as you are able." Kate got to her feet. Although Penelope remained seated, they shook hands.

"Thank you very much Penelope. I can't tell you how excited I am about the prospect of living here. But I do have one small condition of my own, if I may."

"Go on."

"If I am to call you Penelope, then you must please call me Kate. The only person who still calls me Catharine is my grandma, Roisin."

Penelope chuckled. "All right, it's a bargain."

The bell pull summoned Tom Gerrard, who escorted Kate back out to her car and expressed his delight at her taking on the tenancy. He handed over a sheet of paper with the solicitor's details, wished her a safe journey home, paused as if to say something else, shook his head and walked away.

Kate barely noticed his hesitation, too submerged in the fantastic certainty that, even if only for a year, Hawkswell House was about to become her new home.

Chapter 2

Two weeks later, a visit to Strand, Cowper and Geggs, Miss Townshend's solicitor in Bath, secured a twelve-month lease on the flat. The paperwork was signed and witnessed under the lugubrious gaze of the senior partner before Kate handed over a cheque for the first month's rent. After a round of handshakes, the keys were finally handed over.

A small self-drive van was all she needed to transfer all her belongings down to Hawkswell. She had seen the flat for the first time on a bright, early spring day but, as she drove down the M4 on Good Friday through the drenching rain that so typically blighted English bank holidays, she began to wonder if it would still feel so friendly.

But she needn't have worried. As soon as she opened the door with her bright new key, she knew everything was going to be all right. Someone, she was sure it must have been Tom Gerrard, had already been in and lit the wood-burning stove. In place of the acrid tang of fresh paint, this time she was greeted with a gentle warmth and the seductive scent of wood smoke.

Moving around her new home for the first time, Kate was filled with an overwhelming sense of well-being. As she tried to pin down the feeling, the best she could come up with was that it felt like coming home. She laughed at the thought. Home was hundreds of miles away, across a hideous stretch of sea, while she was deep in a foreign countryside surrounded by some very strange English folk. But there was no getting away from the fact that her new flat felt a whole lot more than merely comfortable.

With the bed made up, the wardrobe and chest of drawers filled and the kitchen as sorted as possible without a major shopping expedition, she pushed the remaining boxes out of the way and settled down on the sofa by the fire with a mug of tea. The rest could wait.

Late in the afternoon, the rain clouds cleared as the forecast had promised, the sky painted a hundred shades of graduated blue and pink as the sun dipped behind the wooded ridge above the house. No-one knocked on her door, and she tried to work out whether she was grateful or sad that there was no opportunity to invite someone in for a cup of tea or perhaps a flat warming drink. But after a few minutes' consideration, she concluded that a little bit of loneliness was character building and that she was glad that her privacy was being respected.

After spending the best part of half an hour trying to get a picture on the TV using her coat hanger aerial, Kate decided that she'd have to have a proper one installed as soon as possible. The snow storm would have to do until then.

Unpacking a few more bits and pieces, she built up the fire as the temperature outside fell away and cooked herself a first meal in her brand new kitchen.

Deciding to test the oven another day, she used the hob to cook herself a wild mushroom risotto as a moving-in treat. From the very first mouthful, she knew she'd made the right choice. This was proper country food, perfect for Hawkswell.

While she ate, she jotted down a list of things to do. The first few items concerned practicalities – telephone, TV aerial, post, grocery deliveries, Sunday newspaper, nearest shop – things that she'd ask Tom about the next time she saw him.

There was another list on the next sheet, more serious this time in that it described a list of things she was determined to find out, and right at the top of that list was a question: What is behind the heavy door in the downstairs corridor? The damned thing intrigued her a little more every time she passed it.

She also intended to find out all she could about the Townshend family and Hawkswell House itself. If she was going to be living there for the next twelve months, she felt that she at least ought to discover some of the history behind the place.

Having closed the shutters when darkness fell, the flat quickly warmed up and Kate found her eyes growing heavy. Eventually she stopped fighting the inevitable and took herself off to her new bed. The last sound she heard as she slipped off into a deep, contented sleep was that of an owl quartering the meadows on the far side of the river.

She drove the empty van back to London the following morning, locked the door of the cellar flat for the last time at twelve thirty on Easter Saturday morning and drove her Mini back down the M4 to Somerset, singing all the way.

The following morning Kate woke from a deep and dreamless sleep and glanced at the clock on her bedside table. 6.30. How come it was so early? And on a Sunday morning too! Then it came to her where she was and she also remembered that she'd opened two of the shutters wide to let some air in overnight. Even though the sun hadn't yet made it onto her side of the house, her bedroom was filled with a dazzling golden light.

She lay back and let her eyes close again. Ah, what the hell.

The flat felt cool but not cold. Even though she hadn't turned on any of the night storage heaters, she'd banked up and closed down the wood burner before going to bed, like Tom had showed her, and it seemed to have done its job well.

Then she listened.

Instead of the grumbling roar of the city that had greeted her for the last three years, on this morning of her new life in the countryside, all she could hear was wall to wall, high fidelity birdsong.

It sounded as if two or more pigeons were trying to outdo each other on the roof above her head, while the noise from the woods and the orchard suggested that every blackbird, thrush, sparrow and robin for miles around was competing for her attention.

The old house creaked around her as the sun warmed its roof and gutters while an aircraft droned high overhead, its engine noise softened by distance and fading as it passed. Kate breathed in, smelling a hint of wood smoke and musk from the joss stick she'd lit the night before – warm, dry smells of the type she had missed so much since leaving her Ireland home.

She drifted in and out of sleep until her bladder and a raging desire for a mug of coffee forced her out of bed. While organising her breakfast, she opened up the fire, the previous night's embers roaring into life as if hungry for more logs. Seated on the floor, her back against the sofa, she absorbed the friendly warmth of the hypnotising flames as she planned her day.

For the next few days of her week's relocation leave, Kate settled into a relaxed routine. After a token trip round the flat to tidy the bedroom and clear away the breakfast crocks, she would take a coffee down to the early triangle of May sunshine at the far end of the terrace. The air was still cool enough to make sunbathing a truly sensual pleasure rather than the endurance test it would become later in the year. For a few minutes she could lie back, eyes closed and absorb the warmth, the clean air and the peace – a combination of experiences impossible in London.

But more often than not, after less time than she intended, the sheer vitality of Hawkswell would force her into action.

That Wednesday morning, she headed for the walled garden where she came across Tom busy at one end of the long greenhouse. He must have heard her coming for he spoke before she even had a chance to say hello.

"Good morning Miss, and how are you settling in like?"

Kate smiled at the 'Miss', at the fact he didn't look up from what he was doing, knowing it was her.

"Really well, thank you Tom. Oh, and thanks for lighting my wood burner on Friday, I really needed it in the evening even though it does feel as if summer might be here at last."

As he tapped out another handful of tomato seedlings, his thick fingers stained dark with compost, he shook his head slowly, concentrating on his work.

"I wouldn't be so sure about that, Kate. It is only May you know. We had snow here one June, thick it was. Lasted three days, and we lost a lot of lambs." He paused, as if remembering, then qualified his caution. "That was back in the thirties, mind."

Enjoying the concentrated steamy warmth, Kate inhaled the fresh green tang of crushed tomato leaves that overlaid the earthy background smell of the old greenhouse. From where she stood, two levels of wide slatted wooden shelves ran down both sides of a central walkway right to the far end of the structure. Countless pieces of dusty string and ancient cobwebs hanging from the roof timbers swung gently in the faint breeze. While most of the glass was intact although green with lichen, some panes had overcome their lead spacers and slipped out of place, leaving clear, bright gaps for the sunlight to slice through.

Although Tom was using barely a quarter of the available area, she was astonished at the variety and quantity of plants and cuttings all neatly potted, labelled and laid out in orderly ranks along the shelves.

"This is amazing, Tom. Surely there's far too much here for just this garden."

He turned towards her, scrubbing his hands together to clean off mud and compost.

She thought she could sense a hint of pride as he said, "Oh, it's not all that much. But you're right, quite a lot of this'll go to the farm shop in the village. Brings in a few bob, which helps these days. 'Course, it wasn't always like this. Used to be four under-gardeners and two apprentices here in me father's day, with two boys from the village. We even used to take on casual help during the busy times, mostly gypsy families what used to park up in the woods. This whole place was packed from end to end with cut flowers, fruit and vegetables, all sorts. And the orchids, of course. The Master as was, Mr Townshend, used to love his orchids, he did."

"Was that Miss, er Mrs, Townshend's husband?"

"Lord bless me no. Old Mr Edward Townshend was her father, and as fine man as you'd ever want to meet, in my opinion."

"So, it really is Miss Townshend. She's never married then?"

"Ay, there was someone once, back in the war, an RAF officer. Didn't work out. Proper devil he was, if you'll pardon me saying so. The mistress don't like to hear mention though, s'why she went straight back to her maiden name." As if to forestall any further discussion about his employer, Tom picked up a tray of plants.

"I don't suppose you'd fancy giving me a hand planting a few of these out, would you? If you're not too busy unpacking, that is?"

Kate grinned. "I'd love to, Tom. I'm pretty much organised and I've got the evenings to unpack what's left. Just let me go and change. I won't be a minute."

She spent the next two hours on her hands and knees in the sunshine, happily working her way along the carefully prepared beds, planting out tender young tomato plants for hardening off. Once they were all heeled in and watered, she helped Tom with the heavy old glass cloches.

By the time they'd finished, it was nearly one o'clock and Kate was delighted to be invited for what Tom described as 'a spot of lunch.'

It seemed to Kate as if the Gerrard's kitchen had hardly changed in a hundred years. Dominated by a huge black cast iron range, its front and top peppered with various sized oven doors and lids, the whole thing was overhung with every conceivable shape of pot and pan, from giant copper preserving pans to black iron saucepans and skillets. Two ceiling high dressers were loaded with plates, serving dishes and piles of saucers with matching cups hung from hooks.

The 'spot' of lunch – home baked bread, butter, cheese, pickles and a flagon of cider was laid out at one end of a well-scrubbed and scarred kitchen table.

Mrs Gerrard who, although having been at last introduced to Kate, still hadn't acquired a first name, bustled about the kitchen while Tom and Kate helped themselves. The simple food was delicious and she quickly discovered a fresh air and hard work appetite. After a few minutes, Kate gradually became aware of an uncomfortable silence. In fact, apart from a polite yet cursory welcome, Mrs Gerrard had hardly spoken a word, and Tom – who seemed to consider conversation as necessary as breathing – was conspicuously silent.

Maybe they need a kick-start, she thought. Her cider finished, she placed the empty glass on the table in front of her with deliberation.

"Tom, that was the most delicious cider I've had in years. Is it homemade?"

Reaching for the flagon, Tom shook his head.

"Oh no, not for years now. You'll have some more?"

Kate smiled, nodded and held out her glass.

As he filled her up, Tom continued, "Must be back in the forties when we last made a mash here. We had the pickers then you see…"

"Fifty two it were," interrupted Mrs Gerrard with a waspish snap to her voice.

"And it weren't nothing to do with the pickers, neither. Her just lost interest, that's all." She flicked her head towards the main house. "Like all the rest of it, she just give up."

Kate glanced at Tom just in time to see him shake his head ever so slightly – a clear signal not to ask any more questions.

"Time we were getting back to work, Kate," he said, pushing his chair back and easing his back as he stood up. "Got plenty to do while this fine weather holds."

Before following Tom out into the yard, Kate thanked Mrs Gerrard for lunch and received a curt nod from the woman. As soon as they were out of earshot of the kitchen, Tom slowed.

"Sorry about that. The wife and the mistress haven't seen eye to eye these last forty years or more. May's particular upset right now about her letting the flats if you must know. It's nothing personal, nothing against you, Kate. It's something from way back, although I'm damned if I know what. She'll get over it, never you mind. I'll see to that."

May, Kate thought. May Gerrard. An old fashioned name.

She wasn't sure it suited the woman, and was just as certain that she would never be asked to use it.

After helping prepare another bed for planting, they packed up in the vegetable garden and Tom headed off on the gang mower.

With time to kill, Kate took a book down to the river and found herself a sunny spot under one of the willows. She had only been reading for a few minutes when she was surprised to see Penelope Townshend, leaning heavily on a walking stick, making her way slowly down from the house towards her.

As the old lady approached, Kate closed her book and started to get to her feet.

"Sit down! Sit! You look so comfortable." The instruction, accompanied by much stick waving, was delivered as if to a dog.

Already halfway to her feet, Kate decided she couldn't slip back down again, so she picked up her book and stood, brushing bits of grass and leaves from her jeans.

"It's all right, Penelope, I was about to head on back. It's getting a bit chilly."

The old lady, obviously painfully out of breath, waved a hand dismissively as she stopped by the tree and for a moment looked as if she might collapse against it. Instead, she propped her walking stick against the trunk, rummaged in the pockets of her ancient woollen coat and brought out cigarettes and lighter.

Two lung filling drags and a brief coughing spasm restored her voice, although it was still ragged, her words coming in short bursts.

"Must get myself... some kind of a buggy... Can't walk as well as I... used to... these damned smokes, you know." She waved the offending cigarette about as if she was going to throw it in the river but replaced it in her mouth instead and talked around it. "I would very much like you to join me... for tea tomorrow afternoon... if you are free that is?"

Kate wasn't entirely sure whether she was being issued with a request or a command.

"Thank you. I'd like that very much. What time should I...?"

"Three fifteen prompt... Mrs Gerrard won't make it any earlier or later... God knows why three or even three thirty won't do. Always been the same. Bloody woman. See you tomorrow then."

As suddenly as she had arrived, the old lady turned and walked away along the river bank leaving a thin trail of smoke drifting out across the water, and Kate even more intrigued than ever about the relationship between Penelope Townshend and May Gerrard.

Tea was served in the same cluttered room where Kate had first met Penelope. No sooner was she settled in an armchair than in came May Gerrard with the tea trolley. This time, instead of staying to serve, she was summarily dismissed,

"We'll look after ourselves now Mrs Gerrard, thank you."

Kate had to bite her lip again. It was all so Victorian, so feudal. Mistress and servant.

"I hope you'll take Darjeeling, some won't. It's the only tea I'll have in the house. Can't bear those damned bags, revolting things."

So if you don't like it, tough, Kate thought. She thought about her box of PG Tips tea bags in the kitchen cupboard and determined not to rise to the old lady's provocation.

"I hear you've been helping Tom in the garden."

"Well it was such a lovely day, I could hardly bear to be indoors." The minute Kate spoke, she regretted the words. The curtains drawn against the sunlight, the electric light, all spoke of very different needs. She hurried on, "And there's so much to do at the moment, planting out and preparing..."

Penelope interrupted. "Yes, yes. Well, Tom seems happy enough. Reckons you know what you're about."

Kate would have enjoyed the praise more if it hadn't sounded so grudging. The two sat in silence for a minute until Penelope asked, "So, what are your passions in life, Kate? What gets you out of bed every morning?" The question came as such a surprise that Kate had to think for a moment before answering.

"Wow. Er, that's a tough one. I suppose I would have to say my job. It's what I've always wanted to do, ever since I was at school, and here I am getting paid to do it."

Penelope leant forward in her chair. "I see. Maybe this would be a good time for you to tell me a bit more about precisely what it is that you do, my dear. I asked Tom to request a copy of your magazine in the village newsagent's the other day but they had never heard of it."

Kate smiled. "I'm not surprised. It's subscription only. People register with us and we mail the magazine to them every month. Newsagents won't stock it because our circulation is too low. Although it's growing every month we've got some way to go before that happens."

"I assume that, despite its name, *GreenGauge* is not devoted to fruit or vegetables."

Kate laughed this time, recognising Penelope's attempted humour. "Not entirely, no. Although we do feature a lot of articles that relate to horticulture and farming in one way or another. No, *GreenGauge* is a campaigning magazine aimed at people who care for the environment."

Penelope raised her eyebrows. "The environment? How on earth do you define the environment?"

Kate laughed again. "Just that. You said 'how on earth', and that's just it, the earth. This planet and everything that lives on it. Plants, trees, animals, fish, birds, and people, of course."

"So it's a nature magazine, then."

"Well… no, not really. I'll tell you what, I'll let you have some back issues. You'll understand when you've had a look through a couple."

"No, no. Don't bother to do that. My old eyes aren't up to too much reading these days. It's all I can do to get through the crossword clues. When you say campaigning, do you mean protesting?"

"In a way, yes. Except that we protest in print rather than marching up and down with banners."

"So what do you protest about?"

"Oh, goodness me. Loads of things – pollution, waste, deforestation, cutting down hedgerows, overuse of pesticides and fertilisers. If it's bad for nature or people, we campaign against it."

"It sounds to me as if you are just opposed to any kind of progress."

It was such a dismissive comment that Kate felt her hackles rise a little. "No, that's not quite fair. There's nothing wrong with progress at all, except when it's not thought through thoroughly and turns out to be detrimental to the environment."

"All right, give me an example."

Kate didn't have to think for long.

"Over-packaging. That's the big issue right now. Remember when people used to take their own paper bags to the grocer to have them filled with sugar or tea or whatever?"

The old lady nodded.

"Now everything comes in packets and boxes and bottles which are then put in polythene bags and all thrown away. You must have seen all that kind of stuff at the side of the road. Those polythene bags won't go away you know. They don't rot. They will probably last for hundreds of years. Food companies package items in plastic or glass pots and then place the pots in cardboard and cellophane boxes. It's nothing more than advertising and it all gets thrown away. We used to be able to take our empty pop and beer bottles back, now they just get thrown into huge holes in the ground. A complete waste."

Suddenly Kate realised that she was lecturing and to an increasingly restless audience.

"I'm sorry, Penelope. It's something I'm passionate about. I get carried away."

The old lady lit another cigarette. "Those times weren't quite as rosy as you make out, my dear. It must all seem rather quaint to you, looking back to when everyone had a pig at the bottom of the garden and nothing was ever thrown away. They didn't do it because it was good for the planet, you know, they did it because they had no choice. They had so little, you see. Without that pig they would have gone hungry, simple as that.

"I do wish everyone would stop harping on about how much better things used to be. They weren't. People used to die of illnesses we hardly give a thought to these days. My mother died giving birth to me, and that hardly ever happens nowadays, at least not as often as it did."

Kate opened her mouth to speak and her face must have given her away because she received the now familiar wave.

"Oh, don't say you're sorry. I don't need it any more. I'm past all that. My brother died too, in 1915, during that pointless bloody war. We didn't learn from that either. Then my father not long afterwards, from a stroke. The fact is they were hard times. Not for me, of course. I was born on the right side of the tracks as the Americans say. I was privileged, sent to the very best schools and then on to finishing school in Switzerland, all of it.

"I didn't know what it was like to be hungry, or to have no proper shoes or clothes. But life was really hard for most people back then. No-one had the time or energy to campaign or protest, they just got on with their lives as best as they could. It seems to me that people today have far too much time on their hands. None of you know you've been born, if you ask me."

And then she stopped.

"You had better be getting on now, Kate, I'm rather tired."

And that was that… again.

Penelope laid her head back into the corner of the wing chair and shut her eyes. Kate thanked her for the tea but got no response. So she let herself out and closed the door softly behind her.

That'll teach you to deliver lectures, Kate O'Donnell, she told herself as she let herself back into her flat. Still, she'd learned a few things along the way, especially what had happened to the rest of Penelope's family. Poor old thing. If Tom was right about her only being married briefly, then it sounded as if she'd managed Hawkswell pretty much by herself for the last sixty years.

No wonder she was a bit crabby, Kate thought.

I'd be the same myself by now, watching this place gradually falling down around my ears.

Over the next few weeks, Kate settled into her new life as if she had been born to it. She had quickly found a traffic-avoiding route to and from work, and one of the few remaining back streets where she could park for free. Since the one time she had taken afternoon tea with Penelope Townshend, she had hardly set eyes on the old lady.

On the other hand, she saw Tom regularly, seeking him out to check if he needed any help in the garden at the weekends. Work was relatively quiet during May and so there were no late nights. She got her books sorted, put up pictures, hung curtains and had a TV aerial fitted and phone installed.

Just like Tom's precious seedlings, she started to put down roots.

One glorious Sunday in early June, while she was helping Tom in the walled garden, the old man suddenly stopped what he was doing and groaned, holding his back and obviously in a great deal of discomfort.

Kate hurried over to him, "Are you all right, Tom?"

He nodded at first then, slowly and painfully, he bent and stretched a couple of times before answering, "Sciatica. Always gets me this time of year. Could hardly get out of bed this morning."

"Oh Tom. Why on earth didn't you stay there if it was that bad?"

He grinned ruefully. "This stuff won't plant itself, lass. Should've been put out a week ago, but what with the weather last week and all… Anyway, you know what they say, you'll never plough a field by turning it over in your mind."

Kate laughed. "That's exactly what my mother always used to say. But surely that's not a Somerset expression, is it?"

"No. You're quite right. It's an old Irish saying, or so I was told."

Kate was gently puzzled. "So how…?"

"Ah, I reckon it must have been that Jamie what I got it off."

"Jamie?"

"Young lad, worked here for just afore the first war. I was but a kid back then, barely six years old, but we become friends and he told me a lot about Ireland and taught me all manner of expressions and sayings and that. Seems some of 'em must've stuck."

"So he was from the old country, this Jamie?" Kate asked.

"Lord, he was Irish as you and more so. Lovely lad. Tall and broad shouldered, stronger than two men of his age. Good looking too, with his long, curly hair. Like yours it was, Miss, only darker, more brown than red if you know what I mean. His green eyes was like yours too, if you don't mind me saying."

"It's an Irish thing, Tom. Goes with the hair. So what exactly was this Jamie doing at Hawkswell?"

"He was orphaned, or so he told me. Shipped over here to work for old Mister Townshend for some reason. Turned up here at Hawkswell... let me see, must have been early in 1913. Dreadful day it was, bitter cold with rain and sleet. I remember it 'cos I seen him through the window when he arrived. Like an alley cat he was, soaked from head to toe, and like as not freezing cold after his journey. He didn't exactly get a warm welcome either as I heard it..."

Chapter 3

North Somerset, February 1913

A bitter east wind caused Jamie to shiver violently as he stepped down onto the almost deserted station platform. Pulling his fisherman's cap down over his ears, he hunched his shoulders inside his jacket and looked up and down the train.

There were no other passengers, only the station master wreathed in steam from the stationary engine, and a porter who, after giving a quick glance left and right, scuttled back into the warmth of the waiting room.

Although only mid-afternoon, the light was already gone from the day and overhead lamps glowed a sickly yellow as they swayed in the wind, sending shadows lurching grotesquely across the walls and platform.

There seemed to be activity around the guard's van towards the rear of the train so, picking up his oilskin sack of belongings, Jamie headed that way. At least there might be someone to tell him how he was going to make the last leg of his journey.

A short, stocky man in a filthy ankle-length raincoat and wide brimmed hat had just slammed the tailgate of an open cart full of milk churns, causing the wet and miserable looking horse strapped between the shafts to flick its ears and stamp a hoof.

Jamie caught the man's eye. "Excuse me, sir, please can you tell me how I might get myself to the Hawkswell Estate?"

The man deliberately finished dropping the locking pins in place before turning and looking Jamie up and down with undisguised contempt.

"So you'll be the Irishman, Kirkpatrick."

It was a statement, not a question, and Jamie was surprised that anyone thereabouts knew of his existence and his business.

"That's right," he answered politely. "I am James Kirkpatrick." He offered his hand, as he had been brought up to do when meeting a stranger. The carter looked at the hand, then back at Jamie's face, while both his own hands remained jammed firmly inside his coat pockets. He tipped his head towards a small space beside the milk churns. "In there." Then he strode to the front of the cart and swung himself onto the driving bench.

So there was to be no handshake, no smile either. No please, no welcome, no invitation to sit up front, and not even a cursory backwards glance as Jamie slung his sack over the tailgate before heaving himself up after it.

Without giving his passenger a moment to settle into the cramped space, the carter whipped up the horse, which snorted and bucked against its harness before jerking the cart forwards. Jamie crashed hard against the tailgate as they lurched out from under the station's canopy, away from its swinging lights and into darkness and the bitter, wind driven rain.

It seemed as if he was to be 'the Irishman' from then on, maybe 'Kirkpatrick' if things went well. For a young man who had been known by his given name all his life, it felt strange and somehow sad, yet another reminder of how much he had so recently lost, and the terrible extent to which his life had changed in so short a space of time.

Born the son of a boat builder in Poulnadree, a creek-side hamlet on Ireland's Galway coast, Jamie's earliest memories were of crawling happily around his father's feet in his boatyard home. His first playthings had been springy coils of freshly planed oak and pine wood, bits and bobs of rope, canvas and sea shells.

His playground had spanned the ever changing space between the tide-washed slipway and the warm, simply constructed house behind his father's workshop. Not merely an Irishman there, he had been 'young Jamie', the much loved son of well-respected parents.

By the time he'd reached the age of eight, he was helping in the yard whenever dreaded schooling didn't beckon. By the time he was twelve and master of his letters and numbers, he had become apprenticed to his father, thus fulfilling each of their respective dreams.

Life for the Kirkpatrick family and their neighbours was hard but simple, and brim full with love and laughter. At his father's side, the boy came to know the many ways and uses of timber, copper, brass and iron, tar, canvas and rope along with how all those materials could be best deployed. In a few short years he absorbed and practiced the slew of skills necessary to build a range of craft from tenders and dinghies to small fishing boats for both river and open sea. He also learned to sail, row and scull those boats as easily and as effortlessly as he knew how to walk and run.

Sheltered from the growling tensions of the wider world, Jamie's life, and the lives of those around him were ordered and directed by the weather, the seasons and the tides, and by the rising and setting of the sun.

All was well in the life of young James Kirkpatrick until, the day before Christmas Eve 1912, many folk in the hamlet, including both Jamie's parents and two of his three younger sisters, began to fall sick. A doctor, summoned from the nearby town, swiftly diagnosed enteric fever. Within hours, the village well was tested, found to be contaminated and swiftly sealed off. While fresh water was brought in barrels from a nearby village, a new well was dug on the far side of the village, fifty yards upslope of the original.

Although the remedial action was swift and effective, it was tragically too late for many. Out of a village population of ninety-one souls, thirty-seven died directly as a result of the outbreak, sixteen of them young children.

Jamie and his youngest sister, Rosie, were the only members of the Kirkpatrick family to survive. Within days, the girl, barely five years old, was swiftly appropriated by an aunt from Limerick and Jamie was never to see her again. She was collected and taken away on the 12th day of January 1913, and for the first time in his seventeen years on earth, Jamie found himself completely alone.

A week later he would be homeless and without a job.

Numb with grief, he'd watched his parents and two of his sisters buried side-by-side in the little churchyard above the harbour, company for the many other victims of the outbreak. To Jamie it felt as if the village and everything he had ever known had been devastated by a tidal wave of tragedy. To add to his grief, the banks wasted little time in calling in the mortgages and within days a bailiff arrived to serve notice on the house, the boatyard and all they contained. Without a shred of sentiment, Jamie was given twenty-four hours to pack the few belongings to which he was entitled, and leave.

With no last will and testament, there was neither inheritance nor final words of love, comfort or farewell from beloved parents. Jamie found a few Irish Punts and a handful of loose change in the bottom of the biscuit barrel, along with a tightly folded piece of paper with the name and address of a Dublin solicitor. Hastily scrawled and unsigned, it had probably been placed there in case of such a tragedy, never expecting to be needed. Above the address was written, 'If anything should ever happen to your mother and me, this man will help you and your little sisters.'

When he read those words, the dam broke, and Jamie wept at last.

Two days later, shocked into a state of mute acceptance by the speed with which such a tumultuous event had overtaken his world, Jamie presented himself at the address in Dublin, resigned to whatever fate had in store. Although he probably should have considered himself lucky to have any future at all, the prospect with which he was faced held little appeal.

It appeared that an unknown uncle with a legal practice in a place called Bristol was owed a small favour for services rendered but un-invoiced, the upshot being that his equally unknown nephew was to be provided with a position in settlement of the debt.

The Dublin solicitor was brief and blunt, squinting through tiny, thick-lensed eyeglasses at the young man.

"You will work for your food and a roof over your head, Master James, and not a penny paid for five years. I have it on good authority that Mister Edward Townshend, for it is he to whom you are to be indentured, is a kind and fair man, at least as kind and fair as any Englishman can ever be. It is a generous offer by your Uncle Kevan which I have accepted on your behalf by telegraph this morning."

When Jamie asked to know exactly where he was to be sent, the man answered, "England, of course, as I am sure I have already said. A place called Hawkswell, in the county of Somerset. I cannot tell you more since that is all I know myself."

Although Galway enjoyed more than its fair share of rain and inclement weather, Jamie was quite unprepared for an English winter. From the moment he descended the ferry's gangway he'd been engulfed in a thick and bitter fog that raked his throat, causing him to cough and choke before he had even set foot on the dockside.

Prior to his brief passage through Dublin, the largest conurbation Jamie had ever experienced had been Limerick, and that just once a year since he had been old enough to accompany his parents. While he had been shocked by the hugeness and the noisy bustle of both those places, nothing could have prepared him for the sheer ferocity of Liverpool.

Thousands of people, all rushing from one place to the other at breakneck speed on foot, in trams and automobiles, buses and wagons, all seeming to know their business and none caring what or who they mowed down in the process. The place was filthy, smoky, deafeningly noisy and, had it not been for the bitter cold, would have been Jamie's perfect idea of hell.

After asking directions and being snarled at and cursed more times in thirty minutes than in the entirety of his life before, he'd at last found his way to the railway station and the long, uncomfortable Third Class journey to Bristol and then on to Bath. Then, after a long and tiring wait, a branch line had taken him to the station a few miles from Hawkswell where he had joined the milk churns and their surly driver in the cart.

The journey from the railway station to Hawkswell took forty long and excruciatingly unpleasant minutes. Forced to cling on hard to the side of the cart with one hand, Jamie held onto his belongings with the other as the creaking, clanking cart lurched in and out of ruts and potholes.

Bitter rain found its way into and under every last nook and cranny of his shivering body. At each jolt and swing of the cart, the empty churns clanged and boomed against each other until he thought his head would burst with the noise.

When, after half an hour, battered, bruised and chilled almost to insensibility, he shouted above the din "How much further?", receiving no response. Perhaps if one of the milk churns had opened its lid and called out the question, he wondered, maybe it would have got an answer. His wry smile dripped away with the rain at the thought that it probably would.

At last the carter pulled off the public highway into a gateway in a high brick wall. Barely visible in the feeble glow from the carriage lantern, ornate iron gates twice as tall as a man stood open onto a broad, gravelled drive that swept away between banks of vegetation.

"The house is down there."

The carter pointed with his whip.

"You're to report to Roberts, the Head Groom. He'll be in the stables at the back of the house."

Soaking wet, frozen stiff and exhausted, Jamie dragged himself down from his perch and pulled his sack after him. He thanked the man for the lift but might as well have saved his breath.

Without another word, the carter whipped up the horse, turned the cart around and lumbered off into the darkness.

Gravel crunched under Jamie's boots as he started off down the drive. Luckily what little daylight remained enabled him to find his way. Too tired and miserable to think about much more than placing one foot in front of the other, he didn't notice that the foliage had lessened until he caught his first shadowed sight of Hawkswell house ahead of him, its lighted windows reflected in some kind of a lake. Even in the dark the place looked impossibly grand to Jamie's eyes, and he couldn't help but wonder what he was walking into.

Taking the broad drive across the front of the house, he made his way around the side, avoiding the broad swathes of light from the lighted windows, until he came at last to the very rear of the house. There were lights there too, in occasional windows and doorways, but they were like fireflies compared with those at the front. The sound of stamping hooves brought him to the stable block and a lad of about his own age hefting a bale of hay up into a rack.

Jamie introduced himself.

"Where might I find Mister Roberts?"

At first it seemed as if he hadn't been heard or understood, but when he started to ask again, the lad held up a hand to stop him.

"All right. I heard you the first time. And what business might one such as you have with Mister Roberts?"

The lad, an inch or two shorter than Jamie, had small, dark eyes set close together in a mean, rat-like face. Under any other circumstances, Jamie might have stood his ground, but that night he was too tired and dispirited to do anything other than state the obvious and hopefully find somewhere warm and dry to lie down and sleep.

"I'm come here from Ireland, to work for Mister Townshend. I've been told to present myself to Mister Roberts, the Head Groom."

"I know who Roberts is," the lad snarled, "You don't have to tell me that, Paddy. Out of 'ere, turn left and the tack room is the last door on the left. Go on, get along with you."

The tack room door was opened after Jamie's fourth attempt at knocking and he introduced himself for the third time that afternoon, asking, "Are you Mister Roberts?".

"I am," said the man, studiously ignoring Jamie's extended hand, causing him to wonder whether that was how things were done in Somerset. Comforting aromas of wood smoke and pipe tobacco emanated from inside the room, reminding Jamie painfully of home and his father, but the man standing four square and belligerent in his shirt and braces obviously had no intention of inviting him inside.

Roberts stared for thirty long seconds, obviously enjoying the sight of Jamie shivering and dripping onto the cobbles, before delivering what sounded like a familiar and well-rehearsed speech.

"You will sleep in the hay loft above the stables along there," he pointed to his left, "and you will take your meals in the servant's hall along with the rest of the staff. Breakfast's at six thirty, when you will also collect your lunch pail. Dinner is at seven p.m. You will wash at the pump in the yard and there is an earth closet next to the dung heap behind the stable block.

"Your job is to keep the loose boxes spotless, with new straw on the floor every day and fresh hay in the mangers. The water buckets are to be kept filled and cleaned out regularly. You will also assist in the cleaning of the carriages and wagons and the tack and harness."

Almost by rote, as if he was reading from a list, Roberts continued.

"You will answer to me directly, but if any of the grooms, the footmen or the other stable lads give you an order, you will carry it out unless it interferes with your other duties, in which case you will inform me immediately. Is that all understood?"

Jamie nodded even though in truth he had hardly understood a word that the man had said, his head full of questions he was too exhausted to voice.

Roberts then leaned forwards and spoke directly into Jamie's face.

"You will speak to no-one unless absolutely necessary, and you will keep yourself out of sight as far as possible. This is for your own good, is that clear?"

Jamie nodded again, it seemed like the best thing to do whether he understood or not.

"Your kind are not popular in these parts and especially not on this estate. We've been plagued with thieves and poachers this last twelve-month and folk are sick and tired of it. So mind me, you just keep yourself to yourself, if you know what's good for you."

When he asked about dinner, he was told that he was too late for that evening but that he might get some bread and cheese if he went to the kitchen door.

Then, without another word, Roberts stepped back into his room and shut the door in Jamie's face.

At least the stable loft was dry and warmed by the horses below. Jamie fell asleep that night amongst the hay with a full stomach but an empty heart. For as long as he could remember, he had been at the centre of his family and his family had, in turn, been at the centre of their small community. Everyone knew everyone else and mostly liked each other.

Even the most miserable of the old folk had a smile for young Jamie Kirkpatrick, who was not just 'an Irishman'.

But what of this place?

He wondered where and how in God's name he was going to fit into such an alien world with not a glimpse or a smell of the sea, and not a boat for miles around.

How would he ever understand these English people's ways and follow their rules? He could barely understand a word any of them said. His new master, Roberts, was a fine example with his thick Somerset accent. And what was all that about thieving and poaching? What in heaven's name had that to do with him?

Then there were the horses.

Dear God, horses.

What did he know of them except what went in at one end and what came out the other? But he would learn, out of necessity.

"Well," he spoke into the darkness, "there's no-one lookin' out for you now Jamie boy, you're well and truly on your own and no mistake."

As he fell asleep, he reckoned he was going to need all his wits about him in the coming days and weeks if he was to survive at all.

Woken at six by the stamping of the horses in the boxes below his makeshift bed, he enjoyed a freezing cold wash under the massive iron pump in the yard. At least he'd slept well and his clothes had almost dried overnight. The rain had stopped, leaving a well washed sky that promised a glimpse of the sun. The earth closet was no better nor worse than many others and Jamie had headed off to the servants hall for his breakfast, a spring in his step, determined to make the best of his lot.

His breezy "Good morning" brought no response from the assorted household staff gathered around the long wooden table. Then he spotted the stable lad he had met the night before and guessed that his arrival was anticipated and that he was being deliberately ignored.

A single empty chair stood at the near end of the table, carefully separated from all the others. Ah well, he thought as he sat down, feck the lot of you. A man's got to eat!

The breakfast was surprisingly good and very welcome. Hot porridge and plenty of it, with as much tea as he could drink. He might as well be alone on a desert island, but at least he wouldn't starve to death.

Edwards was waiting for him as he headed towards the stables and wearing a thunderous look that suggested his day was not off to a good start.

He was right.

It seemed that he was supposed to feed and water the horses before even thinking about feeding and watering himself. It didn't matter that he'd received no instructions to that effect, he was somehow supposed to know.

When he tried to tell Edwards that he had never worked with horses before and didn't know the requirements of his job, he was shouted down.

"You're here to work as a stable lad. I didn't ask for you. I was told that you are to replace a lad who ran off a fortnight ago. If there is something you don't know, ask either of the other lads, or one of the grooms. You will not ask me because I don't care about your problems, is that clear?" Jamie nodded, not trusting himself to speak. "Good. Now get on with your bloody job!"

If the path Jamie was treading had seemed steep until then, it was about to become far worse.

Of course Tooms, the first lad he'd encountered on his arrival, wasn't going to volunteer any useful information. In fact, when Jamie asked him to explain his duties to him, the lad spread his hands wide to encompass their entire surroundings, horses and all.

He raised his eyebrows above a feral grin. "All this, Paddy, needs cleaning. The horses need watering and feeding. The muck needs shovelling out and barrowing. What else is there to know?"

Jamie's workload would have been hard enough but, no sooner had he cleared the old straw from the floor of the first loose box, and despite having little experience of either horses or their stables, it became obvious that his predecessor had cared little for his work or his charges.

The cobbled floor was caked with layer upon layer of compacted manure and rotted straw. Inches thick, its ammoniac stink was eye watering. Jamie knew straight away that he had a choice on his hands – he could either ignore the state of the floor and merely replace the old straw and move on to the other boxes, all of which were likely to be in no better shape, or he could clean the box out thoroughly and probably reap a bollocking for his trouble.

Somehow there was no choice. As far as young Jamie Kirkpatrick was concerned, there was only ever one way to do a job – to the best of your ability – regardless of the consequences.

It took dozens of buckets of water and two hours hard scrubbing and scraping to get that floor clean. The moment it was done, he washed down the wooden sides of the box before spreading fresh, clean straw on the floor and replacing the musty old hay in the manger. By the time he'd finished, the place looked how he thought it should.

He had just started on the second empty box when Tooms arrived.

He took one look at what Jamie was doing and stood as if he had been shot through the head.

"Please tell me this isn't all you've done this morning, Irish, just this one box."

Instead of answering, Jamie pointed at the piece of floor immediately beneath his feet.

"The job took so long because this place hasn't been cleaned out properly in months, look."

Tooms shook his head, not for a moment taking his eyes from Jamie's face.

"Oh, no. I don't want to look at nothing. You should have cleared out all eight of these boxes by now because the horses will be back from their morning ride in half an hour. And where will they go, eh?" Tooms' face was growing redder by the second as his anger took hold. "Back into their stinking stalls because our Irishman can't stand a bit of shit on the floor. You haven't got a bloody clue have you? Well, I'm going to give you a piece of advice right now, Paddy. You get those other seven boxes cleared out afore those horses come back or Roberts'll have the hide off your back. Then, with any luck he'll send you back to potato land where you fuckin' well belong."

Jamie had the other boxes cleared and ready five minutes before the horses returned. Of course they were done as poorly as they had been before, but it didn't seem as if anyone cared one way or the other.

Finding a corner to sit and eat his lunch, he wondered what his predecessor had done with the rest of his morning, if it only took half an hour to prepare seven loose boxes.

Over the next few days, Jamie cleaned out the rest of the stables thoroughly, concentrating on one box each day, leaving himself plenty of time to prepare the others before the horses returned from their ride out.

He was disappointed but not altogether surprised when no-one seemed to notice the change that was gradually coming over the place, even though it must have been obvious to anyone with even a minimal sense of smell. But if anyone did notice, Jamie didn't hear about it. The tack and the wagons were in a similar condition to the stables. Whereas those elements that might be visible to Mister Townshend looked just about passable, the rest were caked with mud and filth and desperate for wax and oil, soap for the leather and elbow grease for the brass. Jamie took on an individual piece of restoration work each day, completing the rest of his tasks easily in the time allowed.

Gradually, the carts and the carriages began to gleam like new, along with the harness and the tack. As Jamie finished each item, he painstakingly cleaned the shelves and the racking in the tack room until the place began to look as if someone actually cared for it.

Of course his efforts weren't going unnoticed.

But, far from receiving praise for his efforts, Roberts started to find fault where there was none, insisting that jobs that didn't need repeating were done again, and again, and again. He kept Jamie working late into the nights for no good reason before dreaming up yet another filthy, and quite unnecessary, task to add to the young man's burden.

And all the while, not one person spoke to him except to shout for him to get out of the way or to fetch this or that for one of the grooms or footmen. He continued to eat alone at his end of the dining table, although conversation between the rest of the staff resumed as soon as they realised he was going to make no effort to join in.

In spite of everything, he slept well enough in his hayloft bed and took each day as it came, resigned to his role as kicking boy for the Godless Roberts and his underlings. Then, two months into his placement at Hawkswell, just as the first signs of spring were brightening up the landscape, his luck changed, although in a way he could not possibly have foreseen.

A fortnight of persistent and drenching rain had turned the paddocks and meadows into swamps and the roads and lanes around Hawkswell into muddy rivers. The horses and ponies were confined to their stables, doubling Jamie's workload and making his life, along with that of all the other outdoor staff at Hawkswell, thoroughly miserable.

Despite their best efforts at drying their clothes overnight, everyone started work in the morning as cold and damp as they had ended the previous day, while most were soaked to the skin again by lunchtime.

As a result, tempers were even shorter than usual.

The undeclared war between Roberts and Jamie had been escalating steadily. The fact that the stables, the wagons and the tack were, thanks entirely to Jamie's diligence, better maintained than they had ever been since Roberts' arrival at Hawkswell, only seemed to make matters worse.

For some reason known only to Roberts himself, the single focus of his existence had become to make Jamie's life as unpleasant and intolerable as humanly possible. But every time he thought he had at last brought the lad to his knees, Jamie bounced back.

The day it all came to a head, Jamie had been told to clean the Townshend family carriage, recently returned from a visit to Bath. Liberally spattered with fresh mud, its wheels and running gear were caked with thick layers of dripping, greasy filth.

Telling him that the carriage was required again that afternoon, Roberts had given Jamie an impossible hour to clean it from top to bottom, inside and out.

When he arrived to inspect the results ten minutes earlier than promised, he could hardly believe his eyes. The carriage was immaculate.

How Jamie had managed it in the time, and to such a high standard, even he didn't know. As a result, even when forcing his aching back straight and clenching his fists on blistered palms, he couldn't quite hide a small smile of satisfaction.

Whether Roberts had taken one too many bottles of ale that lunchtime or he was just in a worse frame of mind than usual, Jamie's ghost of a grin that dismally wet afternoon proved the last straw for the man.

He was quite unprepared for the vicious right jab that caught him squarely on the nose, snapping the cartilage in an instant, sending a bright flash of pain to blind his eyes, and a rush of blood down his chin and across his chest.

Thrown back against the wall of the carriage shed by the force of the blow, Jamie barely managed to stay on his feet, although it might have been better had he not. In a blind rage, Roberts followed his first punch with a merciless rain of blows to Jamie's face and head, blacking both eyes and splitting his eyebrow and lip before the young man was able to bring up his arms to protect himself.

Luckily for Jamie, Roberts was shouting and screaming abuse at the top of his voice as he beat the lad, the noise bringing rescue before he could inflict more permanent damage.

While the protesting Roberts was dragged off to his quarters to calm down, Jamie was hustled off to the kitchen where a horrified cook did what she could for his injuries while demanding to know what had provoked such a violent assault.

Jamie tried to mumble that it was nothing more than a misunderstanding and got a sharp dab of iodine on his lip for his trouble.

"If this is just a misunderstanding Master Kirkpatrick, I pray I never have to deal with anything more serious. I am going to send for Doctor Marshall right away. He'll need to re-set that nose and you're going to need a stitch or two in your lip and eyebrow. Mister Townshend is going to have to be informed."

In too much pain to protest, with raw slabs of liver pressed to both eyes and a blood soaked towel in his lap, Jamie could only sit and dread the outcome of his beating. He knew enough about the workings of the world to be certain that Roberts would come up with some plausible story to justify his actions, equally certain that anything he said in his defence would be dismissed out of hand, just as his own dismissal would inevitably follow.

It was only at that moment that he realised how little and how much he had to lose. His father's words echoed in his head, 'A roof is a roof when it's raining, and a meal is welcome at any time'.

It might not have been much of a life since he had arrived at Hawkswell, but he had enough wisdom to know that things could have been a great deal worse. When he first arrived, the doctor was brusque and unsympathetic, seeing only the results of yet another pointless scrap between young men who should know better. The fact that it was Wednesday afternoon and not Saturday night apparently passed him by. It wasn't until the cook took him to one side and explained what had transpired, that he started to treat Jamie with a little more compassion.

With his nose roughly set and heavily taped and spider like clusters of horsehair stitches decorating his eyebrow and his lip, Jamie was helped upstairs to a hastily prepared bed in an empty attic room. There he was settled down to sleep off the pain killing sedative administered by the doctor.

He slept right through until ten o'clock the following morning.

His first sensations on waking were a confusing mixture of unfamiliar comfort and overwhelming pain. The pain radiated from his broken nose outwards to his eyes, his lips and his jaw. The comfort pretty much covered the rest of his body with the exception of his blistered palms. Unable at first to open either of his eyes, he explored his surroundings with his remaining senses.

He was lying in a bed, between clean, starched sheets, with thick woollen blankets on top, something he had not experienced since leaving his home in Ireland. He could just make out that the room was bright with daylight. But above all, it was quiet. No snorting horses and clumping hooves, no cockerel in the yard, nobody screaming at him to fetch this and carry that.

Eventually, not being in any particular hurry to re-join the rest of the world, he managed to force his least damaged eye wide enough to take a better look. The room, distempered white and with only a few cobwebs draped in the corners, was, judging by its steeply raked ceiling, situated in the attic of the house, with a small dormer window in one wall and a closed door in the other. A plain wooden table stood beside the bed with a glass of water and a white cardboard pillbox. On the other side of the bed a spindle-backed chair had his clothes neatly folded on its seat. Although tiny, it was a pleasant place and Jamie wondered what it must be like to sleep in such a room every night. As he dreamed about such an impossible future, there was a light knock on the door, which opened before he could respond. One of the kitchen maids put her head around the jamb and, seeing Jamie roll his head in her direction, spoke to someone over her shoulder.

"I think he's awake now, if you please sir." She moved aside to allow the tall, burly figure of a man attired in an expensive looking tweed suit to duck under the lintel and stand awkwardly. Leaning over the bed, he practically filled the room, blocking out the light as he stared down at Jamie's prostrate form.

"Mister Kirkpatrick, I am Edward Townshend. I have received a report from Roberts, the Head Groom, about yesterday's unfortunate occurrence and I wish to hear your version of events before I decide upon a course of action."

The man's deep, rich voice was devoid of either sympathy or malice. It was so cold and impersonal, Jamie feared that no matter what he said or how he phrased it, his fate was sealed.

Nevertheless he told his story, awkwardly and painfully through bruised and swollen lips. About how he had cleaned the carriage in an impossibly short space of time because it was required again that afternoon and how Roberts had punched him without provocation and then continued to beat him until help arrived.

When his story was finished, Edward Townshend asked for no clarification except to see Jamie's hands. He took each one in turn and looked carefully at the inflamed and blistered palms before turning them over to examine the undamaged knuckles. Then, without further comment, he expressed the wish that Jamie would soon recover, and left. Jamie listened to his booted feet clumping slowly down the stairs like a funeral drum.

To his surprise, his next visitor was the cook with a tray of hot buttered toast and a large mug of tea.

"So Mister Townshend has been up to see you. You are honoured, young man. I reckon that's the first time he's set foot on this floor in five years or more." All the while she was fussing about, propping Jamie up on his pillows and settling the tray. "Now, the doctor says you're not to move an inch until tomorrow morning at the earliest and you must take two of these." She handed Jamie two of the pills from the box on the bedside table. "You're to take them three times a day."

After dutifully swallowing the pills, Jamie asked what she thought might happen to him.

"Oh, don't you go worrying yourself about anything like that. Mister Townshend will do what's right, you can be sure. He's a fair man and used to dealing with such things, after all he is a Magistrate."

At the word Magistrate, Jamie's spirits sank without trace.

Magistrates dealt with the law, and the law was almost always cruel to those such as himself. The cook left him to his tea, his toast and his despair, saying that someone would be up with his lunch later in the day. She told him where the bathroom was and that apart from that he was not to leave his bed.

Probably because of the effect of the pills, Jamie dozed away the rest of that morning and when, much later, the cook arrived with his lunch, he was soundly asleep. Gently shaking him awake, her first words could not have warmed him more than the flush of spring sunlight flooding through the dormer window and across the bed.

"I really shouldn't be telling you this because I'm not at all sure what will become of it. Malcolm Roberts has been dismissed. He's been packed off with his traps, a week's wages and no reference. I don't suppose we'll ever be seeing him around here again." Jamie could hardly believe what he was hearing. "But... I mean..." She hurried on. "It was your hands as did it. No marks you see. Roberts told Mr Townshend that you had gone for him and that he was only defending himself. Silly blighter had only gone and hit himself about the face with something to make his story more believable. Give himself a black eye, he did. How daft is that? Trouble was, his knuckles are all broken and bruised while yours aren't any more marked than anyone might expect with your job. Oh, and all that about the carriage being required again that day, that was complete and utter nonsense. Mister Townshend didn't need no other proof."

Her beaming smile seemed to match the sunshine outside.

"So how do you like that, young man?"

Jamie tried to grin, winced and said he was glad.

"I am sure you must have put in a word for me, and I am grateful for it, truly grateful."

"Well I can tell you here and now, young man, that I did no such thing. I told what I saw and nothing more. But I can also tell you that I never could bear that Roberts creature, nor could anyone else at Hawkswell. We're all well rid of the man and that's the truth."

"I suppose they will get another head groom and I will work for him now."

"Ah, no. Not as I understand it. You see, one of the under-gardeners as works for my husband, he's got experience of horses and he's taking up Roberts' duties straightaway. He's taking his lad along with him to help in the stables along with that Tooms wretch who'll be doing your job."

"My job? So... I mean... what am I to do?"

"Well, that's where we come to the good news and the bad news. The good news is that you are to take over the under-gardener's job and work for my husband. The bad news," she grinned at him to take any sting out of the words, "is that he is a hard task master and you'll have a dreadful lot to learn about gardening in double quick time."

Jamie didn't quite know what to think. He had only seen the head gardener at a distance and knew nothing of his manner, but if he was anything like his wife, he should have no fears of mistreatment. Hard work and fast learning gave him no cause for concern at all. Maybe his luck had changed at last. But then, just as Mrs Gerrard was preparing to head back downstairs to her kitchen she dropped one more delightful bombshell into Jamie's day.

"Oh, I nearly forgot. I have sent one of my girls to collect your things from the stable loft and bring them up here. It's not much of a room, but it's yours if you want it, young man. An improvement on your previous accommodation I'm certain."

Chapter 4

North Somerset, May 1979

When Kate got back to her flat after hearing the enthralling story of her fellow Irishman's arrival at Hawkswell, she lay for a long time, curled up on her settee, mulling over everything she had been told. After a while, she found herself a notepad and a pen, brewed a mug of tea and settled down at the breakfast bar.

At the top of the sheet she wrote 'James – Jamie – Kirkpatrick', underlining the name Kirkpatrick several times. Directly below the name, she put 'Galway coast – Poulnadree?' and underneath that, the final item in her list, a date: '1913'.

Three things – a name, a place, and a year.

Her own grandmother Roisin had been born in a village called Poulnadree on Ireland's Galway coast, and her maiden name was Kirkpatrick. Born in the year 1908 she had been orphaned at the age of 5 – in 1913.

It all fitted perfectly.

Except that none of it made any sense at all because Roisin, or Rosie as she might well have been known as a child, had never had a brother called James or Jamie or anything else. Nor had she had any sisters. In fact, according to everything Kate had ever been told, Grandma Roisin had been the Kirkpatrick family's sole offspring. So the whole thing was nothing more than a mildly interesting coincidence.

With a deep sigh, she tore the page from the pad. But instead of screwing it up and tossing it in the kitchen bin, she put it aside and started to write a long overdue letter to her mother, well aware that she too would be as intrigued by the story.

Determined not to be too disappointed, Kate hoped that her ma might be able to suggest something, such as Jamie being a long lost cousin, or from a forgotten branch of the family. After all, it wasn't as if Kirkpatrick was an uncommon name in the west of Ireland.

She filled four pages, describing everything that had happened since moving into the flat and her determination to find out everything she could about Hawkswell, Penelope Townshend and now the intriguing Jamie.

Three weeks after Kate's arrival, an assortment of builders, plumbers, electricians and decorators turned up to commence work on the second flat. Luckily, each day Kate left for work just as they were getting started and she didn't get home until long after they were finished. Apart from a little extra dust and the smell of sawdust and fresh paint, she hardly knew they were there.

Then, one Friday evening in late May, all the tool boxes, ladders, paint pots and materials were gone. The flat was apparently finished.Nothing happened for two weeks until one Monday evening she found a note on her doormat from Tom telling her that her new neighbour would be moving in the following weekend. As things turned out, Kate was up in London attending a conference that Saturday and didn't arrive back at Hawkswell until gone midnight. It wasn't until late Sunday evening that she heard footsteps on the stairs and the sound of cases or boxes being dumped on the other side of her sitting room wall. She thought for a moment about introducing herself but was too comfortable to be bothered to make herself look decent. It was late and it could wait.

As she headed for work the next morning, she found a dark green Rover 2400 parked alongside her Mini. She took a peek through the passenger window. Leather upholstery and walnut trim. Not a student then.

That evening, as Kate ferried her shopping in out of the rain, she noticed half a dozen long metal cases stacked against the wall of the entrance hall. Certain they hadn't been left by the builders, she wondered whether they might be something to do with her new neighbour. On her final trip down to collect the last of the shopping bags, curiosity made her take a closer look. Instantly she wished she hadn't.

Although well battered and dusted with dried mud, the cases were unmistakably British army issue ammunition boxes. She knew what they were because her father had used one as a tool box, explaining to her once how they had been designed for ease of access after a British military disaster in the Zulu wars.

And there they were, metal clips at either end of the lids — clips easily knocked off with a rifle butt.

What in God's name was Rover man doing with a damned great pile of ammo boxes?

Kate didn't actually get to meet her neighbour until the following weekend. The intervening five days were so unremittingly wet and windy that her exposure to the world outside the GreenGauge offices and her flat was limited to quick dashes to and from her car.

The dismal weather cleared away overnight allowing the Hawkswell valley to awaken to a crystal clear blue sky and sunny Saturday morning. As soon as she'd finished her breakfast coffee, Kate set off to find Tom in the walled garden. As she stepped out into the courtyard, she came across what she presumed was her new neighbour cleaning his car.

Wearing nothing but a pair of disreputable denim shorts and sandals, he was busily sponging down the passenger side of the car when Kate called out a cautious but cheery "Hi."

As soon as he spotted her, he dumped his sponge in a bucket and straightened up. Kate was struck by a number of things straight away — the guy was tall and broad shouldered without an ounce of surplus fat that she could see, his fair hair looked something like a disaster in a mop factory and his smile was bright and wide and included his eyes. He wiped his hands on his shorts before stepping forward to shake hands.

"Hi to you too. You must be the girl next door, Catherine isn't it?"

She took his hand which was large, strong and still a bit wet.

"It's actually Catraoine, but I'm better known as Kate. Welcome to Hawkswell."

"Hi Kate. I'm Daniel, better known as… er, Daniel."

"So no-one ever calls you Dan?"

His face tensed for a fleeting moment, as if she'd touched a sore spot.

"Well, my parents call me Danny. But seeing as how I don't get on particularly with my parents, I don't answer to that one. At school, which is a period of my life I prefer to forget, I was called a lot of things, including Desperate Dan, Dan, Dan, the lavatory man and… I'm sure you've got the picture."

Kate laughed. "Fine with me. Daniel it is then."

As if anxious to change the subject, he asked, "So, how long have you been living here at Hawkswell?"

"Let's see, I moved in at the end of April. That's what, six weeks now, I suppose."

"And how do you like it so far?"

She opened her mouth and, to her complete disgust, gushed, "Oh er, really great. I mean it's brilliant. I love it here. Couldn't be better. So how's your flat?"

"Oh, right. Well it's fine, I guess. Yes, it's really nice."

"You don't sound too sure."

What puzzled Kate was that he looked unsure too.

"No, really. It's great. I mean, it's a flat."

"And the rest of the place?"

"You mean the grounds and all that?"

"I don't suppose you've had much of a chance to look around yet."

He shook his head. "No. What with the weather and work… You know how it is."

"Yeah, tell me about it. Say, have you anything planned for this afternoon?"

He shrugged.

"Not really, not after I've finished here."

"OK, so how about I give you the grand tour? Sometime after lunch maybe."

He looked surprised but pleased. "Sounds good to me. What, say about two thirty?"

"I'll meet you down here."

She was about to walk away when Daniel lifted his empty bucket, "I don't suppose you have any idea whether there's a tap or a hosepipe anywhere around. It's a real pain carting buckets up and down those stairs."

"To tell you the truth, I haven't a clue. But I'm off to see Tom and I'll ask him."

"Is he the old retainer?"

"Tom Gerrard, yes. Have you met him yet?"

"Only when he showed me round the flat."

"And Miss Townshend, Penelope. You must have seen her."

"You mean the old biddy?" Kate nodded, although she reckoned that Penelope deserved a little more than 'the old biddy'. "Barking."

At first she thought she hadn't heard him right. "Sorry?"

"Barking mad. She must be. I mean, look at this place. It's disintegrating around them and yet they carry on as if nothing's changed since the turn of the century. They're living in cloud cuckoo land. The old dear should have sold up long ago and booked herself into a home. A property developer would bite her hands off for this place."

Kate tried hard to keep her smile level. "Well I'm sure she's not quite as crazy as you think. I'm certain you'll change your mind once you get to know her better."

She ignored his look of frank disbelief.

"I'll go and see if I can find out about the tap."

They met in the courtyard as arranged.

Before setting off on the promised tour, Kate led Daniel over to a nondescript wooden door to the left of the gateway. It opened onto a dark and cobwebbed interior packed with ancient gardening tools, old wheelbarrows, plant pots, vegetable boxes and a tap with a coiled hosepipe just inside the door.

"Tom said you're welcome to use the hose whenever you want but please make sure you turn the tap off properly afterwards."

As Daniel checked that the tap worked, Kate wandered across to a magnificent cast iron pump propped against the far wall of the shed. A moment later Daniel joined her.

"Wow, that's a bit of a brute. I didn't know they even made them that big. They must have had to draw the water from a hell of a depth."

Kate looked puzzled so he explained.

"There's a maximum height you can lift water in a single stage. I think it's about 90 feet or so. And the higher the lift, the bigger the pump. Hence this monster."

Kate looked back at the impressive lump of rusting iron.

"So this means that there must be a well somewhere."

Daniel didn't answer for second or two, but when he did there was something in his voice that would niggle at Kate for the rest of that day.

"I guess there must be, and a deep one too."

It wasn't that there was anything specific in either his words or the way he had spoken. The closest she could come to was that his voice carried a sense of yearning, as if he wanted there to be a well very much indeed.

After closing up the shed, they set off down the slope towards the river where a broad footpath ran alongside the bank, shaded by willows. At that point the river was wide and slow as it wound its lazy way past the estate with long tresses of lush green water grass snaking in the current.

Nearest to the house, the outer curve of the meander was swept deep and clear by the current, the occasional splash and swirl betraying an unseen fish while moorhens, swans and mallards trawled up and down the far bank in search of nesting sites.

After a few minutes, they came to a low stone bridge crossed by a farm track.

"Tom reckons that the bridge is Roman and that the track used to be the main route between Bath and Salisbury."

Daniel looked suitably impressed. "I'm sure he's right. That stonework's ages old. There's a very similar bridge near my parent's place in Marlow and that's definitely Roman."

Marlow, Kate thought, on the Thames. Posh country.

They followed the track gently uphill away from the river for two or three hundred yards until, just short of the main road, the brick boundary wall started its long march around the eastern boundary of the estate.

At the road, they turned sharp left again to follow the gently climbing bridleway until they came to the main gate with its lion topped gateposts. Beyond the right-hand gatepost Kate picked up a path that forced its way through the undergrowth and continued along the estate side of the wall to reach the pastureland high above the house.

As the slope grew steeper, Kate's leg began to complain so she made as if to head back down towards the house. But Daniel, who hadn't noticed her discomfort, had other ideas.

"Come on, let's keep going. We should get a really good view of the house from the top."

A clump of wind-ravaged Scots pines marked the highest corner of the estate and the point at which the boundary wall turned sharp left again before heading downhill to lose itself in the broad swathe of conifers that blanketed the slopes beyond.

A fallen tree provided a welcome seat with the perfect view of the house that Daniel had anticipated. It lay directly below them, four square in its landscape, its broad frontage in deep shadow. Mixed woodland stretched down the hill from the edge of the forest to the northern edge of the walled garden.

Daniel spread his arms wide.

"Now that's what I call a view. Those guys really knew how to build houses in the perfect spot. Imagine what it must have been like, to own entire landscapes to choose from, acres and acres of land."

"And equally obscene amounts of money to build them with. The kind of unbelievable wealth that ordinary folk couldn't even dream of."

"There is that, I guess. So how does this landscape compare with Ireland?"

She thought for a moment. "It's not bad, I suppose. For what it is. But it can't really compete. What could ever compare with home?"

"You were obviously born over there."

"Of course. I've only had to suffer this heathen land for three years, thank God."

"So you don't like it here?"

"Oh, I'm only joking, mostly. It's not the same, that's for sure. Life is very different where I come from. Very different."

"So what's your work, Kate? How do you earn your corn?"

"I work for a magazine."

"OK. What sort of magazine?"

"It's called GreenGauge, all about ecology and the environment."

"Hey, I know it. You did a piece on river drainage management a while back. It was really good."

"That was before my time, I'm afraid. I only joined the team a few weeks ago. So how come you were reading an article about river drainage?"

"Because it's part of my remit – natural sciences. I lecture to university students."

"Here in Bath?"

"No, Bristol. I was in London until a couple of years ago."

"Hey, me too. But isn't Bristol a bit of a thrash from here every day?"

Again, just like when she had asked him about the water pump, Daniel looked a tiny bit uncomfortable.

"Oh, it's not too bad. Anyway, I prefer to live in the countryside. And the journey makes a nice break from work, keeps it at arm's length so to speak. No, it's great here, honestly."

"And when you're not working?" she asked.

"Oh, this and that. Nothing in particular. I used to do a bit of caving once but I don't really get the time these days."

"Caving, you mean like potholing?"

"Yeah. In fact, most weekends I used to head up to Derbyshire or down here to the Mendips. And here I am living only a few miles away and I haven't been underground for months. Crazy, huh?"

Kate agreed but had the distinct feeling that she hadn't quite heard the full story.

After a while they set off downhill towards a high barbed wire fence that marked the edge of the forestry. Within fifty yards Kate was suffering on the uneven ground and soon she had to stop. Daniel couldn't fail to notice this time and asked if she was OK.

She shrugged and tried on a grin she didn't really mean.

"It's my frigging leg. It's fine most of the time but it really doesn't like going down hills or stairs."

"So, what, did you break it?"

"Something like that. It'll be fine if I take it slowly. You go on ahead if you want."

"Hell, no. You take your time. I sprained my ankle once, really badly. I know what it's like."

No you don't, she thought, but managed a smile as if they were sharing her pain.

"So what was it, skiing?"

Kate started walking again, getting ahead of Daniel so he couldn't see the pain in her face.

"No. It's something I'd really rather not talk about if that's OK."

Luckily, he took the hint.

Soon the forest and the fence angled back sharply to their right, giving way to grazing land that continued all the way back down to the river.

Kate's walking improved as soon as they were back on level ground although she knew her leg would need a long hot soak in the bath that night.

A path led alongside the row of poplars and back to the walled garden and its greenhouses. Daniel gave the impression he was politely interested although Kate sensed that he had more on his mind now they were closer to the house because he kept on glancing around as if searching for something.

Eventually Kate dragged him away and down across the lawns back to the river and the finale of the walk, the boathouse.

He was immediately fascinated.

"Wow, it looks as if it's been here forever. What a fantastic old building. Have you had a look inside yet?"

"Not yet, no. I'd love to but Miss T seems a bit fond of no-go areas and this seems to be one of them. I so wish there was a boat in there, something I could get on the river. I'd love to do some rowing again."

"Rowing?"

Daniel's response sounded to Kate as if she had suggested something obscene.

"Yes, rowing. And what's so strange about that?"

"Oh, nothing. Nothing at all. It's just that… I mean, you don't really look the rowing type, that's all."

"So exactly what might the rowing type look like, then?"

Unaware of the hole he was getting himself into, Daniel kept right on digging.

"Oh, I don't know. I can't quite get my head round you in a boat, that's all. Sorry."

"Well I know I'm a little out of shape right now, but let me tell you I was brought up on the water. I could row almost before I could walk, and I rowed for my university, very successfully too."

Daniel held his hands up. "OK, OK, sorry, again. I guess the short fuse goes with the red hair." He grinned as he spoke and Kate was forced to smile back and climb down from her tower.

Daniel tried again. "Can I ask where you studied?"

"Queens, Belfast."

"Ah. So when did you graduate?"

"Seventy two."

"So you were there during…"

She interrupted him. "Bloody Sunday and all the rest of that shit. Yes, I was there and it wasn't a lot of fun, I can tell you. In fact I was… Ah, Jesus, I really don't want to talk about any of that now. Especially on such a lovely day. It all seems so far away from here, if you see what I mean."

Daniel nodded, "I understand, honestly. Sometimes it's hard to believe it's actually going on. My dad's with the Foreign Office. He and Mum have to check under their cars for bombs before they drive anywhere."

To end that conversation in a hurry, she started back up the slope.

"OK, that's enough of that. Let's not let it spoil today or this place, please."

Hardly another word was spoken as they headed towards the house. Unasked questions were left hanging, casting long shadows across their respective thoughts, and the day. Without anything specific being said, they had both realised that they were potentially on opposing sides in that squalid little war; it was something they were going to have to deal with sooner or later.

But as things turned out, Kate wouldn't see Daniel again for more than a fortnight.

Chapter 5

Kate was entirely unprepared for what she walked into that Monday morning. At five past nine, she and the rest of *GreenGauge's* staff were summoned to their small conference room. Everyone brought their early morning coffee with them and they took their places round the conference table with varying degrees of anticipation and trepidation.

Andy quickly picked up on the mood.

"Don't panic folks, at least not yet. I know that early morning meetings often mean bad news, but I can assure you all that this is not the case today."

They all relaxed a little while Jenny, their graphic designer, helped Andy set up the slide projector and screen. As soon as everything was working, Kate drew the blinds. The first slide was a logo, the stylised globe of the Summerquest Institute, a high profile lobbying and campaigning organisation.

"Right, you all recognise this, I hope."

They all nodded or murmured assent. Summerquest had been a major supporter and contributor to *GreenGauge* for the last six months, providing over three quarters of its advertising revenue and, in effect, paying all their wages.

Andy pressed the remote and the next slide clicked into place, a full face photograph of an elderly gentleman with steel grey hair swept back from a high forehead, a full beard and a pair of piercing eyes, a dead spit for Richard Attenborough.

"Sir Arthur Summers, founder, Chairman and Chief Executive of the Institute. He is the reason we are all gathered here this morning. I received a phone call on Friday evening inviting me to Sunday lunch at Sir Arthur's home in the Cotswolds. The first item on the agenda was that the Institute has been so impressed with our work these last few months that they have invited us to become their official mouthpiece."

After a moment's stunned silence, the room erupted with questions.

Andy held up his hands for silence.

"OK, OK! This is a democratic organisation and I promise that you will all have your chance to vote on whether or not to accept their offer when it becomes official."

Kate dived in with the question on everyone else's lips.

"So what's in it for *GreenGauge*, Andy?"

"Oh, nothing much. New, larger premises, job security, sick pay, an in-house print facility, almost unlimited resources and the potential to get ourselves on the shelves of national newsagents within our first six months. But as I said guys, it'll be your call."

The room kicked off like a hornet's nest again until Andy banged his desk.

"There's more, and believe me, this part of the deal is a little pressing. For reasons that I am not at liberty to divulge, the Institute wants us to arrange a dinner for five hundred invited guests at the Assembly Rooms here in Bath. There will only be one speaker at the dinner, Sir Arthur himself."

Kate asked the obvious question. "And exactly when is this supposed to take place?"

"Thursday week."

Only Kate actually threw her note pad up in the air, everyone else just looked as if they were about to.

"That's just ten days! I hope this is just another of your wind- ups, Andy."

He shook his head.

"I wish it was, folks. The whole thing has come as a complete surprise, believe me. For starters, I don't know why we have been given the job over and above the Institute's own PR team, although I guess we should all feel flattered in some weirdly masochistic way. I also don't know why it's all got to happen at such short notice, except that I have been told that it is one hundred percent time critical, so there's absolutely no way to put it back. And believe me, I checked that point very thoroughly. Oh, and by the way, the only thing booked so far is the venue."

For the next few minutes Andy fielded a barrage of questions, each answer prompting yet another query until he held his hands up in surrender.

"Let's take some time out here and try to calm down a little. I can't emphasise what a terrific opportunity this is for all of us and I can't think of another group of individuals who I could trust to pull this off. So let's get to it. We'll meet again at three this afternoon and start calling in some favours."

The rest having retired to their own corners and cubby holes to mull things over and consider their own involvement in the project, Kate spent what remained of the day closeted with Andy, preparing a detailed plan of action. By the time the team packed up on Wednesday evening, the full extent of the task facing them had become all too real.

They got there in the end, but it entailed the entire staff working sixteen hour days and an extraordinary slice of luck when their favoured caterer had a last-minute cancellation. Each night, Kate arrived back at Hawkswell any time between eleven and one in the morning, leaving again at six thirty each morning. She didn't get to see or speak to anyone during those ten days, neither her new neighbour Daniel, Tom nor Penelope Townshend. She fell exhausted into her bed every night, only to drag herself out of again it only five or six hours later, with barely enough time for a coffee and a shower before she was back behind the wheel and on her way to Bath.

So much for finding the perfect flat in the perfect setting, she thought more than once, I'm never here to see it!

Sir Arthur's reputation preceded him and the popular story was that if intimidation ever became an Olympic event, he was a shoe-in for a gold medal. One beetle browed scowl had been known to send even Cabinet Ministers scurrying for cover. His monumental rages were legendary and Kate was becoming increasingly terrified as the event approached.

The evening was an outstanding success right from the off. It seemed that the combination of *GreenGauge* and the Summerquest Institute had resulted in a dream ticket. Out of the five hundred invitations issued, only six declined, and all for very good reasons.

The *GreenGauge* team had created as informal an atmosphere as possible while still maintaining a coherent structure to the evening. The hall's entire floor area was taken up with circular dining tables which, depending on size, seated between eight and twelve delegates. The top table, situated centrally in front of the stage was the largest, accommodating all the big fish including key Institute and magazine staff and the evening's hosts, Sir Arthur and Lady Summers. Kate's action station was on a side table, seated between Andy Travis and Sue Penhalligon, Sir Arthur's PA. She learned later that the food was excellent, although at the time she couldn't remember tasting anything for nerves.

The service too was faultless, as efficient and discreet as it should have been from a team used to dealing with Palace garden parties, Royal Ascot and Henley. The four courses passed off with military precision. Eventually the time came for Sir Arthur to take the stage and such was the level of anticipation, the silence that settled across the room as he reached the microphone was profound.

"Ladies and gentlemen, fellow activists and *GreenGauge* supporters. I believe you all know who I am, just as I believe that most of you are aware of the Summerquest Institute and its work, so I'll cut straight to the purpose of this gathering.

"The western world's increasing reliance on science and technology is placing the future of our planet in greater jeopardy than ever before. Natural resources are being squandered at an unprecedented rate while pollution levels are spiralling out of control. Animal and plant extinctions are accelerating year on year as rain forest deforestation continues unchecked. And while eight hundred million people are actually starving and one third of this planet's population exists on less than a dollar a day, we in the so called developed world are becoming ever more concerned with the implications of an obesity epidemic."

He paused for effect and patted his ample belly reflectively. No-one laughed. "It isn't fair, it isn't right, and it has to change." Although spoken quietly, the words carried to every corner of the silent room.

"But this disgustingly unbalanced state of affairs is not going to change by itself, especially now that this great nation of ours has decided to vote a Tory government back into power!"

This was greeted with a ragged chorus of boos and a single, hastily silenced cheer.

"And nothing is going to improve while hundreds of isolated pressure groups, charities and agencies have to compete against each other for limited funds and support. The only way that uncaring, greedy corporations and unseeing, complacent governments will ever be shamed into caring for the environment and its inhabitants – whether they be human, animal, bird, plant, fish or insect – is by joining forces and combining their efforts. That way, instead of a few irritating guerrilla groups nagging away at the establishment's shirt tails, they'll find a full size international force – more than equal to their threats and intimidation – camped on their Godforsaken doorsteps, ready to take them on, on equal terms."

He was really socking it to them now, each word punched into the air, drilling into the hearts and minds of everyone present. Probably not what some of them had expected or wanted to hear, but they certainly weren't going to forget a word of it in a hurry.

"We all know the truism about workers united never being defeated. Well, we should take note of that and, regardless of our political, social or religious beliefs, our nationalities or our individual agendas, join together. Only then will we be strong enough to take on the forces that are inexorably destroying our planet. *GreenGauge*, like many other similar publications and organisations, is doing a magnificent job…"

Sir Arthur's upraised hands quickly silenced a polite ripple of applause.

"...but would they realistically stand any kind of chance against even one of the national broadsheets, or the BBC, or a single government department if any of them really decided to cut up rough? No, of course they wouldn't, no matter how committed are these wonderful folk sitting around this table. They would be blown away, smashed into the dirt. They wouldn't stand an earthly.

"And why not? Lack of cash, of course. The cash to mount and sustain an all-out legal campaign, the cash to support staff through a publishing embargo, the cash to buy airtime and column inches and, through managed publicity, hearts and minds. Because that's what this fight of ours is all about.

"It's not simply a case of giant corporation taking on giant corporation, or even government against government, it's all about one little person fighting to save another little person. It's one old lady in Brighton or Shepherd's Bush digging into her purse for fifty pence so that we can lobby to change the life of a similar little old lady in Ethiopia or Ghana or Palestine. Little people helping little people."

Kate could hardly believe what she was hearing, they were her very own words, taken straight from a recent piece she had written for *GreenGauge* that had, much to her delight, been picked up by some of the nationals. She didn't have time to consider the implications of such blatant plagiarism because the man responsible had an even bigger bombshell to drop.

"And that, ladies and gentlemen, is why the Summerquest Institute is to be floated on the London Stock Exchange in exactly thirty days' time."

There was a moment's stunned silence before the hall erupted like a well-kicked beehive. Sir Arthur held up both hands again for silence and, after a lengthy pause, achieved it.

"I know, I know. It sounds like getting into bed with the enemy. But think about it for a moment. What's the best way to raise the level of financial support we are going to need to fight this war? By a massive share issue. By fighting these organisations on their own turf. I want all the little people to put their fifty pence pieces and pound coins where they can do the most damage. As of this evening, I have managed to accumulate enough rock solid pledges to guarantee a 15% capitalisation on every £1 ordinary share sold – that's an immediate profit for anyone who wants to sell straightaway, as some no doubt will.

"Although I, along with the many individuals and institutions who have pledged to support this venture, do not believe that many will exploit this offer, certain assurances have been put in place. Firstly, we will not sell to institutions and, secondly, the issue will be restricted to a maximum of 10,000 ordinary £1 shares per individual shareholder. With ten million shares released in the first tranche, that's a fighting fund of forty million to get us started. And, as we start to achieve results, much more will come, of that I am certain."

The remainder of the speech was bound to be an anti-climax. More details about the Institute's terms of reference and a brief list of its primary targets – international oil companies, corrupt third world regimes, inefficient and ineffective aid agencies.

The final applause was mixed, most of it ecstatic, but some merely polite, depending on whose hands were doing the clapping. Still seething with indignation about the cavalier high-jacking of her material, Kate's was of the polite variety, but she was not allowed long to simmer. With the structured part of the evening complete, legs were stretched and bladders relieved while tables were cleared and coffee served.

Kate felt a tap on her shoulder and turned, ready to tell someone where the loos were, only to come face to face with Sir Arthur Summers.

"Ms O'Donnell, I believe I owe you a rather large apology…"

Caught completely off guard, Kate found herself blushing for a number of very different reasons. Firstly, Sir Arthur was most definitely not a giant, their eyes were on a level. Secondly, those eyes told her immediately that he was not an ogre either – they were dark blue, bright as ice chips and full of humour. And finally, the voice that had thundered around their heads barely minutes before was deep, warm and gentle. If this sounds as if she was bowled off her feet by the man, then that's because she was. She would have forgiven him anything right then.

She must have looked like she'd been sandbagged because he carried on as if she hadn't understood, "…about using your words just now without asking your permission. I am really very sorry but there wasn't time before we sat down. I was putting the finishing touches to my speech in the car on the way here when I came across the piece you had written. It was precisely what I needed."

As he spoke, he took her arm and carefully eased her into a quiet corner. She caught a glimpse of Lady Summers deep in conversation with Andy, and of Sue Penhalligon and a few other Summerquest people forming a polite but impenetrable barricade against the throng. But she was caught in a bubble, held apart from all the rest. She wasn't even nervous anymore.

"There is absolutely no need for an apology, Sir Arthur. On the contrary, you do me great honour."

"Catraoine, or may I call you Kate?"

"Kate please, Sir Arthur. Catraoine is such a mouthful."

He laughed. "Only as long as you drop the Sir. I am plain old Arthur to my friends, something I believe we shall very quickly become."

If it had been anyone else, Kate would have run a mile, certain that she was being blatantly, and publicly, seduced. But at that very moment she couldn't have felt more at ease. All her instincts told her that this was a man she could trust, implicitly.

He went on. "And I don't agree that an apology isn't in order. I was watching your face when I came to the little people passage. You would have shot me through the head right where I stood if you'd had a gun."

Kate laughed, she couldn't help herself.

"Yes, I probably would have. It was a bit of a shock. Especially as that piece meant a lot to me. I still don't quite know where it came from, but it was one of my first pieces to be picked up and, you know…"

He put a hand on her arm. "I know exactly what you mean. It was a remarkable piece of writing, and not just in my opinion. It was that piece that lifted *GreenGauge* head and shoulders above the competition as far as I was concerned. And it was no flash in the pan either, from what I've discovered since."

She felt the blood rush to her face, hoping the light was too dim for anyone to notice.

"Well, er, thank you very much. It's only that I write what I feel. It kind of makes it easy in a way."

"There's nothing easy about it, my dear, I know that. Excellent journalism is a combination of diligent research, passionate belief and damned hard work. But you have the ability to make it appear effortless, and that's why you are so good at what you do."

They say that flattery will get you anywhere.

Kate's trouble was that she had no idea right then where she wanted or needed to go. All she could remember the next day were the hundred things that she forgot to say at that moment. Someone whose shoes she didn't feel qualified to shine had just praised her to the roof, and all she could say was, "I hope you enjoyed the food".

Convinced that she had missed one of her life's greatest opportunities by a country mile, Kate could only watch as the great man was spirited away to commune with more sentient beings. Afterwards she mooched around feeling like a complete prat until Andy cornered her and asked if she had been offered another job.

She laughed enough for him to help her into a chair in a corner, "God, far from it Andy. After my totally inarticulate performance I'll be lucky if he even says goodnight."

And he didn't.

As the evening blew itself out, Kate found herself rushing about from one mini-crisis to the next – lost keys, lost coats, lost wife. Sir Arthur and Lady Summers were long gone by the time she made it to the cloakroom to collect her own coat. Still, it had been a great evening and, at two o'clock in the morning, she had no intention of setting her alarm that night. She wanted to sleep for a fortnight.

Sadly for Kate, the rest of the *GreenGauge* team and their various partners had other ideas.

Three horrendous hours later, back at Andy's flat, Kate, well aware that they were both more than a little bit pissed, slumped into one his battered armchairs and slammed her head back against its cushions.

"Dear God, if I ever have to listen to another 'happy couple' dribbling on about how much they 'enhance each other's' lives', I swear I'll throw up all over them. What in God's name is the imperative that insists that we all have to go round in pairs? If that's how life was meant to be, we'd have all been born Siamese twins, joined at the hip."

Andy, stretched out on another sofa opposite her, laughed.

"Jesus, Kate, why are you so determinedly anti-relationship?"

Kate gave him a slightly skewed frown. "I'm not anti-relationship. I'm not against any of it, the dreaded marriage thing included. I just can't see why it's so unacceptable to not be in one, a relationship that is."

"So you really like being on your own, do you?"

"Course I do. Love it. If I wanted to share my life with someone, I'd do it. I'd go out and find someone. It shouldn't be that difficult, there are enough sad lonely bastards out there who'd jump at the chance."

"You mean jump into bed."

Kate stuck her tongue out at him.

"There you go. That's what it all comes down to in the end, doesn't it? Sex. No-one can get their sad little heads around someone who can get along very well without regular nookie. Well that's their problem. I don't miss having some great hairy man cluttering up the place and that's an end to it."

"What, not at all? Don't you ever climb between those cold sheets at night and wish there was someone there to cuddle up with, to tell your troubles to? Don't you ever see or hear something wonderful and want to share it with someone? We weren't meant to stumble through life on our own, Katie, we're just not wired that way."

"So how come you're so concerned about my welfare all of a sudden, boss?"

Andy thought for a moment before replying. "I don't want you to feel that it's cool to be on your own, Kate. It's not. I'm on my own because no-one could ever replace my late wife Mel, you included. So you can stop looking worried, I'm not about to make a pass at you."

"And why should I be worried if you did? You're a very attractive man."

"Because you, my dear Kate, deserve so much more than a sad old widower, far too many years your senior. You're beautiful, intelligent, witty and fun to be with. I mean it's criminal that you're not with anybody!"

It was Kate's turn to hold her hands up. "All right, all right. That's enough of the bullshit compliments. They're all nonsense anyway. I'm damaged goods and you know it." She slapped her bad leg for emphasis. "I've got a temper on me that makes hand grenades look like kiddie's toys, and I can't stand idiots. It's as simple as that, Andy. I can't cope with fools and, as most men are fools, I reckon I'm better off on my own."

This time it was Andy's turn to look affronted.

"Hey, hey, hey. Most men are certainly not fools! That is way beyond a generalisation."

"OK, sorry. Point taken. Maybe not all men are fools. The trouble is that all the gorgeous ones I've ever met turned out to be idiots and most of the intelligent ones were geeks or gay. Why is that? I mean, you meet a hunky guy at a party. Wow! you think. Maybe he's the one. You get talking, and then what? All he can talk about is football, cricket or rugby, or how fast his frigging car or motorcycle goes. Mention literature, music or art and you can watch the membrane sliding across their eyeballs. They're gone. At the other end of things, you've got some balding, geeky nerd who can talk about all the right stuff but even the thought of them with their kit off is enough to make you run a mile."

Andy laughed.

"So what you're really looking for is a beautiful Olympic athlete with a PHD and a Nobel prize for literature."

Kate sighed.

"God no. Just someone who looks half way decent and who's got more than two brain cells in their head. I don't understand how testosterone seems to dissolve brain cells. How come no-one's ever come up with an answer to that?"

"So, what about your new neighbour?"

"My what?"

"The guy who's moved into the flat next door to yours."

"Daniel?"

"So you know his name already?"

Kate's tongue came out again.

"His name is Daniel Lewis. His father's 'something in the Foreign Office', he lectures at Bristol University and drives a big, shiny Rover. I mean, what more do you need to know?"

"Surely he can't be all bad. What's he look like?"

"Oh, Andy. I really don't care. I haven't noticed, and that's the truth. Jesus, I haven't even set eyes on the guy for the last fortnight."

"Wow. So you're missing him already. That was quick."

When Kate got back to her flat later that morning and crawled into bed, Andy's voice still rolled around her head like distant thunder, "Don't you ever climb between those cold sheets at night and wish there was someone there to cuddle up with, to tell your troubles to? Don't you ever see or hear something wonderful and want to share it with someone?"

The trouble was that her answer to both of those questions was a resounding 'yes'. The only trouble was in finding the right someone. Sure there might be plenty of fish in the sea, as she was so often told, but all she ever seemed to meet were either sharks or flounders.

Andy had given everyone the Friday off and so, with no alarm, Kate didn't wake until 10:30. After a leisurely breakfast, she set off to collect her post only to discover that Daniel had left it neatly outside her door. Despite her exhaustion she felt quietly touched by the gesture. About to leave it on the breakfast bar for later, she spotted an envelope with a familiar Limerick postmark.

She quickly tore open the envelope and flopped onto the sofa.

My Dearest Katie,

So wonderful to hear from you. Now that's what I call a letter! It sounds like you have found yourself a little bit of English paradise and no mistake, and so cheap too! So what's wrong with it? (Only joking.)

And what amazing news about that Irish boy. By the way we're all well here and I'm just dashing this off before going to work. As a result of your letter, I'm taking some time off later this month. I've decided to visit cousin Maeve in Dublin for a few days to do some digging in the national archives – something about all those coincidences makes me think this might be worth looking into. Leave it to me! Your father will probably be glad to have a few days peace from my nagging, so it'll be like a little holiday all round. I'll let you know what I find as soon as I can. But don't get too excited. Your grandma Roisin was never a one for keeping secrets so I'm completely certain that she never had a brother. There are probably hundreds of Kirkpatricks in Galway but I'll see what I can find all the same.

God bless and look after yourself,

Mum and Dad (who's asleep in front of the telly right now)

Kate sat back and closed her eyes. Dear old Mum, any excuse to do a bit of fossicking. She would enjoy herself and no mistake. The thought of her and cousin Maeve on the loose in Dublin made her smile.

Chapter 6

It was gone nine by the time Kate woke on Saturday morning. She dozed for a while before making herself a large mug of coffee and climbing back into bed. Propped up on her pillows, she looked across to the meadows on the far side of the river where black and white cows grazed contentedly. A flock of crows pecked around them, occasionally swirling into the air like wind-blown autumn leaves before redistributing themselves back onto the ground.

Meringue-like clouds slid slowly across the bright blue sky, their shadows hardly disturbing the scene. From the far side of the house came the sound of Tom on one of the motor mowers. She felt a stab of guilt at the sound and decided that, unless something else cropped up, she'd go and give him a hand that afternoon.

When Kate got downstairs, she found an extension lead snaking out to the courtyard from one of the power points in the hall. She stepped into the sunshine to be confronted by Daniel's backside as he vacuumed the inside of his Rover's cavernous boot. She waited until he straightened up and saw her, and straightaway he switched off the cleaner.

"Hey Kate. Haven't seen you for a while. How's things?"

"Really good, thanks. Just had a couple of crazy weeks at work. I've hardly been here except to sleep. Oh, and if it was you, thanks for bringing my post up this morning."

"No problem. I knocked a couple of times during the week to check things were OK, but as your car wasn't here, I reckoned you must be working. Who'd be a journalist, eh?"

"Tell me about it. Look, I'm sorry in case anyone was worried, maybe I should have left a note or something."

"Why should you? It's your life after all."

"Reckon it is at that. Although it'd surely be nice to live some of it now and again instead of working all the bloody time."

He laughed. "I know just what you mean. I get my fair share, don't you worry."

"Look, I'm just off to invite Miss T over for a spot of tea later this afternoon, if she can make it. I don't suppose you'd like to – "

He finished the sentence for her. "Join you, for tea? Er, nice idea, but I've got a hell of lot to do this afternoon. Fact is, I'd better crack on. Thanks anyway. Another time maybe?"

Only slightly disappointed, she said, "Sure. I don't suppose tea with an old biddy and a crazy Irish woman are right at the top of your agenda anyway."

He grinned. "Not exactly. Although a cold beer or two, or maybe a nice bottle of red wine for two might sound a bit more appealing."

Kate put that one away for future reference.

As they were talking, Kate couldn't help notice that both Daniel's hands were bruised and the knuckles grazed, with a large piece of sticking plaster across the back of his left hand. It looked as if teaching in a university wasn't the cushy number she thought it was, or maybe he'd been working on his car. She couldn't see any tools anywhere, so maybe he was just clumsy.

"Catch up again soon, yeah?"

As Kate went off in search of Penelope, she caught his answering grin as he bent to switch the vacuum back on.

Walking round the side of the house towards the front door, she tried her damndest to work out what it was about Daniel that continued to puzzle her. Of course the last thing he'd want to do on a Saturday afternoon was to sit making small talk with

Miss Townshend. In all honesty, Kate wasn't exactly looking forward to it herself, but she had an ulterior motive.

Eventually she realised what was really bugging her.

Why on earth would someone like Daniel want to live at Hawkswell?

Penelope was delighted to be invited for tea and confessed to a sneaking desire to see what the flat looked like now that it was occupied.

"You know, my dear, I have often considered taking a sneaky look while you were out at work, just to satisfy my curiosity. But as that would have constituted an unforgivable invasion of your privacy, I have been quite cross with myself for even entertaining the thought. However, I will look forward to seeing you at three o'clock."

Kate almost said, "Don't be late," but managed, "Lovely, see you then," instead.

There wasn't much to tidy or clean, since she'd hardly set foot in the flat for the past two weeks, but she hoovered around and dusted all the same before shifting some of the half-empty book boxes through into her bedroom out of sight.

Standing in the middle of the sitting room, she was quietly pleased with the way the place looked. Some pictures on the walls, a couple of hangings she'd bought in London, and some carefully placed ornaments made all the difference.

Penelope was as punctual as Kate thought she would be, and seemed genuinely delighted with the look of the flat.

"You've made it very homely, Kate. I was a little worried because these rooms were so cavernous when they were empty, so cold. But this is delightful. Well done."

With Penelope settled on one of the sofas, Kate produced her best teapot and the two cups and saucers unpacked specially.

"Darjeeling?" she called from the kitchenette, "Didn't you say that's what you liked?"

"Well remembered, my dear, thank you."

"I'm afraid these little cakes are straight from Marks and Sparks." Kate set down a loaded plate. "I'm sure they won't be a patch on Mrs Gerrard's." At the mention of the name, Penelope's face stiffened, albeit briefly, yet it was as clear as if someone had flicked a switch off and then on again. The list of Hawkswell mysteries seemed to lengthen by the day.

After dealing with all the niceties of conventional afternoon conversation, including the weather, Penelope's health and Kate's tough couple of weeks at work, she couldn't keep her news to herself any longer.

"I was talking with Tom the other day and he mentioned that there was once an Irishman working here shortly before the First World War, someone called James or Jamie Kirkpatrick."

Penelope sipped at her tea and answered without looking up.

"Yes, I believe there was someone of that name here for a while."

Something in the old lady's voice made Kate immediately want to say, "Oh, it's nothing really." But she soldiered on, determined to discover as much as she could. "Well, if this Jamie is who I think he might be, I have got something quite astonishing to tell you." A puzzling look flickered in Penelope's eyes before she asked Kate to continue.

Thinking about it later, she would conclude that the old lady was afraid of something. Right then though, Kate blamed her own imagination. "You see, my great aunt on my mother's side is Roisin Kirkpatrick. She was also born in a place called Poulnadree on the Galway coast of Ireland and orphaned in January 1913. That's all I know so far, but my mother, back in Ireland, is trying to uncover as much as she can."

Expecting a dramatic reaction from Miss Townshend, Kate was disappointed when the old lady hardly seemed interested.

"How interesting. If what you say turns out to be true, it will indeed be a coincidence that you should find yourself living here. I'm afraid I cannot tell you very much about Mister Kirkpatrick. I recall that I was away at school for most of the time he was here at Hawkswell."

Apparently wishing to change the subject, Penelope indicated a group of Kate's rowing photographs hanging above the fireplace. The biggest, in the centre of the group, was a black and white close-up taken during a race. Shot by a fellow student from one of the chase boats, so far as Kate was concerned it graphically summed up all the pain and effort involved in competition rowing.

"Goodness me, Kate, do I recognise you in that picture?"

"Er yes, you most certainly do. Not looking my best I'm afraid. If it had been in colour you'd have seen that my face was the colour of a beetroot."

"Where was it taken?"

"On the Lagan river, to the south of the city, Belfast that is. There's a regatta there every summer. I was rowing with my university crew."

"Did you win?"

Kate laughed.

"Of course we won! We were the best crew in the whole of Ireland by a country mile. God knows we worked hard enough for it."

"How do you mean?"

"Training. It was hell on earth. We were up most mornings during the season at five thirty to be in the gym by six. We did an hour of circuit training and then another half hour in the boat, no matter what the weather. Then it was a quick shower, breakfast, and off to lectures. And that was during the week. Weekends were even more punishing."

"My goodness. I can't imagine anything worse. I don't know how you managed it my dear. You must have loved your rowing very much."

"I still do. I get on the water whenever I can. I have joined a club in Bath but, what with work and living here, I haven't got down there yet."

"That's a shame. You mustn't let your work take over your life, my dear. I did, in that running Hawkswell was a full time job. And I regret it bitterly when I reflect on everything I have missed."

Penelope leaned forward slightly as if she was about to get up. Kate didn't want her to leave straight away, feeling she was getting close to something even though she hadn't a clue what that something might be.

"How about another cup of tea, Penelope?"

The old lady thought for a moment before settling back against the cushions.

"Another small cup would be very welcome my dear, thank you."

As Kate filled the kettle and rinsed out the pot and cups, Penelope hauled herself to her feet to take a closer look at the photographs on the wall.

With fresh tea poured, Penelope pointed at the photographs.

"Tell me Kate, what is it that makes you so passionate about rowing?"

Kate thought carefully for a moment. "I'm not sure that passionate is quite the right word. The fact is, I grew up with boats. Mum reckons I could row before I could walk, but all mums talk nonsense sometimes, don't they? Having said that, I was on the water ever since I can remember. Our house is at the top of a creek and needless to say there were all kinds of boats down there. I used to go fishing with my dad at first. Then, the moment I proved to him that I could row against the strongest tide he let me loose in one of the skiffs. I learned to canoe and sail too, but always preferred the rowing.

"A club at school gave me the opportunity to race for the first time. I reckon they must all have thought I was cheating somehow because I won everything going. When I went up to Queens, it was natural that I'd join the club there. I started out in the single skulls and did quite well, then one day I was invited to join an eight."

Penelope held up a hand. "I'm sorry to interrupt my dear, but I have a couple of questions if I may."

"Sure, go ahead."

"Firstly, why did you go to university in Belfast? Wasn't it rather dangerous?"

Kate paused for a second and thought hard about her answer.

"It still is, believe me. But I don't remember us paying much attention to all that back then. It was well before Bloody Sunday, and I think we in the Republic mostly believed it was something and nothing, just a bit of local nonsense stirred up by the Brits and that it would soon settle down. And, of course, there hadn't been any serious bombings then. As to why Belfast, that's simple, Queens was the only university offering the combination of courses I wanted. I could have come over here to England of course, but the north seemed more like an extension of home I suppose."

"I understand. Thank you. Now please will you explain what an 'eight' is?"

"That's easy. You know the boats that compete in your boat race on the Thames, between Oxford and Cambridge?"

Penelope nodded. "Well they're eights. They should be called eight and a bits really if you include the little one who steers, the cox. Anyway, they're exactly the same as that, except that ours was an all-girl crew. And that was something else. I wasn't sure about joining the crew at first. I suppose I never really saw myself as a team player and I thought it might be a bit, well... you know, girly. But after a couple of sessions, I was hooked. What a crew! Rampant feminists the lot of them. Jeez we had such a time. I'm not sure when we were at our most dangerous, on the water or off it!"

As she spoke, she realised for the first time in many months how precious those times had been and how much she missed the close company and being on the water.

Penelope, sensing something in her words, must have wanted to know more. "These other girls, you must all have become very close friends I would imagine."

Kate smiled wistfully. "They were the best any girl could have."

"Something happened, didn't it?"

Kate nodded and swallowed hard before she answered.

"There was a car bomb in the city centre. I was badly hurt and... and Annie and Eileen were killed along with too many others." Penelope leaned across the space between them, put her hand on Kate's knee and squeezed.

"I am so sorry, my dear. I shouldn't have asked."

Kate sniffed, dug out a tissue from her jeans pocket and blew her nose. "It's OK. You weren't to know. I'm fine, really. It was a while ago now, but it finished us as a crew. We'd all been so close you see, we couldn't just find two more girls. It wouldn't have been right. And anyway, I was… "

She tailed off. Penelope prompted her.

"You were?"

Kate shook her head and slapped on a smile.

"Nothing, really. I graduated later that year and came straight over here to try and find a job in London."

"Do you miss it, the rowing?"

Kate glanced through the window, to the bright daylight and the river. Especially the river.

"I don't miss the racing. Not really. It was damned hard work staying competition fit right through the season. Didn't leave much time for anything else except studying. All a bit too single- minded looking back on it. But I miss being on the water. Yes, I do miss that a lot. Back home, my favourite thing was to take one of the boats out at daybreak, when the creek was still as a mirror and layered with early morning mist. It was the most magical time of day, with the ducks and coots, the moorhens and the swans all drifting about. It used to be so quiet, just the whispering sound of the water against the boat's hull, the drips from the oar blades. God, I really miss that. Once or twice I've walked down to the river here before leaving for work. It's so lovely down there by the boathouse. I don't suppose –"

"You don't suppose what?"

Kate braced herself and threw caution to the wind. "I don't suppose there might be a boat or two tucked away in there?"

Penelope was silent for so long that Kate was sure she'd blown it. When she eventually answered, it was with a voice so distant, so faint, that Kate barely caught what she said.

"There is a boat, at least there used to be. But it's so dangerous, too dangerous."

A moment or two later, without saying another word about the boathouse or the boat, the old lady struggled to her feet, thanked Kate for the tea, the cakes and the conversation, and left.

Kate had her fingers tightly crossed as she said goodbye.

After an early night and an excellent night's sleep, Kate woke refreshed on Sunday morning, determined to spend at least part of the day helping Tom in the garden. She found him in the tool shed refuelling one of the mowers.

"Hi, Tom. Sorry I haven't been around for a while. How are you keeping?" He put down the fuel can, carefully replaced the cap and straightened up slowly.

"I'm fine, lass, apart from this blasted back of mine. Been playing up something chronic this last week. Suppose I'll have to go and get some more horse liniment before it'll get any better."

Kate could see the pain in his face and wished she'd offered to help earlier.

"I'm really sorry to hear that. Is there anything I can do? I'm free all day."

"Ah, well. Maybe you can. There's something strange going on around here that I don't understand at all."

Kate frowned, unable to figure out what he meant. "Strange, in what way?"

"Well, peculiar anyways. The mistress come to see me first thing this morning and asked me to take you down to the old boathouse to see about a boat what's supposed to be in there."

He must have seen the excitement in Kate's face. "Now don't get your hopes up, young lady. Her told me as how you like getting on the river and I can understand that. Trouble is, no-one's been inside that there boathouse since I don't know when. Tell you the truth, I'm surprised it's still standing. By rights, it should've fallen into the river years ago." He took a step closer to Kate and lowered his voice in his customary way.

"Between you and me, I know exactly what boat she's

talking about and let me tell you that nothing good'll come of seeking it out, even if it's still there. And even if it is up there, it's hardly likely to be in one piece after all this time. Most likely eaten away or long rotted to dust. But that's by the by. I been asked to take you down there and that's what I'll do, whether I like it or not." After collecting the key from a rack in the tool shed, Tom picked up a torch, a crowbar and a can of penetrating oil. "For the boathouse padlock," he told Kate, and led the way down towards the river.

Level with the carriage gate, they met Daniel coming the other way. Once they'd all said their hellos, Kate let on where she and Tom were going and Daniel asked if he might tag along.

Nestled within a gap in the willows, the boathouse leaned tiredly away from the river bank, forming a bridge between land and water, anchored to both, yet part of neither. Its wooden shingles were grey, curled with age, as decorated with moss and lichen as the surrounding tree trunks, its pantiled roof dipping alarmingly from gable to gable.

The wide double doors facing the riverside path were secured by a single iron hasp and an enormous rusty padlock which required liberal doses of oil before the key would even turn, and another few squirts before the thing could at last be prized open.

The hasp and staple were rusted together so Tom wrenched them apart with the crowbar before he and Daniel could heave one door open just enough to enable them to squeeze inside. Decades of accumulated soil and debris would have to be cleared away before it could be opened further.

The interior was dark and damp, daylight reflected in the water of the little dock sending flickering patterns dancing across the tightly boarded roof. Tom and Daniel stepped forward carefully, checking each board before trusting their full weight to it, inviting Kate to follow a yard or two behind in case something gave way.

Surprisingly, despite being soft and green with age, the planking seemed quite sound. A wide deck extended down both sides of the dock which was choked with weed and river debris, the skeletal remains of what might once have been a punt hanging forlornly from a rotted mooring line. Kate was bitterly disappointed that there was no sign of any other craft although there was racking on the wall obviously intended for oars and spars.

A flight of wooden steps to one side of the entrance led up to a large square hatchway in the roof. Kate gave the structure a good shake before starting up cautiously.

Tom called out a warning. "I'm not at all sure that's safe."

Three steps up, Kate flexed her knees and gave the structure another shaking. She grinned down at the two men.

"Solid as a rock. No problem."

She climbed on up to the metre square hatch but, when she tried to lift it, it wouldn't move at all. After reassuring himself that the structure would hold, Daniel climbed up beside her and added his weight to hers, but to no avail. He squatted down on his heels and gave the hatch a good look over.

"It can't be locked, there's no keyhole, no padlock, nothing."

At that moment Tom called up. "I'll leave you to it then. Nothing more I can do here, and I've got plenty enough else to be getting on with. You both take care, mind."

As he eased his way out through the narrow gap in the doorway, Kate and Daniel exchanged puzzled shrugs before turning their attention back to the hatch.

"Maybe there's something on top of it, holding it down," Kate suggested.

Daniel looked at her sideways. "So if someone put something on top of the trapdoor, how did they get out of the loft?"

Kate paused for a moment, as if she didn't really want to admit to the ridiculous thought that was creeping around in her head.

"Maybe they didn't."

"Didn't what?"

"Didn't get out. Maybe that's the mystery. Maybe that's why Tom's cleared off."

Daniel's response was almost convincing.

"Hey, come one. That's crazy. Why would anyone want to seal themselves up there for heaven's sake?"

As if goaded by his own slight discomfort, Daniel gave the hatch another heave of his shoulders and felt it give a little in one corner.

"Come on, Kate. It's moving. Get beside me and push."

Having cracked the seal, the hatch couldn't resist their combined efforts and, with a shriek of rusted hinges, it sprung open, dousing them in a cascade of thick white dust and debris.

Coughing and sneezing and slapping the dust out of their hair, they stepped up into the loft space which was as dry and aired as the area below was damp.

Deep wooden louvres in each gable end provided a steady flow of fresh air, while stripes of green tinted daylight filtered through panels of mildewed glass set in amongst the roof tiles. A small window at one end overlooked the river, with a substantial looking work bench running the width of the loft beneath it.

The opposite gable, above the river bank, had a wide set of double doors similar to those found in hay lofts.

The deal planked floor, the cracks tightly caulked to prevent damp penetrating from below, was covered in a thick layer of dust which swirled at their every movement.

To one side of the work bench, a rusty old pot-bellied stove poked its crooked flue out through the roof, while on its other side stood three sturdy looking wooden chests and a number of saw horses, all similarly cloaked in thick grey dust and countless years of cobwebs. Bolts of what seemed to be canvas lay scattered along one side of the loft while the opposite side was occupied by a long, tarpaulin covered shape.

In the farthest corner, tucked in under the eaves, snug and comfortable, lay what looked as if it might once have been a bed. Some kind of mattress had been covered with a square of tarpaulin or sail cloth. A couple of dusty old blankets and a faded striped bolster lay rumpled and discarded as if abandoned in a hurry and never revisited.

A rusty hurricane lamp and a couple of jam-jars and saucers with traces of candle stubs completed the picture. It looked as if someone had once slept in the loft, maybe a tramp or a gamekeeper's assistant.

Kate wondered if they would ever find out who.

The long shape of what she so desperately hoped was the boat that Penelope had mentioned could not be ignored for long and she quickly dismissed the mystery of the loft's former occupant as she lifted away one end of the tarpaulin cover.

Even in the dim, dust filtered light, the deeply polished wood glowed like liquid honey. Pulling the sheet away completely revealed a magnificent rowing skiff, inverted on a set of six wooden trestles, obviously made specifically for the purpose.

The craft was broad and elegant, her richly coloured, shapely flanks exposed to the bright mosaic of daylight for the first time in how many years? The thickness of dust and guano on the canvas cover suggested decades. As they looked closer, it was clear that she had been laid up with exquisite care, the wood itself heavily varnished and waxed, all the iron and copper components sealed with thick plugs and strips of wax or tar.

A long and tightly wrapped oilskin bundle had been cleverly slung beneath the hull to keep it clear of gnawing rodent teeth.

The boat's name was picked out in hand painted gold lettering on both bows and transom 'ANNABELLA', the lettering so fresh and clear, the paint might only have dried a few hours ago.

Kate's voice was hushed with amazement and respect.

"Dear God, but she's beautiful. It's as if she was put up here yesterday. She's an old boat though – you don't see craftsmanship like this anymore. Look, every joint, every seam is perfect."

As her hands moved over the silky smooth surfaces of the *Annabella's* hull, Kate felt a faint tingling in the tips of her fingers, like a static charge but not uncomfortable at all. Then, as she ran her palm along the boat's keel, the sensation became almost unbearable. But as soon as she tried to pull her hand away, some force held it tight against the timber, as if there was another hand on top of her own.

She closed her eyes, concentrating all her awareness into that single point of contact, that bridge between the past and the present, between herself and whoever had built the boat. She felt the pressure on her hand ease and fade away as if, now that contact had been made, she had been granted permission to move on to the next stage of the process, whatever that might be.

And she was immediately certain what the next stage must be, to get the *Annabella* back in the water as quickly as possible.

She realised that she had hardly been breathing and took a long, shuddering breath. Something extraordinary had just happened, something she couldn't fully comprehend right then, but hoped she would in the fullness of time. What surprised her most was a complete absence of fear, superstitious or otherwise.

To break the spell, she crawled underneath the hull to examine the seats and inner ribs. Daniel, for the moment forgotten, was busying himself by taking another look at the corner with the makeshift bed.

Kate called him over. "Can you come and give me a hand with this please, Daniel?" It was the oilskin wrapped package. Having released the bundle from its careful suspension she was sliding it out from beneath the trestles. "Take the end before it tips and I'll slide the rest out. I want to see whether the hull's damaged at all. We must get this lot out of the way before we can turn her over."

Daniel was uncharacteristically nervous. "Are you sure we should move it? It looks really heavy and I'd hate to drop it. Besides, isn't it very fragile? It looks ages old."

Kate tried to sound reassuring. "It'll be fine, Daniel. Trust me. It doesn't weigh half as much as you think. Look."

She grabbed hold of the bow with both hands and easily lifted it clear of the trestles.

"She's as light as a feather."

Despite his reservations, Daniel gave in to Kate's enthusiasm and ten minutes later they had the *Annabella* resting upright on her keel in the centre of the loft and looking as if she'd been taken out of the water only moments before.

Unwrapping the oilskin bundle revealed a beautifully made set of four oars, a boathook and a rudimentary mast and boom wrapped tightly in its own crisp, white sail.

Kate was lifting out the bottom boards and looking for any sign of rot or damage when Daniel called out, "Look, here in the back, sorry, the stern. There's some writing. I can't quite make it out, it's carved into the wood."

Carefully, they swivelled the hull round until one of the broader shafts of light enabled them to read the deeply carved characters – JCK, 1914.

"Nineteen fourteen. JCK must have been the builder."

In the excitement of the moment, Kate completely missed the significance of the initials.

Later that afternoon, she called round as requested to let Penelope know how they'd got on. After she had described the condition of the decking planks and the staircase, she told her about the *Annabella*.

"It's one of the most beautiful pieces of craftsmanship I've ever seen, and it's in absolutely perfect condition even though it looks as if it's been up there for decades."

"Sixty-four years, almost to the day."

Kate stared open mouthed at Penelope, astonished at what she had just heard. The old lady continued.

"She was laid up there in the autumn of 1914 and has neither been touched nor seen since. I believe one of the staff used to check the loft every now and then to ensure that the roof was still watertight and that sort of thing. But that must have stopped years ago. I am surprised that everything up there hasn't rotted away. Are you absolutely certain it's all right?"

Kate swallowed her astonishment. "Well, yes. As sure as I can be without actually getting her in the water, but I can't see any obvious damage. Of course her planking will have dried out and shrunk, but I'm sure the joints will soon close up once she feels some river water."

Penelope studied Kate over the top of her glasses. "Am I to understand from what you have said that you would like to take her out on the river?"

Kate tried to hold back her grin but failed. "Well, yes, absolutely. I mean, of course. If that's all right with you. We'll need to clear out all the rubbish from the boathouse dock first and work out a way to get her down safely, but yes, I would very much like that."

It was Penelope's turn to smile. "Good. I'm glad. You had better talk to Tom Gerrard about anything you need. Perhaps, er, your neighbour might like to help. Maybe we can all have a picnic on the river someday. I would very much like that."

Just as Kate was about to leave, she remembered the work bench and the tools.

"The loft, where we found the *Annabella*. It looks a bit like a workshop. Surely she wasn't built here at Hawkswell?"

"As a matter of fact she was. Not up in the loft of course, but on the riverbank directly in front of the boathouse."

"But who…?"

"Who built her? Why, James Kirkpatrick of course, the man you think may be your great uncle."

Kate felt her chest tighten and her heart skip several beats.

The initials, JCK, James C Kirkpatrick, she didn't know then what the C stood for. Of course. The static charge, the sensation of a hand on hers. It had to be Jamie, who else? But then how…?

"I'm sorry, but I don't quite understand. I thought that Jamie, er James, worked in the stables and that he was a bit of an outcast here."

"Oh, he was that all right. I believe that Tom told you all about the, how shall I put it, unpleasantness with the dreadful Roberts person. Well, after he had recovered, Jamie was, in many ways, able to start his life here at Hawkswell all over again." For someone who hadn't reckoned she could tell Kate much about Jamie, maintaining that she had been away at school during most of his time at Hawkswell, Penelope was surprisingly forthcoming.

Chapter 7

North Somerset, April 1913

Jamie's new life had begun on a damp and overcast mid-April morning which, in the absence of even a breath of wind, looked unlikely to improve. His instructions were to meet his new master, Brian Gerrard, in the tool shed in the walled garden.

As a mere stable lad, Jamie's working environment was strictly delineated and, as a result, he had never set foot in the walled garden until that morning. Even though it was shrouded in drifting curtains of misty drizzle, the sight that confronted him couldn't fail to impress.

The overwhelming impression was of order and industry. There were greenhouses ranged all along one wall, with carefully trained fruit trees covering another and a row of substantial brick buildings completing the third side of the square.

Two of the garden staff were already busily barrowing coal around to the boiler room, situated at one end of the row of greenhouses, while others were shifting soil and manure between the plant beds. No-one paid Jamie any attention as he headed towards the tool shed, but by then he was used to being invisible

His knock was answered with a loud and cheery, "Come in."

He stepped inside to a sight that conjured up memories of his father's workshop back in Ireland. Although few of the countless tools racked on boards and stands and shelves around the place were familiar to him, Jamie spotted immediately that they were all well cared for.

Each item enjoyed its own allotted place and glistened with oil and polish. Pegged boards held dozens of different shapes and sizes of secateurs and pruners, along with saws and axes, sickles and scythes, ditching and hedging tools, watering cans, hoes, rakes, forks and spades of every size and shape. Here was an order and a passion entirely lacking in the stable yard.

A burly, ruddy faced man with bushy side whiskers, a full three inches shorter than Jamie, stepped forward and gripped his proffered hand firmly.

"Mister Kirkpatrick, I do not believe that we have yet been introduced, although I am sure you already know who I am. Otherwise you wouldn't be here at all, would you?"

Jamie couldn't help returning his friendly smile.

"Yes, sir. You are Mister Gerrard, the Head Gardener."

The man nodded vigorously. "That I am. And you are the poor devil newly rescued from the clutches of the recently departed and un-lamented Malcolm Roberts. You've not had a good start at Hawkswell, young man, and I am sorry for that. But since you're here to work, then work you shall. You'll quickly discover that I'm a hard task master, but I'm a fair man, and will only beat you when absolutely necessary."

Jamie's disappointment at the man's words must have been evident in his face because Brian Gerrard grinned and punched his shoulder lightly.

"Don't look so worried, lad. I was pulling your leg about the beating. You'll work hard, make no mistake, but you'll be treated fairly, that I guarantee."

Jamie felt his tension ease as he realised how his life might be about to change. He grinned and said, "I have to tell you, I know nothin' at all about gardening, Mister Gerrard, sir. But I'm quick to learn and have skills in my hands. I'll try my best not to let you down."

His new boss placed a calloused hand on Jamie's shoulder and steered him towards the back wall of the shed where the majority of the tools were racked.

"I couldn't help but notice your face as you walked in here, young man. All these tools must appear frightening at first sight, so many blades and unfamiliar objects."

Jamie spoke up immediately. "Oh, no sir, not frightening at all. I am well used to such things. The chisels, saws and planes that I used in my father's yard were quite as sharp as these, I'm sure. I'm pleased at seeing things so well cared for. Something my father taught me before I learned much else – look after your tools and they'll look after you, is what he used to say."

As he expected, Jamie's early duties were entirely menial, comprising the barrowing of coal, logs, timber, soil, compost, manure and cuttings from one end of the estate to the other and sometimes back again. He forked over the mountainous compost heaps, raked the last remaining autumn leaves into huge piles for burning, and fetched and carried for any of the other gardeners whenever and wherever instructed.

At that time, the gardening staff comprised Brian Gerrard, three under-gardeners, all of whom lived in Hawkswell village, and two full time trainees who were billeted in the house along with the rest of the servants. Jamie quickly learned how lucky he was to have even a temporary position in the garden, such posts being highly sought after and jealously protected.

One lunchtime at the beginning of his third week, instead of having to find himself some isolated spot to eat his bread and cheese, he was invited into the shed where the others kept their coats and boots, and the place in which they congregated for their breaks. It seemed he had passed a test of sorts and had at last gained himself a place at Hawkswell.

Six years previously, Brian and Emma Gerrard had, to everyone's delight not least their own, produced a son, Thomas, known to everyone almost since the moment of his birth as Tom.

One particularly hot afternoon, while Jamie was busy barrowing muck from behind the stables to the vegetable garden, Brian Gerrard tasked the boy with taking a water pitcher around to all the garden staff. After completing his round, Tom returned the almost empty pail to where his father was working in the greenhouse.

"Has everyone had their fill, Tom?" The lad nodded, his head down, unwilling to look his father in the face.

Brian was immediately suspicious. "Everyone?"

Still without meeting his father's eye, the boy mumbled something.

"Come on now, son. I didn't hear a word of that. I'll ask again. Has everyone had their fill?"

"I couldn't find, er… Mister Kirkpatrick."

Brian sighed. So that was it – Jamie Kirkpatrick, the gypsy.

He'd heard enough stories at his own mother's knee to know how gypsies were reputed to snatch children and take them off into the forest, never to be seen again. He shook his head angrily as he remembered the superstitious nonsense. And there was Jamie with not an ounce of gypsy in him.

He swallowed his anger, not wanting to take it out on his own son. After all, being afraid wasn't Tom's fault, there was more than enough misguided and malicious gossip circulating amongst the rest of the staff. Although Jamie had proved himself a willing and diligent member of the gardening team, he remained an outsider, a foreigner.

He might be tolerated, but he was unlikely ever to be accepted.

Brian made a decision.

"Come along with me, young man. We're going to sort this out right now."

He led the boy around behind the stable block to where they found Jamie loading his barrow.

"Ah, Mister Kirkpatrick. I'm glad we've found you at last. My young son Tom here has been searching for you to offer you a drink of water. Isn't that right, Tom?"

Jamie plunged his pitchfork into the pile and straightened carefully, easing his back and shoulders. He looked down at the young boy staring up at him with saucer eyes.

"Well now, a drop of water would be very welcome, especially today. I'm as dry as a summer hayloft and no mistake."

He squatted on his haunches until his face was level with Tom's and held out his hand.

"I'm very pleased to meet you Master Tom. My name is James Kirkpatrick, but you may call me Jamie, if you like."

The boy looked up at his father, then back at Jamie's enormous, grimy hand, and back to his father again.

Brian nodded, watching his son's reaction carefully. "Go on son."

Jamie took Tom's trembling hand in his as gently as he might have held a tiny bird in fear of breaking its bones.

"There now," said his father, "that wasn't so bad, was it?"

Strangely, Tom didn't pull his hand away as might have been expected. Instead he left it where it was and looked directly into Jamie's eyes. Whatever he saw there that afternoon must have eased his fears, for when Jamie smiled, the boy smiled back before asking, "Are you a real gypsy?"

Jamie laughed. "So you think I'm a gypsy do you? And what is it makes you think that then?"

"Well, you speaks like a gypsy, and you looks like a gypsy."

"Ah, I see. Well, it's true that many gypsy folk come from Ireland, just as I do, and they probably sound and look a lot like me. But no, Tom, I'm not a gypsy and I have never lived in the woods either. I am the son of a boat builder and I would have been a boat builder too if… well, if things had turned out differently."

"So why didn't you?"

Jamie answered before Brian could intervene. "Because my father died, young Tom. Along with my mother, my two sisters and many others in our village."

The boy's eyes widened with delicious horror. "How did they die?"

"From drinking bad water from the village well."

Tom's eyes widened even more before his father tapped him gently on his shoulder.

"Now come along Tom, let's leave Mister Kirkpatrick to his work. He'll be getting into trouble with his boss if we're not careful."

Tom spotted the joke and grinned up at his father before releasing his hold on Jamie's hand.

"If I come and see you again, Mister… er, Jamie, please will you tell me about the place you come from?"

"I'd be pleased to Tom. If you'd like to come and find me when I'm having my lunch, maybe we can speak then."

In saying this, Jamie looked towards Brian Gerrard, who smiled and nodded.

"I'm sure we can arrange something. Come along now."

As the two walked away, Tom turned and, hopping backwards on one booted foot, grinned and waved back at Jamie, all his earlier fears blown away.

And Jamie smiled too.

Both Brian and Tom had called him Jamie that afternoon. It was the first time he had heard his given name spoken aloud in many long months.

When, later that day, Brian explained his reasoning behind the introduction, Jamie understood and said that he was pleased with the outcome.

"He's a fine lad. Will you mind if we meet?"

"Not at all. I'll be glad of it. Speaking with you will broaden the boy's mind and put an end to his fear of strangers. I have arranged for him to take his lunch with you tomorrow, if you're willing?"

Jamie smiled.

"More than willing, sir, I'll be glad of the company."

Brian took a moment to compose his next words.

"I've noticed that you have little to say to anyone, Jamie. You keep very much to yourself. Is this something you choose to do?"

Jamie's reply sounded matter-of-fact but was revealing in its simple honesty.

"My father always told me that the less you say, the less can be held against you. I also know that my manner of speaking marks me out as different so, as I have little knowledge of the world outside my home to speak about, I say little."

From then on, whenever possible, Tom managed to be near to wherever Jamie was working around the time he stopped for his lunch. The two would sit together and talk for the duration, Tom ever careful not to interfere with Jamie's work for a moment longer than was acceptable.

During these discussions, he leaned about a place called Ireland.

"It is an island, exactly as its name suggests," Jamie told him, "although so huge that it takes many days of travel to get from one side to the other."

He picked up a stick and scraped two shapes in the clinker of the path, one to represent Ireland and the other England, with Wales and Scotland lumping top and side. And between the two he drew some lines shaped like giant waves, telling of a wide, wild ocean that could only be crossed in a huge ship which would most often be troubled with much danger and sickness. Thomas ignored the reference to sickness, but couldn't resist more questions about huge ships, oceans and danger.

Some eight weeks after first starting in the garden, Jamie was summoned to the estate office to meet with Brian Gerrard.

"Close the door, young man, and sit down please."

The older man's face was unreadable, Jamie unable to detect any hint of a smile or a frown. Dreading that his life might be about to change again, he sat down as requested, his heart heavy. Despite the hard work and long hours, he'd enjoyed his time on the gardening team. They had been good, satisfying days, a time in which he'd grown fond of young Tom too, learning as much about Hawkswell as he himself had passed on about his own early life in the as yet un-faded memory that was Ireland. Surely all that couldn't be coming to an end?

His fears were groundless.

Far from ending, his position as under-gardener was being confirmed with the entirely unexpected wage of two shillings a week. He would never learn how hard Brian Gerrard had pressed Edward Townshend to confirm Jamie's employment and to get the lad any wage at all.

His new-found status confirmed, Jamie settled even deeper into the life and fabric of Hawkswell, soon discovering that the gardeners' responsibilities extended far beyond the immediate environs of the house.

From the rhododendrons bordering the approach road, to the formal planting fronting the house, the orchards in the west, the back spinney, the paddocks and the trees that lined the boundary wall, the team were kept busy pruning, mowing, planting and clearing from dawn to dusk, all except for Sundays.

Sundays at Hawkswell, along with most other country estates at that time, were different, especially the afternoons. Mornings were, in some respects, no different from a normal working day, there being numerous chores to complete. But in the afternoon, the work often became more social and recreational.

On one particular Sunday early in the summer, the day's task entailed clearing the winter's accumulation of weed and debris from the creek separating the river bank nearest to the boathouse from the island a few yards beyond. To Jamie's initial surprise, it seemed that this annual exercise involved the entirety of Hawkswell's staff, with the operation commencing immediately upon their return from church. Also, that day's lunch was to take the form of a picnic.

Edward's son, Charles, was in charge though everyone seemed so familiar with their tasks that they required little or no direction. Although obviously popular with the household staff, Charles was entirely unfamiliar to Jamie. He assumed that the young man was not a horseman or they would have come across one another during Jamie's time as a stable lad. His alternative assumption was that Charles spent little time at Hawkswell, something later confirmed by Brian Gerrard.

"Spends most of his time in Bath or London, although I've no idea what he does in either place. Nice enough gentleman though, from the few times I've met him. He'll give you the time of day, unlike some."

Tall and with an unruly mop of straw coloured hair, Charles was clad that morning in a pair of ancient looking cricket flannels, and an off-white collarless shirt tightly buttoned at the wrists.

As the young man strode up and down the river bank, offering advice and encouragement wherever he deemed necessary, Jamie observed an easy confidence and a sense of belonging that he could only marvel at, and envy. This, after all, was the man who would one day become master of Hawkswell.

It was such a warm and sunny afternoon that, ignoring propriety for once, most of the younger men were soon stripped to the waist, with their trousers rolled up to their knees. Using long handled hay rakes and pitchforks, the weed nearest the bank was quickly harvested and heaped up ready to be carted off for composting.

The broad mat of weed farther out could only be gathered by wading waist deep into the channel. It was only the youngest and tallest men who went into the water while the rest stayed on the bank with the women and children to collect and stack the gathered weed.

It wasn't long before someone lost their footing and slipped under, only to lurch to their feet again, spluttering and shaking the water from their hair and eyes, much to the amusement of the rest. Inevitably, mud was thrown and returned until everyone in the creek was liberally plastered. Jamie threw and caught his fair share, soon becoming as anonymous as the rest in their coating of mud.

Later, with all the weed cleared and the churned sediment swept away by the current, it was time to open the boathouse doors for the first time that year. Charles unlocked the padlock, opened the door with a flourish and disappeared inside.

Some minutes later, to a raucous cheer from those assembled on the bank, an ancient looking rowing boat emerged into the sunlight, the young man inexpertly flailing the oars to draw the craft round towards the river bank.

Then it was 'all aboard the skylark' – men, children and women, all lugging picnic baskets and large brown jugs of beer, cider and lemonade, taking turns to be rowed out into the main river and around to a small gravel beach on the far side of the island.

When Jamie's turn came to step down into the boat, he was shocked by its appalling condition. A number of the timbers were rotten and split, the caulking dried and come away in places allowing the river to seep in. After each round trip, six or eight inches of muddy water had to be emptied with a bucket.

After three round trips, Charles, obviously exhausted, leaned on the oars, closely examining his blistered palms. Spotting this, Jamie respectfully asked if he might scull the boat across the channel on its next trip.

Although puzzled at Jamie's request, a grateful Charles handed over the single oar as requested and stepped up onto the bank. He watched with trepidation as, with his four passengers settled, Jamie stood upright in the stern of the little boat, legs wide apart to brace and balance himself, and poled away from the bank.

As soon as there was room, he laid the inboard end of the oar on his right shoulder, tight against his neck, and with both hands began to sweep the blade back and forth with long, powerful strokes. To everyone's delight and amazement, the small boat cut away from the bank, sped out into the river and round to the beach.

His passengers in the boat clapped as did everyone else who was watching as Jamie, his face hot with embarrassment, sculled the boat backwards and forwards between the island and the river bank. Charles was so impressed that he took Jamie aside and, after introducing himself, looked Jamie right in the eye.

"As soon as everyone's established on the island, I absolutely insist that you teach me how to do that."

While those on dry land enjoyed their Sunday picnic, the two young men worked up a sweat while Jamie attempted to communicate a skill that to him was instinctive. To stand upright in the stern of a tippy rowing boat is hard enough. To control an eight foot oar with no other fulcrum than your own body is something altogether more tricky. To move the boat in the direction you wish it to go is another matter entirely.

Of course, no sooner had Charles taken his position ready to have a go, than the boat was over, pitching both men into the river. They dragged it to the bank, tipped out the water and re-launched it, but soon they were over again, and again, and again.

Such a performance made even the mud-slinging pale by comparison.

That particular picnic would be remembered for years to come for aching sides and tears of laughter, and also for a strange sense of awe as Hawkswell's staff watched Jamie's magical boat handling skills. While Charles took a break to get his strength back, he sat on the centre thwart, open mouthed in admiration while Jamie spun and pirouetted that tired old boat up and down the river, his balance and control almost supernatural.

He could speed in a straight line, the craft weaving along to the sweeping thrust of the oar that seemed like an extension of his arm. He could carve tight turns and bring the graceful bow of the old boat to rest, barely disturbing the grass of the bank.

Somehow, his performance was so artless that not one of those present that day imagined for a moment that he was showing off.

By the end of the afternoon, Charles had learned just enough to maintain his dignity, his final attempt culminating in a burst of speed that propelled them clear across the river and into the far bank with enough force to send them both over the side.

And, just for a moment, the insurmountable social barriers that existed between those two young men evaporated in a tangle-limbed storm of unquenchable laughter. A unique friendship was born that summer afternoon that would, within a few short months, carry both men to the very gates of Hell and beyond.

Two weeks after the river picnic, Brian Gerrard conveyed a message to Jamie to the effect that, if he felt it could be done, he might care to effect repairs to the old rowing boat so that the Townshend family might once again enjoy picnics on the river.

"That there river was once the late Mrs Townshend's passion," he was told, "but ever since her death, the boathouse and its craft have seldom been used. In fact, the place has only been opened up for a couple of weeks these last few summers."

Later that day, Brian and Jamie strolled down the wide slope of lawn to the boathouse. Although shaded by willows, the inside was bright with evening sunlight reflecting off the water between the wide open river doors. There were two craft harboured there – the old rowing boat moored against the left hand side of the little boarded dock and, against the opposite side, the waterlogged remains of a river punt.

With a lot of heaving and grunting, the two men managed to manhandle the old boat out onto the dockside and turn it on its side, an accumulation of river water cascading over their boots. Once the bottom boards were removed, the true condition of the timbers was revealed.

With a sadness reserved by some for animals and people, Jamie knew right away that it was beyond saving. It was a miracle the poor old thing had lasted the day of the picnic without literally falling apart. Presented with a similar circumstance, another man might have attempted some fist of a repair, if for nothing other than to gain the approval of his master. Maybe another man, but not Jamie.

He gave Brian Gerrard the simple unvarnished truth. All the boat was good for was firewood. And that was precisely how the state of affairs was reported to Edward Townshend.

There then occurred one of those remarkable turns of fate that occasionally re-shape all our lives. Far from Jamie's honest appraisal losing him the chance of working with the little boat, it gained him far more – something that was to alter his life and the lives of those around him beyond recognition. Barely a week after declaring the rowing boat beyond repair, Jamie was summoned to a meeting with Edward Townshend. On his way there he reminded himself that this was the man who put food in your belly and a roof over your head, and who could as easily cut off the supply of one and remove the other, as proved by his summary dismissal of Malcolm Roberts.

In all the time since Edward Townshend had visited Jamie while he was recovering from his beating, Jamie had neither spoken to, nor been addressed by the man. The gulf that existed between master and servant is today almost impossible to imagine –the immaculately dressed, wealthy land owner on the one hand, and the almost penniless under-gardener on the other.

Jamie could not imagine anything good resulting from such an unprecedented meeting. The encounter took place in Hawkswell's library, from which most of the estate business was conducted. That morning, the high ceilinged room was flooded with sunlight streaming unchecked through wide, floor to ceiling windows. Furnished with dark green leather upholstered armchairs and settees, the library had a broad, leather topped desk at its centre, behind which the lord and master of Hawkswell was seated.

Brian Gerrard, who had escorted Jamie through the house, stepped up to the desk and coughed politely, causing Edward to look up from his papers before staring long and hard at Jamie, as if weighing a decision. Regardless of his own misgivings, Jamie held the man's gaze, his hands at his side, trying his best to look unconcerned.

"Thank you, Mister Gerrard." Brian turned and left.

Now it comes, thought Jamie.

"Mister Kirkpatrick. I am glad to see you fully recovered from that unfortunate incident with Roberts. I hear that you are doing well in your new position and I am glad for you." Jamie remained silent. Edward Townshend's next words were so unexpected as to be almost incomprehensible. "I am told you know of boats." Although a statement rather than a question, Jamie felt it deserved an answer.

"My father was a shipwright, sir, back home in Ireland."

The man nodded. "Aye, lad. I am fully cognisant of your origins. The question I have for you is simple, could you build me one, here at Hawkswell?"

"A boat, sir?"

"Of course a boat. A rowing boat, for the river. Well?"

The idea crashed into Jamie's head like a lightning bolt. A boat. Merciful God, the man wants me to build him a boat.

"Oh, yes, sir. I most certainly can. I will build you as fine a boat as you'll ever see."

The man behind the desk gave him a faint smile. "Well, we'll see about that. You will need materials of course, Edwards the bailiff will see to that. And I am led to understand that there is a full complement of woodworking tools in the boathouse loft, left there by Dan Lapways. I shall want to see what you propose before you make a start. I am sure someone can find you some drafting materials."

"Yes, sir. Thank you, sir."

A slight nod of the man's head told Jamie it was time to leave but, as he turned for the door, Edward spoke again, as if there was something he needed to make clear.

"This boat. It is for my daughter, Penelope. It is to be a birthday present. She will be returning here in time for Christmas and I require the boat to be finished in time for next summer, by, let us say July at the latest."

Jamie was at such a loss for words that he could only nod and bow slightly as he closed the door behind him.

Two days after Edward Townshend had issued his remarkable request, his son Charles took it upon himself to show Jamie around the workshop above the boathouse. Jamie got the impression that in some way he considered the place his own private domain.

The loft itself, reached by climbing wooden steps that led up from the little dock, was spacious and well ventilated. At one end were two large barn-type doors, while the opposite end was given over to a woodworking workshop with a wide, strongly constructed bench running the full width of the space below a cobwebbed window in the gable end which, once cleaned, would provide plenty of working light. Numerous clamps were set into the front edge of the bench with a mighty steel vice bolted to one side. Beneath the bench were ranged a set of four iron bound tool chests secured with heavy brass padlocks.

Charles held up a set of keys on a ring.

"Pretty sure we'll find that some of these fit the padlocks. I'm afraid it'll be a bit of trial and error."

Jamie felt lucky when the second key he chose turned smoothly and opened the first padlock. Opening the lid of the chest, Jamie stared in awe at the magnificent array of woodworking tools inside. Almost reverently, he lifted a spoke shave from its nest, marvelling at the way it came to his hand, the steel burnished with use, the blade keen and blue with oil. The culture of care exhibited in the garden tool shed had obviously extended as far as this workshop.

He laid it back alongside its fellows and turned to Charles, asking who the tools belonged to, well aware that there was no carpenter on the staff.

"These were all old Dan Lapways'. He died four, no… five years since. Funny old chap. Wouldn't give you the time of day, smelled like a wet dog, but could turn his hand to almost anything. Made all our toys – rocking horses, dolls' houses, sledges for the winter, you name it. Furniture too, along with wheelbarrows, gates, in fact anything that could be made from wood. The old boy used to scare my poor sister half out of her wits."

"Did er… this Lapways make the rowing boat below?" Jamie asked.

"Lord no! Father had that shipped from Bristol, I believe. It was for Mother one birthday. No, he might have been good at most things, old Dan, but boats were beyond him. Are you absolutely sure you know how to make one, Jamie? Damned if I'd know where to start."

"With a drawing, Mr Charles. That's where you start."

Jamie's confident words belied his inner turmoil.

The contents of the four chests alone were enough to overwhelm him with doubt. Any man who could accumulate and master a range and variety of tools of such quality must have been a craftsman indeed. Suddenly, all his earlier confidence and excitement evaporated in a puff of doubt, and it was a thoroughly chastened Jamie Kirkpatrick who followed Charles Townshend back to the house.

Over the next few days, pencils, erasers, rulers and set-squares were hunted down from various hideaways along with two rolls of heavy lining paper. And so, on the Sunday afternoon after agreeing to build the boat, Jamie found himself stretched out alone on the floor of the boat house workshop confronting a wide, blank sheet of paper and a dreadful certainty that he was bound to fail.

There was nothing in his head. No starting line. No feel for form or shape. Sure, he had watched his father lay down those graceful lines that, when scaled up, became the formers for ribs and strakes, gunwales, stems and transoms. Had he not handled a hundred such workings, helped with the scaling himself as a boy, dragging the heavy pantograph stylus across the surface of the master drawings? But now he came face to face with the frightening realisation that he had never actually drawn the first line, that deep enduring cut that opened up a map or a plan.

For the twentieth time he reached out, the sharpened pencil an inch from the surface, his hand trembling with uncertainty, only to pull it back again. There was no shape in his mind to follow, nor line to trace. His father was never as dead as at that moment, and Jamie never so alone.

Over the course of the next fortnight, he tried and tried again to make a start, often taking himself up to the loft with a lantern after finishing work for the day, desperate for some hint or inspiration. Countless designs were started only to be scrubbed out, the paper scored and torn.

Then, on the second Sunday, he was surprised by a visit from Charles. Evening sunlight was pouring through the window and roof lights, painting the loft gold and firing the tracery of cobwebs that adorned the raw timber rafters.

Too despairing even to be aware of the beauty of his surroundings, Jamie didn't hear Charles's approach until he hauled himself through the hatchway.

"Hello, Jamie. Just popped up to see how things are coming along."

The blank paper and Jamie's face told far more than his answering words.

"Not well, Mister Charles, not well at all. I can't seem to get started somehow."

Charles sat down heavily on one of the tool chests, his sympathetic expression masking a well of doubts. Could he have been wrong in persuading his father to commission the boat? Perhaps Jamie had exaggerated, or even been untruthful about his past experience. He tried a direct question, dreading the answer.

"Have you never made a boat from scratch, Jamie?"

Jamie winced, knowing precisely what the question implied.

He was being asked far more than the simple question, and a quick bright flare of anger sharpened his voice.

"I am the son of a son of a boat builder. I helped my father build as many boats as he helped his father before him. Why would I lie?"

Startled by the vehemence of Jamie's response, Charles was quick to calm him.

"Good Lord, man, I'm not for one moment accusing you of lying. Of course I'm not. It's just that, well, helping someone isn't quite the same as doing it yourself, if you see what I mean."

They sat in silence for a minute or two until Jamie sighed, his anger replaced by contrition.

"Please forgive me, Mister Charles, I shouldn't've spoken like that. You are quite right to question my abilities. Right now I doubt them even more myself. I feel sure that I could draw a building or even a carriage right away, although I know little of such things. But a boat is like a creature, a living thing. It is as much a thing of water as of wood and metal."

Charles moved from the chest and stretched out alongside Jamie on the dusty floor.

"I think I know what you mean, old man. It must be like trying to make a cloud out of a piece of stone, or a bird's feather out of clay."

Jamie rolled to one side and sat up, the faint trace of a grin flickering in his eyes.

"By God, Mister Charles, there's a poet inside you and no mistake."

At that they laughed together and talked about all the things that could not be made out of other things, and all the things that could not be made at all, like love and laughter and beautiful girls. But soon they returned to the boat and its construction, except this time from an entirely different direction.

And Jamie soon found words inadequate to describe how the vessel should sit upon the water, the way its stem should slip through the current and ride the small waves, so that he soon had to resort to pencil and paper to clarify his thoughts.

At first glance, his sketches looked simple. But that was deceptive. The boat was to be a skiff with a broad transom seat, a wide beam and a river vessel's shallow draught. She would be clinker built, with overlapping planks – her ribs, keel and bottom boards to be fashioned from best English oak and her planking from seasoned beech. It was only later, when Jamie started to translate his sketches into quarter size drawings of the many individual elements that the intrinsic beauty of his design began to reveal itself.

The curves Jamie drew late into those summer nights were the lines of life itself, of wind bowed branches, curling leaves and flowing water. Their shapes came from deep within his memory and his soul, coursing through his wrists and fingers as they once had through his father's.

And as the lines took shape on the paper, so the boat itself took form within his head, so that when he came to cut and plane, he knew with a profound certainty that his hands would know their way.

In early November, Jamie and Edwards the bailiff travelled to Bristol by train and carriage to choose and order the timber and materials from a specialist merchant and chandler. For Jamie, the journey was as cold and uncomfortable as his companion's company, Edwards so aloof that Jamie felt more like a prisoner being escorted to gaol.

The actual selection and ordering of the timber however proved a joy. It took only moments for the merchant to recognise Jamie's knowledge and eye, and soon the two were crawling amongst racks of seasoned timber, sharing their passion for nature's most versatile construction material.

The selected materials were scheduled to be delivered in time for Christmas, which would allow Jamie to start construction in the New Year. He planned to trace and draw the templates for the keel and ribs throughout the winter months before precurving the planking in the early spring, a process that, although long winded, would produce a hull so sound that, with care, it would last a hundred years or more.

The wagon arrived exactly ten days before Christmas and less than twenty-four hours ahead of Penelope Townshend, the daughter of the house. Its arrival passed almost unnoticed and Jamie was left with only the carter to help him unload and manhandle each and every item up into the boathouse loft.

Penelope Townshend's arrival on the other hand, could have been likened to the onset of a tropical storm.

When Jamie first arrived at Hawkswell, Penelope, then fifteen years old, was away at school in Switzerland. The anticipation of her homecoming that December threw the entire household into turmoil as rooms were aired, carpets beaten, bed linen washed and ironed to perfection. The activity in the kitchen was frenetic.

Jamie, although aware that Charles's younger sister was returning from school, remained blissfully unaware of the approaching cataclysm.

With gardening activity scaled down for the winter months, he had been able to spend more of his time in the boathouse loft, sorting and preparing the newly arrived timber and materials in preparation for the commencement of boatbuilding.

The unbridled joy that greeted Penelope's arrival up at the big house, and the string of parties, balls and general merrymaking that continued unabated right up until Christmas Eve, passed largely unnoticed by Jamie other than by virtue of Charles's continued absence.

Those long, lamp-lit evenings were spent scaling up the painstakingly drawn plans into full sized templates for keel, ribs, stem piece, transom and rudder. As Jamie worked, he carefully constructed a scale model from his original drawings to satisfy himself that his design would translate into reality.

A number of seasonal celebrations involved the entire staff, notably the cutting and dressing of the tree that dominated the main hall of Hawkswell. Carols were sung and a variety of events took place in and around the village and the church, in not one of which did Jamie take a part.

As far as he was concerned, Christmas had always been about families, and all those closest to Jamie's heart were recently dead and buried, their graves distanced by a grey unforgiving ocean.

So it was that the preparations for the building of the boat provided a welcome escape from those achingly jolly gatherings, the cosy boathouse workshop quickly becoming a haven from well-meant but unwittingly painful festive frivolity.

Late on Christmas Eve, while Jamie was deeply and pleasantly engrossed in the finishing touches to the scale model of the boat, Charles's voice startled him from the hatchway.

"Thought we'd find you up here, old son. I've persuaded my sister to come down and have a peek at how the great work is coming along. Took a bit of dragging down here, mind you, she absolutely loathes the place. Still, here she is at last."

After so long working within a pool of lamplight, Jamie's eyes struggled to adjust as he attempted to focus on the figure barely visible against the darker extremities of the loft. To make matters worse, Charles held a bull's-eye lantern which was, at that moment, directed full in Jamie's face.

"Come on up, sissy. Jamie won't bite. He's not a bit like old Dan."

There was a rustle of fabric and a sharp intake of breath as someone struggled to pull themselves through the hatchway. Charles turned and directed the lantern towards his sister to help her over the last step.

Jamie's first sight of Penelope Townshend was of a tumble of glistening black hair surrounded and framed by a boil of bright blue silken fabric that poured through the loft hatch behind her.

"Oh, for heaven's sake Charlie, you're standing on my dress, you oaf! Now look, it's all covered in dust and filth. Goodness knows why I let you persuade me to – " Petulant, shrewish, strident, penetrating; a voice redolent with education and privilege, if not, at that precise moment, with breeding; a voice full of authority and annoyance, and a voice that stopped as soon as its owner caught sight of Jamie, sitting on a milking stool in his corduroy trousers, rough canvas shirt and leather gilet.

"I thought you said he wasn't anything like Dan Lapways. Looks like he might be his son for all I know."

Charles shuffled forward and attempted to make introductions. "Jamie Kirkpatrick, may I introduce my beloved sister Penelope, recently arrived home from school."

The slight emphasis on the word 'school' was missed by neither Penelope nor Jamie, who nevertheless stood to offer his hand, which was pointedly ignored.

Penelope addressed her next remark directly to her brother. It seemed that Jamie did not warrant her attention at all.

"And what is this person supposed to be doing up here?"

Annoyed and embarrassed, Jamie spoke just as Charles opened his mouth.

"I am building a boat, miss, that is intended for your use on the river. It was requested as a birthday gift from your father who obviously thinks more highly of you than you do of me."

Silence.

There are silences and there are silences.

This was a silence that could have frozen raindrops in flight. With a visible effort, Penelope Townshend clamped a pair of bloodless lips against whatever violent retort might have sprung to mind. With eyes as bright and sharp as knife points, she turned in a swirl of silk and, brushing her brother aside, struggled clumsily through the hatch and away down the wooden steps.

Charles, for once lost for words, muttered a goodnight to Jamie that might or might not have contained an embarrassed apology, and hurried after his sister.

Jamie remained standing for another moment or two, listening to the high pitched, wordless sound of a furious female voice receding into the night. Then he sat back down and lowered his face into his hands, overwhelmed with the certainty that he would looking for another job come Boxing Day.

Chapter 8

North Somerset, May 1979

"But he wasn't sacked, was he?"

"And how on earth would you know that?"

Penelope's response was far more abrupt than Kate was prepared for. So she smiled to take any sting out of her next words.

"The boat, the Annabella. She wouldn't have been built if..."

Penelope nodded slowly, looking slightly embarrassed. "No, you're absolutely right. Of course he wasn't sacked. Although I will admit that I was in a terrible rage when I left the boathouse that evening, so much so that that it was my overwhelming intention to see him dismissed. I had no good reason to be angry, of course. You must understand, my dear, that because no-one had ever been so rude to me before, I found it hard to believe and didn't know how to deal with it. I felt outraged, even humiliated. I know it must sound pathetic now, but circumstances were very different then.

"The social order was so rigid, so inflexible, that it's almost impossible to imagine in today's terms. We were so powerful I suppose. It wasn't as if we had the power of life or death over our staff and servants but we might as well have. If someone found themselves dismissed without a reference, and especially if word was put around that they were a bad lot, they would never be able to obtain work in the locality again. And even if they moved far away, their lack of a reference would make their lives extraordinarily difficult."

To Kate, Penelope's outpouring sounded strangely like a confession, as if she was unloading a lifetime's remorse. Her voice was harsh at first, as if the very act of speaking the words was painful, but as she continued – as if the worst was over – her voice softened and Kate saw her relax.

"And you have to remember, Kate, there was no welfare state in those days. If you were out of work, you either starved or you fetched up in the workhouse, and I'm sure I don't need to tell you how dreadful those places were. You see, as a member of that hierarchy, to be addressed in such an insolent manner by someone as lowly placed as Jamie was a bitter pill to swallow. If my father had discovered what had happened, Jamie would undoubtedly have been sacked immediately, Christmas or no Christmas. Nor would the boat have saved him either. My father valued civility second only to honesty."

Kate found what Penelope had described almost too easy to understand. Her own temper and lack of discretion had let her down on far too many occasions. Even so, the reminder of those days of social injustice left her with a feeling of deep discomfort that was only relieved by the fact that things had improved immeasurably since those times.

She took a long, slow breath and asked, "So how come you didn't tell your father if you were so angry?"

This brought a faint remembering smile from Penelope. "My dear brother Charles talked me out of it. He was absolutely convinced that Jamie meant no harm with his words. I didn't believe him of course. It wasn't just that he looked a bit like old Dan Lapways, whom I used to loathe as a child, Jamie had something about him, something that made me want to strike him, knock him down… " Her words tailed off into silence.

"Ah, but that was all so long ago. How strange that it seems so clear, so… so recent. Sixty-four years. Goodness me, what a long time."

Suddenly she sat up straight in her chair as if she had changed up a gear. "Now then, Kate. The Annabella. When do you think you might try and get her down from the loft?"

Surprised by the sudden change of direction, Kate had to think fast before answering.

"Well, er, any time that Tom and Daniel are free to help, I suppose. I know Daniel's quite busy right now, but he might be free at the weekends. I'll ask, see what he can do."

Penelope nodded. "Good. Please keep me informed. It will be lovely to see the old boat back on the water. I wish you the very best of luck."

Kate reckoned the only way she had a chance of securing Daniel's help would be to tell him all she knew about how Jamie came to build the Annabella and that the young Irishman was almost certainly her great uncle. His reaction was quite unexpected.

"Wow, that's excellent. Does that mean you get to inherit the boat?"

Her response tumbled out before she had time to modify it.

"Jesus, Daniel. Do you ever think about anything but money?"

He looked genuinely hurt. "Whoa! Hold on there. Just when did I say a single word about money?" She shook her head slowly without speaking. "No, I didn't. I thought that if you love this boat so much, maybe the old girl might give it to you, or maybe leave it to you in her will since you have such a close personal link to it. Nothing whatsoever to do with money, OK?"

Kate flushed with embarrassment. "I'm sorry. It's just ... Oh, I don't know. It's been a long day. I guess I'm a bit strung out. I meant to ask you to help me and Tom get the boat down from the loft, but it looks like I've blown it."

Once more, Daniel's response surprised her. "I'd be delighted to help you get her down. I'll be travelling quite a bit over the next couple of weeks and I've a lot on at the weekends too, especially... Oh, it doesn't matter. If it won't take more than a day or two, count me in. Although from what I saw yesterday, you'll need to do something about the boathouse dock and the little creek. Even if she comes down all right, you'll not be able to get her in the water without a hell of a lot of dredging."

Penelope had already tasked Tom with giving Kate as much help as he could, and the next Tuesday evening, they met down at the boathouse to talk things through. By the end of the week they had a plan worked out.

Kate, Daniel and Tom assembled down by the river at nine-thirty on Saturday morning, ready to commence operations.

Tom had already laid a four foot thick layer of straw on the towpath directly beneath the external doors to the loft. Their first job involved covering the straw with an old rick cover and pegging it down securely.

"It's not so much for the boat, I don't want any one of us to break no bones neither," Tom explained.

The ancient, rusted padlock securing the loft's double doors gave easily to a few strokes of a hacksaw, enabling them to swing outwards, the squeals of protest from both hinges and timber sounding as if they were about to collapse onto the carefully arranged safety mat.

Thankfully they held and, although sagging alarmingly, were propped in place with two lengths of timber. Now all they had to do was lower the Annabella to the ground.

Had the boat been any less beautifully made, they probably would have had it down on the towpath inside fifteen minutes. They might even have taken a chance and dropped it straight down onto the safety mat.

But the Annabella was something special, something so inherently precious that they all treated her like they would a priceless art treasure. Two long and anxious hours later, the Annabella's beautifully raked bow kissed into the canvas covered mattress and sank into the straw bed.

By the time they had lowered the stern down to ground level, manhandled her back into the boathouse and laid her back on her original trestles beside the empty dock, the afternoon was well advanced and they were all completely exhausted.

Despite her tiredness and a few aches and pains, Kate felt as excited as a five-year-old on Christmas Eve.

"We'll get her on the water tomorrow. I'll take you both for a row."

Neither Daniel nor Tom had the heart at that moment to remind her of the solid mat of weed and silt that blocked the boathouse creek, nor about the dire weather forecast.

Kate woke to the sound of rain lashing against her bedroom windows and cascading in a series of waterfalls from the ancient guttering. Once up, she made herself a coffee, resigned to writing off the day, and the fact that the Annabella's re-launch would have to wait another week.

After all, she thought, what's another week after 65 years?

However it seemed that Daniel had other ideas.

Just after ten o'clock she opened her door to a loud, impatient knock and stared in open mouthed astonishment at the figure in the hallway. Daniel was clad from head to foot in a disreputable suit of overalls which barely concealed what looked like an equally tatty neoprene wetsuit. In one hand he held a battered pair of boots.

"What in God's name?"

"Ah, the suit. Do you think it's a bit too formal? I considered wearing the white tuxedo, but I thought this ensemble would be better suited to the job in hand."

Kate eyed him with a mixture of disbelief and irritation.

"Jesus, Daniel. Must you always talk in riddles? It's Sunday morning, it's pissing down with rain, in case you hadn't noticed and, much as I'm ever partial to a joke, can you please tell me what you have in mind dressed like that."

He answered by flicking his head in the general direction of the river. "The boathouse dock and the creek."

"So what about them?"

"They need clearing, right? And that's a process that will involve getting very wet and muddy, so what better time than right now, while it's raining cats and dogs? Or have you got other plans for today?"

"Dear God, it sounds like you might be serious."

"Absolutely. So, do you want to help or will you just come down and watch?"

At that moment, all Kate wanted to do was shut the door and curl up on the sofa with a book. Flailing around in muddy water in pouring rain lay right at the bottom of a long list of things she didn't want to do that day. But there was something so earnest about Daniel, so positive that, in spite of her reservations, she shrugged.

"But I haven't got anything to wear."

"Oh, come on Kate. That's such a girly thing to say. If you really want to help, I'm sure I've got some old overalls that'll fit you. You'll probably have to roll the trousers up, but they shouldn't be too bad. Have you got waterproofs and an old pair of trainers or wellies or something?"

She nodded, reluctantly. Maybe just for today she'd let Daniel take charge.

He proved as good as his word and, half an hour later, feeling ridiculous and very uncomfortable in an oversize set of overalls and a waterproof anorak that came down to her knees, Kate trailed him down towards the boathouse through swirling curtains of rain.

They stopped first at the tool shed in the walled garden to pick up a pair of long handled rakes and two shovels. Tom, who she thought would laugh at Daniel's plan and try and talk them out of it, hardly batted an eyelid, commenting instead, "There's plenty of water in the river today, I 'spect the flow'll help clear the channel once you get started."

The little creek should have been swept clear of weeds and silt by the action of the river alone, but rivers seldom behave as they're supposed to. What Kate and Daniel were faced with that Sunday was a strip of swamp with bits of tree and heaven knows what embedded in it. It certainly wasn't dry, at least not enough to walk over to the island without getting wet feet. Nor was it a stretch of river either, and definitely not deep enough to float the Annabella.

The task looked daunting viewed from the bank, but as soon as Daniel slopped his way out into the middle of the channel, the true scale of the job became clear.

"I don't reckon there's more than six inches of water at the deepest point Kate. And even that's pretty much choked with weed."

Kate's tried not to sound too discouraging as she called out.

"We'll need at least two feet of water to float her."

Daniel shrugged. "It's not so much the depth. You'll need width to use the oars. You could pole her out through a narrow cut I suppose, but I'm not sure you'll even be able to turn her out of the boathouse unless we clear the full width of the channel."

At that moment he stopped and stared past Kate up the slope towards the house.

On hearing the guttural throb of a powerful diesel engine grinding its way towards them, she too turned.

Out of the rain, over the brow of the hill strode Tom Gerrard, swathed in waterproofs and, looming out of the rain behind him like some prehistoric monster, its bucket held high above its cab like a banner, trundled a bright yellow JCB. The machine hissed and rocked to a halt a few yards short of the towpath and Tom walked over to them with a mile-wide grin splitting his weather- beaten face.

"I thought you might need a bit of help, like. This here," he nodded towards the face barely visible through the streaming windscreen of the digger, "is Ted Walton. He's done a few heavy jobs for me in the past and I keep him and his family well stocked with winter vegetables. He's got a free day and feels he owes me a favour, like."

Suddenly, the task didn't seem so impossible any more.

However, having the JCB there didn't mean they could all stand back and watch. There remained a great deal of shovelling and barrowing to do, trundling the dredged gunge two hundred yards along the towpath and dumping it in another weed choked inlet. Try as they might, the three of them barely kept pace with the machine.

Steadily, Ted worked his way downstream, shifting the digger a vehicle width at a time and dipping his bucket with effortless precision to scoop up more sludge in a single go than any individual could have shovelled in an hour.

Two and a half hours later, the JCB's bucket scoured its way across the final band of silt that lay like a narrow dam across the lower end of the creek. With a gleeful rush, the river swept through the breach, taking all the mud and remaining detritus with it. Kate, Tom and Daniel whooped and cavorted about on the bank like a bunch of five-year-olds.

They waved off Ted Walton and his digger before traipsing back up to the house for some much needed food. Half an hour later, leaving Tom to sleep off his lunch, Kate and Daniel returned to clear the dock. During their break, Daniel had suggested that Kate would feel much more comfortable in a wet suit and had lent her one that fitted really well.

She desperately wanted to ask who it had belonged to, but something in Daniel's attitude stopped her.

The rain had stopped and the sky was clearing by the time they got to the dock, the strongly flowing river having already scoured away most of the flotsam.

A bit of shoving with a rake cleared the rest and the little dock started to look quite purposeful. Dragging out the remains of the old punt, they stacked what was left of the rotting wood on the towpath to dry.

Kate tried the depth with one of the Annabella's oars but there was barely enough water to cover the blade before it reached the silty mud on the bottom. She shrugged, sloshed the mud off the oar blade and laid it back alongside the boat.

"Time for some shovelling, I reckon."

The water felt cold as it crept up her legs, and Kate was glad of the wetsuit. Each taking a shovel, she and Daniel started pushing muddy gloop out of the open end of the dock and into the fast flowing stream, the water in the dock quickly taking on the consistency of brown Windsor soup.

It wasn't particularly hard work and it quickly became fun, especially as they warmed to the task. They only cleared the left hand half of the dock, just enough to get the Annabella well afloat, but even so, by the time they had finished, it was six o'clock and so they returned to the house for a shower and a bite to eat. The hard work had given them both an appetite.

Kate could hardly contain her excitement, bolting her cheese and tomato sandwiches before heading straight back down to the river. The rain had stopped, a break in the clouds revealing slabs of bright blue summer sky.

By the time Daniel arrived, twenty minutes later, the Annabella was floating serenely against the side of the dock, rowlocks and oars in place and a grinning Kate sitting on the centre thwart.

He looked down at her, horrified. "Please tell me you didn't put her in the water all by yourself?"

She laughed. "Doddle. All I had to do was swing her round and slide her in. It felt as if she couldn't wait, as if she'd been away from the water for too long, if you know what I mean."

"Are you sure she's watertight?" he asked, somewhat nervously.

"She soon will be. There's a bit of a trickle here and there because the seams are all dried out. But now she's in the water it won't be long before the planks swell and close up again. It's amazing how tight all the joints were, even after being dried out for so long. The planks must have been made with unbelievable skill to fit this well."

Daniel stood looking down at her until Kate patted the seat beside her.

"Do you fancy a turn up the river? I've just got to take her out, even if only for half an hour."

He hesitated fractionally before replying. "Er, no thanks. Another time maybe?"

Kate nodded and tried not to show her relief. She so desperately wanted to spend time alone with the boat and the river.

"Next weekend maybe."

Daniel remained on the dock while Kate handed the boat along until the current carried the bow round into the creek. She deployed the oars as the Annabella slipped out into the evening sunlight and headed straight down the middle of the narrow channel and out into the river as if she knew her way.

After making a wide arcing turn out into the stream, Kate rowed easily upstream against the current and around the sweeping bend behind the house. As the Annabella's bow began to push through the water, wind ripples set up a cheerful chuckle that harmonised with the regular splash of the oars.

Kate knew from her first full stroke that the Annabella had been superbly crafted. As well as being beautiful to look at, she was balanced, responsive and light as a feather to row. And as they moved gently upstream, Kate realised what she had been missing all those months away from the water. Rowing, after all, was what she did, who she was, and always had been.

OK, she might earn her living as a journalist, but everything in the end drew her back to the water. She determined there and then that she would try and stay at Hawkswell for as long as possible. And, whenever the time came to move on, she would make certain that her next place was as close as possible to a river, a lake or the sea.

After thirty minutes hard rowing, she turned to drift gently back downstream, rowing just enough to maintain steerage, daydreaming of gardens running down to little jetties, houseboats and mill houses and all those things people dream about when they are happy.

The first tendrils of evening mist were already threading themselves between the reeds that lined the shady side of the river as she arrived back at the house. The sun, setting behind the orchard, projected long swathes of golden light across the shadowy lawns.

After turning, she rowed cautiously upstream into the boathouse creek and, as she did so, caught sight of a figure midway between the house and the river, watching her approach.

It was unmistakably Penelope Townshend. Kate waved but received no response, and before she could try again, she had eased into the boathouse and nestled the Annabella up against the smooth green timbers of the dock. While considering the pros and cons of leaving the boat in the water, she heard a scrape at the door.

Penelope stepped gingerly into the shadowy interior, tapping the boards ahead of her with her stick. Kate hurried over and made as if to take her arm but the old lady waved her away.

"Just came to see how you were getting on. She floats then?"

She tapped her way along the dock until she could look down into the Annabella, and what appeared to be several litres of river water lapping her bottom boards.

Kate was reassuring.

"She's bound to take on a little until her timbers swell a little. Anyway, most of this has dripped off the oars." She hopped aboard, lifted one of the boards and started to bail the water out.

"I don't think she's shipped more than a gallon or two. Sure and that's not bad for a sixty-five-year-old boat, is it?"

Penelope nodded. Kate couldn't see her face, but she seemed to be deep in thought. I wonder how the old girl feels, seeing the Annabella back on the river after all these years?

Penelope waited until Kate had finished bailing.

"I think it's best to leave her in the water. She'll be safe as houses in here and it'll help to close up her planking. Maybe you would like to come for a row one day, Penelope. It's so beautiful out on the river, especially in the evening."

The old lady stood for a moment, apparently lost in her memories. Kate expected her to agree, to be charmed by the idea, but instead she started to shake her head, slowly at first then more forcefully.

"No, no. I think not. It's been too long. No, no."

She turned and, without another word, shuffled away and out of the door.

The summer settled into a series of long, hot sunny days and life at Hawkswell slipped quietly into a gently heat-hazed routine. The warmth even winkled Penelope out of her dismal sitting room.

A surprised Kate discovered her one particularly beautiful Saturday morning stretched out in an old steamer chair tucked away in a corner of the terrace. She was wearing an ancient print frock that looked at least three sizes too big for her, sunglasses that wouldn't have looked out of place on Marilyn Monroe, and a huge, raggedy edged straw hat.

Kate nearly laughed but thought better of it.

The stillness of the old lady's head, coupled with the impenetrability of the sunglasses meant that Kate couldn't tell whether she'd been seen or not. She scuffed her feet a little on the old stones and cleared her throat as she approached. Penelope's head inclined an inch or two and a frail, blue veined hand beckoned her over.

"What a beautiful morning," Kate said as she approached.

The hand flapped in its familiar dismissive fashion. "Too damned hot, inside and out. No getting away from it. There's thunder in the air, you mark my words. It always brings on thunder, this kind of weather."

Kate decided to stay positive. "But it's lovely while it lasts. This must be the best summer we've had in years. Like summers used to be when I was growing up."

Penelope took off her sunglasses and rubbed her eyes. "Like summers used to be! And what would you know about it? Believe me, summers were a hard time when I was growing up. Not the excuse for dashing off all over the place on foreign holidays like everyone seems to these days. No, summer was all too often a hungry time in the country, let me tell you, especially during the two wars. Even without rationing, the grain stores were empty and the crops weren't ripe enough to harvest. And everyone all worn down with the heat and the dry and praying for rain as their vegetable gardens dried up and withered before their eyes." She stared across the sun scorched lawns.

Kate couldn't think of anything sensible to say so joined Penelope in looking out from the shade of the terrace towards the heat rippled meadows above the far bank of the river, meadows dotted with fat, contented cows and edged with leaf heavy trees. It looked so right to her, like summer countryside should look, as it always must surely have looked. She couldn't quite bring herself to imagine anyone going hungry in the country, it seemed inconceivable. And as for thunder storms…

"I wouldn't worry about thunder, Penelope. They said on last night's weather forecast that this dry spell is due to last well into next week. I expect Tom will soon be getting anxious about his vegetables."

The pale eyes under the straw brim refocused on her face for a moment before ranging up towards the hills behind Kate, the hills that formed the eastern rim of the valley. And when Penelope spoke, Kate could barely make out her words, even though she would remember them all too clearly in just a few days' time.

"This summer will end in a storm my dear, just like it always does. Just like everything ends – with a storm."

On Monday morning, her post included the letter from her mother that she'd been eagerly anticipating. Tearing open the envelope, she settled at the breakfast bar to read:

Dearest Katie,

Remember me saying that I would take a trip to Dublin to do some research into this mysterious Jamie person of yours? Well, I've just got back. (Aunt Maeve sends her love and hopes you are not settling too well into the English way of life!)

What a time I've had! You wouldn't believe how many Kirkpatricks there are in Ireland!

First stop was the registry of births, marriages and deaths. I struck gold straight away by discovering my great grandparents, Patrick and Maire Kirkpatrick. They died and were buried in January 1913, in Poulnadree, Clare, but to my astonishment there were also two young lassies died at the same time; Dierdre, aged eleven and Allana, thirteen, both Kirkpatricks. What do you think of that!?

If I'm honest I can't quite believe it. Why would Grandma Roisin make a secret out of something that simple? Well, I went straight back the next day to look through the record of births and you'll never believe what I found in addition to the records of the two little girls – James Connell Kirkpatrick, born on 7th January, 1896 to Patrick and Maire.

Astonishing! There's a record for Grandma Roisin there too, of course.

I've never been more shocked about anything in my life. All these years without knowing. Next on my agenda was to find a record of uncle James' death, but there's nothing. He's vanished. Grandma's death is recorded, but no sign of a James or a Jamie. I must confess, I'm baffled.

Of course, we can't be completely certain that the Jamie Kirkpatrick that worked at Hawkswell and the one born in Poulnadree are the same, but it seems very likely.

Imagine if it is! What are the chances of you pitching up at the very place he worked? Millions to one I reckon. There must be a reason for it, if it is the same person.

Mind you, I've always said that fate is a strange thing. Drives your father mad when I do say it. He seems to think it's blasphemous for some unfathomable reason. I can't imagine why.

I'm not at all sure whether this news is exciting or just perplexing.

I must be getting on.

Do you think you might be able to find out more from that Miss Townshend or your nice friend, Tom?

Dad sends his love and says to tell you that his back's much better now.

God bless and look after yourself,

Mum

By the time Kate had thoroughly considered the contents of the letter and their implications, her coffee was almost cold.

Could it be, she wondered? Might the Hawkswell Jamie really be her great uncle? And if so, whatever happened to him?

When she was first handed the task of liaising between GreenGauge and the Summerquest Institute during the latter's stock market flotation, Kate had no idea what she was taking on. As things turned out, the demands on her time quickly became overwhelming, so much so that one day she tackled her boss about it.

"They're using me as a one girl press office, Andy. I must have written sixty press releases already this week. What's wrong with their own press relations people?"

Andy's response was typically robust. "They're crap, Kate. At least from what I've seen. OK, maybe that's a bit unfair. Maybe they're not used to handling this kind of a pitch."

"Hey, neither am I. Don't forget that. I'm a journalist, I don't do PR."

"Yeah, but you're a natural communicator, Kate. It seems to me that you've really got a handle on what they're trying to achieve and the ability to put it into the kind of language everyone can understand. You're really putting their message across right now. They like what you're doing, it's as simple as that."

"So what about the rest of my work load, Andy. I've got three major projects sitting on my desk gathering dust."

"Hand them over to me. I'll either farm them out or bin them. From now on you just concentrate on Summerquest. I've got a feeling that catching hold of their shirt tails is going to take us on a very exciting ride."

Penelope's thunder storm arrived at the end of that week. The temperature and humidity that had been building steadily throughout Thursday eventually became unbearable. By Friday lunchtime, the desk fans in the GreenGauge offices were merely pushing the hot, moist air from one place to the next. Tempers were shortening and Andy suggested everyone get away early before the storm broke.

In fact, it didn't break until nine o'clock that night, but when it did come, it came with a vengeance. By seven, the sky had turned the colour of old pewter, with mountainous thunderheads soaring upwards in all directions. As Kate attempted to watch TV the programme was peppered with the white noise crackle and pop of approaching lightning.

Gradually, the daylight turned a bilious yellow as the entire landscape lay like a beast resigned to its fate, as if awaiting the executioner's blow. The cloud cover had become so thick and impenetrable that it was almost dark before the first marble-sized raindrops thudded into the dusty earth of the meadows and onto the hot, dry stone slabs of the terrace.

With little warning, the thunder and lightning that had been flickering and booming in the distance was right on top of them, producing a ragged series of blinding flashes and window rattling detonations that at last released the full ferocity of the rain.

And that was the moment when Kate's world went crazy.

She had been sitting next to a wide open window to catch as much air as possible, but when the storm struck, a number of things happened at once.

Rain hit the window ledge so hard that she had to slam the casement down to prevent the room from being flooded. Then, on the second lightning strike, every light in the house went out.

Far from being plunged into darkness, Kate's room was transformed into some kind of nightmare disco venue, full of blinding, flickering strobe flashes and the overlapping crashes of the continuous thunder. It rolled and crashed along the ridge above the house as if determined to flatten every tree and building. Rain roaring onto the roof and against the windows quickly became deafening. Mesmerised, Kate stood at the window to watch the show. In the flickering light, the terrace slabs disappeared under a seething white mass of water while waterfalls cascaded past her window where the guttering couldn't cope with the flow from the roof.

Lightning skipped around the horizon, individual forks lancing down to earth like science fiction death rays. It was magnificent and terrifying at the same time. Suddenly her lights came back on and a split second later there was a knock at her door. It was Tom Gerrard, in streaming oilskins and carrying a big yellow torch.

"Is everything all right, Kate? I been checking for leaks and there's plenty coming in over the other wing. You should be all right here though, the roof was thoroughly repaired before the flats were done."

"I'm fine, Tom. Thanks. Although I'm relieved the power's back on."

"Ah. That's the old genny, the generator. It's in the cellar. I just been down to check it's got plenty of fuel. It comes on automatically when the power goes off for more than five minutes."

"A generator. Wow. That's a bit posh, isn't it?"

"Not so much as it sounds. We used to run a herd of dairy cattle here right after the last war and made some of the best butter and cheese for miles around. There was milk coolers and fridges all over the place. Couldn't afford to have them going off every time we had a storm or someone put a digger through a power line, could we? So the missus got a generator installed, and it's come in useful more often than I can say, trusty old thing."

"Will it stay on all night?"

"Aye, until the electric boys sort out the problem. Doesn't usually take them too long, but it's nice having the back-up in the meantime." As they spoke, Kate suddenly remembered the Annabella.

"Do you think the boat will be OK in the dock?"

"Oh, she'll be fine. I went down earlier to check she was secure. Safe as houses she is. The river never comes up more than a foot or so before it breaks out onto the floodplain downstream from here. The old Annabella's got plenty enough slack in her lines to cope with that, don't you worry."

Grateful not to have to venture out into the storm herself, Kate thanked Tom and asked if he'd like to come in and dry off.

To her delight he agreed and soon they were both sitting either side of her fireplace nursing large mugs of liberally doctored coffee.

"By God lass, that's a warming brew and no mistake."

After a few minutes, when Tom looked properly settled, Kate took the unexpected opportunity.

"Er, Tom. You know Penelope told me that Jamie Kirkpatrick built the Annabella for her as a birthday present in 1914?" Tom nodded noncommittally. "Well, she also told me that you and he became quite good friends."

"Aye. That's true enough. I often reckon that I was the only real friend that lad had at Hawkswell. 'Course my old father, Brian, had always been very fond of him, but he was in a bit of an awkward situation, being his boss and all."

"So do you remember anything about the actual construction of the boat?"

"Oh aye. I used to get down to the boathouse as often as I could to watch him working. Fascinating it were. But there was so much other stuff happened at that time, stuff between him and the mistress. She had a real problem with the lad, though to this day I've never quite understood what it was all about…"

Chapter 9

North Somerset, December 1913

Christmas Day arrived along with a vicious winter storm. Wave after wave of wind driven sleet and snow swept up the Hawkswell valley, lashing the old house with a ferocity that shook windows in their casements, lifted tiles off the roof and chilled its occupants to the bone.

The last remaining autumn leaves were ripped from the trees and added to the blizzard of debris that peppered windows and doors, as the ravening wind howled through the chimney stacks in terrible disharmony with the high pitched wail from the trees on the ridge overlooking the estate. Those sheep, cattle and horses that remained in the fields and meadows huddled in the shelter of buildings, trees, walls and banks.

Jamie joined the rest of the estate staff for the traditional Christmas lunch with reluctance, and thereafter avoided all other aspects of the festivities, his heart and mind far from Hawkswell.

It was a whole week before he could dare to hope that he was not after all going to be sent away. No news was good news, and it seemed as if the incident in the loft had been forgotten.

1914 arrived as winter tightened its icy hold on the valley. In late January, snow fell heavily for four consecutive days and nights and brought most work on the estate to a standstill. A bitter north easterly wind built deep drifts against walls and buildings, blowing it under the eaves and through even the tiniest gaps in window and door frames.

During that long, harsh introduction to the New Year, countless bitter hours were spent clearing pathways and tracks, rescuing stranded livestock and sawing and splitting logs for heating.

Jamie did his fair share and more.

An old potbellied stove in the boathouse loft – its flue poking up through the tiles of the roof – warmed the space just enough for work to continue whenever Jamie could be spared for an hour or two, although those occasions were infrequent during the worst of the weather.

It wasn't until the last week of March that the bitter cold began to ease its grip at last. Spring arrived on a welcome southerly breeze that swept the sky clear of its blanket of grey and washed the landscape with balmy warmth. Primroses, late snowdrops, cowslips and daffodils jostled for space on the lawn edges and in the hedgerows. At last, despite the heavy workload in the garden, Jamie was able to resume work on the skiff.

One Sunday afternoon in April, he took advantage of the sunshine and set up his saw bench immediately outside the wide open doors of the boathouse, where it was sheltered from a keen wind cutting across the river.

Busy sawing lengths of timber for the many ribs that would make up the framework of the boat, he had abandoned his shirt for the first time that year, delighting in the feel of the hot spring sun on his back.

At the sound of a horse approaching along the river bank, he looked up to see Penelope Townshend, mounted on Josephine, a grey mare he recognised from his time in the stables. As they approached, Jamie put down his saw and brushed the sawdust from his apron. Penelope reigned in a few yards from where he stood and the mare whickered as she caught sight of Jamie.

When no greeting was forthcoming, Jamie was left to open the conversation.

"Good afternoon, Miss Townshend. What a fine day it has turned out to be."

For a moment, it seemed as if the immaculately dressed figure had not heard him for she seemed to look around as if searching for the speaker. After a few long seconds, she at last allowed her gaze to fall upon Jamie and he found himself looking directly into her eyes. Although shadowed by the brim of her riding hat, he could see that they were a deep, rich grey like sunlit thunder clouds, the surrounding whites clear and bright.

But they were angry eyes in a flushed and tight lipped face.

Her words, when they came, cut like a whip.

"Today is Sunday, Master Kirkpatrick, and you are improperly dressed. You will replace your shirt immediately and I must insist that such a blatant breach of propriety does not happen again."

Having delivered her petulant admonition, the girl attempted to drag Josephine's head around with a harsh jerk of the reins, seemingly intent on riding back the way she had come. Unfortunately for her dignity however, the mare, objecting to such harsh treatment, rolled her eyes and immediately dropped back on her haunches, preparing to rear.

All too aware of what was about to happen, Jamie leaped forward and grabbed the reins right where they joined the bridle, using his body weight to hold the mare's head down before she could throw her rider onto the hard path or, even worse, into the river.

"Whoa, Josephine. Steady girl, steady. There now."

Holding her head firmly, he stroked and calmed the mare until her breathing slowed and her ears flicked forwards again.

When he spoke, he could barely repress his fear and anger.

"If you saw with the bit like that Miss, she'll send you flying will this one. She has the mouth of a lady sure enough, but she has a temper to match."

Swiftly regaining her balance, if not her composure, Penelope flicked the reins out of Jamie's hands, and with a great deal more care, completed her turn and settled the mare back on the path. Although she kept her face averted, Jamie had already seen a bright embarrassed flush spread from her neck to her eyebrows at the realisation of how close she had come to complete disaster.

As Penelope tapped with her heels to urge the horse forward, Jamie spoke just loudly enough to ensure that he was heard.

"Take care of the mistress now, Josephine."

Walking into the servant's hall for his dinner that evening, Jamie was immediately aware that something was seriously amiss for no-one would meet his eye. Before he even had a chance to take his place at the table, Brian Gerrard, his face a thunderous mask of barely suppressed anger, took a tight hold of Jamie's sleeve and dragged him straight back out into the yard.

As soon as they were out of earshot of the rest of the staff, he pushed Jamie against the wall of the building.

"What in God's name were you thinking of, you bloody fool! She could have been thrown and killed. I thought you of all people would have known better. Now I suggest you take yourself as far away from here as you can until the master has had a chance to calm down."

Despite being shocked and confused by his master's behaviour, Jamie stood his ground, desperately trying to make sense of what he was being told. He opened his mouth to speak, but Brian Gerrard hissed,

"Go, now, for all our sakes, or there's going to be hell to pay!"

But instead of running off to hide, Jamie lifted his chin in defiance.

"I have done nothing to fear anyone's anger, Mr Gerrard, sir. Josephine reared because the mistress sawed at the reins and I stopped her taking a fall, that's all. I caused nothing, nothing at all."

Brian Gerrard, listening all the while for any sound of his approaching master, heard Jamie's words and saw the honest outrage in his face.

"That's not what I was told half an hour since. Mistress Penelope was in a terrible state of fright at her narrow escape.

She says that you jumped out in front of her and caused the horse to rear. Her father is furious."

Jamie became more outraged with every word.

"I did no such thing. As God is my witness, it happened exactly as I told you. She rode up to where I was cutting timber and tore me off a strip because I had no shirt on. Then she sawed Josephine's bit to turn her and the old mare reared and would have thrown her had I had not taken the reins and calmed the horse. I saved her from a certain fall and possible injury."

Brian Gerrard shook his head.

"Well, that's not what she's saying. And who will they believe? Answer me that, who will they believe? You'll have to go lad. Get out of sight and I'll see what I can do."

Jamie stepped away from the wall.

"I'll not run from something that's not of my making. If I run, it will only confirm her version and prove my guilt. I'm going to go and set this right with Mister Townshend himself!"

Brian tried to stop him but Jamie was too strong and elbowed him aside before striding away through the carriage gate. At that moment, the old gardener felt certain he had seen the last of the boy at Hawkswell.

Jamie's arrival at Hawkswell's front door – puffed up with righteous indignation and determined to prove his innocence – might have proven one of the worst decisions of his life. But, as luck would have it, he arrived just as Edward Townshend was leaving. Perhaps the fact that no-one else was involved in their conversation made the difference, or maybe it was because the confrontation took place outdoors.

Whatever the reason, Jamie managed to present his case without losing his temper and his lord and master, despite his own anger, heard him out. As soon as Jamie had finished his piece, Edward Townshend stood for a moment in thought before sending Jamie back to the boathouse where he was told to remain until summoned.

We can never know the details of the ensuing conference between Penelope and her father that occurred that evening within the high ceilinged rooms of Hawkswell House. Even Charles would say nothing of it to Jamie, considering it far too private and personal to divulge. Suffice to say that Jamie was summoned to the house an hour later and told to wait in the library. Even then, he couldn't bring himself to believe that he would be dismissed.

After five anxious minutes, the door swung open and a chastened looking Penelope stepped into the room, closely followed by her father, who closed the doors behind him. Jamie had not been asked to sit, and was left standing in front of the heavy kneehole desk as he had on the day when he had been asked to build the rowing boat.

The two Townshends, father and daughter, ranged themselves on the far side of the desk. They too remained standing. Edward Townshend cleared his throat.

"It appears that an incident occurred today on the river bank by the boathouse, in which you young people were involved and about which you have each given me a conflicting account. Are you both agreed that a horse bearing my daughter shied and that she was nearly thrown?"

Both Jamie and Penelope nodded, although hers was an almost imperceptible bob of the head whereas Jamie's was a vigorous gesture of assent.

Edward continued. "Was it the case, Mr Kirkpatrick, that you were at the time of my daughter's arrival inappropriately dressed?"

Jamie answered quietly and carefully, realising that much might hang on his answer.

"I was not wearing my shirt, sir. It was hot and sunny and I was sawing timber for the – "

Edward Townshend interrupted him. "I am not interested in what you were or were not doing, man. You were without your shirt, is that correct?"

"Yes sir, that is a fact."

"And did you frighten the horse my daughter was riding and cause it to rear and nearly throw her to the ground?"

This time, far from embarrassed, Jamie looked his inquisitor straight in the eye and spoke loudly and clearly.

"No sir, that is not what happened. The mare was perfectly calm until Miss Pen..., your daughter, that is, attempted to turn her and then... something must have spooked the horse and she began to rear."

"You told me earlier that my daughter sawed at the mare's mouth with the reins and that is what caused her to rear."

"I did say that sir, but I may have been mistaken. She was making a turn when old Josephine reared, and that's the truth of it. I took the reins to prevent your daughter from being thrown, sir. It may have seemed that I frightened the horse and that would be an easy mistake to make, especially as your daughter must have been frightened by the possibility of being thrown. But Josephine, the mare, knows me well. I often take her carrot tops from the garden when I'm passing. She's a dear old horse but she is highly strung."

As he spoke he tried to catch a glimpse of Penelope's face to discover his fate perhaps, but her freshly brushed hair concealed all but her nose and chin. The room fell silent as his last words were absorbed by the book lined walls. He waited in dread for the words that would send him away. Instead, Edward Townshend addressed his daughter first and Jamie second with two distinct inclinations of his head.

"A misunderstanding. That is what we are looking at here. The horse became frightened by we know not what, and started to rear. Mister Kirkpatrick's move forward to take the horse's head was misinterpreted as the cause of the fright. An easy mistake to make in such a circumstance. Are we all agreed?"

Delighted and not a little stunned by the outcome, Jamie fought back a grin and nodded. As Penelope looked up at her father, he fully expected to see a face suffused with indignation, but was surprised to catch the faintest suggestion of a conspiratorial smile when, for the fleetest of moments, their eyes met.

"Yes, Father. I believe I may have been mistaken."

"Then you will apologise to Mr Kirkpatrick for your accusation and instead, thank him for saving you from an almost certain fall."

Her face flushed a little then, and Jamie sensed that this might be a rather less bearable humiliation than the admission of error. But when she spoke there was no trace of anger or dismay. There was little warmth either.

"I am sorry for misinterpreting your actions, Mister Kirkpatrick, and I thank you for your timely intervention."

Edward Townshend looked at each one of them in turn, before squaring his shoulders inside his dark suit.

"We shall let that be an end to the matter then. Thank you Mister Kirkpatrick. You may return to your work."

A storm in a teacup? Maybe, but a storm nevertheless.

Although Edward Townshend's final verdict on the incident allowed for nothing worse than a misunderstanding taking place, both Jamie and Penelope knew that she had tried to get him disciplined at best, dismissed at worst.

Over the ensuing days the incident faded into memory, although Jamie had to keep reminding himself that he would need to be very cautious in his dealings with the young mistress of Hawkswell.

Charles visited the boathouse a few days later and apologised for what had taken place in a manner that indicated that he was not fully aware of all the facts.

"I have had trouble with that Josephine myself, Jamie. Spooks at the slightest thing. Almost had me on my back more than once, I can tell you. Must have frightened poor Penelope almost to death I shouldn't wonder. Nearly as much as you without a shirt I reckon." He then gave Jamie a most peculiar smile before asking about progress on the boat.

Right then, Jamie was involved in putting the finishing touches to a steaming box. The long wooden case rested on trestles and was connected by a heavy rubber pipe to an ugly looking tank mounted above a smoke blackened brazier.

When Charles arrived, Jamie was in the middle of fitting a solid looking door to the open end of the box with heavy brass hinges.

"What on earth is this contraption for, Jamie? It looks like some instrument of medieval torture."

"It is for steaming the timbers Mister Charles, to make them more easy to bend into shape. I shall fill that boiler with water and fire up the brazier. When the prepared lengths of wood are in the box, I will close this door tightly and the thing will fill with steam to soften the fibres."

"But won't it soften the timber of the box as well?"

"No, I've lined it with sheets of zinc, look."

They both peered into the confines of the long dark box.

"So when will you begin?"

Jamie thought for a moment.

"Well, it's too late to start today. I'll need a full day to make the most of the process. Saturday maybe, as long as the weather holds."

"So which part of the boat will you start with?"

"The keel. It will be in three sections and I will bend each section around a series of iron stakes hammered into the ground. Positioning the stakes is the hardest part, they have to be an inch perfect."

"And after that?"

"All the ribs. Sixty of them. I'll do them in pairs, left and right, around the same stakes to ensure a perfect match. That will be a long job because each pair of ribs requires a specific set of stakes. I think I've got enough to prepare five pairs at a time, so the ribs alone will take at least a week."

Jamie caught Charles' look of disappointment.

"Don't be impatient Mister Charles, these things take time, especially as there's always so much work to be done in the garden."

"Supposing you were free of your gardening duties. Could things move much more quickly then?" Jamie nodded, not quite sure what Charles was getting at.

"Oh, yes, of course. But I have to earn my keep, don't forget."

Charles looked thoughtful for a moment.

"We'll see. When might the boat be finished if you can only work in your free time?"

"If all goes well, August maybe. Perhaps a little later. It's busy in the gardens in the summer leaving me little time to spend down here."

Charles nodded. "That's exactly what I thought. But if you had all the time you needed, how long then?"

"Goodness me, six weeks, maybe less. All being well and if nothing goes badly wrong. Yes, six weeks I should think."

Charles smiled and gave Jamie a knowing wink. "Leave it to me, old son. I'll have a word with Papa, see what I can arrange."

And so the course of Jamie's life took yet another turn.

He wasn't summoned up to the house this time. Instead, a handwritten message was delivered to Brian Gerrard stating that Jamie was to be released from his duties in the garden until such time as the rowing boat could be finished.

Brian was to recruit additional help from the village or employ one or two itinerant labourers to cover for Jamie's absence.

At first, young Tom was only allowed to visit the riverside construction site with his father in close attendance, there being far too many sharp tools around, and especially while the river itself presented a potentially lethal attraction. But after a few visits, and with Jamie promising that he would not let the lad out of his sight, Brian relented. From then on, whenever Tom was allowed to visit, he behaved impeccably, watching in awe as Jamie worked.

The steam box was fired up for the first time at the beginning of May and, after a few leaks had been repaired and the door mechanism adjusted, it proved a great success.

Both Charles and Tom were on hand to watch the first of the long keel sections removed, blisteringly hot and gleaming wet from the bowels of the box. The length of malleable timber was laid carefully between two stout iron stakes that Jamie had driven deep into the firm ground alongside the riverbank path. Then, to both onlookers' amazement, he took the free end and drew it back with ease to notch behind a third stake. After a little fine-tuning with a stout crowbar and some wooden wedges, Jamie stepped back, satisfied. An arrow straight length of English oak had become one of the elegantly curved keel sections of a rowing boat before their scarcely believing eyes.

It already looked beautiful.

"Once cooled, Mister Charles, it will keep its shape forever."

Entranced, Charles rolled up his sleeves, put on a pair of heavy leather gauntlets, and helped Jamie with the other two sections that had been left in the box, while Tom watched from his usual position atop one of the saw horses and well away from any danger.

Both lengths of timber were dealt with in a similar fashion and soon the entire profile of the rowing skiff could be seen outlined on the bright green grass. The two men shook hands, pleased with their work. What had for so long been mere lines on paper and a stack of ill-assorted timber was at last taking on a form and life of its own.

Over the following days, with the weather holding fair, construction moved forward at an almost dizzying pace. Able to concentrate fully on the job in hand, Jamie could often be found working long into those early summer evenings by the light of hurricane lamps. Once the keel sections were firmly screwed and glued together, they were propped upright on a line of timber billets to keep them clear of the ground, and secured within a temporary timber framework.

At that point, Brian Gerrard helped Jamie rig an old rick cover between two of the bankside willows so that it could be drawn across the entire working area in case of bad weather.

By the end of his third full-time week, the boat was beginning to take shape, although to an outside observer, that shape remained tenuous and insubstantial. It was in reality a skeleton, waiting only for the flesh and muscle of its planking to make it whole. Charles, on his third visit after arranging for

Jamie to work full time on the project, was astonished and delighted at his progress.

"My goodness, Jamie. She's beautiful, so fine and light. Are you sure it will be strong enough?"

Jamie laughed. "Don't you worry, Mister Charles. The strength does not lie in the ribs. Once the planking is in place, she'll be as sound as sound can be, you can be sure."

Charles was so taken by Jamie's achievements that he lost no time in persuading his father and sister to accompany him down to the work site later that same afternoon. The trio arrived just in time to find Jamie removing one of the long gunwale sections from the steam box. These were the longest and, in some ways, the most critical sections of the hull, for they would hold the ribs firmly in place while the planking was applied. By that time of day, Jamie was hot, dirty and anxious as the party approached. He was also not a little resentful at being interrupted at such a crucial stage of the operation. He nodded a greeting to Edward Townshend and Penelope, politely requesting that they keep their distance while he eased the length of steamed timber into place.

There was a lashing already prepared to take one end at the extreme tip of the keel section where it formed the graceful prow of the boat. With that end firmly secured, Jamie drew the timber along the line of ribs, bending it as he went, all the way along to the broad transom piece at the stern. It was hard work and soon sweat was pouring down his face and under his shirt.

As soon as the right hand gunwale was firmly fixed to the transom he quickly started to remove the second piece from the box.

Charles called out. "Jamie, can you please explain what you are doing to Father and Penelope."

Jamie scowled into the steam that enveloped his head as he drew the section of timber from the box.

"I'm very sorry, Mister Charles, but this is a particularly demanding stage in the construction and I cannot afford to make a mistake. I also have very little time to complete this task before the timber loses its pliancy, so if you wouldn't mind – "

Charles got the message and suggested quietly to his father and his sister that they might refrain from talking for the next few minutes.

So, in almost complete silence, Jamie repeated the mirror image of the task he had just performed until the insubstantial looking twin lines of ribs were enclosed by the two gently curved pieces of timber. He then proceeded to place a series of pre-prepared spacer bars across the width of the boat to keep the gunwale strips evenly spaced, tapping each piece carefully into place with a wooden mallet until the entire structure was firm and sound.

Only then did he turn to face his audience.

"Mister Townshend sir, Miss Penelope, Mister Charles. Please accept my apologies if I appeared rude, but I am sure you can understand that there are some tasks where it is impossible to stop midway through."

Charles stepped forward. "Don't worry Jamie. I was explaining to Daddy and Penelope how the steam softens the wood and that it has to be bent into shape immediately. They both understand. May we take a closer look now?"

To Jamie's surprise and delight, all three seemed genuinely fascinated with the embryonic craft, ignoring the heavy smell of glue, hot wood and the occasional cloud of wood smoke that drifted across from the dying embers of the boiler fire. He stayed as far back as he could, aware that both his clothes and his body were ripe from his day's work.

But, despite his best efforts, he suddenly found Penelope standing close at his side as she leaned across to view how the gunwale boards were notched into the transom piece and held fast with oak dowels. He watched with dismay as he saw her nostrils dilate for a brief moment and braced himself for a caustic comment.

Instead, she leaned even closer, speaking so softly that he barely caught her words.

"My goodness, Mister Kirkpatrick, what a resourceful man you are."

Shortly, Edward Townshend spoke some kind and encouraging words and Charles basked in Jamie's reflected moment of glory. But for many hours after the little party had left him to his endeavours, Jamie could remember not a word of what had been said. All he could recall was Penelope Townshend's sweet breath on his cheek as she spoke those enigmatic words into his ear. He had to force himself to remember the incident with the rearing horse as a reminder to maintain his distance from that unpredictable, and probably dangerous, young lady.

It took a further two days to fix the ribs to the gunwale strips, each joint carefully cut and drilled before being glued and finally pinned with a pair of copper rivets. Only then could the task of planking the outer shell of the craft begin.

Planing, shaping, steaming and nailing the individual planks onto the ribs was to prove the most demanding and time consuming part of the project. Jamie worked from first light until his strength and patience ran out, often long after dark. As June's long days and short nights set in, it seemed to him hardly worth making the short journey back up to the house at the end of each working day, although he did admit to himself that it was more the solitude he craved than the convenience.

So one fine morning, after first obtaining permission from Brian Gerrard, Jamie hauled a spare mattress and some bedding down from the servant's quarters and set himself up a place to sleep in one corner of the boathouse loft. The time saved by being close to his work was negligible, whereas the peace and quiet were priceless.

Those first nights, lying on his mattress so close to the river and its myriad soft and gentle sounds, were some of the happiest and most contented that he had spent since leaving the place of his birth.

Right from the beginning of the boat building project, intrigued members of the Hawkswell staff would find excuses to pass along the riverside path to take a look at progress. During the early stages, when little appeared to change from one day to the next, the frequency of visits soon slowed to a trickle.

It was only after the visit with her father and her brother that Penelope Townshend herself began to take a more regular interest in the work. She would often appear, either on foot or on horseback at least twice a day and, as each subsequent day passed, would spend a little longer observing, often from a discreet distance, Jamie at work.

Right from the outset he adopted a polite but distant attitude, answering questions when asked but not otherwise offering information or opinions.

Penelope's increasingly frustrated attempts to start any sort of conversation were met with what appeared to her to be studied indifference.

But, instead of being put off by Jamie's attitude, she became, to his surprise and consternation, even more determined, and would often sit for as long as an hour, asking question after question and generally making a thorough nuisance of herself.

As day followed day and against his better judgement, Jamie found himself looking forward to Penelope's visits with increasing pleasure. He even began to relax his previously taciturn manner and offer more detailed answers to her questions.

However, he studiously maintained his distance and took no liberties with either speech or action. He kept his shirt on at all times, never swore while she was within earshot, no matter how good a reason he might have had for so doing, and always addressed his visitor as Mistress Penelope, despite being asked to drop the Mistress on numerous occasions.

Penelope also discovered that she too could hardly wait to get away from the house and down to the temporary boatyard beside the river. The tranquillity and calm industry of the place began to weave all sorts of spells within her being that could, of course, have nothing at all to do with the handsome, although often irritating, young man who was constructing her birthday present.

Conveniently forgetting the way she had treated him when her horse shied, she began to realise with a subtle mix of annoyance and dismay that the young upstart Irishman quite plainly didn't like her very much. But then, she thought, why should she care one jot whether he liked her or not?

While the weather remained warm and clear, Jamie completed the boat's planking and, with a small pressed gang of helpers, lifted and inverted the hull before carefully placing it onto a set of trestles under the tarpaulin shelter ready for rubbing down and the first of its many coats of varnish.

The very next day, for the first time in six weeks, the weather broke with an almost tropical rain storm. With so much moisture in the air, varnishing was out of the question and so Jamie covered the upturned hull with dust sheets and another tarpaulin and moved operations into the shelter of the boathouse. There he began fashioning the bottom boards and the thwarts – the wide wooden seats that ran from one side of the boat to the other. There was to be one deep seat up in the bow below which Jamie intended to construct a locker to contain mooring lines and fenders. The broad centre thwart would need to be positioned with great care for that was the seat for the single oarsman and needed to be a precise distance forward of the boat's centre of gravity. For the stern, Jamie would fashion a wide, curving bench that would flow around the entire aft section of the boat enabling three of four individuals to be seated in comfort and safety.

It was on this seat that he commenced work that afternoon.

The rain had become steadily heavier as the day wore on and Jamie became ever more engrossed in his work, shaping and planing in comfortable isolation. He did not expect anyone to make the journey down from the house in such weather. Through the partly open doors of the boathouse, he could see long curtains of rain sweeping up and across the lawns, sometimes obscuring the house altogether. He knew he had some bread and cheese and the makings of a pot of tea up in the loft so he decided not to make the journey up to the house for lunch.

It was at that moment that he realised how much he was enjoying his time down on the river bank. Having the house even fleetingly disappear from view made him aware of how he had become divorced from both the place and its people and customs. He was doing what he had been born to do. And that was the moment when he resolved to return to Ireland at the earliest opportunity and take himself back to Poulnadree to make boats.

He knew it might take years for him to save enough money for the fare alone, let alone start a business, but he knew he had a plan at last, an aiming point for his life.

Soon the last coat of varnish was applied to the boat and its fittings and Jamie's task was all but finished. All that remained was to fit her mooring lines and seat cushions, give her a name and launch her.

After church one Sunday, the entire Townshend family, along with any of the estate staff who could be spared from their duties, and a few interested folk from the village, arrived at the boathouse for the naming of the newly built skiff. A sign writer from Bath was due on the Monday morning to paint the name on each bow and the stern of the boat. Edward Townshend made a short speech of welcome to his guests before stepping forward and laying his right hand on the boat's bow.

"I name this rowing boat the Annabella, in loving memory of my dear departed wife and the mother of my children. Mister Kirkpatrick, you have built a craft that is worthy of carrying the name of such a beautiful lady. It will be a fair tribute and a reminder to us all of how she loved the time she spent on this river."

There were tears shed that afternoon, none more so than by Penelope. Glasses of beer and porter were passed around and a toast proposed to the Annabella. Another toast was proposed to Jamie himself as her builder, which caused him great pleasure and embarrassment.

The following day, while Jamie finished binding leather sleeves around the pivot points of the oars, the sign writer painted the skiff's new name in clear gold letters on both sides of her bow and again across the full width of her stern. She was due to be launched the following Saturday, so Jamie had plenty of time to tidy up the boathouse and construct two greased rails for her to slide down into the river. He also spent a very happy hour carving his initials deep into her transom, JCK 1914.

The launch went smoothly and, despite an overcast sky, a fine time was enjoyed by all. Jamie's first passengers were the three Townshends who sat on soft cotton cushions especially prepared by one of the maids for the stern seat. The Annabella performed faultlessly although Jamie quickly became aware that he would have to move the oarsman's thwart a few inches towards the bow to even up the balance of the boat.

There was to be a picnic party the following afternoon, down river at an island known to the family for many years. Jamie would of course supply the motive power. It turned out to be an easy, happy day. The picnic site was ideal and Brian Gerrard had set everything in place under a bright white canvas pavilion. Jamie was not invited to lunch with the family.

Britain declared war on Germany on the 14th of August, exactly twenty-one days after the final picnic of the summer. On that fateful day, anyone could have been forgiven for thinking that nothing momentous had occurred. The sky remained blue, the grass kept growing and life carried on undisturbed at Hawkswell. Although popular wisdom held that the war would be over by Christmas, this was not a view held by the recruiting Sergeants who had already set up shop in most towns and cities.

This jingoistic mood reached Hawkswell within weeks of the outbreak of hostilities and brought with it a mad gaiety that infected everyone on the estate. Suddenly everyone wanted a turn up and down the river in the Annabella and Jamie was glad to oblige. Those trips usually took place either late in the evening or on Sunday afternoons, and were often riotous occasions.

One of the very last outings involved just Jamie, Penelope and Charles. A pleasant enough trip down river was followed by an uncomfortable and awkward picnic, with Charles attempting to treat Jamie almost as an equal and Penelope seemingly insistent on maintaining the social division. During their journey back to the house, Charles began expounding on his excitement at the prospect of getting involved in the fighting in France. When he tried to involve Jamie in his enthusiasm, Penelope asked him to stop.

"I am already sick and tired of hearing about this beastly war, Charles. I honestly don't understand why all you young men are so determined to go and get yourselves killed anyway."

Charles pressed on regardless. "But it's such a great adventure, sis. Everyone's going. We'll give the beastly Hun a damned good thrashing and be home in no time, you'll see."

And that was when young Penelope Townshend, to her brother's considerable surprise and dismay, screamed, "That's enough! If you two are so set on adventure, you can bloody well swim back to Hawkswell!"

And with that, she threw the picnic hamper over the side and, grasping both gunwales and throwing herself from side to side, capsized the Annabella and tipped all three of them into the river.

A potential tragedy almost descended into farce as Jamie and Charles struggled to their feet, barely up to their waists in water. However, Penelope, floundering nearby in her waterlogged skirts and petticoats, remained inconsolable, and, even after the Annabella had been righted and emptied, sulked all the way back to the boathouse. As Charles had so eloquently expressed, the war in Europe was seen as nothing more threatening than an exciting overseas adventure.

Within a very few months, however, the conflict would reveal its true horror, reaching out to touch the lives of each and every inhabitant of the Hawkswell valley.

Chapter 10

North Somerset, May 1979

Tom's voice caught as he described how the war impacted on the people of Hawkswell.

"They was dreadful times and no mistake. Can't hardly bear to think about it even after all this time. When I hear about folk being killed in Northern Ireland, it brings it all back. It's like no-one ever learns, not even after two world wars, Korea, Vietnam and God alone knows what else."

In the silence that followed, Kate became aware that the storm had passed and was rumbling its way into the distance. She glanced at her watch, astonished to find that it was nearly one o'clock.

"You'd better get off home, Tom. May will be wondering where you've got to." Not receiving a response, Kate touched his shoulder lightly. "Tom?" He lifted his head, eyes unfocused, half asleep and lost in a world of memories.

"I'm sorry Kate, I was miles away. You're right, I'd best get back. But don't you worry yourself about May, she'll be sound asleep. Take more'n a bit of thunder to wake her."

Kate accompanied him downstairs and into the courtyard. It had stopped raining and the air was cool and fresh, with only an occasional distant rumble of thunder. A closer, richer symphony played itself out as countless drips and gurgles of rainwater found their way down from the roofs and gullies.

"Oh Tom, doesn't it smell lovely? Everything's all so...
washed, so clean."

"Aye lass. It's part of what makes this place so special."

Kate looked across at him, his face a pale shape in the
darkness. "You couldn't bear to leave Hawkswell, could you
Tom?"

"As long as the mistress is alive, I hope that'll never happen.
But after her's gone... well, let's hope she's got a few more
years left in her. Goodnight, my dear."

Kate watched him walk the few paces to the far side of the
courtyard and let himself in. It amused her when, despite what
he'd said about May's heavy sleeping, he closed the door softly
behind him.

While making herself breakfast the next morning, Kate
spotted an envelope on the floor inside her door. It hadn't been
there when she'd gone to bed the night before, so it must have
arrived some time during the night or earlier that morning.

Praying it wasn't bad news, she tore it open to find a note
from Daniel.

Dear Kate,

*Now that we are neighbours, perhaps we ought to get to know each
other a little more. To that end, would you please have dinner with me
either tonight or Sunday evening? I know a great place not far from here.*

No strings.
Daniel

Now, exactly what kind of strings might he be talking about,
she wondered. She hadn't been taken out to dinner in years. Not
since Andy had treated her after confirming her job with
GreenGauge, and that had only been to a rather dodgy
Tandoori.

So why not?

Before she could change her mind, she knocked on his door
to accept, but there was no response. She hurried back to her
place, grabbed a pen and scrawled on the back of his note.

'Tonight would be great, thanks. Formal or casual?'

Then she slipped it under his door.

Too late now. Job done.

To stave off an unexpected wash of nervousness about the evening ahead, she dragged on a pair of shorts and a singlet and set off down to the river. Penelope had told her she could use the Annabella whenever she chose, and right then seemed too good an opportunity to miss.

Rowing steadily upstream against the current she was quickly aware of the extent to which the night's torrential rain had swollen the river, now dark with mud and sediment, small branches and other debris swirling in countless miniature whirlpools and eddies.

Soon her arms began to ache and she began to sweat. God, I'm not used to this, she thought. I must be losing my touch.

Spurred on by the realisation, she rowed even harder, lengthening her stroke and upping her rhythm. And the Annabella responded willingly, shouldering aside the rich brown water as they rounded the long, wide bend and entered the long reach below Hawkswell village and its road bridge. As she pulled through the centre arch, a familiar voice called down from the parapet.

"Hi, Kate."

She looked up, squinting against the sunlight, to see Daniel looking down at her. With a couple of skilful strokes, she eased the boat sideways out of the main channel and into an area of still water immediately upstream of the bridge. She watched as Daniel made his way down the steps to the towpath.

"Hi," she said, "I got your note."

"Oh, good. So are you OK for dinner?"

"I slipped a reply back under your door, seeing as how you weren't there."

"And… dare I ask what that reply was?"

She laughed. "It's a yes, of course. I mean, tonight would be fine, if that's OK with you?"

He grinned across at her. "Of course it is. I'll book a table to be on the safe side."

"Nowhere too formal I hope."

"Course not. You can come like that if you want."

Kate was suddenly conscious of what she must look like in her sweaty rowing singlet and shorts. She also realised that her injured leg was in plain view for the first time, its ugly scarring livid and obvious.

"Ah, now, come on Daniel. You know what I mean. Posh or casual?"

"Casual. Relaxed. It's only a pub. But I happen to know that they do a cracking nut roast."

She must have given him a look because he hurried on.

"No, seriously. I'm not taking the mickey, honestly. It really has got a great reputation for its vegetarian menu. That's why I thought you might like to go."

Warmed by the fact that he had remembered, the evening began to sound a lot more appealing.

"Thanks. That's very thoughtful of you. Us veggies usually get an omelette and chips if we're lucky. So what time?"

"How about seven? It'll give us a chance to have a drink first."

Kate eased the Annabella back out into the stream and aimed her bow at the bridge's centre arch. As she pulled away she gave Daniel a parting wave.

"See you at seven then."

He'd seen her leg in all its scarred and gnarly glory.

She had watched his face closely for any hint of revulsion or pity, and seen neither. Maybe it didn't bother him after all.

As she pulled back down river to Hawkswell, the last remaining clouds cleared away and the sun blazed down on the lush green, rain washed landscape. Kate felt like singing for the first time in years and, safe in the knowledge that there was no-one to hear, belted out one of her favourites:

Oh Mary, this London's a wonderful sight,
With people here working by day and by night.
They don't sow potatoes nor barley nor wheat,
But there's gangs of them digging for gold on the streets.

At least when I asked them, that's what I was told,
So I just took a hand at this diggin' for gold.
But for all that I found there, I might as well be,
Where the Mountains of Mourne sweep down to the sea.

Not once during the half hour journey back to Hawkswell did she question why she felt so happy. Approaching the boathouse creek, Kate spotted Penelope watching from the river path. She waved and got a raised hand in return. The old lady was waiting by the dock as Kate eased the Annabella alongside.

"I came down earlier and saw that the boat was gone. I thought it might have been washed away by the river at first, but then Tom told me you'd taken her out. Have you had a good row? You look very hot."

Kate laughed. "I had a really nice trip thanks. And yes, it's pretty warm out there on the water, especially going upstream. It wasn't too bad coming back, but the river's running so fast that I had to keep up quite a pace just to maintain steerage."

"Couldn't you have sat there and drifted along?"

"Absolutely not. If you stop rowing even for a few seconds you spin round and round, especially in a current this fierce. You're completely out of control and that's when you tend to hit things and damage the boat. You need to be moving a bit faster than the water so the rudder will work." She realised she was lecturing and plucked at her singlet. "I reckon I'm in need of a shower." Just then she realised that Penelope had caught sight of her damaged leg. "Bit of a patchwork isn't it? Don't reckon they'd have won any prizes for their embroidery."

The old lady shook her head slowly. "It must have been very traumatic for you, my dear. And painful too, no doubt."

"Oh, it was that all right. Although I would have put up with even more just to keep it."

"So they considered amputation then?"

"More than once. It was touch and go from the start. One surgeon would say it's got to come off and then another would step up and reckon he could save it. Luckily he was the guy that won out in the end. And I'd surely prefer this tatty old thing to a metal one." She laughed as she stepped up onto the dock. "It might ache a bit sometimes but at least it doesn't rust!"

As they started back up towards the house together, Penelope asked her if she'd like to join her for a glass of Pimm's after her shower. Kate looked at her in amused delight.

"Pimm's? Dear God, I haven't had a Pimm's for years. What a lovely idea. Can I bring anything?"

"Just yourself, my dear. Shall we say in half an hour?"

"I'll be there, you can count on it."

Four cast iron picnic chairs with sun bleached cushions were arranged around a matching table covered with a startlingly white linen cloth. A pair of elegant cut glass tumblers sat beside a huge glass jug of the promised Pimm's, complete with its sprig of mint and raft of cucumber slices and ice cubes. Penelope matched the day in a daffodil yellow sundress topped with her wagon wheel sized straw hat that not only shaded her face but half the table as well.

As soon as the drinks were poured and glasses clinked, Kate proposed a toast to the Annabella.

"She's such a lovely boat. I've never rowed anything quite like her. The racing skiffs I've been used to are mostly made of fibreglass or laminated wood. They're great pieces of kit of course, but something made entirely by hand is really special, especially when it was made by a real craftsman such as Jamie. Tom told me all about how she was eventually finished and named after your mother. He also said she was launched only a few weeks before war was declared and I guess those must have been truly awful times."

Penelope took a long pull of her drink before carefully placing the glass back on the cloth with a trembling hand. Kate could almost feel her pain as she spoke again.

"They were. The very worst. Everything happened so quickly. I still can't quite believe how complacent everyone had become. The whole thing seemed like a great adventure, with the men talking about how they were itching to get involved, how they wanted to give the Kaiser a bloody nose. It all sounds so dreadfully crass now, knowing what actually happened. But they had no idea, at least most of them didn't. But the women did – especially the mothers, wives and girlfriends. They knew, somehow. Maybe it was something we inherited from our ancestors, that feeling of foreboding, that knowledge that we'd wave our men off and maybe never see them alive again."

Kate squeezed her arm lightly a second time to communicate her empathy.

"Don't talk about it if you'd rather not, Penelope. It was all so long ago. Maybe it's best left to rest."

Penelope gave her a sad old smile. "Oh, I don't mind, my dear. Now it has all come to the surface, I'd rather get it off my chest I suppose. You see, it has all lain buried for so long, as if it didn't really happen, and was nothing but a bad dream, a nightmare. But there are so many reminders. Remembrance Sunday, the names on the war memorial in the village – so many men who used to work here – and now the Annabella, of course, after lying forgotten in the boathouse all this time.

"You see, one minute it was late summer and all was well, and then, in the space of so few months, everything had changed and so many men and boys had joined up and been marched away. Kitchener wanted 100,000 volunteers, you see. My brother Charles went first. Up to staff college in Camberley to be trained as an officer. Then the village men joined up, one by one, along with staff from Hawkswell. Those from here were formed into what they called a 'pal's battalion'. They were very keen on that idea at first. What better than a group of men all known to each other? The powers that be must have believed that they would look out for one another. Maybe they did."

Her voice trailed into silence.

"So, how many men went from here, Penelope?"

"If I remember rightly, twelve in all. Of course they had to be in good health, over nineteen and under thirty years of age, although I know of more than one lad who lied about his age. Some were from the Home Farm, the rest were household staff. How I remember their excitement as they were driven away to a training camp. There was a band playing, with everyone waving and calling out, flags and bunting everywhere. It was like a village fete."

Kate asked the question she had been holding back. "And Jamie...?" The shadow that crossed Penelope's face was swiftly masked.

"Yes. Jamie went with them. My father had arranged things so that he was able join up. I don't know what he did precisely, but it must have had something to do with him getting British citizenship or something like that."

"So he actually went to France?"

"Yes, they all did. After three months' training on Salisbury Plain I believe, they all got a weekend's embarkation leave before they were shipped over there for further training. I don't think any of them got to the actual front until February of 1915 or even later than that."

The word 'front' hung in the air like smoke.

Neither woman seemed able to ask or voice the next question. Eventually, it was Penelope who spoke again.

"Only three came home to Hawkswell. Three out of twelve and two of them were never the same again. One, Thomas Cooper, was blinded by gas, and young Jack Pettit's lungs never fully recovered and he died in 1918, only weeks after the armistice."

"So Jamie wasn't one of those three?"

"No he wasn't. Although he did come back to Hawkswell for a while. He was wounded in June 1915 and shipped back to England to recover. My father arranged for him to convalesce here. I have always supposed that was because he wanted to know more about what happened to Charles. He was Jamie's Lieutenant, you see." The old lady's eyes watered and she dabbed them with a handkerchief tugged from a pocket. "You see, my brother was killed only days before Jamie himself was hit." For some reason, Kate missed the warning note in Penelope's voice.

"I'm sorry, about Charles I mean. I take it Jamie went back after he had convalesced?"

"Oh, yes. As soon as he was declared fit enough, he went back to the front. We… we never heard from him again."

"But – "

"Enough!"

That single word held more grief than Kate could imagine. It was like Penelope had ripped something from her insides, as if something had broken. The sun continued to shine, but that summer day had chilled.

Kate kept silent, knowing there was nothing more to be said.

Then, without warning, Penelope slumped forwards across the table. Horrified, Kate hurried around and crouched at her side.

"Penelope? Are you all right?"

But there was nothing, only the slow rise and fall of the old lady's breast to show that she was still breathing. When, after a few seconds, she was able to speak, her words were so quiet that Kate could barely hear what she was saying.

"I am very tired, Kate. Please will you help me indoors."

As soon as she'd settled Penelope as comfortably as she could in her sitting room, with a rug tucked around her legs, Kate rushed off to find May Gerrard. Halfway across the courtyard she met Tom, who took one look at her face and hurried over.

"What's wrong, lass?"

Kate, out of breath from running, gasped out, "I'm fine, Tom. It's Penelope… Miss Townshend. I think she's had some kind of an attack. I was looking for May. I don't know what to do."

Tom hustled her into their kitchen and called May in from the sitting room. As Kate recounted the story of the afternoon's conversation, she watched a look of tired recognition spreading across May Gerrard's face. Tom looked as though he was hearing something completely different, because he kept on looking to his wife as if she was the only one who might understand what Kate was saying.

As soon as Kate finished, May asked, "Were you talking specifically about that Jamie Kirkpatrick when she had this attack, as you call it?"

"Yes. I'd just asked her what happened to him after he went back to his Regiment, after he'd recovered from his wounds."

May's breath eased out in a long, slow sigh. "All right. Enough now. I'll go and see to her. She'll be herself again in a day or two, God willing."

Kate wasn't satisfied. "But what...?"

May's answer came like a slap in the face. "I said enough, for goodness sake! No more questions. I hope to God your meddling hasn't done too much damage. I always knew that having strangers in the house would lead to this. Why can't you people leave things alone? Why do you always have to poke your noses into things you don't understand?"

Then, without another word, she flew from the room and could be heard stamping off into the depths of the house.

Kate, shocked at May's outburst, looked to Tom for some explanation. But he just shrugged and raised his eyes to the ceiling.

"Don't ask me, lass. I've never known what goes on between those two. Whatever it is, it goes back years, ever since the mistress was first in hospital."

"Hospital?"

Tom paused for a moment. "Now there, I've gone and said too much already. Look, if you want a word of advice from an old man, you'll do exactly what May says, and leave things be. There's all kinds of stuff about this house that you don't need to know and it's best left that way. Understand?"

Kate didn't, but nodded anyway.

"And before you ask, I don't know what happened to the lad either, and that's the truth of it. Now, best make yourself scarce before the missus gets back."

Kate tried to follow Tom's advice by clearing her head of all the questions surrounding Jamie and Penelope and concentrating instead on her impending evening with Daniel.

Four o'clock found her standing in the middle of her

bedroom throwing clothes around like a mad woman at a jumble sale. At last she shouted with frustration at the mess she'd made.

"Jesus. It's not as if it's even a proper date. I'm hardly out to impress the man, just being friendly to my neighbour. So why the fuck can't I find anything to wear?"

In the end she settled on an old but favourite Laura Ashley top, her usual jeans and her best boots. She stopped herself from doing something different with her hair but spent at least half an hour on her make-up. The whole ensemble was set off with her favourite leather jacket.

Kate was ready by five past six. They weren't due to meet until seven.

Settled at their table, Kate read her way through the extensive menu with increasing amazement.

"This is astonishing, Daniel! It's as if the carnivores are the underclass for once. You've no idea what it's like normally. This is fabulous. Can we have two meals?"

He laughed. "You can have as many meals as you want, but only if you tell me what happened to your leg. I can tell that it's troubling you and I really want to know, to understand."

"OK, OK. If you insist. But can we order first?"

"Fine. What would you like to drink?"

Kate thought for a moment.

"Well, seeing as you're driving, I'll have a pint of Guinness please."

"You sure? Wouldn't you rather have a bottle of wine?"

"Maybe later. But I'm really thirsty right now and us Irish girls are partial to a drop of the Liffey."

They took their time ordering the food, Kate spoilt for choice for what felt like the first time ever. But after sending the waitress away for the second time, she realised that her delaying was only putting off the inevitable, the time when she would have to recount the painful story of how she came by her leg injury.

Eventually she made a decision and, as soon as Daniel's lager and her Guinness arrived, they clinked glasses and Kate dived straight in.

"Right, I studied at Queen's in Belfast. But then you already knew that. At this point I need to tell you that I'm a Republican sympathiser. I even joined one of the more radical groups at uni and went on a couple of marches. Of course, that was before British squaddies started shooting at us." While Daniel tried not to look too shocked, she carried on before he could comment.

"But, and it's a big but, I have never actively supported the IRA and all their various affiliates, and I absolutely abhor their methods, always have done. I loathe violence in all its forms, and that includes against animals as well as humans, but I don't agree with the partition of Ireland." She fiddled with her knife, took a sip of her drink, carefully licking the froth from her top lip.

"All the while I was in Belfast, I found it damned near impossible to bear those bloody aggressive Orange men with their apprentice boys and their marching bands. I mean, what a bunch of pricks, strutting about like that. No wonder the Republicans are so pissed off."

Daniel reached over and gently stopped her tapping. "Go on."

She put the knife down carefully.

"Isn't this where you're supposed to defend your country?"

A grin took the edge off her words.

He shook his head.

"I can't. Not really. I think they're all as bad as one another. They know they'll have to sit around a table one day and sort everything out. What I can't understand is why they keep on killing each other in the meantime. You see, I'm a pacifist too. How's that?"

Kate looked relieved.

"Good start. At least neither of us has walked out yet. Maybe they ought to get us around that table. I'm sure we'd have it all sorted out in no time at all."

The humour helped. So far, so good, Kate thought. Then Daniel brought her crashing back to earth.

"Right, Kate. So we've sorted out the Northern Ireland problem, but I'm still waiting to hear what happened to your leg."

"Damn. Thought you'd forgotten about that. Ah well, they say patience is a virtue."

She took a deep breath before continuing. "Although all kinds of activism took place on campus, most of us managed to keep fairly well away from the worst of the Troubles, even though the Falls and Shankill were right across from the campus. We all knew what was going on, but learned to avoid most of the trouble spots. I managed to stay clear of the worst of it until one particular Monday in March 1972."

"Wasn't that when…?"

She nodded slowly. "Sure. That was when the IRA set off a huge car bomb in the centre of the city. Apparently they'd called in a hoax that made the security forces direct people right onto the bomb. Seven died that day and over a hundred and forty were badly injured. The dead included two very close girlfriends of mine."

"God, I'm sorry, Kate. But how come you were involved?"

"Funnily enough, I was buying some new knickers in a shop not thirty yards from where the car was parked. There was this huge bang, a great rush of air, and the whole place came down on top of me. My friends were waiting for me right outside the shop."

Daniel reached across and held her hand. "OK Kate, I've heard enough." She didn't remove her hand, just looked into his face. He could see the pain, the tears barely held in check. But he saw defiance there too, it was in her voice when she spoke.

"It's all right, Daniel. Shit happens. I'm glad I've told you. I mean, nothing I can do will change anything. The dead are dead and the injured have to live with it, and that's that. I was one of the lucky ones. Trouble was that I was completely trapped for four hours. Couldn't move, couldn't see. Luckily I could breathe or I'd not have got out of there alive, simple as that. They had to lift a massive slab of concrete off my mangled leg to get me out, cranes and everything. Made me quite a celebrity I can tell you, the last person pulled out of there alive and all that crap."

"And your face?"

Kate only just stopped her hand going to her scar. "Oh, that. According to the docs it was a fragment of the car that blew up, red hot metal. Hurt like hell at the time, much more than my leg. How crazy is that?"

"So you didn't get your knickers."

Kate looked at him in astonishment for a split second, opened her mouth to call him every name she could think of, but something in his eyes told her that he actually understood, that joking was his way of dealing with the shittier aspects of the world. So she sighed instead and smiled.

"No. I didn't get the knickers."

They laughed then, and it was good, shared laughter.

The food was as good as the menu had promised and Kate's opinion of Daniel climbed another notch or two as he ate his way through a vegetable curry, insisting it was delicious. While they waited for their coffees to arrive, something reminded Kate of the ammunition boxes. Maybe it would have been better if she'd forgotten all about the damned things. There was no way she could have foreseen the Pandora 's Box she was about to unlock.

"Can I ask you something, Daniel?"

He nodded, "Go ahead."

"The day you were moving in to your flat, I noticed a pile of old ammunition boxes in the hall. I don't suppose they were yours by any chance?"

Without answering, he drained his beer in one long swallow, caught a waiter's eye and waved the empty glass.

"Would you like another Guinness?" he asked Kate, his face giving nothing away.

"Yes please, a pint again. Something tells me I might need it."

As soon as the drinks arrived, Daniel asked what at first sounded to Kate like an absurd question.

"What do you know about Howk's Well?"

"Whose well?"

"Howk, Thomas Howk. It's where the name Hawkswell comes from."

"You mean there is a well after all?"

"Oh, there's a well all right. And a hell of a lot more besides."

Kate's intrigue racked up a notch or two.

From no more than a foot away they studied each other, while Daniel seemed to be making his mind up about something. Right then, with a belly full of good food and a pint and a half of Guinness inside her, Kate would have been quite happy to get even closer. She only held back because Daniel seemed more serious than he'd been all evening.

"Kate, I want you to promise me that you'll not repeat a word of what I'm about to tell you to anyone at Hawkswell. In fact I'd prefer it if you don't mention it to anyone at all, OK?"

She crossed her heart with a finger. "Hope to die."

And so Daniel began. "Sometime in the late twelve hundreds, no-one's quite sure precisely when, a man named Thomas Howk discovered a well. The story goes that right in the middle of a long dry summer, some of his sheep fell down a hole. Apparently there was a hollow underneath an old thorn tree where the flock used to shelter from the sun. Thing was there'd never been any sign of a hole there before so it looks as if the ground must have just opened up and swallowed them. Must have scared the shit out of the poor guy. Anyway, after lobbing a rock down and hearing a splash, he lowered a bucket on the longest piece of rope he could find and brought it back up brimming with clean, fresh water."

"You make it sound more like he'd discovered gold."

"Even diamonds wouldn't have been more valuable that summer, Kate. With the river nearly dried up, farmers were apparently fighting each other for access to every stream and pool, so any new source of water would have been beyond price."

"Of course, Thomas didn't own the land, his local Lord did. But he held some kind of a tenancy and that was the important bit. It meant he controlled access to any water found on his patch. So, he found himself a band of itinerant masons, and they cleared the covering of soil and loose stones away to reveal an almost circular hole in the bedrock, what we now call a pot hole. It was reportedly more than big enough to swallow a sheep or a careless man."

Kate interrupted him. "So what exactly is a pot hole, Daniel. And how come you know so much about all this?"

"OK. A pot hole is a hole formed in limestone by water action. The rock all around us here is limestone which is soluble in water, especially acidic water, which includes the majority of rain. What also happens sometimes is that a small pebble of harder stone finds its way into a hollow in a stream bed and gets swirled around gradually, sometimes over hundreds if not thousands of years, wearing away at the softer limestone. Eventually, after carving itself through the underlying bedrock, the stream breaks through into another cave and you're left with a vertical pipe with water roaring through it." He paused. "OK so far?"

She nodded. "Go on."

"Over time, the stream changes course or dries up, leaving the hole high and dry. I know all this, Kate, because I'm actually a hydro-geologist."

"A what?"

"A geologist that specialises in water courses, aquifers, rivers and such like. Everything I'm about to tell you has been thoroughly researched over the last ten years by Bristol University. Don't worry, you'll soon find out why."

"Ah, I see now. Hence the caving."

Daniel grinned. "Hence the caving. Anyway, Thomas arranged for stone to be brought down from a quarry up on the hillside – traces of it are still there by the way – and a circular retaining wall built around the lip of the hole. The masons then built the wall up until its top was level with the surrounding meadow and, voila, they had their well. All they needed to complete it was a winding mechanism and a large leather bucket."

"Leather, why leather?"

"Lighter than wood, easier to haul such a long way. With an apparently limitless supply of fresh water, the well quickly became the envy of the valley. Thomas charged a nominal amount for each bucket raised, the proceeds allowing him to build a new house for his family and outbuildings for his animals. Finally he constructed a wooden housing around the shaft with a thatched roof and a lockable door to protect his newly discovered asset.

"What's fascinating is that neither Thomas nor anyone else appears to have questioned the source of the water. Maybe they thought it was a gift from God and that was enough. Anyway, over the next few hundred years, Howk's farm grew until it covered a five mile stretch of the river valley. The farmhouse was enlarged, barns and other outbuildings grew up around it until, towards the end of the fifteenth century, the farm became an estate and the farm house became a Manor – Howkswell Manor."

"Which grew into what is now known as Hawkswell?"

Daniel nodded. "Eventually. But before that happened, another dry spell hit the west of England, far worse than the one back when Thomas Howk first discovered his well. This drought went on for three consecutive years. First the crops died and then the livestock. The situation was becoming desperate, with people succumbing to hunger and disease. Water became more precious than ever before and Howk's Well soon became the target of raids from surrounding farms.

"Worried about losing control of his nice little earner, Matthew, Thomas Howk's descendant, constructed a much more substantial structure over the well shaft. Blocks of granite were carted up from Cornwall and a chamber with a vaulted stone roof was built during the second spring of the drought. A massive oak door with an iron lock ensured the security of Howkswell's water supply. Over the next decade, the two wings were added, one to accommodate the increasing number of staff required to run the house, and the other, originally intended as a guest wing, was built specifically to include and encompass the well chamber."

Suddenly Kate realised what Daniel was saying. "You mean that big, heavy door downstairs is…?"

"Yes. I'm certain it's the entrance to Howk's Well."

"Jesus, Mary and Joseph. Go on."

"During the civil war, the Howk family sided with Cromwell. Ten years later, their decision came back to haunt them when they found themselves disgraced, their house and lands forfeit. The entire Howkswell estate was gifted by Charles II to a chap called Nigel Townshend, a man with a modest fortune but little property, who had had the good sense to follow his instincts and support the crown no matter how futile that must have seemed at the time. The house and its estate were substantially remodelled and renamed Hawkswell, probably to distance the place a little from its original owners.

"For the next two hundred and fifty years the Hawkswell estate prospered while the well continued to supply clean, fresh water and remained a benevolent presence at the heart of the house. But everything changed at some time during the First World War."

Kate waited, but Daniel didn't seem to have anything else to say. "So what happened then? You can't just leave it there!"

"Not a lot, only that your Miss Townshend, who had by then inherited Hawkswell from her father, had the original pumps replaced and new electric ones installed to draw the well water into a holding tank, after which she had the chamber sealed off."

"But why?"

"No-one knows, or at least no-one's telling. That door hasn't been opened since then and I've checked. It fits perfectly, with a hermetic seal, must have been made that way. There's not even a breath of air from the other side."

"All right. So that's the story of the well. But where do you and the university fit in?"

"We think we know where that water's coming from. There's been a huge amount of research done in the last few years to try to explain how all the water gets off the Mendip plateau. The trouble is, there's not enough flow in any of the rivers to account for all the rain that falls on the high ground."

"So where's the rest going? No, wait. I think I see where this is headed. You reckon it's all going underground."

"Dead right we do. You know Cheddar Gorge?"

Kate nodded.

"Where's its river?"

"What do you mean?"

"Bloody great gorge like that. It had to have been cut by a river, so where's it gone. There's not even a trickle. It's got a road running right down the middle of it now."

"So what?"

"So the river that cut the gorge has gone deep underground. Heaven knows how far because no-one's found it yet. But if that's the case on the southern flank of the Mendips, why shouldn't the same thing be happening here?"

"OK. So you want to find out if there's some kind of underground river at the bottom of Howk's Well. So why don't you ask Miss Townshend for permission to check it out?"

Daniel spread his arms wide. "That's what they've been doing for the past six years."

"And?"

"She refuses. Absolutely. Won't even discuss it. In fact, a year ago she took out an injunction to prevent us from ever approaching her again."

"Hey, it's her house Daniel, even if I don't understand what her problem is. But what can you do?"

Daniel lowered his voice.

"Ah, now, that's the thing. Why do you think I took the flat? I remember you saying it was a bit far from my job."

Kate didn't like what she was hearing. "Please don't tell me this is all part of some scheme?"

"Dead right."

"What, you mean you want to break in?"

"No breaking and entering necessary. I've got a key."

"You've what?"

"I knew there had to be one somewhere. So I waited until Penelope had gone into Bath with Tom that time, you remember, about three weeks ago?" Kate waited. "It took a while, but I found it in the end. It was hidden in a bureau in her sitting room. I got one of the engineers at the University to make me a copy." When he saw the look of horror on Kate's face, he hurried on. "Don't worry. The original's safely back in place now."

Kate's next words came out in a rush. "That's not what I'm worried about, Daniel, and you know it. Jesus Christ, man, that's trespassing. Creeping around someone else's house like that. And Penelope an old woman too. If she'd come back she might have had a heart attack."

Daniel began to look as if he wished he'd never started the conversation. "But she didn't. I was careful."

"So what exactly do you plan to do with this key now you've got it?"

"Find out if it is the well chamber for starters. Then get inside of course, and see if our theory's right."

"And just how do you plan to do that without being discovered?"

His face lit up again. "Simple. I'm going to have the guys come round for dinner one night. As soon as Miss T and the Gerrards are tucked up in bed, we'll open up and get all our equipment inside. We'll take everything we need to spend forty eight hours in there – food, drink, sleeping bags and all that kind of stuff. We'll close and lock the door behind us, so no-one need ever know we've been in there."

"But why, Daniel? What's so bloody important about an underground river?"

"Because it's hugely significant, Kate. Apart from helping to explain the geology of this whole area, it could provide a new drinking water supply for Bristol and Bath for instance. But I suppose the biggest thing is helping us to understand what goes on beneath our feet. This whole region is riddled with cave systems, with only a fraction of them unexplored. I suppose that now I should confess a bit of an ulterior motive in being involved in all this. I volunteered for the job because of my passion for caving. It's what got me involved in geology in the first place."

"So you've been crazy for a long time then?"

He grinned. "Since I was fifteen. A friend's father took us down my first cave, Goatchurch cavern in Burrington Coombe. I was hooked right from the start."

"I'm sorry, Daniel. I can get my head round lots of things, but potholing isn't one of them. I don't get how crawling around in a dark wet sewer pipe can be anything but hell."

"Oh, it can be pretty hellish at times, I agree, and some of the places I have been have been a lot smaller than a sewer pipe I can tell you. I'm sure you won't believe me, but it can be breathtakingly beautiful down there. There's a place near here called Fairy Cave where there's a massive cavern full of pure white stalactites of every shape and size. It's wonderful. Just imagine being the first person to ever see something like that."

"I'm sorry Daniel, I still don't get it. After all, what's the point?"

"I can't believe you're saying that, Kate. It's a bit like saying why bother to go to the moon or why bother to explore the ocean deeps or the Arctic. Can't you see that if the human race ever stops doing stuff like that, it'll be the end of us. It's discovering new places and things that keeps us going." After his passionate outburst, Daniel sat back in his chair. He looked completely deflated.

Kate knew that she should still have been annoyed with him for coming up with such a devious project, even more furious at the way he was going behind Penelope's back. But, despite all her instincts and the countless alarm bells going off in her head, she couldn't help but admire his passion and energy.

"And you're absolutely sure it can be done without anyone finding out?"

Daniel sat forward again, the light back in his eyes. "Absolutely. We've planned the whole thing down to the last detail over the past six months. All the equipment is already stashed in my flat... "

"The ammunition boxes, at last!"

Daniel nodded. "And the rest. I've been ferrying stuff down from Bristol for weeks. All we've got to decide is when to go."

Kate looked long and hard into his eyes. Was there over-confidence maybe, some more complicated, more devious motive? Whatever she was searching for, all she found was rock hard determination and excitement.

"Daniel, I'm really not happy about this. Maybe you guys took the wrong approach with Penelope. I can't imagine why she's kept on refusing like that. I mean it's not as if the well's even used any more. Hawkswell gets all its water these days from a spring up on the hill. Tom told me that it was set up years ago when the pumps in the well-kept failing. It was when I asked about the hose to wash your car, remember? He said that there's only so much flow from the spring and there's some kind of a cistern up by the gates. If too much water gets run off in a hurry, they get silt in the pipes or something. So it just doesn't make sense that she won't let you check the place out and explore if you have to."

Daniel sat back and folded his arms. "So you agree we've no alternative."

"No. No, I don't. I still think it's underhand and sneaky. I mean, what if something goes wrong?"

"How do you mean?"

"Suppose someone gets trapped down there, or has a fall and breaks a leg. What then?"

"It won't happen. We'll make sure of that. We're good at what we do, you know. We've years of experience between us."

"But it might. Shit happens, Daniel. Don't ever forget it."

She took a second or so to think. "How about if I have a word with Penelope?" Daniel looked horrified.

"Shit, Kate. Don't do that! You'll blow the whole thing wide open. I'll be thrown out of my flat in ten seconds flat and she'll probably have me arrested into the bargain."

Kate shot him the kind of look you give a five-year old who's just asked why they have to go to school.

"Of course I won't mention you, or your plan. I'm not entirely stupid you know. I'll tell her that I know someone who mentioned that the university want to take a look, for geological research. That's not exactly going to come as news to her, is it? So what's the harm? And I might even learn why she's so dead set against you guys."

Daniel gave a reluctant nod. "OK, you win. It's worth a try, I guess. I have to confess I'd much prefer it if we can get access legitimately. So when do you think you could ask her?"

"I'll try and work it in next time we have tea or something."

"How about tomorrow?"

"Jesus, Daniel. Where's the fire? Anyway, I can't. Not straight away. She had a bit of a funny moment earlier today and I don't expect she'll want to see me for a while. I think I touched a raw nerve when we were talking about Jamie, about how he was killed in the war." She then had to relate her entire conversation with Penelope and explain May Gerrard's reaction. By the time she'd finished, the landlord had called 'time'.

Kate only allowed Daniel to pay for the meal on the strict understanding that she would pick up the tab next time.

"So, there's going to be a next time, is there?" he asked, with an almost annoying grin.

"Only so long as you promise me not to even think about that well shaft until I've had a chance to talk to Penelope."

When they stepped out into the pub car park, the soft night air was tinged with a hint of bonfire smoke, a timely reminder that autumn was on its way.

During the short drive back to Hawkswell, Kate promised that she'd try and catch Penelope as soon as the old lady was sufficiently recovered. Just how on earth she was going to bring up the subject of a well she wasn't even supposed to know about without raising suspicions was quite another matter. She didn't ask Daniel in for coffee, which seemed fine since he made no attempt to invite her to his place either. A quick hug and a peck on the cheek outside Kate's door brought a fascinating but bewildering evening to a close.

Half an hour later, alone and naked in her bed, Kate allowed herself to imagine Daniel in a similar condition barely yards away. As her imagination considered a possible alternative, she shut it down. Don't go there, Katie girl. Don't even think about it. But of course she did. And when she did, she couldn't help smiling.

Chapter 11

Kate was woken for the second morning in a row by the sound of rain pattering against her bedroom windows. Although it was only 8.30, one look at the heavy grey clouds hanging in the treetops told her that it was most likely in for the day, so that was the end of her plan to take the *Annabella* out again.

After a lazy and slightly disconsolate breakfast, she tidied the flat before settling down to read her Sunday paper. Four pages in she came across an article describing how the War Graves Commission were in the process of restoring a World War I cemetery at Zillebeke in Belgium.

Any other day she might have turned the page, but not then.

Suddenly she knew there was something she had to check out. It was only a ten minute drive to Hawkswell village and when she arrived shortly after eleven, there was plenty of room to park in the centre, right outside the Red Lion Hotel. A pretty enough place, even in the pouring rain, it boasted all the amenities that make up a sleepy little Somerset village – a tiny post office, a small supermarket, a second-hand bookshop, the hotel and a duck pond, its inhabitants blissfully unconcerned with the weather. A small triangular patch of chain bordered grass surrounded a modest war memorial that bore the all too familiar legend:

To the gallant men of this village who gave their lives in the Great War, 1914 – 1918.

Two columns of names, twenty in the left hand column and nineteen in the right, had been carefully chiselled beneath the dedication. As she stood and stared, Kate couldn't help wonder at the loss of thirty-nine young lives from one small community. And there are thousands of similar memorials, she thought, in countless towns and villages throughout the country.

Dear God, all that remembrance and not a scrap of sense learned. For there, directly beneath the first panel was another, detailing lives lost during the Second World War. Fewer names this time, yet still telling the same harrowing story. By then, the rain had turned to a heavy drizzle, but Kate hardly noticed as she began to read her way down the first list:

Abel, P Private, North Somerset Yeomanry
Alinson, B Flight Sergeant, Royal Flying Corps
Atkins, C Corporal, North Somerset Yeomanry

She read slowly and carefully until she stopped at:

Townshend, C A Lieutenant, North Somerset Yeomanry

Charles. Penelope's brother.

Her throat tightened and an unexpected heat burned her eyes, as if seeing his name there, etched into that block of stone, somehow made him more than just a name. She looked again.

No names began with K, so no Kirkpatrick, J C.

Maybe he... maybe what?

Maybe he had never existed at all. Perhaps he hadn't joined up, hadn't gone to war. Because, surely, if he had and he'd been killed, his name would be there. Then she had another thought. If he hadn't changed his nationality after all, maybe he wouldn't be entitled... Her thoughts were interrupted by a voice close behind her which made her jump.

"I thought it was you, Kate."

She turned to find Tom Gerrard, his wax jacket darkened by the drizzle, standing there, a half empty pint pot in his hand.

About to say something silly about the rain watering down his pint, Kate realised that he was looking past her, at the names on the memorial with eyes so full of sadness that she kept silent.

Tom nodded, as if to thank her for understanding. And when he spoke, his voice was as soft as the rain.

"I knew most of them lads. Some was older brothers to a few of my pals at school, others worked up the house or in the garden. Good to see their names up there. Means they'll never be forgot." He stood for a moment or two before turning to Kate and tipping his head towards the hotel.

"Come on in out of this weather lass, and let me buy you a drink."

The public bar of the Red Lion wrapped itself around them like a warm hug that morning, its cosy, smoke-filled interior redolent with the smells of men, beer, pipe tobacco and wet dogs.

Tom didn't introduce her to anyone although they all raised their glasses or muttered a greeting to Tom himself. To them, Kate just happened to be there with him, like a Jack Russell. The lack of a reception didn't upset her, far from it. It was how things were back in her home town bars, so much so that the place felt even more familiar and comforting.

Tom got himself another pint, and a half of Guinness for Kate which he set on a small, round table in the bay window that overlooked the war memorial.

"So you was searching for your Jamie, then?" It wasn't a question, more a statement of fact. Kate nodded. "Not there is he? I could have told you that if you'd only asked. And before you ask, I don't know why neither. The way her ladyship tells it, he was declared fit and left early one morning without so much as a by-your-leave. Not a word to no-one. Next thing we hear is he's been reported missing, presumed killed. And that's the beginning and the end of it. I'm sorry if he was your relative, because it's not much to remember him by."

Kate sipped her drink. "It's all right, Tom. I'm not that bothered really. He left us the *Annabella* and that's a pretty amazing legacy. And let's face it, a couple of months ago I didn't even know I had a great uncle! I suppose I hate mysteries, that's all."

They sat for a minute or two in companionable silence until Kate said, "Tom. You remember you told me about the water supply at Hawkswell coming down from a spring up in the woods?" The old man nodded. "Well, I'm a bit puzzled. You see, when I was showing Daniel where to find the tap and the hose to wash his car, we came across an enormous pump in the shed. Surely you need a well to have a pump?" Tom stared down at his pint for a moment and when he looked up again, Kate thought he was about to tell her to mind her own business again. But instead, he smiled.

"There's not much gets past you, young lady, is there? Aye, there's a well. It's how the house got its name."

"You mean Howk's Well?"

The moment she spoke the words Kate could have kicked herself.

Tom's voice sharpened a notch. "So how come you knows about that, if you don't mind me asking?" It was time to improvise.

"Oh, er… I read about it. There's a book I came across in the library in Bath. I think it was called Manor Houses of North Somerset, or something like that. It's got loads of information about the history of Hawkswell and there's a bit about the well."

Tom eyed her suspiciously so she hurried on, "I only thought that, seeing as I'm living in the house, it would be nice to know a bit more about its history, that's all."

He seemed to relax a little.

"So you know where it is then."

Kate thought quickly.

"No, not really. The book just says it's somewhere inside the house, that's all."

"Well, you know that big old door in the downstairs corridor below your flat? It's behind there. Damned great chamber all made of stone. Even thinking about that shaft makes me shiver. My old dad took me in there and held me up so's I could see down it once. Fair scared the life out of me it did. It just goes down and down so far that when you shine a light down, the water at the bottom's no bigger than a sixpence. Bloody terrifying place it is. Dangerous too. That's why it's all sealed up, to stop anyone falling to their death. Of course there used to be all kinds of pipes and stuff what went down and joined up with the two big pumps. There was one right in the middle of the courtyard and another in the big kitchen. But, as you saw, it's a long time since they were last used."

Kate knew there had to be more. "It said in the book that the original well never dried up and that it was the best water for miles around."

"Aye. That's true. The level never changed an inch, winter or summer, rain or drought. In the early days there was a mark on the winding rope that showed when the bucket was submerged. They never had to move it."

"If it was so reliable, why didn't they keep on using it?"

"What d'you mean?"

"Instead of going to all the trouble of getting water from the spring up in the woods?"

Tom suddenly looked resigned. "Truth is, I don't know, lass. I was only a youngster when it all happened. As far as I can recall it was the mistress who thought it represented too much of a danger. On top of that she'd had enough of folks turning up from all over to…"He stopped abruptly.

Kate gave him a moment then asked, "To what, Tom? Why did people keep turning up?"

The moment he spoke, she feared she'd pushed him too far.

"For heaven's sake, lass. Why can't you let things lie?" Kate sipped her Guinness, not daring to say a word. After a few moments, Tom sighed. "If yer must know, there used to be some stupid legend about the water from Howk's Well. Load of superstitious rubbish if you ask me, but there was plenty as believed in it. Them's the ones what become the bloody nuisance."

This was far more than Kate had bargained for and she wasn't going to let him leave it there.

"Oh, come on Tom. What was the stupid legend all about?"

"All right. But if I tell you, you keep it to yourself, understood?" She nodded eagerly. Tom took another couple of pulls at his beer and sighed again. "Someone come up with the idea that if two lovers drew a pail of Howk's Well water and drank from the same pitcher, they'd never love another."

Kate, expecting something much darker, was disappointed.

"And that's it?"

"Aye, that was what folk believed. Course it meant that every courting couple for miles around wanted to give it a try. The lads wanted to take the lasses there as much as the lasses themselves. They must've thought it was some sort of guarantee that their marriage would last. I've no idea who started it, or when. It was part of local folklore long afore I was born."

"There must have been quite a fuss when Penelope sealed the chamber."

"Oh, aye. Folk was put out right enough. But don't forget, that all happened in 1919, right after the end of the Great War."

"So?"

"So… There weren't hardly no young men left to go a'courting, was there?"

After buying Tom another pint, Kate left him to the tender embrace of the Red Lion and drove slowly and thoughtfully back to Hawkswell, her head crammed with unanswered questions about just what became of Jamie Kirkpatrick. The drizzle was petering out as she approached the house, but the sky remained a sullen grey. Before heading up to her flat, Kate knocked on the Gerrards' door.

May answered, looking as if she'd just woken up, her eyes puffy, hair all over the place. Kate apologised for disturbing her and asked after Penelope.

The woman's reply came as a shock.

"Doctor's been out this morning and give her something. She was bad in the night, I had to sit with her." Kate couldn't believe what she was hearing.

"Oh dear God, I… I'm so sorry. If I'd known…"

May flapped a tired looking hand. "Oh, it's not all your fault, don't get to thinking that. Her's bin like this for years. More mad than sane some reckon. She'll be right as ninepence for months, sometimes a year or more, then something happens

and she has another of her turns. Tell the truth, I been expectin'
this, ever since you gone and got that blasted boat out again. It's
some kind of nervous illness, at least that's what the doctor says.
She'll never be rid of it, not now. It's only the pills as keeps her
going most of the time and that's only when she remembers to
take the blasted things."

The woman was obviously half asleep on her feet and Kate's
guilt washed over her like a wave.

"You were asleep and I woke you up. May, I am so very,
very sorry. If there's anything at all that I can do, please…"

"There is one thing you can do, young lady, and that is stop
meddling. I'm not being unkind. I know as how you're
interested about this place and its history and all, 'cos Tom
keeps telling me, but there's too much pain still, 'specially her's.
If you want to help, just stop asking questions."

Back in her flat, Kate threw herself down on the sofa. You
and your prying, Kate O'Donnell. Now see what you've done.
Stirred up a hornets' nest and no mistake. At that moment, she
was tempted to pack a bag and get clear away from Hawkswell
and its ever darker mysteries. Just get in her car and drive.
Maybe Andy would let her stay for a couple of weeks while she
found somewhere else to live. If not, she could try a bed and
breakfast for a while. Anything to escape the mess she'd stirred
up.

But then she thought of Daniel and knew she'd have to stay.

She tried to tell herself that it was because she needed to
stop him going ahead with his planned expedition down Howk's
Well, but even as she did so she realised that she was kidding
herself. There were many things about Daniel Lewis that she
didn't really understand, but one thing was all too clear, he was
by far and away the most attractive and charismatic man she'd
met in many a long year. And to complicate matters even
further, he might even be a little interested in her.

She let out a long, anguished sigh.

Keep on digging Katie girl, you just keep right on digging.

After a quick glance out of the window to check that
Daniel's Rover was parked in the courtyard, Kate knocked on

his door, determined to tell him about Penelope's vulnerability before he took his plan any further.

When he opened up, he took a quick look up and down the corridor before inviting Kate in.

She realised why as soon as she stepped across the threshold. The well shaft exploration plan was loads more serious and further advanced than she'd first thought. Most of his sitting room, which was the same size as hers, was littered with equipment, some of which she guessed had been emptied out of the ammunition boxes which stood open along one wall.

Coiled ropes in a multitude of colours and thicknesses, tightly rolled aluminium ladders, wet suits, helmets, lamps, battery packs and all sorts of canvas and oilskin wrapped packages covered virtually every square inch of floor space.

Daniel stood in the middle of it all, rather obviously a man in his element.

"Sorry about the mess. After last night, I got so fired up I thought I'd have a good sort through to make sure we haven't forgotten anything."

"Ah, right. Looks like you're really serious about this."

"Never been more serious about anything. This is huge, Kate. The potential is staggering. If there's any sort of a system down there and especially if there's a river, we need to know about it."

"And we need to talk."

His exuberance faded. "What, now?"

"Right now, if you don't mind."

"OK, would you like a drink. Wine, coffee…?"

"A glass of wine would be good, thanks."

Soon they were sitting facing each other across a pile of sleeping bags and rolls of foam mats. Kate barely had time to taste her wine before Daniel prompted her.

"So, talk."

"I met Tom in the village this morning and I asked him what he knew about Howk's Well."

Daniel looked horrified. "You're kidding. Please tell me you didn't mention – "

Kate shook her head angrily. "Of course I didn't. He's not got a clue. I told him I'd read about it in a book in the library. No, it was what he said about the reason why the chamber was sealed. It seems like it just got too dangerous."

"Dangerous in what way?"

"He didn't know, or he wouldn't say. I just wanted to let you know what he said. And there's more. Penelope's really sick. From what May Gerrard just told me, she's had some kind of a nervous breakdown. They had to call the doctor out this morning. It sounds serious."

If she'd expected Daniel to show concern for the old lady, she was disappointed. He sat forward on his chair and asked Kate to tell him everything she knew. As soon as she'd finished, Daniel slapped his hands on his thighs.

"Right. That's it. I'll set the operation up for as soon as everyone can make it."

Kate couldn't believe what she was hearing.

"You'll what? Jesus, Daniel, haven't you heard a word I've been saying? Old Miss Townshend is ill, very ill. She's vulnerable right now. If anything happens, the shock could be disastrous. Have you stopped for a single moment to think about what that would mean? Have you?"

"No, but…"

"No you haven't. Not for one fecking minute. If the old girl ends up in hospital, what will happen to Tom and May? And what about us, these flats? Oh shite, forget I said that. Of course, you're only here because of the bloody well, aren't you? Well I'm not, Daniel. I like living here. No, more than that, I really love living here and I can't bear to think of you doing anything to jeopardise that. Do you understand?"

Daniel sat and stared at her for an uncomfortable thirty seconds, the atmosphere cooling steadily.

"Kate. I really don't think you quite understand where I'm coming from here. The river system that feeds Howk's Well could open up the way to one of the most dramatic geological discoveries ever made in this part of the country. It's not only me that wants to find out what's going on down there, and not just the team either. There are some serious geologists and academics, not only in Bristol, but all over that have been working for years to try and work out the underground geography of this area." He paused for a moment to let Kate absorb what he'd said. "All I want to do is get this expedition done and dusted, without it affecting anyone else."

As Kate looked closer, she saw what she'd been missing ever since she'd first met Daniel – the signs of strain etched across his face, the way his skin was stretched a little too tightly across his cheekbones, the faint bruises under his eyes. What shocked her even more was how sorry she felt for him.

"You're really caught between a rock and a hard place, aren't you, Daniel?" He nodded and she relented a little. "OK. Let's consider a couple of things shall we? How absolutely certain are you that you can get down there, explore what you need to and get out again without being discovered?"

He sat forward then. "One hundred percent. Look, that well chamber is built like a nuclear bunker. The walls are feet thick solid granite and that door is massive. We could hold a party in there and no-one would hear a thing. With your help, we can be in and out without anyone being any the wiser, job done. I don't care what happens afterwards. I'll have fulfilled the task I volunteered for and it'll all be over."

"And then you'll give up the flat?"

He gave her a rueful smile. "Not straight away. I'll have to give a month's notice. But yes, I'll have to go back home then."

"So you've got another place?"

"In Bristol. Clifton, up by the Downs."

"Nicer than here?"

"Well, the flat's a bit nicer. I mean it's got all my stuff in it, so I would say that, wouldn't I? But I guess this place has even the Downs beat for surroundings. It's beautiful here, what with the river and the woods. And before you ask, yes, I'll miss it. But much more than that, I'll miss you."

In the resulting silence, Kate wondered whether she'd heard right. But when she saw the look on Daniel's face she knew she hadn't been mistaken.

"Daniel, I – "

He hurried on, "Kate, this has absolutely nothing to do with the well exploration, nothing at all. I'm not trying to get round you. I like you, Kate. In fact, I've come to like you a lot. And when I leave here, whatever happens in the meantime, I'd like to think that we might somehow be able to carry on seeing each other."

Kate drew breath to tell him he was mistaken, that she didn't want any kind of relationship, but instead found herself telling him, "I'll miss you too. Though I'm not quite sure why. Oh, Daniel, I don't know what's happening here. It's as if we've both got ourselves caught up in some kind of a storm, and neither of us are quite in control anymore. I like your company and I'm really glad that you like mine. But I don't think I can cope with anything more right now. I'm sorry."

Daniel stepped over the pile of sleeping bags until he was immediately in front of Kate. He hunkered down and took both of her hands in his. They felt strong and safe to Kate and all she wanted to do right then was give in, to let him scoop her into his arms. But she held back, afraid of letting go of what little sanity remained in her world. Daniel spoke softly and persuasively.

"Kate. Let's get this exploration done. It can all be over by this time next week. Then we'll be able to take our time and decide whether there's something here worth taking further, OK?" He squeezed her hands and she turned hers so that she could answer his pressure. And when she did, it felt good, as if by doing so, they'd each said things that words might have ruined.

Everything's going to be OK, she told herself.

And she kept on telling herself the same thing right through every waking minute of that endless week.

Then, one evening she found a note from Daniel on the floor inside her door.

If you get in before midnight, please knock on my door.
It's important. D.

Although she knocked quietly, Daniel must have been waiting because he opened the door almost immediately.

"Hi, Kate. I heard you drive in. Sorry it's so late. I won't keep you long, promise."

The room was back to being a sitting room, all the caving equipment gone. There was no sign of the ammunition boxes either. She didn't ask where they'd gone. She turned down a drink and, as soon as they were sat down, Daniel threw a rock into her day.

"It's on for this weekend, the expedition. The plan is for me to bring the last of the equipment and supplies back here during the week. Then, on Friday evening, I'll meet the three other team members in the village and drive them back here. It'll be better if we don't have suspicious looking cars parked around the place.

"As soon as Penelope and the Gerrards are settled for the night we'll get everything set up and shift all our gear into the chamber. Then we'll lock ourselves in and get on with it."

Although much too tired to take in most of what he'd said, Kate did home in on what she saw as the only flaw in the plan.

"You'll be making a right idiot of yourself if that door doesn't lead to the well chamber."

He grinned. "But it does. I checked last night. Mind you I thought I'd blown the whole thing right then, it made such a racket when I opened it. I've oiled the hinges so let's pray it doesn't happen again. I did the lock too. It was damned near rusted solid."

Kate's head was spinning. "You mean you've actually been in there?"

"Only to do a quick recce."

"But what about the windows in the corridor? Anyone could have looked in."

He grinned. "Simple. I've made up some wooden frames that fit inside the windows and covered them in light-proof fabric. I wanted to test them last night so I blacked out the two windows nearest the door and left a torch switched on while I went outside. They work perfectly. Not a glimmer. It was the perfect opportunity for a dry run."

"Wooden frames? What… I mean where are they now?"

"Under my bed. All neat and tidy. Everything else is packed into the wardrobe and the kitchen cupboards in case anyone comes in."

In spite of her exhaustion and her anxiety about the whole crazy scheme, Kate was beginning to find Daniel's excitement infectious.

"You've really thought this through, haven't you?"

"Every last tiny detail. And before you remind me, I know how important it is that no-one knows it's happening. Having you on the surface, so to speak, completes the last piece of the puzzle. We've got three VHF walkie-talkies. One goes down with the underground team, one will stay with the safety guy at the top of the shaft and you'll have the third. If anything goes wrong – which it won't – we can let you know, and vice versa. We've left absolutely nothing to chance, so there's nothing to go wrong, honestly."

The thought of taking a part in the expedition, albeit a passive one, held little appeal except that it might in some way give her a measure of control over events.

"So what's the chamber like?"

Daniel grinned.

"It's like a small chapel, with a domed stone roof. It's incredibly solid, beautiful stonework. The shaft at the centre's amazing. I only took a quick look but I'm guessing it's eighty or ninety feet down to the water, absolutely solid all the way. Only the top ten feet or so is masonry and that looks really sound. The rest of the shaft is solid limestone, like a big drain pipe, beautiful. God knows why anyone would think it was dangerous."

"Is the original winding mechanism still there?"

"The framework is, and solid oak by the looks of it. Everything else's gone, including the bucket. I expect it's around here somewhere, I'd love to find it."

Kate failed to stifle a yawn. "Sorry, it's been a hell of a day and – "

"Hey, don't apologise. Blame me for keeping you up so long. Just one final question, are you sure you're on for the weekend?"

"I hope so. We've got a lot on right now so there's a small chance I might have to work late on Friday or maybe even Saturday morning. But I should know by Thursday. What will you do if I can't help?"

He shrugged. "We'll go anyway. We're all set. I'd much rather you were there, but if not, it won't be the end of the world."

If Daniel had picked his words a little more carefully, Kate might have slept better that night. As it turned out, she couldn't get the idea of the end of the world out of her head.

By the time Friday evening arrived, Kate was wound up so tight she could barely think straight although she had at least rationalised her involvement in the well exploration plan. Maybe by taking part she could help minimise the risk of discovery.

Even though Daniel insisted that he would deny her involvement if it did go belly up, Kate was far more concerned for Penelope's welfare.

Unable to get to see the old lady since she suffered her turn the previous Saturday, what few reports she'd managed to prize out of Tom had told her nothing more than that she was doing as well as could be expected and that the doctor was happy with her progress.

As the moment of commitment edged ever closer, Kate found herself pacing her sitting room, fingers firmly crossed. When Daniel tapped lightly on her door at 10.30, it was already dark outside.

The other three team members were with him. Barry, a small, dark, bushy bearded Welshman who looked as if he'd been born underground, Pete, six foot two, bald as an egg, with an ear-to-ear grin, and Tony, small and wiry with black, curly hair, who described himself as the 'fourth musketeer'.

Crowded into her sitting room, making polite but pointed comments about how tidy it was compared to Daniel's, Kate was relieved they didn't all look like lunatics. In fact, the strongest impression was of a bunch of academics on the brink of some world-changing discovery.

Daniel ran through the plan one more time for Kate's benefit.

"First off we'll get the frames downstairs and put them in place at the last possible moment. If you can help me with that job, Kate, the others can start ferrying stuff downstairs to the corridor immediately outside the shaft door. Once the frames are up we'll open the chamber and move everything inside. Even with the windows blanked out, we use only head torches, agreed?

"Kate, once we're established and the corridor's clear, you can start taking the frames down again and moving them back upstairs out of sight. Don't worry, one of us will give you a hand. I hope we'll be able to rig some kind of blackout curtain inside the chamber door, which will allow us to come and go without being compromised.

"When it's time to pull out, all being well that'll be Saturday night, we'll do the whole thing in reverse. Of course, it might take a little longer because we'll probably be muddy and wet. Hopefully we'll all be able to change before we leave the chamber, so it shouldn't be too big a problem.

"Any questions?"

Kate put her hand up. "Can we run through the walkie-talkies please? I've never handled one before."

"Thanks Kate, I'd forgotten. Barry's your man for that. They're really simple but he'll show you everything you need to know."

There were no other questions, so, while Kate received her radio instruction, the others started ferrying the cumbersome blackout frames downstairs, pausing frequently to listen and check outside in case someone decided to take a late night stroll.

While the equipment was being carried downstairs, Kate

filled two of the enormous thermos flasks she'd been given with hot, black coffee and a further two with soup.

Her nerves almost stretched to breaking point, she insisted that they wait until midnight before opening up the chamber. Although Tom often took a late night tour of the vegetable garden, she'd never known him to be out later than eleven thirty, even in mid-summer.

They spent that last hour in Kate's sitting room mostly in silence, so keyed up that no-one felt like chatting. The moment the minute hand of Daniel's watch touched the hour, he led the team into the upstairs corridor. What light there was came from a scattering of stars and a sliver of moon glimpsed between slow moving clouds. It took barely fifteen minutes to put all the blackout panels in place in the windows. Insisting on checking from the outside, Kate was relieved that they looked exactly as Daniel had promised, as though nothing was going on.

Carefully closing and locking the door to the courtyard, Kate arrived at the well chamber door just as Daniel was preparing to open it. The large key grated a little until the lock tumbled with a muffled clunk. Holding onto the key, Daniel pushed gently with his shoulder and the door swung slowly open, with only the smallest protest from the hinges.

A wash of cool air flooded the corridor as the team crowded into the entrance. Daniel told them to stay put while he erected the blackout curtain inside the door. A few seconds later, they eased themselves one-by-one between the door jamb and the curtain until they were all inside the chamber.

Kate waited outside, horrified to hear a few seconds later a ragged chorus as the team took their first look down the shaft.

"Bloody hell, it must be nearly a hundred feet to the water."

"Is that a calcite flow down there? There, near the bottom of the pipe?"

"There's a cavern definitely, maybe even a lake, come on Kate, let's —"

Kate hissed as loudly as she dared through the open door.

"Will you guys keep it down for Christ's sake, you'll have the whole place awake!" The voices eased to a whisper and Daniel's head came around the edge of the curtain.

"Sorry, Kate. We got a bit carried away. I forgot the door was still open. Do you want to come in and take a look?"

Kate shook her head. "I'm not sure. Are you sure it's safe?"

"As houses. The place is absolutely solid and there's plenty of light now we've lit the pressure lamps."

She hesitated but knew she'd regret it if she didn't take the chance. "Just a quick look then." As the curtain dropped into place behind her, she was dazzled by the glare of the two big lanterns they had slung from either end of the winding gear cross beam. Once her eyes had adjusted, she was able to look around. The chamber was much bigger than she had expected, its barrel vaulted ceiling extending to ten or twelve feet above a floor paved with massive slate slabs, polished to a dull shine by countless booted feet.

The well shaft itself, right in the centre of the space, looked to be a little over six feet from one side to the other, surrounded by a thigh-high retaining wall with a perfectly circular slate parapet. The winding gear was an impressive construction featuring two massive uprights set into the retaining wall with an equally substantial cross-bar. Various heavily rusted iron hoops showed where the winding handle had been attached. As Kate watched, the team busied themselves with their individually appointed tasks. Barry and Daniel were rigging slings and ropes from each of the uprights and the crossbar. Pete was coupling up and testing a box full of head torches and batteries, while Tony loaded stuff into large canvas sacks, each with lowering straps attached.

No-one paid her any attention as she stepped gingerly towards the mouth of the shaft. As soon as she was near enough, she placed both hands on the slate parapet and, taking her weight on her arms, leaned forward to peer down the shaft. The stonework, green with age, glistened with countless tiny beads of moisture. It was easy to spot where the masonry finished and the natural rock shaft began. Kate was astonished at how smooth it was. Expecting to see ferns and moss, the well, like the rest of the chamber, appeared devoid of any sign of life. Of course, she thought, there's no light. No light, no life.

As her gaze slid slowly down towards the coin-like gleam of water far below, she felt as if she too was sliding down an enormous throat and into the belly of some sleeping beast. As the throat widened, drawing her in, Kate felt herself pulled forward and down. Far away, someone was shouting, screaming.

She couldn't make out the words, wondering who it was while wishing they'd be quiet and let her go, down into that peaceful place, that dark and watery sanctuary, that darkness.

Her face hurt. Someone was shaking her hard enough to rattle the teeth in her head. She felt sick and cold.

"Kate, come on! You're OK, Kate! Snap out of it."

She opened her eyes and looked into Daniel's frightened, wild-eyed face. She only saw it relax with relief when she spoke.

"What happened? Where am I?"

"You're in your flat. You're OK. You've got a bit of a bump on your head, but nothing else. Thank God you're all right."

He held a glass to her lips and she took a sip. As the liquid hit the back of her throat, her whole head seemed to explode and she had to cough away tears.

"Jesus Christ, what is that?"

"That, dear girl, is a very good quality Cognac. It was all I could find, sorry."

After she'd wiped the tears away, she pushed herself up on one elbow. "What happened? The last thing I remember I was looking down the well shaft."

"That was nearly the last thing you ever remembered. You fainted. Maybe it was fumes from the lamps or an attack of vertigo or something. Next thing is you're pitching forward over the parapet. We only just managed to catch you."

She lay her head back down again. "So how did I get up here?"

"I carried you. You were out cold. I was going to give you another thirty seconds and then call for help. The guys are ready to get everything out of the chamber."

"God, no. Don't do that. Not now you've got this far. I'll be fine now, honestly."

Daniel squatted down until his face was level with hers. "Are you sure?"

She rustled up a smile. "Course I am. Really."

Then Daniel did something she wasn't expecting. He leaned forward, took her face in his big, capable hands, and kissed her like he meant it.

When he moved away to draw breath, he whispered, "I thought I'd lost you." Then he stood, squeezed her shoulder, and walked out of the room.

She thought about what he'd said. It was enough. By the time Kate felt recovered enough to go downstairs again, all the blackout panels had been removed and were stacked inside the chamber ready for the following night. The coffee, soup, stoves and other supplies including a five gallon jerry-can of drinking water were already inside and they were getting ready to close the door.

After a quick radio check, Kate insisted on one more kiss from Daniel out of sight of the others before they closed the door. She heard the key turned in the lock and then withdrawn. With the metal flap in place over the keyhole, not a glimmer of light or any hint of sound escaped.

The house seemed unnaturally quiet as she climbed the stairs, silently thanking whoever built the well chamber door for doing such a thorough job while offering up a hatful of prayers that nothing would go wrong.

It was gone two o'clock and she was suddenly aware of her own exhaustion. Her legs felt like rubber as she crawled into bed, the walkie-talkie radio on her bedside table. Convinced that she was too wound up to sleep, she ran the tip of her tongue over her lips, certain that she could still taste Daniel.

She woke seven hours later to a loud hiss from the radio and a crackly voice.

Chamber to Kate, chamber to Kate. Come in Kate. Over.

Chapter 12

Still half asleep, she made three wrong hits before finding the walkie-talkie's transmit button.

Kate to chamber, Kate to chamber, who's that? Over.
Hi Kate, it's Barry. Just letting you know that everything's going well. Daniel, Pete and Tony have established a base on a small beach. Everything's going to plan. Over.
Morning, Barry. Did you say beach, as in seaside? Over.
Yes, beach – Bravo Echo Alpha Charlie Hotel. Over.
Does that mean there's a lake down there? Over.
It most certainly does. It's in a huge cavern at the bottom of the shaft. The others are exploring a subsidiary passage. Oh, and there's an underground river too. Over.
Er, wow, that's brilliant. You guys take care down there, OK? Over.
Will do. I'll call again at mid-day. Over and out.

Despite an impenetrable ceiling of low, grey cloud and swirling, wind-blown drizzle, reminiscent of the worst kind of weather at home in Ireland, Kate was determined to do as much as she could to maintain an air of normality at Hawkswell. She sought out Tom Gerrard and, ignoring the wet, helped him dismantle four rows of runner bean poles and uproot the dead plants. As they worked, she asked if there was any more news about Penelope.

"May's been taking her meals in three times a day and reckons that the cantankerous old bat – her words, not mine –

is being her rude and fussy self as usual. So I reckon 'er's on the mend."

Kate grinned at that. "I'm glad she's making progress."

She crossed her fingers as she hoped the old lady wouldn't fully recover until after the caving team had finished and left.

Back in her flat for the scheduled mid-day call, the ten minute delay until the walkie-talkie crackled into life felt like an hour.

She recognised Daniel's voice straight away, despite the distortion.

Chamber to Kate, chamber to Kate. Come in Kate. Over.

This time she got the transmit button first time.

Kate to Chamber. Hi Daniel. How's it going? Over.
It's amazing down there. Shame you can't see it. The lake cavern is absolutely beautiful. We'll have done everything we can by six this evening. Leaving the kit in the chamber... probably be out before it gets dark. Can you stand watch, let us know when the coast is clear? Over.

She clicked the transmit button.

Did you say you're leaving all the equipment in the chamber? Over.
Yes. Over.
Why? Over.
Tell you later. See you at six. Over and out.

The radio popped into silence.

Kate sat in the echoing silence, heart thumping, fists clenched in her lap. If they're leaving everything in the chamber, it means that they're planning to go down again. I'll go away next time, she thought. I'm not going through all this again.

She remained in her sitting room for the rest of that afternoon, listening to the radio, watching the teeming rain and conjuring up a hundred different reasons why the cavers might have changed their plans, not one of which was enough to alleviate her sense of betrayal.

Daniel had been so adamant that they would be in and out again in twenty-four hours. Just the one trip. He'd promised. So why would he renege on the deal? Maybe he was nothing special after all. As the thought flicked through her head it brought a wave of disappointment and sadness.

Just when…

Just when what, she thought? So you've been out to dinner once and he's kissed you twice. You're hardly engaged for Christ's sake. Pull yourself together Katie O'Donnell.

Already in position outside the well chamber door, Kate heard the key scrape in the lock. It was still raining heavily and she'd seen Tom head indoors half an hour earlier. She hoped he was done for the day.

The door opened enough for Daniel to whisper, "Hi Kate. How's it looking out there?"

She tried to keep her voice calm. "It's clear at the moment, but you'll all have to crawl along the corridor in case Tom or May happen to be looking this way."

Daniel chuckled. "No problem with that. Crawling is what we do best!"

One-by-one, and looking pathetically like a line of kids playing hide-and-seek, the team wormed their way out into the corridor and across to the wall below the windows, each dragging a large waterproof kit bag. Safely out of sight below the sills, they scuttled along to the far end and disappeared up the stairs.

Finally, Daniel dragged out his own kit bag, and closed and locked the door behind him. Kate looked puzzled about the bag.

"Muddy clothes and wetsuits, got some washing to do."

Kate took her first good look at him, liberally plastered with ochre mud which had dried in his hair and eyebrows and beneath his fingernails. She failed to hold her big question back a minute longer.

"Daniel. What's all this about a second trip?"

He slid across the corridor on his bottom until he was sitting with his back against the wall. She was surprised at how good it felt to see him again.

And that made her even more annoyed at his duplicity.

"You promised me you'd be in and out and that'd be it. Twenty-four hours you said, and it's over." She watched his shoulders slump and realised that whatever decision had been made, it hadn't been his alone.

"It's the river. It's in a tunnel below the lake, about thirty feet down. We dropped some dye markers and a weighted line. It's incredibly powerful, a torrent. We want to get a couple of divers down to investigate. I know it means breaking my promise, but it's too big a discovery." He sounded exhausted, mentally and physically.

Kate allowed her caring side to take over. "Well talk about it later. Right now you look like you could do with a hot bath and something to eat."

"I think we all could." His grin appeared half-hearted.

She then surprised herself. "Looks like it's going to be a bit of a crush in your bathroom. You're welcome to use mine, if you'd like to, that is." She turned away and headed towards the stairs before he could answer.

While Daniel soaked the mud away in her bath and the rest of the team sorted themselves out next door in his flat, Kate used her biggest casserole dish to prepare a huge vegetable curry for everyone. She knew that they would probably prefer something with meat but hey, principles were principles, and she knew it would taste good.

An hour later, scrubbed and ravenous, the team reassembled around Kate's dining table. As they demolished the food, she listened with a mixture of horror and astonishment to their rambling account of the expedition, made even more confusing by them all talking across each other in their excitement, shooting off on tangents, cutting back to earlier moments. Despite the shambolic nature of the story, Kate eventually managed to piece together the sequence of events.

The moment the well chamber door had been closed and locked, the tension had racked up a notch or two as the four men went about their final preparations for the descent. They had all had been shaken by Kate's near disastrous encounter with the shaft and reckoned that the sooner they were harnessed up and clipped on to the safety ropes the better.

Wetsuits, overalls, harnesses, helmets, lamps and boots. All pulled on, checked, laced and ready. After thoroughly examining and testing the winding gear framework, Daniel reckoned it was more than strong enough to take their abseil ropes and safety lines. As he worked, he became aware of a gentle but steady draught of air from below. When he mentioned it, Barry took out a cigarette, lit it and held it out over the gaping mouth of the shaft.

They all watched in amazement as the thin smear of blue smoke spiralled upwards to disappear through an almost invisible hole in the centre of the arched roof. Barry pulled the cigarette back and took a drag.

"That's deliberate, some way of keeping the air circulating when the door's closed. It probably feeds into one of the chimney stacks."

Whatever the mechanics behind the draught, it was welcome, as with the heat from four bodies and two pressure lamps, the air in the chamber would have quickly become unbearably hot and stale.

As soon as Daniel was happy, he and Pete clipped their friction brakes onto the two separate abseil ropes while Barry and Tony prepared to belay them with the safety lines. Daniel was first to swing out over the drop and commence his descent.

As he looked down between his legs, the tiny disk of reflected light from the water far below appeared to wink at him as his shadow flickered across its surface.

A pair of rusty iron water pipes were clipped at irregular intervals to the stonework, Daniel guessing they were the pipes that must once have supplied the two big iron pumps. Ten feet down, the closely fitting stone blocks gave way to water smoothed bedrock where the jointed pipes hung unsupported until they disappeared into the darkness. Sliding down the nylon rope, he spun like a spider on the end of a thread until he jammed a boot against the wall. He looked up. Pete was twenty feet above him, following him down. The up draught blew ever more strongly across his face and he breathed in deeply, tasting the cool, fresh, underground air.

"Everything OK down there?"Barry's voice boomed in the shaft.

"Not so loud!" Daniel hissed back, "no problems so far. I think I can already see where the shaft bottoms out." Peering down, it was becoming clear that the well shaft stopped long before it reached the water. Sure enough, a few feet further down, the shaft flared out to become the roof of a cavern.

Daniel estimated that the water was still at least another thirty feet below his boots. He could see where the abseil ropes broke the crystal clear surface before spreading out like languid snakes.

He called up to Pete. "Hang on where you are a minute, mate. I'm going to see if I can get something in here to make a staging belay."

Level with his knees he could see a horizontal crack in the rock that looked like it might take a couple of pitons. Easing down until his legs were hanging in space below the bottom lip of the shaft he locked off his friction device to free both hands.

The crack was perfect. Removing two hard steel pegs from his belt, he hammered them home before clipping a pair of aluminium karabiners into their rings.

"Bomb-proof!" he called up. "You could hang a steam engine from those two beauties!"

As Pete slid down towards him, Daniel rigged up some foot loops. Once his weight was off the abseil rope, he made a knot and secured it to the pegs. Shortening the drop would make the final section of the descent to water level much steadier, taking a lot of the stretch out of the rope and preventing them from swinging around.

As soon as Pete was level with him, Daniel outlined the next stage of the operation.

"If they lower the inflatable down to us now, it'll be much easier to inflate it here and lower it into the water rather than trying to do it down once we're down there. Agreed?"

Pete nodded, adding, "Just one thing, will there be enough room to get it past us?"

"No problem. I'll descend until I'm below the mouth of the shaft and lock off there. I'll be in a good position to unpack the boat and crack the CO2 bottle." Ten minutes later, the tightly packed rubber dinghy scraped and slid its way down the shaft until it was dangling level with Daniel.

"That'll do! Hold it there." It took Daniel another ten minutes to release the clips and straps that restrained the unwieldy mass of rubber fabric. Soon it hung below him, gleaming black in the light from his headlamp. "OK," he called up to Pete, "here goes."

He twisted the release valve on the canister until he heard the roar of gas. Almost instantly the shapeless mass seemed to come alive, twisting and writhing as the carbon dioxide unbuckled its folds until the fabric was drum tight. Now, something resembling a massive black doughnut twisted slowly in the darkness. After making sure that the bag containing the paddles, emergency kit and mooring lines was still attached, Daniel called up for Barry to carry on lowering. As soon as the boat began to move downwards, he released his brake and slid down alongside it towards the still, black waters of the lake.

With the inflatable safely settled on the surface and secured to the two abseil ropes, Daniel took his first chance to look around. The lake stretched away in all directions to the limit of his headlamp's beam, its surface as clear and flat as a sheet of glass, disturbed only by the concentric ripples caused by his movement in the boat.

The two iron pipes hung free from the mouth of the shaft and stopped where their lower ends kissed the surface of the water, rusted away as if cut with a knife. When he gave them a tug they swung alarmingly and he called up for Pete to secure them to the wall of the shaft somehow. A few seconds later he heard the sound of more pegs being hammered home, and watched as the pipes were shifted a couple of feet away from him before becoming still.

Above his head, the roof of the cavern arched down in all directions away from the mouth of the shaft which appeared as a soft edged disk, backlit by the lamps in the chamber above.

Sweeping the beam of his light across the roof, it was as if it was covered in tens of thousands of tiny diamonds. Looking more carefully, he saw that the diamonds were in fact individual water droplets, each hanging from the tip of a thin, straw like stalactite. It was one of the most beautiful underground sights he had ever seen, made all the more precious because he was almost certainly the first person ever to have laid eyes on it.

As he sat in awed silence, he became aware of the sound of hundreds of individual droplets pattering onto the lake's surface all around him. Underground rain, he thought, and laughed aloud with delight. Playing his head-torch vertically down over the curved side of the boat, he could just make out the floor of the cavern sloping down out of the darkness to converge at another shaft, a perfect mirror image of the one above his head, plunging ever deeper into the earth.

Aware that there was only the smallest movement in the water, Daniel reckoned that, if there was a river, it must lie further down, possibly even beyond the continuation pothole. If they were to discover more, they would definitely need divers.

As soon as Pete joined him in the boat, Daniel spoke to Barry and Tony on the walkie-talkie. He needed the first of the equipment packs that contained the flood lights and cameras.

Before commencing the lower, Barry got them to paddle the boat away from the bottom of the shaft for safety. As soon as the bundle of packages came into sight, they eased the dinghy back into place so that it dropped neatly between them onto the rubberised floor.

With the floodlight attached to its battery pack, Daniel switched on. The broad beam of dazzling white light exploded into the farthest corners of the cavern illuminating a scene never before seen by man. Aimed over the bows of the boat and scything thirty yards or more in front of them, they saw where the roof curved down to continue below the surface of the crystal clear water. Free of stalactites, it plummeted downwards until it met the floor curving up to meet it.

Panning slowly right, the point at which the roof of the cavern met the water stayed constant for about ninety degrees of arc until it began to recede.

At its most distant point, it maybe averaged fifty or sixty yards away from the bottom of the shaft. At that point, roughly over the stern of the boat, they saw that the floor of the lake rose up to break the surface. The roof remained higher in that direction, leaving a small rock beach and an intriguingly dark area beyond that looked as though it might be a passage leading away from the main cavern.

Still more fascinating, they spotted what might be the mouth of another substantial passage feeding into the far end of the lake, some fifteen feet below the surface. After taking a series of photographs, Daniel called Barry up on the walkie-talkie and suggested that Tony came down with extra rope and a couple of lightweight ladders.

After stowing the extra kit he had brought, they called Barry to let him know they were moving out of line-of-sight. That done they paddled away from the shaft heading for the little beach, trailing the two safety ropes behind them.

Prior to descending from the well chamber, Daniel had carefully chalked the points of the compass onto the parapet around the shaft to enable them to orientate themselves before venturing underground.

The two water pipes were set on the south side of the shaft with a bearing of 195°, or roughly SSW. He'd also indicated the direction to the main road entrance to Hawkswell, 100°; the stable block, almost due north; and the boathouse, 180° due south. Paddling towards the beach, Daniel approximated their direction from the point the water pipes entered the water.

"I reckon we're travelling directly beneath the front part of the house," he told the other two, "headed towards the main gate." The moment the boat grounded on the gently sloping limestone of the beach, Daniel scrambled out and took one of the mooring lines up the slope to a convenient boulder. They attached the two safety ropes in the same way before lifting the boat clear of the water.

One of the floodlights showed that the cave continued to slope upwards for another fifty yards at least, its floor levelling before turning sharply left. Tony said he'd stay with the boat.

"I can maintain contact with Barry in the well chamber while you guys explore the passage." They carried out a quick radio check, agreeing it was adequate even though the reception was scratchy. When they checked the time, they were amazed to find it was already 3 a.m.

"Back here no later than six, agreed?"

Daniel and Pete each took a rolled up ladder and a coil of rope plus oilskin bags with spare battery packs and survival gear. They shook hands and swapped grins with Tony before heading off up the slope.

They were able to walk fairly easily to the point where the passage turned, but as soon as it did so the roof began to descend, reducing them to a crawl. At the same time, the tunnel started to climb steadily. Aware of a strong, fresh breeze blowing in their faces, both men were eagerly anticipating the discovery of another entrance into the system, one that could make any future exploration much less hazardous.

The tunnel soon became slot-like, widening as it became shallower. As the headroom steadily reduced, the breeze became stronger. After a difficult hundred yards being forced to shuffle forwards in a space barely high enough to accommodate their heads, the gap narrowed even further.

Eventually, Daniel attached a safety rope onto his harness and handed it to Pete.

"I'm going to see if I can get a bit further. It might open up, you never know. If I shout, you know what to do."

Pete grinned. "Pull like hell."

Daniel shuffled forwards as far as he could before he had to take off his helmet and slide it along beside him. Although the slot – known as a bedding plane – continued its upward trajectory, its height remained constant long enough for Daniel to get his hopes up. Maybe, just maybe they might be able to get through into another system or, even better, all the way to the surface.

But after another fifty feet of exhausting shuffling, he was forced to admit defeat. The slot was blocked with rubble and he could see that a few feet further on it narrowed even further, making further progress impossible. He twisted to reposition his head torch and nearly became wedged as his boiler suit caught on a sharp edge of rock. As soon as the rope stopped moving, Pete knew that Daniel had come up against a problem. After a while, he gave a couple of gentle tugs and called ahead into the darkness.

"Are you OK, Daniel?"

Instead of an answer, the rope twitched three separate times signalling that Daniel was coming back. Pete pulled the rope in as it came and coiled it at his side. Soon he could see Daniel's light as he struggled towards him, stopping every now and then to catch his breath and rest. Eventually, he eased himself alongside Pete and lay there panting.

"Bloody hell, that was tight. Thought I was well and truly jammed for a minute back there. Not nice."

"So it doesn't go."

"No way."

"Diggable?"

Daniel shook his head. "No. It closes up right across its full width. It's down to less than eight inches and narrowing even further."

"So that's it?"

"Yeah. Shame. Come on, let's get out of here."

Reluctantly, they turned around and slithered and crawled their way back down the passage, heading back for the beach and the lake. Despite examining every promising looking crack and fissure they came across, they were forced to the conclusion that the Howk's Well cavern did not connect with any other navigable system, at least not above water level.

"So that's why you want to get divers down."

In the relative safety of Kate's sitting room, it was Barry who answered.

"Yes Kate. It's the only way we're going to be able to find out where all that water comes from and where the hell it goes to."

"Sorry, I don't understand. What exactly do you mean by all that water?"

Barry borrowed a writing pad from one of the others and drew a rough cross section of the lake cavern.

"OK. All we know so far is that there's a hell of a lot of water coming in at the north east end of the cavern and disappearing down the pipe that continues on below the well shaft."

"But how do you know?"

"Dye. We dropped dye markers in at various points around the lake and watched what happened. For most of it there's hardly any movement at all, just a very gentle clockwise circulation. But when we dropped some in right by the beach, here," he marked the place on his drawing, "where we could see the other passage coming in, it went off like a rocket straight towards the continuation of the well shaft pothole. Damned stuff dived down it like a frightened rabbit down a burrow."

He swept a biro line across the page to where he had drawn the mouth of the continuation shaft.

"God knows what the flow rate will turn out to be, but I'll bet you could run a fair sized hydro-electric generator down there!"

"So what happens to all the dye?"

Daniel answered. "It's only food dye, Kate. Nothing to worry about. And it's all flushed away by now. That's why the water from the well is always so fresh. It's being constantly renewed from the source. And that reminds me. Didn't Tom say that the house is now supplied by a spring up in the woods?"

"That's what he said, yes. There's some kind of a cistern up by the gates."

Daniel slapped the table in his excitement. "I'll bet anything that the spring is an off-shoot of the source that supplies the lake. The alignment's perfect." And that kicked off a whole new debate about exploring the woods and trying to locate the spring. Kate took herself off to make coffee, realising with a sinking feeling that the exploration had developed an energy all of its own and was slipping rapidly beyond her control or influence.

As soon as everyone had finished their coffees, Daniel suggested that it might be a good time to take the other three back to their cars in the village. After saying their goodnights to Kate and thanking her for the curry, the others filed out.

Daniel lingered a few seconds. "Would you mind if I pop in when I get back?"

Her heart skipped. "Sure, no problem."

"There's something I want to show you. I didn't want to involve the others, it's kind of... I can't really explain now, but it's personal. See you in about half an hour?"

He was so preoccupied he didn't kiss her, even though she hoped he would. He wasn't back in half an hour either.

Kate cleared away the crocks and washed up, eagerly listening for Daniel's knock. An hour later she was still waiting.

He eventually arrived a few minutes after ten and started apologising as soon as she opened the door.

"The guys wanted to have a drink and there was such a lot to talk about. I only meant to have a quick pint but I guess I kind of lost track of the time. I am so sorry. Look, if you'd rather do it some other time..."

Kate was annoyed at his lateness and even more so by the dreadful predictability of his excuse. But there was something so earnest about him, so endearing that she dropped her shoulders and her frown and asked him if he'd like a drink.

"Er, a coffee would be good. Thanks."

"Coffee, this late?"

He gave her a look she couldn't decipher.

"I think you might need one too, if not something stronger."

In the end she broke out a bottle of Jamesons to beef up the coffee, sat down on the sofa opposite Daniel and waited to hear what he had to say.

"When we were in the well chamber today, I found something."

It was only then that she noticed the carrier bag that he'd placed at his feet. He reached into it and pulled out what looked like a solid block of rust, about the same size as a small cake tin or biscuit box.

"This was buried under a loose slab right at the back of the chamber. I only found it by chance when I was shifting one of the ammunition cases and the slab moved. It was completely rusted to the bottom of the stone. Once we'd dug it out, I took a quick look to see what was in it. That was when we all agreed that I'd better bring it to you first."

If Daniel hadn't looked so serious, she would have told him to cut the crap and get on with it. Instead she waited, somehow knowing that the contents held some very special significance.

Daniel settled the tin on his lap and eased off the lid which he replaced carefully in the carrier bag.

"The rust flakes off as soon as you touch it, I don't want to put it down anywhere."

Then, with heart-breaking care, as if he was handling a priceless piece of jewellery, he lifted out a bundle of papers, tied with a faded red ribbon.

"They're letters." He hesitated. "From Jamie. There was a loose one on top. It's how I found out who they were from."

Kate shifted across to sit beside him and he placed the bundle in her hands.

"I thought that, well… with Jamie being your relative, it seemed only right that you should… well, you know…"

Kate realised that they were both whispering, but it felt right somehow. "Thank you, Daniel. God this feels weird." Carefully, she eased the ribbon off the bundle and lifted a single envelope from the top of the pile.

It was addressed to Miss Pattie Tancock, 14 Back Street, Hawkswell Village, Somerset, England. She looked questioningly at Daniel who shrugged.

"Must have been a girl in the village, his sweetheart maybe."

Only the letters on the top half of the pile were readable, the rest congealed into a solid mass by the damp that had penetrated the tin during its time in the chamber. They were heavily censored, whole sentences and paragraphs scored out with an indelible pen. But each one was signed, Your beloved Jamie.

After arranging the twenty or so readable letters in date order, Kate started to read each sheet, passing them one by one to Daniel. And as they read, the raw horror of those dreadful times crept into Kate's cosy Hawkswell sitting room and settled around them like an unseen, chilling fog. There were detailed and often amusing accounts of training on Salisbury plain, of being sent by train to London and, after being moved around seemingly aimlessly for a week, eventually to Dover for embarkation. In each subsequent letter, the anecdotes became less and less amusing, the descriptions more disturbing.

Jamie's regiment were held in reserve, close enough to feel the artillery through the ground under their feet, but far enough away to survive it. They waited for two long months while winter gave way to spring and men began to hope that it would all be over by the time their turn came.

They were not to be so lucky.

Chapter 13

North West Belgium, May 1915

The German bombardment of Bellewaerde Ridge – immediately preceding what was later to become known as the second battle of Ypres – commenced at 2.45 a.m. on the 24th May 1915, Whit Monday, with an avalanche of high explosive slamming into the British trench lines. The garrison, although alert to the possibility of a full scale assault, were ill prepared for the sheer speed and ferocity of the attack.

'Gas! Gas! Gas!' The word was repeated again and again. More screamed than shouted, it skipped along the trench lines from the south, growing louder and more frantic with every repetition.

Jamie hauled his respirator out of its case and dragged the evil smelling canvas and rubber contraption over his head, bracing himself against the instant claustrophobia. Even as he tightened the straps around his head, the first cloud of bile green gas rolled over the lip of the sandbag revetment to cascade into the trench. The soldier immediately to his right lurched against Jamie, clutching at his throat and gasping, his respirator clutched in his other hand, its webbing tangled and useless.

Then the shrill whistles started and those troops around Jamie who had not succumbed to the gas began to fumble their way onto the firing step, their vision obscured by gas mask eye-pieces misted with the cold heat of fear. Bayonets fixed, the long barrels of the Lee Enfield rifles probed towards the as yet invisible enemy advancing behind the rolling wall of gas.

A machine gun's manic chatter to Jamie's left was quickly followed by others up and down the line. A muffled voice shouted, "Steady lads. Hold your fire until you have a target. Here they come!"

And sure enough, as though responding to some insane stage direction, the first grey shapes loomed, masked faces inhuman behind dreadful probing blades, their distinctive pickelhaube helmets removing any shred of doubt.

The enemy.

As the Germans stumbled across the first barbed wire barrier, their line started to break up as the Vickers machine guns swept their fire back and forth like a farmhand reaping corn with a scythe. And, just like corn, the faceless shapes fell in rows and piles. But still they came on, more and more of them. Men either side of Jamie started firing, the sharp cracks of their rounds rippling unevenly up and down the trench, merging with the shouts and screams of charging, dying Germans.

Jamie picked an officer straight ahead of him, waving his men forward with a pistol held high above his head.

"Bloody fool," Jamie shouted into his gas mask as he shot him through the chest and watched him pitch back into the path of the following man. "Bloody fool," he shouted again as he pulled back the bolt, aimed and fired, again and again and again.

A German soldier, hit more than once and barely able to put one foot in front of the other, stumbled over the last strands of wire and pitched head-first into the British trench beside Jamie. The man on Jamie's left stared for a moment as the dying German tried to drag himself to his feet, before skewering him inexpertly with his bayonet. It was a poor blow that took the man in the lower back and made him squeal with agony. The English soldier stabbed again and again until the German's screaming stopped.

Overwhelmed with shock and horror, this English farmhand soldier continued the screaming for him, his hands bright and slick with German blood.

They repelled them that first time, and the next... and the next. Each subsequent attack added to the windrows of dead and dying drifted up against the forward edge of the British trenches. The attacks also exacted a heavy toll from the British defenders. Men died from blast and shrapnel, from machine gun and rifle bullets or, if they were very unlucky, from a bayonet thrust. Not many died from the gas, not straightaway.

There was no time between assaults to make any attempt to clear the British and German dead from the trenches. There was barely enough time to evacuate the wounded and get essential ammunition, water and reinforcements up to the forward positions.

And so the living stood on top of the dead.

They didn't need the firing step any more.

The German offensive went on all that day, only easing off as night fell. There were small breakthroughs at both extremities of the line and only some determined and costly counter-attacks prevented the enemy making a wider breach in the Allied lines.

One of the counterattacks took place late that night – an attempt to relieve a place that the British army, in their skewed wisdom, had named Mouse Trap Farm.

The remnants of Jamie's unit were ordered along the communication trenches to reinforce the already weakened 84th Brigade for the assault. As they prepared, Jamie found himself crouched on the firing step trying to stay in the shadow of the trench wall, bright moonlight already sweeping no-man's land with its unforgiving glare. It was at those times, when the artillery fell silent, that reasoning men prayed not so much to survive, but for a quick and painless death. An officer came haltingly down the trench, doling out words of encouragement in an over-loud whisper, an almost foreign language that referred to other people, in another place, at another time. He stopped by Jamie, looked up and grinned in recognition.

"Hello, Jamie, old man. Here we go again. One more push for home, eh?"

Jamie barely recognised Charles Townshend, the young man's moonlit features bleached and drawn by fear and strain.

"Aye, sir. One more push for home." Sir – Charlie Townshend, his Lieutenant's pips bright upon his shoulders as aiming marks. Poor bastard, Jamie thought. Only his third month at the front and he's leading an assault against impossible odds across a stretch of no-man's land more brightly lit than a bloody dance floor. Some dance! He was probably scared shitless like the rest of them and who could blame him.

As for Jamie's platoon, ranged either side of him, hunched on the firing step for a last quick drag, they were beyond fear. Shelled, gassed or picked off by sniper fire, less than a third of the men who had taken up station two weeks ago remained alive. Afraid once, long ago, fear had long since passed them by, moved back down the line to the fresh faced boys even now marching forward to replace that day's losses.

Both hope and fear had become like dry clothes and hot food – luxuries they could no longer afford. A distant whistle shrilled, immediately followed by a dozen more, rippling down the line of trenches towards their position.

Futile star shells and parachute flares burst overhead as, with countless cries of rage and anguish, the khaki ocean surged up and across the sandbags and into hell.

Stumbling and slipping in the cloying mud, Jamie ran, head down, his rifle a lifeline, his sole link with sanity in a world gone mad. The acrid stench of cordite ripped at his gasping throat, screams tore across the staccato hammer of the scything guns while bullets and shrapnel whimpered and fluttered around his head.

The man immediately in front of him went down, his legs swept away from under him in a shattered mess of bloody fabric. Jamie jinked, lost his footing and fell into a shell hole, half filled with rancid muddy slime that sucked him down amid bloated corpses and rusty barbed wire. Coughing and retching, he struggled to the surface to lie propped against God knows what, too exhausted to move.

The insane rattling hammer of the machine guns reached a crescendo before spluttering into short bursts bracketed with the random popping crackle of rifle fire. The attack had failed and those who had survived the initial assault were staggering back in ones and twos, seeking the relative safety of their own lines, all the while being picked off by the German gunners.

Bullets in the back kill just as effectively.

As the firing became less frenetic, Jamie was suddenly aware of someone groaning close by. After making sure his steel helmet was well coated with mud, he jammed it hard down on his head before risking a quick look over the rim of the crater.

All he could see were the soles of a pair of boots, officer's boots, about an arm's length away. And the boots were moving, as if their owner was desperately trying to bury himself deeper in the mud.

Jamie called out. "Can you move, sir?"

After a moment's pause, a frightened voice gasped. "Who's that? Where are you?"

"I'm in a shell hole right by your boots, sir. I'm going to try and drag you in with me." Then, pressing his face into the disgusting mud, Jamie wriggled himself upwards and forwards until he was able to get a grip on the officer's ankles and started to pull. As soon as he did so, the man screamed, a high pitched, teeth grating sound that Jamie knew would bring every gun to bear on their position.

Sweating with fear, he hissed, "For Jesus Christ's sake, will you stop your fucking wailing!"

The screaming stopped, replaced by a muffled groaning as Jamie continued to slide the man's unbelievably heavy weight towards the safety of the shell hole.

"Come on, you fucker. Give me some help here!" He felt the legs move a little. It helped, just enough until, with a slithering rush, the khaki-clad figure slipped over the edge and down into the slimy pool. As he shot past, Jamie grabbed his Sam Browne to stop him sliding all the way down into the muddy water.

"Welcome to my humble abode," he said, touching the rim of his helmet in a parody of a salute, "Private James Kirkpatrick at your service, sir."

The officer, who had ended up with his back to Jamie, rolled over until they were face-to-face. Jamie knew the man. He'd seen him before somewhere, but couldn't think where. The face was ashen under the mud and filth, a neatly trimmed moustache evident below eyes that were dimmed with pain and shock. The face tried to smile.

"Major Thomas Watkins at your service. Very pleased to meet you, Private Kirkpatrick. I would return your salute but – "

With his left hand, he reached across and touched a scorched and bloody mess where his right arm should have been.

"That used to be a damned good arm," he said, and fainted.

With a wound of that severity, the man had little chance of surviving, and Jamie knew he should leave him where he was to die in peace.

Instead, as soon as a bank of cloud obscured the moon and the shooting died away to nothing, Jamie hauled Major Thomas Watkins out of the shell hole and half dragged, half carried him back to the British trenches. The man was still alive when he handed him over to a pair of exhausted stretcher bearers.

"Look after him lads," he called, as they carried the Major away, "he owes me a drink or two."

The attack failed. No-one had really expected anything different. Losses were light though, if you could call just under a thousand killed and fifteen hundred wounded, light. Some of them would doubtless slip from one list to the other within a day or so.

But, from a strictly military perspective, it had served its purpose, allowing time for reinforcements to make their way along the miles of communication and supply trenches without being shelled into oblivion. The following day, the 26th of May, the shelling died down and the Germans remained in their trenches.

It was all over, until the next time.

Newly commissioned Lieutenant Charles Edward Townshend never even made it out of his trench. He was cut down by a sniper even as he reached the top of the ladder and turned his head to encourage his men. The heavy Mauser bullet took him below his right ear, shattering the lower half of his boyish face. He lived for a while, long enough to be shipped back down the line to an advanced field hospital, there to endure two hours of futile, agonising surgery as they tried to repair the irreparable. He died in a clean hospital bed, far from the scavenging guns and the stench of war. Not that it mattered to him. In the end, death was death, wherever or however it was met.

Long weeks of stalemate followed as torrential spring rain flooded the roads and trenches, rendering all movement impossible. But while the artillery and the machine guns took a break, gas gangrene, pneumonia and snipers kept the grave diggers occupied.

One dismal afternoon Jamie received a surprise invitation to accompany a messenger back to Divisional HQ, which was situated in the remaining half of an artillery shattered Manoir three miles behind the lines. He was told to wait in a room with only half a ceiling. After half an hour, he was summoned through into what looked as if it might once have been a ballroom, packed with officers and orderlies, with trestle tables covered in maps and messengers shouting into telephones while others banged away at typewriters. Taken to the far end of the room he found himself standing to rigid attention in front of a Field Marshall.

"Are you Private James Connell Kirkpatrick, North Somerset Fusiliers?" the man asked.

"Er, yes sir, that's correct, sir." Even as he spoke, Jamie wondered if there had been some dreadful mistake and that he was about to be punished for something he didn't even know he'd done.

"And do you know of a Major T L Watkins?" Jamie must have looked confused because the man tried again. "Thomas Watkins." At the sound of the man's Christian name, Jamie remembered.

"The man who lost his arm? Oh, yes, I remember him. Did he survive, I mean is he all right now?"

"Thanks to you, my boy, he did. But I'm afraid his war's over. He's back home recuperating. What you did was a very brave thing, Private. I have great pleasure in informing you that you have received a mention in dispatches." The man made it sound like he was awarding the Victoria Cross but Jamie knew that it was exactly what it was, a mention, no more, no less.

"Thank you, sir," he said, wondering if that was all they'd dragged him back for.

Then the Field Marshall stepped forward and shook Jamie's hand warmly. "I would also like to give you these. Call it a battlefield promotion. You may sew them on when you get back to your unit. They have already been informed." Jamie looked down and found himself clutching a set of Sergeant's stripes and a brand new pay book. "Congratulations, Sergeant Kirkpatrick. Jolly well done." The Field Marshall nodded, smiled, saluted and turned back to his map strewn table.

Just as the June sunshine was drying the way for yet more ritual slaughter, the newly-promoted Sergeant's luckiest moment arrived. With barely ten days to go before 50,000 troops were to be committed in one of the costliest pushes so far in his sector, he fell to the long distance attention of a diligent sniper.

A low point in the parapet, a moment's loss of concentration and a brilliant snap shot drilled a hole in Jamie's upper chest. Entering an inch or so behind his right shoulder, the shot was angled such that the bullet travelled obliquely across his chest to make an untidy exit hole three inches above his left nipple, carrying away part of a rib and puncturing a lung as it went. It missed his heart and major arteries by less than an inch.

The damage was extensive but, with the big push imminent, the very best medical help was close at hand. Dry roads, a well maintained ambulance and a battle seasoned surgeon saved his life, but only just.

After a month during which he was too sick to be moved, he was transferred via Boulogne to the tranquillity and safety of a military hospital in Kent.

Chapter 14

North Somerset, October 1979

The final two letters had been written and mailed from the hospital. They described how Jamie, although still confined to bed, was at least able to sit up and carry on a conversation, which was more than could be said for many others in his ward.

Blinded by gas, gut shot, lung shot or with whole or partial amputations, the only thing they shared was pain and, for those capable of any feeling anything at all, relief. Certainly those blinded or with missing limbs would not be returning to the front. Jamie, on the other hand, had already been told that, after a period of convalescence, he could look forward to a full recovery and a return ticket to the war.

"So he must have gone back to France?"

Daniel's words were half question, half statement of fact. As though what Jamie had endured wasn't enough, they were still prepared to ship him back for more.

Faintly, in the still quiet of the night, Kate heard the church clock in Hawkswell village strike the hour. It was two o'clock in the morning of Sunday 21st October, 1979. Sixty-four years had passed since that awful war, less than some peoples' lifetimes.

Then she remembered what Penelope had said about Jamie.

"He came back here first, to convalesce. I don't know how long for, but he was definitely here at Hawkswell for a while."

Daniel sighed and slowly shook his head.

"Dear God, what a contrast that must have been. I mean, how can you compare this place with where he'd been and what he'd endured? It's so peaceful here, so safe. We can never really have any idea what they went through, those men and boys, can we? And for what? They were at it again twenty years later."

"They still are."

"How do you mean?"

"Belfast, Iran, Afghanistan, Uganda, all over. No-one ever learns. Sure the Americans and the Soviet Union are palling up to each other right now, but how long will that last? And where's the next big one going to flare up? India and Pakistan, China and Taiwan, North and South Korea? If it's not one place it's another. And it's still young men dying and mothers grieving and kids left without fathers. God I hate it all."

"You mentioned Belfast."

Kate nodded.

"I seem to remember you telling me that you're a Republican sympathiser. How do you square that with your pacifism?"

Kate shunted herself along the sofa, creating a space between herself and Daniel, and turned to face him.

"Jesus, Daniel. How can you ask me that?"

"I really don't see how you can sympathise with the IRA after what they've done these last few weeks. Have you forgotten Lord Mountbatten? Out for a quiet day's fishing and blown to bits along with half his family. Soldiers killing soldiers is one thing, they all put on the uniform, but blowing civilians up, that's murder."

All the while he was speaking, Kate kept her eyes locked on his, even while his words enraged. The moment he finished, she let it all go, her voice whiplashing into the night's calm silence.

"As I told you at the time we had that conversation, whereas I sympathise with their aims, I do not in any way condone their methods. Don't you ever forget that I am Irish, heart and soul. I have no idea how many generations my family go back beyond Jamie and Roiseen, but you can be sure that every man jack of them was at some time or other oppressed by the bloody English.

"Check out your history Daniel Lewis, and find out what an inglorious one it is where Ireland and the Irish are concerned. The Troubles are just the latest chapter in all those years of exploitation and ill treatment. Yes, I do believe in a united Ireland. I also believe the way the Catholics in the north are discriminated against is immoral and unjust. But I do not, nor will I ever believe that the way to solve these things is by killing and maiming people. Will you please understand that!?"

Even in the face of Kate's anger, Daniel held his ground.

"All right, so how else should they achieve their ends?"

"By bloody talking, that's how. By diplomacy. And if the bastards won't sit down and talk, they should blow up a few electricity sub-stations or pylons. Take out the telephone system, the TV and radio masts, railway tracks even. That would bring the bloody place to its knees in weeks and no-one need be hurt. But no. What do they do? They blow up shopping arcades and chip shops, and they kill women and children indiscriminately, Catholic and Protestant alike. And what does that achieve? It makes people scared, sure, but more important, it makes them bloody angry. And it makes them angry with all the wrong people. Instead of the British Army being seen as the villains they undoubtedly are, the occupiers and oppressors, it's the Provos that get all the really shite press. Oh, they deserve it, don't get me wrong."

As she paused to draw breath, she saw something in Daniel's eyes that stopped her words.

"It's not funny, Daniel. I'm warning you – "

But it was too late, Daniel had allowed himself to smile.

Even though it was a kind smile, a sympathetic and understanding smile, it was a mistake, as were the words that followed.

"You know, being angry really suits you. You should do it more often."

"Get out!"

Kate's response was more hissed than spoken.

"Now! Get out of my fecking flat!"

Daniel held up his hands as if to ward off a blow. "Whoa, hold on there, Kate. It was a joke. I was only trying to lighten things up a bit."

Kate lurched to her feet, stepped away and pointed to the door, her arm painfully straight and trembling.

"If you can find anything even faintly humorous in bloodshed and death, you have no business here. Now get out!"

But he didn't. To Kate's astonishment, Daniel stayed put and spoke slowly and calmly.

"No. I'm not leaving until we have sorted this out. I completely agree with everything you have said, every single word. I agree with you about the bloody English, the IRA and warfare in all its forms. But I don't want to end this evening angry and depressed. Kate, this world is full of shit. I know it and you know it. It's packed to the rafters with all kinds of injustice, unfairness and stupidity. But getting angry doesn't solve anything. It just makes things worse."

Throughout Daniel's speech, Kate's arm remained rigidly aimed at the door. Even when he finished speaking, she made no response, standing there like a signpost, already cursing herself for her reaction. He had to go. There was no way she could back down. But a small part of her, way down inside, desperately wanted him to stay, to take charge. And so she kept silent while she prayed that Daniel would prove to be different from all the rest, that he might, after all, be stronger than her.

After an agonisingly long pause, he stood. "It's been a long day and we're both tired. I don't want to leave, Kate, especially not like this. I said the wrong thing at the wrong time and for that I'm really sorry. Our emotions have taken a bit of a battering tonight, especially yours. Maybe you'll feel differently tomorrow."

Kate stood as if carved from stone. But when Daniel went to step past her to reach the door, she turned her head slightly and the light from one of the table lamps caught her face, allowing him to see that her eyes were brim full of tears.

And so he stopped and she prayed harder than ever.

Be strong Daniel Lewis, please be stronger than me.

Slowly, she let her arm drop to her side.

It was enough.

Daniel stepped forward, put his arms around her and pulled her to him. Only when her face was firmly pressed into the safety of his chest did she finally release her tears.

Kate neither knew nor cared how long they stayed like that, arms wrapped tightly around each other, her face buried in Daniel's pullover, his face and lips pressed into her hair.

Neither felt the need to move, to change position, to speak.

It was the holding that mattered, the staying that counted.

In the end it was Daniel who murmured, "I think I'd better go now."

Kate tightened her arms briefly before letting her hands slide down to his waist. She rested them there, reluctant to break the contact while Daniel spoke again.

"I'm truly sorry for what happened earlier. I should have read the mood better I guess. But there's one thing I'm not sorry about and I'm not going to take it back either. You are very beautiful, Kate O'Donnell, angry or not."

Then he kissed the crown of her head gently and eased himself out of her embrace. They stood face-to-face for a hand span of seconds and Kate so nearly asked him to stay.

Instead, she kissed him gently on the lips, took his hand in hers and led him to the door.

As she let him out into the corridor she asked, "Will I see you tomorrow?"

He squeezed her hand before releasing it.

"How about lunch?" She nodded.

"OK. Where?"

"Same place we went the other night." She grinned.

"About twelve thirty?"

"See you then. Goodnight, Kate."

She said goodnight and closed the door softly before leaning against it.

Daniel Lewis. Strong Man. She laughed quietly to herself.

Well who would have believed it?

He called for her as promised and drove them both to the pub. Even the weather played ball because they enjoyed one of those special days that seemed to be left over from the summer, a clear blue sky and comfortably warm sunshine.

The food didn't disappoint and neither did Daniel's company. It felt as if they'd crossed some indefinable boundary in their relationship, not least in the fact that it was continuing to develop. Barriers had been dismantled on both sides and they chatted easily about their respective childhoods, their triumphs and disappointments, favourite films, music and books. In fact, they talked about everything but work, the well, and anything to do with war and conflict.

Daniel proved to be witty and entertaining. He was self-deprecating, refreshingly honest, and shared more of Kate's passions and beliefs than she would ever have believed possible.

After the meal, Kate suggested that they drive up onto the Mendips and down through Cheddar Gorge. Of course there were plenty of places to stop and look around, from ancient quarries to spectacular views, so much so that it was already getting dark by the time they turned for home. Then, because neither of them had anything else planned, they stopped at the Red Lion in Hawkswell village for a drink and a bite to eat before heading back in time for an early night. Both hinted at busy weeks ahead.

Once again, when saying goodnight after a quick nightcap in Kate's flat, Daniel behaved impeccably, more so than she might have preferred. But then, she smiled to herself, with any luck there would be plenty of time for all that.

Chapter 15

Daniel's car was parked in the courtyard when Kate got back from work the following evening and, in need of a boost after a long, hard day, her spirits lifted as soon as she saw that he was in. Even better, he must have been waiting for her because the downstairs door was opened with a flourish as she approached.

"Welcome home milady."

She laughed, dumped her bag and allowed herself to be engulfed in a very welcome hug before receiving an equally delightful kiss. A breathless minute later, she detached herself.

"Sure and that's what I call a welcome home. Hey, Daniel Lewis, I think I could get used to this."

He kissed her again before picking up her bag, closing the door and leading the way along the corridor and up the stairs.

As Kate opened the door to her flat, she abandoned caution and invited Daniel to dinner. An hour and a half later, they were facing each other across her dining table, a pair of candles burning brightly, their flames reflected in two glasses of red wine.

If it wasn't the best meal that Kate had ever cooked, it was a damned close second. Daniel's expression of delight at his first mouthful couldn't have been anything other than a hundred percent honest.

"Now I know why you're a veggie. With food this good, who needs anything else? This is absolutely delicious, what's in it?"

"All good stuff – wild mushrooms, garlic, onion, feta and cheddar cheese, fresh parsley and basmati rice all wrapped up in a filo pastry parcel. It's a bit of a faff putting it together but it's worth the effort."

"You can say that again. I've always thought that vegetarian food was unremittingly bland, full of tasteless beans and shredded carrots. But this really is something else. You might have a convert here. What started you off?"

She laughed. "That's easy. I've never known anything different. Mum and Dad had always grown all their own vegetables and when Dad came back from his three years in Burma, he was so used to eastern food with lots of exotic vegetables that he fell straight into it. So that's how I grew up. Endlessly bland, that's me."

"Now that has to be the very first truly stupid thing I've ever heard you say, Kate O'Donnell. You might be lots of things, but bland you most certainly aren't."

Kate would look back on that evening in years to come, and remember its calm normality. There would be many other similar evenings, but the cataclysmic events that were about to engulf the house and everyone it sheltered would detach that future from everything that had gone before, like drawing a thick line under a paragraph. Before and after – two different worlds.

Comfortably full of food, wine and well-being, they snuggled up together on the sofa in front of the fire. They lay for a while, wrapped in each other's' arms, bathed in the gentle, golden light from candles and burning logs.

The only sound, apart from their own breathing was the occasional pop and crackle from the fire.

After a while, Kate murmured, "This is so scary."

"Did you say scary?"

"Yes."

"What on earth is there to be scared about?"

"It's all too good, too comfortable, too enjoyable."

"Sorry, I don't understand."

Kate shifted in Daniel's arms until she could look up into his face. "Good things have a habit of coming to an end prematurely in my life. I try to avoid them, to push them away. You may have noticed."

He responded cautiously. "Am I one of those good things."

She murmured a yes.

"But I'm not going anywhere. I'm here, with you, in this cosy flat in this crumbling old house. What's to be frightened about?"

She shrugged.

"I don't know. It's something I do when things are going well. I think about how transient this all is, how it's all going to end someday."

"Now that's just morbid. Of course it's all going to end, everything does. It's up to us to enjoy each day as it comes, make the most of what we've got."

"OK. So what have we got, Daniel?"

He thought for a moment. "I was going to say we've got each other, but that would be a bit... I don't know, taking rather a lot for granted. I think we might have something good here, you and me. You're not the only one who's afraid, you know."

Kate could see the candle flames dancing in Daniel's eyes but not beyond, to what he was thinking or fearing. Then he leant down and kissed her, slowly and gently, before pulling away.

"Kate, I must go."

That woke her up.

"Why?"

"Because if I don't go now, I know what will happen. We'll end up in bed together."

"And what's so wrong with that?"

"That's what I'm afraid of, and I think you are too. We don't know each other well enough. It's too early. I don't want to spoil something so precious by rushing."

Kate wanted desperately to understand, but all she could feel was confusion, and worse, a feeling of rejection.

"Daniel, what's wrong with us going to bed? Don't you want to? Is there something else I need to know? Or is it because of this?" She pointed to her leg.

"Of course not, and of course I want to go to bed with you. And how on earth could I object about your leg. It's part of you, part of what makes you who you are. Sure it wouldn't win a beauty contest but who cares? I think you hide it too much Kate. And yes, I want to make love with you and sleep beside you and make love to you again when we wake up in the morning. You are gorgeous. I've fancied you since I first set eyes on you. And, no, I'm not gay, and to put the record straight, I'm not married or in any form of a relationship right now. I have never been married and I have never been able to maintain a long term relationship either."

"So whose was that wetsuit you lent me the other day when we were clearing out the boathouse dock? It certainly wasn't yours."

Daniel was taken off balance for a moment before he answered. "Oh, that. It belonged to a girl called Amy. I thought I was in love with her and we were together for six months, a record for me. I wanted to share everything with her and I persuaded her to come caving with me. That's why I bought her the wetsuit."

"So what happened?"

"She couldn't bear getting mud under her nails."

Kate stifled a laugh. "Just that?"

"Just that. I took her down one of the easiest but most beautiful caves I know, and that was all she thought of it."

"So that's why you…"

"That's why we split up, yes. Or, to be more accurate, that's when I opened my eyes and saw her for what she was, great to look at not a lot else. Oh God, that sounds too cruel. She was a lovely girl but definitely not for me."

"Do you intend to try and take me caving? Because if you do, you're on a hiding to nowhere, pal. Nothing on God's earth could ever persuade me to go underground."

Daniel laughed. "Of course I wouldn't dream of taking you caving if you really don't want to. But you might like to teach me how to row if we ever did…"

Kate stayed silent, knowing there was more.

"Look, I don't want to spoil what we might have here by jumping straight into bed. And that's the truth of it. I want us to get to know each other better. I want us to be friends first, lovers second. Can you see that? I have fallen in lust so many times, climbed between the sheets as quickly as possible and woken the next morning knowing I'd made a terrible mistake. I don't want that to happen with us. And before you ask, no, there isn't a problem. Everything is in perfect working order as I hope you will find out very soon. I'm falling in love with you Kate O'Donnell, and I want to finish falling in love with you before I make love to you. Oh, God, I'm not making any sense am I?"

Kate lifted her head and touched her lips to his.

"You must trust me very much. I want you very badly, Daniel Lewis, but I am trying to understand. My head understands, and I think my heart does too, it's the rest of me that's confused."

They laughed.

"And for what it's worth, I think I'm falling in love with you too, and that's what I'm afraid of, falling. We are so alike, you and me. I've done the same as you, time and time again. Fallen head over heels for some guy and jumped straight into the sack. It's that morning after feeling that hurts so much, knowing, just knowing that you have made a terrible mistake and that you're alone again. I do understand, but can I ask you a favour?"

"Sure."

"Please go right now before I rip off all your clothes and ruin everything."

Chapter 16

Kate couldn't get the events of the previous evening out of her head and barely managed to get through her day's work without making a complete idiot of herself. In a moment of madness, she decided to ask Daniel in the following evening and cook him a steak. She could still hardly believe what she was doing even as she loaded the disgusting chunk of flesh, oven chips and a bottle of single malt into a carrier bag at the supermarket checkout.

She had stayed late at the office and, after stopping to shop, it was gone ten thirty by the time she pulled up next to Daniel's Rover.

With no lights showing from the wing, she let herself into the flat as quietly as possible, reckoning that Daniel was probably already in bed. She was wrong. He turned up at her door fifteen minutes later in his caving gear, brushed past her and closed the door behind him.

"Bloody hell, Kate. What did you have to turn the bloody lights on for?"

She stared at him dumbfounded before she was able to speak.

"Oh, hello Kate. Thank you for thinking of me and buying a hunk of bleeding meat and a bottle of disgustingly expensive malt whisky."

Daniel stared at her as if he hadn't understood a word.

"I was in the well chamber. I've been checking the kit. When I came out –"

"You haven't listened to a word I've said, have you? I don't give a flying fuck where you've been, Daniel Lewis! I have spent most of last night and all of today thinking that we might have found something special here and all you can think about is that fecking well!"

While she was speaking, she reached down for the shopping bag containing the steak and pressed it to Daniel's chest where he clutched it, incomprehension blanking his face.

"Take it! Get out of here and don't even think of talking to me again until you've grown up enough to have something sensible to say that hasn't got anything to do with well shafts or fecking caving."

She pushed him, with the shopping bag still clutched to his chest, out into the corridor and slammed the door in his face.

He knocked, but not for very long. He wouldn't want to make enough noise to attract any attention, especially dressed as he was. He probably phoned too, but by then Kate had pulled the lead from its wall socket.

As she sat and sobbed on her sofa, she missed the sound of a note being slipped under her door, and only spotted it as she turned off lights before going to bed. She turned the folded sheet in her hands for ages, split between wanting to open it and determinedly not wanting to. Eventually curiosity won and she eased the sheet apart, wondering what form Daniel's apology would take. The note consisted of six words:

Divers here next Saturday night, Daniel

She cried like she hadn't cried for years. She sobbed until snot and tears dripped off her chin into her lap and then she sobbed some more. She cried until her eyes hurt but all the time she cried in silence, determined that the cause of all her grief wouldn't hear. And as she wept, she drank the whisky, one deliberate glass after another, steadily and purposefully, praying for the alcohol to dull the pain.

"You single-minded, stupid, insensitive, immature, thoughtless shit. And I thought you were different. I so wanted you to be different."

When the tears at last eased and dried, she threw more logs on the fire and curled up to wonder where it had all gone wrong. Even the bloody fire wouldn't play ball. Instead of bursting into flame, the logs just sat there and smoked.

She reached across and flicked open the dampers.

Still nothing happened.

Sod it. She closed her eyes.

It was the frantic banging on her door that woke her to a vision of hell. Her cosy wood burning stove wasn't looking so friendly anymore. What had once been jet black was now cherry red and crackling and pinging with the searing heat. The fire itself looked like the inside of a blast furnace.

Eventually the shouted words from the other side of the door got through to her fuddled brain.

"Open up, Kate. Hurry or we're going to have to break it down!"

Half stupefied, she lurched to her feet and stumbled across to the door. Only then did she realise that it was shaking in its frame from the ferocity of the pounding. She slipped the latch and Daniel hurled himself past her into the room.

"Soak some towels in the bath, anything, quickly!"

Unable to take in what was happening, she was vaguely aware that Tom had followed Daniel into the flat and was helping him do something to her sitting room. She stumbled into the bathroom and sat down heavily on the toilet, head between her knees to stop herself being sick. Her face felt raw and blistered and it was only then that she became aware of the acrid smell of scorching paint and fabric.

Daniel barged his way into the bathroom and dragged a towel off the rack, plunging it under the cold tap in the bath until it was soaking. He rushed out again. Kate wondered vaguely why he hadn't said hello.

By the time she felt able to move, she staggered out of the bathroom to find Tom crouched in front of her stove, its doors now tightly closed and looking more black than red.

A moment later, Daniel hurried in from the corridor.

"I think it's OK, there's only a bit of steam now."

As Kate stared at the scene, unable to make any sense of what she was seeing, she realised that all the furniture had been pushed away from its cosy arrangement and that there was a mass of canvas spread about on the floor, littered with wet towels and bits of unburnt wood.

Daniel noticed her then and hurried over.

"Bloody hell, Kate. Are you OK?" Taking her head in his hands he gently turned her face towards the light.

"Wow, you're going to be sore in the morning. What happened?" She licked her lips and tried to speak but could only manage a dry croak.

Helping her to one of the sofas, Daniel sat her down while Tom started to tidy up. She shivered. Two of the big windows were wide open to the night. Daniel hurried off and came back with the duvet off her bed which he wrapped tightly around her before handing her a glass of water which he encouraged her to sip.

"I think we'd better get you to hospital, have you checked over."

After exchanging a few words with Tom, Daniel tried to help Kate to stand but she could only slide forward off the sofa onto the floor. Nothing worked. Her legs had gone off somewhere. First she couldn't speak, now she couldn't even stand. She tried to look up, to ask Daniel what was happening to her, but even her head wouldn't do what it was told. Oh, sod it, she thought, might as well pass out. And so she did.

The first thing she saw was light, lots of very bright light. Screwing up her eyes didn't do any good, it stayed just as bright. She tried to put a hand up, but one was too heavy to lift and someone was holding on tightly to the other. Trying to pull it away she managed to mumble, "Too bright. It's too bright."

A voice right by her head said, "Ah! You're back with us then." She turned her head in the direction of the voice and away from the light, which got a little easier to bear. She risked opening her eyes. Daniel was holding her hand. He smiled.

"Hi Kate. How are you feeling?"

She couldn't remember feeling bad, so figuring out whether she was feeling better was tricky. She nodded, or at least tried to.

She had another go at speaking.

"Where...?"

"Where are you? You're in the casualty department at the Royal United Hospital in Bath." She must have frowned because he explained, slowly and deliberately. "You fell asleep in front of your fire, back at the flat. You left it wide open and when it caught, it went off like a rocket. The chimney nearly caught fire and that's how I knew what had happened. I had gone to get something from my car and caught a whiff of burning soot. Your chimney looked like a Roman candle. Very impressive."

"Logs wouldn't catch," she mumbled.

Daniel leaned closer. "Sorry, I didn't hear that."

"The logs. They just smoked. Everything else had gone wrong, that was the last straw. I must have..."

"You fell asleep, or more like unconscious. Seems you demolished the best part of a bottle of rather good malt whisky."

She blinked to re-focus, the earlier part of the evening beginning to fill in. "What are you doing here, anyway? I'm not speaking to you."

"Ah, no. Of course you aren't. But I drove you here, so I can't exactly leave, can I?"

"Looks like I'm bloody stuck with you then."

Daniel squeezed her hand. "I'm not going to escape that easily. Anyway, surely there are better ways of getting rid of me than burning the house down." She tried to grin but it hurt too much.

"My face...?"

"Superficial. Nothing to worry about. More like sunburn, at least that's what the nurse told me. You'll probably peel a bit, but there's no real damage."

"Oh God. So I was drunk?"

"Very."

"Ah."

She ran her tongue around her mouth and grimaced. "Is there any water anywhere?"

Daniel said he'd find some. About to rise, Kate gripped his hand for a moment and held him back.

"Don't think I've forgiven you. You made me cry, you sod. That's why I got drunk because – " Tears stung her face.

Daniel hugged her until a nurse came and everything went hazy again. The next time she woke, Daniel was nowhere to be seen and a nurse was adjusting a drip connected to her left arm.

"Where's – ?"

"Your man? He's down the passage having a coffee I think. We told him we were keeping you in for the rest of the night for observation but he insisted on staying. He's been sitting beside you until a few minutes ago. Wouldn't budge. Wish I had a fella like that." Kate gave her the best grin she could manage with her sore face and asked her what the time was. "Six o'clock, just gone. Hospital wakey, wakey time. Don't worry, you'll be out of here as soon as the doctor's done his rounds."

Later that morning, having been discharged with a thumping headache, a packet of pain killers and a large tub of cream for her face, Kate allowed Daniel to drive her back to Hawkswell.

While he drove, Daniel told her that he had already called Andy at *GreenGauge* and filled him in on what had happened.

"He said you weren't to worry. Apparently everything is under control and he doesn't want to see you until next week."

When Daniel helped her into her flat, the place looked as if nothing had happened. The canvas and the mess were gone, the sofas were back in place and all there was to show for the night's events was a damp patch on the carpet in front of the fire, and even that looked as if it was drying. A large electric fire stood in front of the wood burner, all three bars alight.

Tom must have heard them arrive because he stuck his head around the door a few minutes after they let themselves in, as concerned as ever.

"Now, how are you, m'dear?"

Kate fingered her sore face. "I'm fine Tom. Nothing that plenty of moisturiser and a bit of extra make up won't cure. I'm so sorry about what happened."

Tom waved her down.

"Don't you think nothing of it. It can happen to anyone. I'm sorry about the mess on the carpet, we had to damp the fire down somehow."

Kate walked over and, much to the old man's surprise, gave him a hug and a kiss on the cheek. "You don't have to apologise for anything, Tom. It's me that should apologise for nearly burning Hawkswell down. And look at all the clearing up you've done. Can I at least offer you a coffee?"

Daniel insisted on making the drinks while Kate and Tom sat either side of the electric fire and talked over the night's excitement. A few minutes later Tom put his coffee mug carefully on the floor.

"Now, you mustn't feel bad about what happened Kate. There's nothing as can't be put right. That stain'll be gone in no time, and the fire's fine now. I checked the flue this morning and there's not a scrap of soot left up there. 'Course, it's not the first time Hawkswell's nearly burned down. And strangely enough, it was your relative what saved the place that time. Back in the late autumn of 1915 it was, when Jamie was back here on sick leave. Last night brought it all back.

"It had been a lovely day, with clear skies and bright sunshine but with a bitter wind if I remember it right. Old Mister Edward, who was of course grieving for the loss of his son, had found the evening so cold and dispiriting that he'd asked for a fire to be lit in his drawing room. Seems that, comforted by the warmth, he'd settled down with a hot toddy and a book. As the temperature fell later that evening, he banked up the fire like you did, Kate, and it roared up nicely, drawn by the wind and the draughts and eventually he fell asleep.

"First anyone knew that something was wrong was when my old dad, Brian, ran out of the house shouting to all and sundry to get outside 'cos the place was on fire. I followed me mother out into the courtyard, and soon as I got there I could smell the burning soot, acrid it was. Everyone was pointing up at the roof and there was the source. One of the chimney stacks pouring flames and sparks into the night sky like a bloomin' volcano. And all the while, the wind was blowing great lumps of blazing soot across towards the walled garden and the greenhouses.

"No-one seemed to know what to do although dad had sent one of the grooms off on our fastest horse to fetch help from the village. Then Jamie arrived. Seems he'd heard the din from down in the boathouse where he was bedded down. Of course he was Sergeant Kirkpatrick by then and he took charge straight away, shouting directions to the men gathered all around. He sent two to the greenhouses to make sure nothing caught from the sparks and told some others to fetch as many buckets as they could find. The rest of the men followed him into the house without question, glad to have someone to tell them what to do, I suppose.

"When they got there, the place was in uproar, doors flung wide open and maids screaming and running about like headless bloody chickens. Edward Townshend himself was standing in the doorway to the drawing room staring in horror at the inferno. The fire in the grate was by then completely out of control, the bricks and plaster pouring smoke. Logs stacked to either side were beginning to smoke too.

"Jamie turned to two of the men who'd followed him into the house and told them to fetch tarpaulins and sacking, as much as they could find. He said to soak them all under the pump and get them good and wet. He got the rest to help him move the rugs and the furniture. When the blokes with the tarpaulins arrived, he got them spread out on the floor so they could drag out the smouldering logs with rick irons.

"While my father and two other men worked from either side of the fire, Jamie draped himself in wet canvas, grabbed a bucket and a shovel and rushed in to scoop up a load of blazing logs and embers before rushing out to the front door. He was only near the fire for a second or two, but he was steaming like he'd just come out of a boiler. Once he'd emptied his bucket onto the gravel, he ran back in to do the same again. Five times more he went into that raging heat before the fire in the hearth began to calm down. Each time he passed through the hall he doused himself with more water from a row of pots and pans stacked along the corridor.

"With the source of the fire removed, all that remained was to put out the chimney itself. Jamie said he knew what to do, and that night not a single soul doubted him. First thing he did was thoroughly soak one of the smaller tarpaulins. Then, with my father helping, he hurled an entire bucket full of water up and into the open mouth of the chimney before ramming the balled up tarpaulin into the bottom of the flue to seal it. The effect was bloody amazing. There was such a hiss when he threw that water up! Then, as soon as the flue was blocked with the tarpaulin, the noise stopped altogether, leaving a creaking kind of silence. Suddenly we could all hear the wind outside again.

"Jamie waited for a minute or two before propping the bundle of canvas in place with two of the rick irons. After that he told the rest of the men to fetch ladders and run a hose spray down the chimney to stop it flaring up again. And that was that.

"Of course everyone applauded. Edward Townshend shook Jamie's hand and congratulated him. When he was asked how on earth he knew how to put out a chimney fire, the lad said that his father managed to set fire to their cottage chimney every winter, sometimes more than once, and Jamie'd watched him put it out easily every time. It's the steam you see, it rushes up the chimney and causes a vacuum behind it, snuffing out the fire.

"Now this'll make you laugh, because next thing is Jamie's apologising for all the mess. Of course the old boy wouldn't hear any of it and packed him off to my old mother to get his burns and blisters seen to. So, you see, you're not the first to set fire to this old house my dear, although I do rather hope you'll be the last."

After Tom had left, Daniel made them both a mushroom omelette for brunch. Kate took one mouthful, quickly followed by another.

"Wow, this is delicious."

He smiled across at her. "Looks like last night didn't damage your appetite." She grinned at him and stuck her tongue out, which he ignored. They ate on in silence for a while until Kate at last decided that there were pressing matters that couldn't wait a moment longer.

"Daniel. About last night..." He finished his last mouthful and mopped the plate with a piece of bread.

"I am so sorry, Kate. You're absolutely right, Howk's bloody well has got under my skin. And as soon as I knew the diving team were willing to come and we'd fixed a date, all I wanted to do was to be ready for them. So I went and checked everything, including all the kit we'd stashed on the cavern's beach."

"What, you mean right down the shaft and across the lake, on your own?" He nodded. "Jesus, Daniel! Wasn't that hideously dangerous?" He thought for a moment.

"Maybe that's why I did it, I don't know."

Kate suffered no lasting ill effects from her roasting apart from the fact that her hair and face needed a little more conditioner and moisturiser for a few days.

A quiet weekend with Daniel was a welcome relief, most of it spent taking the *Annabella* out of the water and packing her away for the winter. Thankfully, Tom had asked Ted Walton to bring his JCB down which made lifting her back into the loft so much easier. Once the boat had been thoroughly dried off, they gave it a thorough waxing. Then they placed her back on her trestles and snugged her down under the tarpaulin cover before closing and locking the boat house. Over the next few days, Daniel spent long hours beneath the house, mapping and photographing the well shaft and the lake cavern and making final preparations for the divers.

Just like with the initial exploration, Daniel met the divers in a pub about five miles from Hawkswell. All their gear was carefully packed into the back of a Cortina estate. The two divers, Chris and Simon, were well known to be a little off the wall. As a result, Daniel went to great lengths to impress upon them the seriousness of the undertaking and how essential it was that they remain undetected.

"The old girl who owns the place is more than a bit flaky and right now she's not at all well. She's a nice enough old bird, but she's got a real thing about the well. Can't even bear to have it mentioned, let alone explored. So if we get caught in the act, all hell will break loose and I intend to avoid that at all costs. It's a great place, Hawkswell, with some really nice people living there, so let's get in, do the survey and get out again without anyone being any the wiser, OK?"

Barry and Pete from the first expedition were coming along as support for the divers, so Daniel drove them to the house in his Rover with Chris and Simon following in the Cortina. Once parked in the courtyard, with the tail gate of the estate car as close as possible to the door, they made plenty of noise as they trooped up to Daniel's flat.

Kate had already let slip to Tom that Daniel was having some friends staying over the weekend, thus alleviating any suspicion about the extra car. Along with the thermos flasks of soup and coffee Daniel had asked for, Kate had also prepared another of her curries for the team, this time at Barry's request.

"Bloody delicious, Kate, just what we need to set us up for a couple of days underground." The air of excitement in Daniel's flat grew steadily as the hours ticked by until midnight.

Being a bitterly cold, moonlit night made transferring the equipment from car to corridor easier but more risky. Fortunately there were no hitches, and as soon as the blackout panels were in place, they were able to open up the chamber and move all the diving gear inside. Daniel had already stashed enough food to last the team until Sunday night both in the chamber and at the beach camp where he'd also set up a small tent with foam mats, sleeping bags and a couple of pressure lamps.

"Better to sleep down there than up in the chamber. There's more room. More than that, it'll save a lot of tiring trips up and down the shaft."

After agreeing a radio schedule, Kate kissed Daniel and wished him luck before he closed and locked the chamber door. She wouldn't see any of the others until Sunday night, although Daniel planned to come out during Saturday to help Kate maintain the illusion of normality. Luckily the weekend weather forecast was for rain and sleet, so no-one would be too surprised at not seeing them out and about.

After finishing the washing up, Kate eventually got to bed at two thirty. She lay in the silent darkness wondering what the future held for her and Daniel. In a little over a month Daniel would be moving out of Hawkswell and back to his flat in Bristol. Just in time for Christmas. Terrific.

She couldn't help remembering the first time they had met, back in June. Only six months ago. Not a long time in which to meet the first man you have ever really cared about and then quite possibly lose him. Eventually, after tossing and turning for an hour, she got up and made herself a hot chocolate. Back in bed she read until her eyes closed and the book slipped from her fingers.

At first she couldn't work out what the noise was, or its source. It crashed its way into a very pleasant dream and hissed and crackled like a fire cracker. There were words too. But they seemed to come from a great distance and failed to make any sense. Then she heard a word she recognised only too well – ambulance.

She opened her eyes to pitch darkness.

The noise was coming from the walkie-talkie.

Stupid! She'd left it on the sofa in the sitting room. She switched on the light, looked at her alarm clock. Five fifteen.

Dragging on her dressing gown, she hurriedly picked up the radio and pressed the transmit button.

Hello. Kate here. Is there a problem? Over.
Blasting out of the speaker, Daniel's voice sounded desperate.
Thank God! Kate. Call an ambulance right now. It's one of the divers.
There's been an accident. Tell them he's got a serious head injury. Have
you got that? Over.

Regardless of the consequences, she dialled 999.

And then it all began… and ended.

Chapter 17

Immediately after phoning the emergency services, Kate threw on some clothes and hurried downstairs to the well chamber, flicking lights on as she went, not even thinking about the blackout blinds.

The door was still locked when she arrived, so she hammered on it with the flat of her hand, shouting, "The ambulance is on its way. They reckon about twenty minutes."

The lock clicked and the door swung open.

The chamber resembled a film set for a war movie.

One of the divers was lying on the ground, frighteningly still while the others knelt over him trying to help – one holding an oxygen mask over his face, the other busy cutting away the top part of his wetsuit with a pair of scissors. The floor was strewn with a mess of dressing packs, bloody water, ropes and equipment.

Daniel, having opened the door, stepped forward into Kate's line of sight, his face ashen in the harsh light from the pressure lamps. Still wearing his harness and helmet, water streamed from his boiler suit. When he spoke, he hardly drew breath, words tripping and stumbling over each other in his rush to explain.

"It was their first dive. Simon got caught in the current, slammed against the wall of the continuation shaft and trapped there by the force of the water. We could see what was happening but couldn't do anything to help. Chris eventually got a rope on him but it seemed to take forever before we could pull him free. He's breathing but unconscious."

Kate desperately wanted to help but could only think of one useful thing to do. "I'll go and meet the ambulance at the front of the house and bring them round to the courtyard."

The approaching ambulance could be heard from a long way off, its siren echoing off the hills above the house and ripping the night to shreds. It arrived sixteen minutes after Kate made the emergency call, scrunching to a halt on the gravel in front of the house. Kate ran straight to the driver's door.

"Go down the side there," she pointed with her torch, "Follow the track round and turn right through the carriage gate. There's a courtyard. I'll follow you."

As it drove off, she ran after it, her heart thumping with adrenaline. Lights had appeared in the main house and she knew only too well what they meant. By the time she arrived, the back doors of the ambulance were already wide open and the two man crew were talking to Daniel who beckoned her across as soon as he saw her.

"Apparently there's a doctor on his way by car. Can you go back and keep an eye out for him?"

Kate asked about Simon but Daniel just shook his head.

When Kate got back to the front of the house, two things happened simultaneously – a large black car pulled up in a blaze of headlights, and the front door of the house opened to reveal Penelope and Tom Gerrard, both with dressing gowns over their nightclothes, shielding their eyes from the glare.

Kate ran straight to the car and gave the doctor directions.

As he drove off, she turned and, feeling as if she was about to throw herself off a very high cliff, walked slowly towards Tom and Penelope, who were waiting for her at the bottom of the entrance steps.

"Is that you, Kate? What in heaven's name is going on? Don't you know it's the middle of the night?" Penelope's voice sounded thin but harsh.

Tom stood to one side saying nothing. The light was behind him so Kate couldn't see his face. She took a deep breath and played her one and only card.

"It's nothing really. One of Daniel's visitors has been taken ill and we called an ambulance. They sent a doctor along as well. That was him arriving. Everything's under control, honestly. Why don't you two go back to bed?" She tried to smile reassuringly, crossed her fingers as she spoke and offered up a silent prayer that they'd do as she'd suggested. But the moment Penelope spoke, she knew her gamble had failed.

"How has he been taken ill? Is it drugs or drink? Come on, child, I want to know."

Kate tried again. "He's been taken ill, suddenly. I don't know what it is, but I'm sure it's something they'll be able to put right once he's in hospital. And, no, it's not drugs or anything like that."

Penelope gave her a long, hard stare. She knows I'm not telling her everything. Oh God, what next? She found out soon enough. Penelope spun round and headed with terrible deliberation back up the steps towards the front door.

"I'm going to see what's happening for myself. Come along Tom."

Tom and Penelope gained access to the wing through the door at the far end of the ground floor corridor, the one that usually remained locked. Kate arrived breathless from the courtyard just as it opened. There was no time to warn anyone. All she could do was stand and watch as the very disaster she'd been dreading unfolded before her.

The tableau that greeted the old lady was made up of a uniformed ambulance man, Daniel in his dripping caving gear, and Kate, all three huddled in a tight group at the far end of the corridor, staring into the brightly lit well chamber where the doctor, assisted by the second ambulance man, was working busily to stabilise their patient. There was nowhere for anyone to hide, nothing to be said, nothing to be undone.

Penelope grabbed Tom's arm for support and dragged him towards the scene, her lips pressed into a thin, bloodless line, her eyes glittering with determination and… what? Rage, fear, madness?

Kate neither knew nor cared. At that moment all she wanted was to turn the clock back eighteen hours and start that day again. In desperation, she hurried towards the approaching pair, her arms held out as if in some way she could physically hold back the inevitable. She knew her voice sounded desperate but was beyond caring.

"I'm so sorry, Penelope. This wasn't supposed to happen. You need never have found out. We'll put everything back as it was, I promise. It won't happen again." And as she spoke, she could feel bitter tears pouring down her face – tears of embarrassment and betrayal.

Penelope ignored her entreaties and brushed her aside, coming to a halt a few paces later, directly outside the well chamber. She stood and stared, although whether she could make any sense out of what she was seeing, Kate could only guess.

Daniel stepped forward and tried to speak but Penelope screamed, "Be silent!" without even turning her head in his direction.

Tom moved alongside Penelope and tried to pull her away but she shook him off. By then she was muttering, "What have you done? What have you done?" over and over again.

Deliberately oblivious to what was taking place in the corridor behind him, the doctor stood and beckoned the second ambulance man. He issued quiet instructions before the two uniformed men carefully lifted Simon onto a stretcher.

Followed closely by the doctor and ignoring the group of onlookers, they eased out of the chamber and away to the ambulance. Simon, swathed in a bright red blanket, lay motionless, bright white bandages swathing his head and face, and with an oxygen mask covering his nose and mouth.

The three left in the chamber remained where they were, too shocked and exhausted to move or speak, not knowing quite what to do next. Daniel, Kate and Tom also stood, as if waiting to see who would make the next move or speak first.

It was Penelope. "Get out of my house."

The first time she spoke the words, her voice was low and almost steady. But from that moment on, it grew in volume and pitch with each repetition until she was screaming like a woman possessed, spittle flying from her bloodless lips, one skeletal arm pointing towards the courtyard where the ambulance was pulling away, her other clutching and pulling at her dressing gown.

"Get out! Get out! I want every one of you out of this house right now. That door", she pointed at the chamber, "is to be closed and locked immediately." When no-one moved, she screamed again. "Get out!"

Chris, Barry and Pete started to collect up caving kit but were screamed at.

"Leave it! Leave everything and get out of here before I call the police. Do you hear?"

Daniel stepped forward. "This is all my fault Penelope, I – "

"Miss Townshend, I am Miss Townshend. You are trespassing in my house. You are not welcome here anymore and if you do not leave this very minute I will call the police and have you arrested! Do I make myself clear?"

For a moment Daniel looked as if he was going to call her bluff, so Kate stepped between them, grabbed his arm and pulled him away.

"Come on, Daniel. Let's do what Penelope says. We can sort this out later." She beckoned to the three cavers and they followed each other out after turning off the pressure lamps.

On Penelope's instructions, Tom demanded the key, which Daniel handed over reluctantly. Tom turned it over in his hand, shot a questioning glance at Kate, then shut and locked the door before handing the key to Penelope. She pointed at the three remaining cavers.

"You three will leave my property right now, by whatever means you came here." Then she turned to Kate and Daniel.

"You are both in flagrant breach of the conditions of your lease. You will vacate your flats by this time next week or I will have you forcibly removed."

Kate opened her mouth to protest but Penelope silenced her.

"I trusted you Kate O'Donnell. I trusted you, and this is how you repay me. I never want to set eyes on either of you again. I knew it was a mistake to let these flats. I knew something like this would happen. Now get out of my sight!"

Then, as if she had exhausted the very last remnants of her strength, she collapsed against Tom and would have fallen if he hadn't caught her.

Kate stepped forward to help but Tom pushed her away.

"God knows, haven't you done enough damage for one night? She'll never recover from this, y'know. This is the end of Hawkswell, you mark my words." As he spoke, May Gerrard appeared at the far end of the corridor and hurried to help her husband with Penelope. She ignored Kate and Daniel and helped Tom carry the old lady back to the main part of the house.

The door slammed, the click of its lock harsh and final in the now silent corridor.

The three cavers grabbed whatever they had left in Daniel's flat and, with hardly a word being spoken, climbed into the Cortina and drove away. Daniel had followed them out into the courtyard in time to catch the doctor, also about to leave. When he asked about Simon, he was told that he was being taken straight to the Bristol Royal Infirmary where they had the necessary skills and equipment to treat his condition. He asked Daniel what had happened and Daniel filled in some of the details of the dive. The doctor looked puzzled but didn't ask any more questions before driving off.

Kate was sitting in her flat with the door wide open when Daniel got back upstairs. Minutes later and changed out of his wet caving gear, he walked in and sat beside her. Silence clung like a shroud as the enormity of what had taken place gradually sank in. It was Kate who spoke first.

"Do you think Simon will be OK?"

"I don't know. He looked pretty bad when we got him out of the water. At least he's fit and strong, so maybe – "

"What happened down there Daniel?"

"Truth is, I don't know much more than I've already told you. After we'd locked the door, we ferried the equipment and supplies down the shaft and across to the beach. We made a brew while Simon and Chris checked their gear. It was quite surreal sitting there looking out across the lake. They decided to dive from the beach.

"Simon went first with Chris buddying him. They dropped some dye so they could see where the main current was and managed to keep clear until they were in position above the continuation shaft. By then, Pete and I were stationed directly above them in the inflatable and Barry had returned to the well chamber in case anything went wrong. Luckily, he took the walkie-talkie with him.

"We'd slung two arc lamps over the side of the dinghy so that they were pointing straight down. It was the strangest sensation, the water so clear that it felt as if we were hanging in space, suspended by the ropes from the well shaft. Simon and Chris were finning backwards and forwards above the mouth of the shaft when it happened. Simon must have either strayed too close to the current, or it shifted enough to catch him. It seems as if it was nowhere near as far below the surface as we first thought. Next thing we knew, he was flipped over and pulled down. He hit the rim of the shaft really hard with the side of his face. Thankfully his helmet took most of the force and his air bottles snagged and stopped him being sucked even further down.

"There was a burst of bubbles as he lost his mouthpiece, and we could see him struggling to get it back in. We could see a lot of blood in the water too, so we knew he was injured. As soon as he'd sorted his breathing out, he started trying to pull himself clear, but the current was too strong for him. That was when Chris signalled us to lower a rope. I was worried that the inflatable wouldn't make a stable enough platform, so I took the other end up to the belay at the bottom end of the well shaft. That was when I called up to tell Barry what was happening.

"As soon as Chris was clipped on to the end of the rope, he began to swim closer to Simon while we took his weight. When the current eventually caught him, I was horrified by its power. It felt like he'd fallen off a cliff, it was that strong. Luckily the rope didn't stretch too much and, as soon as he was close enough, he was able to attach a second rope to Simon's harness. Then after we'd pulled Chris clear, we started heaving. We managed to move Simon a few inches but we quickly realised that there was no way the two of us would be able to drag him free.

"Chris surfaced to help but it still took a prodigious effort to get him out of there. I thought we were going to cut him in half with the rope, we had to pull so hard. But then, once he started moving, he came up far too quickly. He had already inflated his life preserver as soon as he knew he was in trouble, hoping that it might be enough to pull him free. So, as soon as the suction of the current was broken, he came up like a rocket. By the time we got him in the boat, he was barely conscious. We knew we had to get him to hospital damned fast. That's when we got Barry to call you up and phone for the ambulance.

"God knows how we managed to haul him up the well shaft. We were exhausted and Chris was freezing cold, so not much help. I guess we were all fuelled by adrenaline by then, but it was a near thing. Back in the chamber, we did our best for him. But there wasn't a hell of a lot we could do. He'd obviously smacked the side of his face quite badly, and even though his helmet took most of the blow, it still looked nasty. Too much blood. Thank God he didn't pass out until we'd got him to the surface. He would have lost his mouthpiece and drowned."

Kate understood most of what she was being told but couldn't begin to imagine what it must have been like down there in the cold, wet darkness. She shook her head slowly and, as she spoke, hot tears squeezed from her eyes.

"I can't really believe all this is happening. Only a few weeks ago we were enjoying Hawkswell and our lives to the full. Now Simon's in hospital and maybe fighting for his life and we've both been thrown out of this beautiful old place. After all the things we've discovered, about Jamie and the boathouse and the *Annabella*. Was it all for nothing? And then there's poor Penelope. Tom said she might never recover. That can't be true can it? Oh Daniel, why has all this happened?"

As she wept, Daniel pulled her towards him, cradled her head on his chest and stroked her hair.

"It's that bloody Howk's well, it's cursed. If we hadn't been so desperate to explore the bloody thing, none of this would have happened."

But Kate wasn't having any of that. She dug her fingers into his back and hugged him hard. "If it wasn't for the well, you wouldn't have taken on the flat and we would never have met. Don't go there Daniel. It's not the well's fault. It's only a hole in the ground, nothing more, nothing less. And that's just the way it'll remain."

"What do you mean?"

"I mean that Penelope is never, ever going to let anyone get within a mile of that well chamber now. I wouldn't be surprised if she has the damned place bricked up, or filled with concrete. Whatever happens, neither of us will ever set eyes on it again, and that's for sure."

Chapter 18

Kate woke at mid-day with a splitting headache. After lying in bed for twenty minutes in the vain hope that it might ease, she dragged herself into the bathroom and swallowed some painkillers. Climbing back into bed she hauled the covers over her head to shut out the daylight. Ten minutes later someone knocked on her door. She ignored it. When they knocked a third time, she crawled out of bed and, without opening the door, called out,

"Not now, Daniel. I've got a hideous headache. I'll see you later."

But the voice that answered wasn't Daniel's, it was Tom's.

Reluctantly, she pulled on her dressing gown and opened the door. But instead of coming in, he remained standing in the corridor. For the first time since she had met him, Tom's face was an expressionless mask, as if he was addressing a stranger.

"I wanted to see if you've had any news about the young man who was hurt last night."

With a shock, Kate realised that she hadn't even attempted to find out. "Er, no. Sorry Tom, nothing yet. Maybe Daniel might know."

"He's gone out."

Kate heard the words but it took a moment for them to sink in.

"How…? I mean…"

"Left early this morning, in his car."

"But, did he say where he was going?"

Tom shook his head.

Kate's vision blurred for a moment, causing her to stumble slightly. Tom stepped forward to take her arm.

"Are you all right, lass?"

Kate tried to smile but couldn't quite manage it. "I think so. It's only a headache and, well… you know, last night."

In the gentle voice that she remembered so well, he asked, "Did you know what they were planning to do?"

She nodded slowly. "Yes, I'm very much afraid I did. I didn't agree with what they were going to do, and I tried my hardest to talk them out of it. But in the end I thought they'd be in and out without anyone knowing and no harm done. And I still don't understand why Penelope was so dead set against them exploring it when they first asked. If she'd agreed back then, none of this would have happened. How is she by the way?"

"Not good. The doctor's been again and given her something stronger this time. We had a bad time with her last night, ranting and shouting until I don't know when. Doctor reckons if she gets any worse, she'll have to go back into hospital and that'll be a right old to do, I can tell you."

Kate leaned against the door frame. "Tom, would you mind if I sit down?"

He helped her across to a sofa where she slumped back against the cushions and closed her eyes against the pounding in her head. He stood over her, concerned.

"Would you like me to make you a drink? Tea maybe?"

"Tea would be good. Thank you, Tom. You'd better shut the door, you're probably not supposed to be having anything to do with either of us right now."

After making tea for them both, Tom parked himself opposite Kate. "Feeling a bit better now?"

She sipped her tea and managed a smile. "Yes thanks, Tom. I think the painkillers are beginning to work. This tea is certainly helping."

Tom looked at her long and hard, as if making up his mind about something. "Kate, my dear. What happened last night. It wasn't all your fault, Daniel's neither. I been kicking myself all night for not telling you earlier. Might have prevented what happened if I had."

"Telling me what?"

"About the mistress, Penelope. It was so long ago, I didn't reckon it was important any more. But all this has gone to prove how wrong I was. Back in 1915 it was, late in the year, maybe August or it might even have been early September. There was a storm, a thunder storm. Like the one we had back along, only worse, certainly the worst I can remember. It was only two or three days since your Jamie had re-joined his regiment. Sometime in the middle of the night the whole house was woken by such a terrible screaming, it sounded like an animal caught in a trap. I heard it from my room at the top of the house and it fair scared the living daylights out of me I can tell you.

"Next thing, the whole place is roused and there's people rushing about all over the place trying to discover where and what the noise was coming from. It was my dad Brian what found out in the end. It was Miss Penelope. Her was sitting on the floor inside that blasted well chamber, screaming and howling like she'd never stop. There was nothing could be done with her, nothing that would stop that dreadful noise. So they called for the doctor and, after he'd tried everything he knew, he sent for an ambulance and they took her away to Wells, to the mental hospital."

Kate could only listen with horror. "Dear God. And did you ever find out what happened to make her like that?"

Tom shook his head. "No. Never. There was lots of theories of course. Everything from the sound of the thunder echoing in the well and affecting her brain somehow, to her having a nightmare and only waking up afore she fell down the hole. But none of them made a lot of sense, tell the truth. Maybe it was the grief of losing her brother catching up with her, I don't know. Whatever it was, it took six months for her to recover enough to come home. And even then she were never quite the same. She seemed to go from a flighty girl to a grown woman in that time, and a sad woman too, if you ask me. Then, to make matters worse, her father, old mister Edward, he upped and died early the following year."

"So she was left completely on her own."

"Aye, lass. There was just her and my mum and dad, and me of course, with a handful of servant girls. Any of the men what weren't already gone off to the war, drifted away to jobs in the cities. Nothing was ever the same after 1918. It wasn't just that all the young men were gone, it was as if we'd entered another age and everything we'd once thought important didn't matter no more. But she kept going, did the mistress. Holding the place together with her apron strings is how my old ma used to put it."

As he tailed off into silence, Kate discovered that her headache had settled down behind the cushion of the pain killers.

"So how has she been since then?"

"Oh, up and down like I already told you. Every now and then things get on top of her and she goes down again. We used to find her sitting outside that well shaft door in her old rocking chair, muttering away to herself and lost to the world. Then she'd be back into hospital where they'd put her right again before sending her back home. It was never the same twice over. Sometimes she'd hardly be gone a couple of weeks and she'd be back, right as rain, if a little slow on account of the drugs what they give her. Other times it'd take months. But she never did no-one no harm, least of all herself. I suppose that's why they kept on letting her come home, because she weren't in any danger."

"So no-one ever discovered what happened to her in the well chamber?"

"Not to this day. Straight after her father passed, she had all the mortar re-pointed and that bloody great door put on. That was about the time we started taking our water from the spring up on the hill. Why we couldn't have gone on using the well, I'll never know. Anyway, one day the door to the chamber was closed and locked and no-one's set foot in there since, until last night that is."

"Oh God, I'm so sorry Tom. We seem to have been nothing but trouble ever since we got here."

"Like I already told you, lass, it's not all your fault. Something was bound to happen sooner or later. I s'pose you just helped it along a bit." He tried a tired smile that made Kate want to cry. "So, what do you think you'll do with yourself, once you leave here, that is?"

Kate looked at Tom long and hard. "I don't suppose there's any chance that Penelope might change her mind?"

"About you and Daniel?" He shook his head sadly. "No, lass. She's already contacted her solicitor. Don't reckon he was too pleased about being called at home on a Sunday neither. She told him what happened and issued her instructions. No doubt there'll be someone round first thing Monday morning with notices to quit. You might argue about whether a week's long enough notice, but I don't suppose you'll want to stick around with all that hanging over your head."

Kate gave a resigned shrug. "No. You're right. If there's no changing it, we'll have to go. It's not a problem for Daniel, he's already got a flat in Bristol."

"Did you say he's already got a place?"

She nodded. "So what on earth was he doing living here then?"

Kate realised that Tom couldn't have any idea about the complexity of the cave exploration plan and so she explained as best she could how determined the university was to get a look at Howk's Well and how, when someone saw the advertisement for the flat, they jumped at the opportunity.

"There were so many people desperate to get a look at what's going on under Hawkswell, that a few months' rent seemed a small price to pay. Of course, Daniel was happy to move here temporarily because he's got no responsibilities at home, no wife or children, I mean."

Tom sat back with a sigh. "I would never have believed it of him. I always thought he was a bit full of himself, if you know what I mean. But taking on the flat to get access to the well, that takes some thinking about."

"The fact is, he's a kind of geologist that specialises in underground water systems. They thought there might be a subterranean river draining water off the surrounding hills and, if that was the case, it would answer a whole load of questions that have been puzzling them for years."

"And is there a river down there?"

"Apparently, yes. A really powerful one, and a huge lake. Daniel says it's quite beautiful. It was the force of the current that injured the diver last night."

"Well I never. I suppose that accounts for why the old well never dried up and how the water was always so good." Kate nodded. "Don't reckon it'll change much though, even if Penelope was prepared to listen. Maybe one day, when she's dead and buried, they'll be able to get down there again and finish their survey or whatever they calls it. Now, you've explained where Daniel's off to, but what about you, Kate, where do you think you'll go?"

"Oh, don't you worry about me Tom. I'm sure someone will be able to spare a sofa while I find myself somewhere. But I'm going to miss Hawkswell, in spite of everything that's happened. I've so loved living here and would have liked to have stayed much longer."

"And I'll miss you too. Having you around the place has brought it alive again, like the old days, especially with you being related to Jamie and all. I know I was against you and Daniel getting the *Annabella* down from the loft. I was afraid of what it might stir up. But it's been lovely to see her back on the water. I know the mistress liked it too. She's shed years while you've been here, Kate."

After that, there didn't seem to be anything more to say and, after wishing her good luck and asking her to keep in touch, Tom went on his way, leaving Kate feeling more lonely than she would have believed possible. She got dressed and made herself a sandwich and a coffee before sitting and staring out at the afternoon light slowly slipping away from the view that had become so familiar and that she knew she would never be able to forget. And as she sat, she spoke into the gathering gloom.

"Where have you got to, Daniel bloody Lewis? Where are you when I need you most?"

Kate was fast asleep when Daniel woke her at six o'clock.

She had dropped off on the sofa and, when she dragged herself to her feet she was so stiff, cold and thoroughly grumpy she hardly noticed that her headache had gone.

"Jesus Christ, Daniel. Where the hell have you been?" The moment the words were out, she realised her mistake. He looked completely exhausted. Unshaven, his eyes swollen and red, hair all over the place.

"I've been in Bristol, at the hospital with Simon."

"Oh, shit. I'm sorry. Come in. I fell asleep on the sofa and feel awful. How about if I brew some coffee while you fill me in?"

It wasn't a long story. Simon had suffered a hairline fracture to his cheekbone and a nasty gash which needed sixteen stitches. Luckily, his symptoms were pretty much all down to his head injury and not, as suspected, down to any degree of decompression sickness. However, he was going to be kept in hospital for observation until the end of the week.

"He looks a lot worse than he is. One side of his face is just one massive bruise. If you can believe it, he's already talking about getting another shot at the system."

"You mean the well shaft."

"I know. Crazy huh? You'd have thought he'd never want to see the place again."

"And you, Daniel, do you ever want to see it again?"

He shook his head. "Not if it means going through what happened last night, not bloody likely."

Kate slowly ran her finger around the rim of her mug. "So you'll be moving straight back to Bristol then?"

"I guess so. What about you. Got any plans?"

"Oh, don't worry about me. I'll find a patch of floor somewhere while I sort myself out. I'm used to dossing around and it shouldn't take too long to find a place."

Daniel placed his empty mug down carefully and turned towards her. "Why not come and stay at my place, if you'd like to, that is." All Kate could do was stare, open mouthed. "No strings. Just until you find yourself another flat, "I've got plenty of space so you can have your own room. It's a really easy commute to Bath, probably won't take you much longer than it takes from here. Look, this has all been my fault and I know how much you have enjoyed living here. It's the least I can do. How about it?"

When she didn't say anything, Daniel drew breath to try again but, before he could speak, Kate touched her fingers to his lips.

"That's a very kind offer, Daniel. And under the circumstances, I'd be insane to turn it down. But I will only come on certain conditions."

"OK. Fire away."

"First, I pay you rent." He started to object but she stopped him again. "Now listen. I will only stay with you if you let me pay at least what I've been paying here. It's only fair. Call it an Irish thing if you want, but I've always paid my way in this life and I'm not stopping now."

He grinned. "OK. Accepted reluctantly. You said conditions, plural. Are there more?"

"Only one."

"Which is?"

"That we share a bed."

Daniel's face said it all. Aha, she thought. That's stopped you hasn't it?

"But…"

"I haven't forgotten what you said the other night about taking our time and not rushing things, but I can't bear the thought of spending the next days, weeks or months pussy-footing around your flat pretending that we're just good friends. It's been bad enough here this last couple of weeks, and here we've got separate front doors. I'm well on the way to falling in love with you, Daniel Lewis, and I'm also fairly sure you like me a bit – "

This time it was Daniel's turn to hush Kate.

"Not one more word. If we're going to share a bed, which incidentally I'm really happy about, I also have a request."

She widened her eyes and raised her eyebrows.

"Which is?"

"If we are going to share a bed in Bristol, don't you think we ought to get to know each other a bit better first, here at Hawkswell?"

"You mean now, here?"

"Well, we could go next door to my flat, but I think here would be far more comfortable."

"Right now?"

"Right now."

And so Kate led Daniel through to her bedroom and there, by the faint spill of light from the sitting room, they undressed each other, slowly and carefully, all the while staring into each other's eyes and watching for any sign that they were making a mistake.

Kate's sheets were cold and so their first embrace as trainee lovers was more for warmth than anything else. But as the bed warmed up, so did they. For such a physical man, Daniel was surprisingly gentle, almost too gentle once Kate had let herself go and allowed passion to take over.

But soon enough, in the quiet of a Hawkswell evening, to the sound of a cold north wind in the eaves above their heads, their bodies merged for the first time, hard and soft together like a hand in a glove. Their loving, although intense, was quickly spent but in its ending there was neither sadness nor guilt for either of them. Instead, both were filled with an overwhelming sense of completeness and well-being, of a profound satisfaction way beyond that of the flesh.

As Kate lay in Daniel's arms with her head on his chest, she murmured, "I think I'm going to enjoy sharing a bed with you, Mister Lewis." There was no answer because Daniel was already asleep. Kate smiled into the darkness. Maybe this time…

With Daniel's assistance it only took Kate a few evenings to pack. They were happy, domestic times bracketed by shared breakfasts and evening meals. Then, one night as they were drifting off to sleep in each other's arms, Daniel realised that Kate was crying.

He pulled her closer to him. "What's the matter, sweetheart?"

She sniffed and brushed the tears away with a hand. "I don't know, Daniel. This is so not me. I don't cry, I really don't."

He hugged her again. "Is it because we're leaving Hawkswell?"

She let out a sniffling laugh. "Yes and no. Oh, I don't know. Everything's so mixed up. Yes, I'm sad to be leaving here, really sad. I'm going to miss it terribly. But at the same time I'm so happy that we've found each other and that, however things work out, we're going to spend at least some time together. It's such a crazy mixture of endings and beginnings that I get lost in it sometimes."

By Friday evening they were ready to go. Kate drove them both to their favourite pub and treated Daniel to a steak supper. She asked him if he was having second thoughts about her moving in, and got a very old fashioned look in return.

"After these last few nights? What do you think?"

She grinned. "I was only wondering if you were having doubts about your stamina."

He grinned back. "We'll see who cracks first."

Neither Hawkswell, its occupants, nor it's well got a mention that evening. Without any discussion, each of them had decided to treat the evening as a beginning rather than an end. They were all too aware that they would both be leaving a great deal behind when they drove away the next day. Kate would be leaving a whole raft of mysteries surrounding her great uncle Jamie, two valued friendships and, of course, the *Annabella* and her times on the river. Daniel, on the other hand, would be leaving an incompletely explored cave system and all the equipment that remained beneath the house.

Despite numerous entreaties to Penelope's solicitors, during which he came clean about his role with Bristol University and explained fully the significance and potential value of the exploration, he had been unable to gain access to the well chamber. No matter what he said or how he put his case, Howk's Well remained firmly off-limits on pain of dire legal action.

Daniel left for Bristol first thing on Saturday and returned mid-morning with a hired van big enough to take their combined belongings. By one o'clock it was time to go and Kate went off in search of Tom to get him to check over the flats and take the keys. She found him, as expected, in the big greenhouse.

He looked up as she approached and she was shocked at what she saw. He seemed to have aged ten years since she had last seen him.

"Hello Tom. I've come to – "

"Aye, lass. I've been expecting you. Sad day this. I been dreading it all week to tell you the truth. What with the mistress and everything, it feels like… oh, I don't know any more. It feels bad, wrong. It shouldn't be happening but it is and that's an end to it."

"How is Penelope, Tom?"

"No better. Her's not eating again and that's driving my missus crazy. Can't bear it, seeing good food wasted. Her's even worse than back in the summer. I don't know what's going to happen."

"Oh God, Tom. I feel dreadful. I know I should have tried harder to talk Daniel out of it."

"Oh, they'd have got in there somehow, sometime. No, all it's done is brought on something that would have come about eventually, one way or another. Her's been going downhill for years now, although she's been better these last months than I seen her for years." He flapped his hands as if to shoo her away.

"You get on now, Kate. Get on with your own life. From what I've seen, you and Daniel look as if you're getting on well enough together."

Kate did a double take. How could he have known?

Tom explained without being asked. "You've had something about you these last few weeks, a glow like. And I seen the way you two look at each other. Well, good luck to you both. I reckon there must be a lot more to that Daniel than I've seen for myself."

Tom followed Kate from room to room as he made a cursory and obviously reluctant inspection of both empty flats.

"I don't see as how she'll ever let them again, so this is all a bit of a waste of time. But I've got to tell them solicitors that I done it and that's that."

Kate took one last lingering look at the view from her sitting room and handed over the keys.

Tom hesitated at the top of the stairs. "You go on now Kate. We'll say goodbye here. I'd rather not watch you go, if you don't mind."

Kate tried to ignore the glint of moisture she'd seen in his eyes as she swallowed hard and gave the old man a quick hug and a kiss on the cheek.

"Look after yourself, Tom. I'll send you a card with my address." Then she turned and hurried down the stairs and out into the courtyard while she could still see through her own tears.

With a quick signal to Daniel who was all ready to go, she got into her Mini and started up as the van eased its way through the carriage gate and out towards the road. As soon as Daniel was out of sight, she wiped her eyes and blew her nose.

Then, as the foliage closed behind her like a theatre curtain, she caught her final sight of Hawkswell in her rear view mirror. When she drove out through the old lion topped gateposts, she was certain it was for the very last time.

She turned left onto the road to find the van waiting to lead her away to Bristol.

Chapter 19

"I thought you said this place was in need of a woman's touch."

Daniel shrugged as noncommittally as he could manage.

"Well, it suits me well enough."

Although sparsely furnished, Daniel's Bristol flat had quite obviously been thoughtfully renovated and decorated. Kate liked it immediately, more so since it occupied the top two floors of a Victorian terrace and enjoyed fantastic views across the Downs in one direction and Brunel's famously beautiful suspension bridge in the other.

Both the decoration and furnishings were a revelation.

Far from what Kate might have expected of a bachelor pad, what few pieces of furniture there were had been carefully chosen and each bore the hallmarks of great design and craftsmanship. In place of the anticipated, and dreaded, chrome and leather, there was lovingly polished natural wood and woollen fabrics, while the walls were adorned with carefully chosen artwork and hangings.

A huge, high ceilinged sitting room, a dining room, a kitchen and a utility room occupied the lower of the two floors while two spacious bedrooms and a beautifully appointed bathroom were located up in the eaves with roof lights and dormer windows letting in masses of natural light.

Off-street parking, an absolute Godsend in the crowded city, was provided by a gated area of gravel immediately opposite, along with a block of garages to one side, the latter discreetly tucked behind a line of trees.

"It looks a lot better than that from where I'm standing. It's gorgeous. Please tell me you didn't do all the work yourself."

He tried to look humble and failed miserably.

"It's taken five years and there's still a lot to be done."

"Such as?"

"Oh, like the bathroom. I want to re-do it completely, and the stairs and the hallway need doing, and – "

"OK, mister DIY. I get the picture. But honestly, I really like it and I think you've done a fantastic job. What's more important and impresses the hell out of me is that you haven't once mentioned what it cost, or how much it's gone up in value since you renovated it."

Her look indicated a joke in there somewhere and they both laughed until Daniel said, "So that was what you really thought about me when we first met. Some kind of money-obsessed materialist."

Her smile stayed. "I suppose I must have. Maybe it was the car. Or it might just have been that you were so bloody good looking and confident. But if you want a truly honest answer, I don't really know." She ran a hand along the back of a sofa, the fabric warm and sumptuous under her fingers. "It all seems rather stupid now."

Apart from some stunningly beautiful and, in one or two cases, alarming photographs of Daniel dangling from the end of a piece of rope and a few rock and mineral samples, the mass of caving equipment that had cluttered Daniel's Hawkswell flat was conspicuous by its absence.

When Kate asked, he replied, "Most of it's still back at Hawkswell, in the well chamber and down on the beach. To be honest, I've resigned myself to never seeing any of it again. The rest is in my garage." To Kate he looked quietly relieved, as if he really had put the events of the past week behind him. "I can't tell you how good it feels now that you can at last see how I really live. That flat was so embarrassing, so not me."

They stashed Kate's belongings in the spare bedroom and, when they were finished and she saw how full it was, she was quietly relieved that the dreadful prospect of separate rooms was well and truly off the agenda.

Her commute to the *GreenGauge* offices in Bath turned out to be as easy as Daniel had suggested, and allowed them to settle quickly into a comfortable routine. But that routine was shattered barely a week after they had moved out of Hawkswell when she got back to Daniel's flat one evening to find him slumped on the settee, a large glass of scotch clasped in his hand and a half full bottle upright between his feet.

Sounding more than half drunk, he waved her over. "Pull up a chair and get yourself a drink, you're going to need it."

Kate dropped her bag and threw her coat across a chair, wondering what on earth was going on, this was so not like Daniel. She got herself a glass and flopped down beside him.

"OK Daniel, out with it. What's this all about?"

"This, my dear Kate, is all about being shafted, royally rogered and well and truly stabbed in the fucking back. I have been sacked, dismissed, given the push."

"What!?"

"Exactly what I just said. I was right in the middle of a lecture when I was summoned to the Vice Chancellor's office. They were all there, the fucking suits and the personnel twat. Apparently I have… hang on a minute, let me read it to you word for word," he dragged out a crumpled piece of paper from his jeans pocket, "Yes, here we are… I have 'brought the university's good name into question by carrying out a treacherous and deceitful exploration of the well at Hawkswell House in direct contravention of a bona fide court order issued by the owner of said house…' It goes on a bit after that, but the message is clear enough. I have been well and truly stuffed. Thank you very much Miss fucking Penelope fucking Townshend."

With that, he drained his glass and topped it up again from the bottle.

"Oh, Daniel. I'm so sorry." She put her arm around him and pulled his head onto her shoulder. "But I thought the university knew all about the planned exploration. Weren't they paying your rent and everything?"

He sat upright again. "Oh yes, they knew all right. Every bloody detail. It was all agreed, but... you've guessed it, absolutely nothing was in writing. It's my word against theirs and that's one I've got no chance of winning."

"But surely...?"

"The truth is, darling Kate, your Miss Townshend's solicitors threatened to sue the university, which would, in effect have meant dragging them through the courts, unless they dismissed me. It's as simple as that. Bloody vindictive I call it, but there's not a lot I can do. They've paid me up until the end of the academic year when my contract was up for renewal anyway. All I had to do was sign a little piece of paper saying I wouldn't attempt to contest the dismissal."

"And you signed."

"Course I bloody did. I would have had no chance if I'd taken them to an industrial tribunal. Their lawyers would have dragged it out until I either ran out of money or died of boredom. I need the money Kate, to pay the mortgage and buy food and all that shit. Jobs for hydrogeologists are like rocking horse shit so God knows where or if I'll ever get another position like I had here."

Later that evening, after she'd helped Daniel into bed to sleep off the whisky, Kate read through all the paperwork. It didn't look good. She'd see what Andy had to say when she got into the office the next morning, maybe the Institute's legal team could help. But she wasn't hopeful.

Sitting in Daniel's beautiful flat she felt his despair and anger wash over her. Damn Penelope! How dare she!

Summerquest's' legal eagles quickly confirmed that Daniel's dismissal was watertight. His signing the waiver was the clincher, but without it he wouldn't have received the generous settlement, so that was that.

Once approached, Penelope's lawyers were quite happy to drop their threat of legal action against the university, although it was a pointless victory with Daniel already dealt with. When

Kate phoned Hawkswell, hoping to somehow persuade Penelope to intervene, the full reality of what had happened was summed up by Tom Gerrard's tersely delivered speech.

"There's nothing more to be said, Kate. I still don't know why you and Daniel did what you did after everyone been expressly forbidden to leave the place alone. But what's done is done and between you and me, it's damage what can't be put right. Penelope's in a right terrible state and if she don't pull out of it soon, she'll be back in hospital and that'll be the end of it. Much as I had become fond of you my dear – and I am very sorry that things turned out the way they did – my loyalties lie with the mistress and this house, God help both of them. So I hope you'll forgive me if I ask you not to call again. Goodbye."

Kate had a good cry when she put the phone down. Tom's voice almost more than his words had been a final reminder that her brief but wonderful association with Hawkswell, its people and its history, was absolutely and irrevocably over.

For the next two weeks, while Daniel set about some of the long-put-off DIY projects around the flat, Kate tried to put Hawkswell firmly out of her mind and to concentrate fully on what was turning out to be one of the happiest and most contented periods of her life. The more she and Daniel spent time together, the more in love they became.

What had started out as an open ended experiment, soon became something more precious than either of them could put into words. For Kate, the realisation that she had at last met a good looking man with brains was soon overtaken by the discovery that he had a heart and a soul too. She still couldn't quite get her head around the fact that he quite obviously loved her as much she loved him, but she was getting there. The only shadow was that, when Daniel eventually found himself another position – if in fact he could – it would almost certainly require him to relocate. And they both knew that that could mean anywhere from Aberdeen to Albuquerque. Kate would then have to choose between her career and her man. Head against heart. She already knew which way that one would go, but hardly dared to admit it to herself.

Then, one frosty winter morning, Sir Arthur Summers arrived unannounced at the *GreenGauge* office and asked to see her. Andy was at a press conference in London so they were able to use his office.

"Don't look so worried, Kate. I've not come with bad news, quite the opposite, in fact. I have only recently learned how the university treated your Daniel and, to be quite frank, if I had my way, they'd all be strung up by their thumbs. I can't bear double dealing or betrayal. But there we are. I'm not about to take on one of our most august academic institutions, but I would like to pick your brains if I may." Kate nodded, wondering what was coming next. "Daniel is, if I understand it right, a hydrogeologist, correct?" She nodded again. "And, from the rather sneaky research I commissioned, a damned good one too."

Kate reckoned she'd nodded enough and found her voice.

"To be perfectly honest, I wouldn't know. He certainly seems to know what he's doing underground, and the other members of the team respect him."

"Quite, quite. I expect he's busy firing off application letters left, right and centre."

"I know he's registered with some agencies and written to a few colleagues at other universities, but to be perfectly honest, he's thoroughly enjoying himself putting in a new bathroom suite in his flat right now."

Sir Arthur laughed. "Good for him. Glad to hear he's not moping. How do you think he'd react if I offered him a job?"

Kate had just taken in a mouthful of coffee and very nearly choked. "A job? But…"

"OK. Without going into too much detail right – which I can't anyway because this is still only an idea – I'll try and give you the gist. As you know, one of the Institute's biggest areas of involvement is sub-Saharan Africa where one of their biggest issues is getting clean water to drink. We are considering setting up a subsidiary operation to go in and drill boreholes, dig wells or do whatever is necessary to provide clean drinking water where it is most needed. I want someone who not only understands underground water, but who is prepared to work hard and get his hands dirty. The job will eventually be based here in Bristol where all the research and organisation will take place, and it will occasionally involve travelling and working overseas. But he'll need to work from home until the Institute relocates, which I trust won't be a problem. So, do you think he might be interested?"

Kate was so excited that she drove straight up to Clifton to give Daniel the news. His reaction was a crushing disappointment.

"Why in God's name would the Summerquest Institute want me to head up an operation like that? I've got no management experience, no organisational skills – I don't get it Kate. I mean I've never met this Sir Arthur of yours, how on earth can he be so sure I'm who he wants?"

Kate could only repeat what Sir Arthur had said to her, adding, "Look, it might not come to anything. You might hate each other, I don't know. But it's got to be worth meeting him and talking it through. And, for what it's worth, I have complete faith in both of you."

From the moment they first shook hands, Daniel and Sir Arthur Summers liked each other. Neither had any side or false pretensions. They were just two practical, straightforward men, one in need of the other's knowledge and expertise.

"There won't be any organisational skills required," Daniel told Kate later, "He's got people who do nothing but. All I've got to do is track down the water source and figure out the best way of getting to it. And we'll be actually helping people on the ground, Kate. Real people, people who have to walk miles every day to collect a couple of gallons of filthy, muddy water that'll probably kill them in the long term. I can't believe I'm being given such an opportunity to do something I've always dreamed about."

Kate decided it was about time he came back down to earth.

"So what about salary?"

"Oh, we didn't get around to discussing that. I'm sure it will be fine."

As things turned out, it was more than fine.

Sir Arthur confessed to Kate many months later that Daniel's seeming indifference to the remuneration aspect of his job offer absolutely guaranteed him the post, adding, "Although there's not many people I would advise to be so cavalier when discussing personal financial matters."

Daniel's spare bedroom, crammed to the ceiling with Kate's stuff, was the only realistic choice for a work space. They were faced with two choices, either find somewhere else to store it all or, perhaps more seriously, spread it around the flat, integrating Kate's belongings with Daniel's.

In the end, it was never even discussed.

Kate merely started to unpack some of her boxes, leaving Daniel to find homes for all the lamps, books, ornaments and cushions, and everything else that personalises a person's home.

It turned out to be a lot more fun than either could have foreseen, with a lot of fooling around. Obviously valued and personal items were held up as 'Hardly fit for a jumble sale, this,' or, 'What do you reckon, throw this in a skip?'

And so 26B Clifton View became Kate's home as well as Daniel's.

From that moment on, it seemed to both of them that any question of their living apart, or anywhere else in the near future was well and truly settled.

Daniel started working for the Summerquest Institute on Monday the 17th December 1979, seven days since Mother Theresa of Calcutta was awarded the Nobel Peace Prize, and less than 24 hours after two remote controlled car bombs in Northern Ireland killed five British soldiers.

The one thing that did detract from his first day in his new role was that he and Kate had not yet agreed how they were going to spend Christmas, a mere eight days away.

When, later that evening, stretched out together on the sofa, Daniel at last confronted Kate with the need to discuss the immediate future, her response came as a shock, but only in the degree to which it matched his own feelings.

"I don't want to even think about the future because this…"
She spread her arms wide to encompass the two of them,
Daniel's sitting room, their entire situation, "…the present, is all
so good. It feels as if making any kind of plans would be
tempting fate, leaving ourselves open to disappointment. I know
it sounds crazy, Daniel, but it's just the way things feel, how I
see it. What we've found was so unlooked for and is now so
precious, I – "

Daniel pulled her to him, cradling her head on his shoulder
and stroking her hair. "It's the same for me. More so than you
can imagine. And I understand what you're saying, I really do.
Look, I've got a suggestion."

Kate shifted in his arms so that she was lying on her back,
looking up into his face. "Which is what?"

"Well, you know how we've been avoiding making plans for
Christmas?"

"Ye-e-e-s."

"How about if we go our separate ways? You go to your
parents, like you normally do, and I'll go to mine."

She slapped on a frown and pushed out her bottom lip. "So
you don't want to spend Christmas with me, is that it?"

Daniel had to look hard before he realised she was pulling
his leg. "It'll only be for a couple of days after all, then I've got
to get back to work and so have you. We'll spend New Year
together. How does that sound?"

Kate reached up and kissed him softly.

"Perfect. To be honest, I've been dreading talking about it
because I've known all along I couldn't possibly let my folks
down. I guess it must have been the same with you. This way we
won't be apart for too long and everyone will be happy. So tell
me, what do your parents know about me?"

Daniel looked into her eyes and took a chance. "Probably as
little as yours know about me."

Kate grinned back at him. "Absolutely nothing is my guess.
A while ago I told them that I'd got some high flying university
lecturer for a neighbour and that he was a bit of a flash git and
not my type at all. I'll have to break it to them someday, but

maybe it can wait a bit. Back to that tempting fate stuff I suppose. So how much do yours know?"

"The same. There wouldn't be any point, even if I did tell them. They wouldn't be interested."

Early on Christmas Eve, Daniel dropped Kate off at Bristol airport for her flight to Dublin and headed east up the M4 towards Marlow and the familiar but tedious ritual of Christmas with his family.

Three days later, Kate exited the airport arrivals gate and threw herself into Daniel's arms with so much passion and energy that he nearly went over backwards.

"I think we'd better start making plans in earnest because I don't want us to be apart again, not even for three days. God, I've missed you, Daniel Lewis."

And as they clung to each other, oblivious of the crowds surging around them, Kate realised that the old adage, home is where the heart is, wasn't so much bollocks after all. Right then, in the middle of a busy airport concourse, Daniel's arms felt like the best home she had ever known. And that was a very pleasant feeling indeed.

Apparently Daniel felt the same because he took her straight from the airport to a restaurant in Clifton for a romantic, candle-lit dinner over which they swapped Christmas experiences. Although the dry and restrained affair Daniel had had to endure in Buckinghamshire could never hope to compete with Kate's warm and ebullient family Christmas in Ireland, both events had one thing in common, a participant who would much rather have been somewhere else.

Kate summed up her feelings. "Much as I adore my parents and the rest of my family, that was the first time I've not cried when I left, I so wanted to get back here to you. But there was something else that kept bothering me all the time I was away, I kept thinking of Hawkswell. I really miss the old place. I'd been so looking forward to spending the winter there, maybe sharing Christmas with Penelope and Tom. Oh, Daniel, I do hope they're going to be OK."

Daniel couldn't think of anything meaningful or helpful to say, maintaining what he hoped would appear as a sympathetic silence. In his heart, he was convinced Penelope would end up in a nursing home and Tom and May in a council flat. Kate suddenly reached in her bag and pulled out a brown manila envelope.

"God, I nearly forgot. Mum has been doing a whole lot of research about Jamie. It's been driving her nuts because she wasn't getting anywhere. Then she tracked down a genealogist in London who specialises in the First World War. You'll never guess what he turned up."

With a flourish, she pulled out an A4 photocopy.

"Jamie's service record."

She turned it round so Daniel could see.

To his surprise, most of the sheet was blank.

It had Jamie's full name at the top, his service number, his date of enlistment and his initial rank, Private. His place of residence was given as Hawkswell House and he was listed as being a Naturalised British Subject. Daniel guessed that that was one of the strings that Edward Townshend had pulled so that he could join up. His mention in despatches and his promotion to Sergeant were also briefly detailed. Then Kate leaned across and pointed to the bottom of the page.

"So what do you make of that?"

Daniel's first reaction was puzzlement. "Sorry Kate, but this just looks like a mess. I can't make head nor tail of it."

She pointed again. "It's much clearer on the original although it took a while. See there, in the box marked Discharge, someone has written what looks like AWOL. Absent without leave."

As soon as Kate voiced the words, the letters seemed to leap off the page. Daniel's intrigue suddenly moved up a notch because he could see that AWOL had either been partially erased or scribbled out and two more words, or what could be seen of them, added, one overlapping the other; ESE TED and ISSING.

"Do they say what I think they say?"

Kate nodded.

"Deserted and Missing. Can't be anything else. The trouble is, no matter how hard Mum and I looked, it's impossible to tell which word was written last. The date's no help either because the day and the month have been overwritten so many times only the year is readable, 1915. At least that fits."

Daniel stared long and hard at that potentially damming piece of paper.

When at last he spoke, his voice was quiet and reflective.

"Absent without leave or missing. They're the easy ones aren't they? It's that other word, deserted. It can't be anything else can it? I mean, maybe someone wrote it on the wrong file and then tried to amend it. It surely can't apply to Jamie – can it?"

Kate stared at him, tears beginning to well up in her eyes.

"But he was a hero. He rescued that officer, he was wounded and he'd been promoted. Why would he have deserted? It's got to be a mistake Daniel, it's got to be."

Suddenly she was crying and Daniel was mopping up. "I'm sorry. It's been a long day and then seeing you and, oh, all this… Please take me home, sweetheart."

The flat was warm and welcoming, the trees outside the windows already glittering with frost. The suspension bridge, decked out in lights, looked like a giant Christmas decoration slung across the Avon Gorge. After unpacking and settling herself in front of the fire, Kate asked Daniel what he wanted to do for New Year's Eve, a mere three days away.

At first he hedged, asking her the same question. "No, Daniel. This is your choice, remember. We agreed about each of us going home for Christmas on the understanding that we'd spend New Year here in Bristol. It's your patch, so your call."

He thought for a long moment. "Do you know what I'd really like to do?"

"Go caving?" Kate offered with a sinking feeling.

Daniel laughed. "No. I've had quite enough of that for a while. What I'd really like to do is have a nice meal and a couple of bottles of bubbles and welcome the New Year in right here in this flat with you. Or is that too boring to even consider? In which case — "

Kate reached out and stopped him with a finger on his lips.

"Daniel. You will never cease to delight and amaze me. That is the most beautiful idea and it's not boring at all, it's totally romantic and... God I love you."

They were already tucked up in bed when 1980 arrived, champagne glasses in hand.

"Any resolutions?" Kate asked.

"No, not really. Last year I might have had some, but not this year. There's not much needs changing now. What about you?"

"Oh, loads of the usual – drink less, get up earlier, lose weight, go rowing more often. I could go on and on, but I know it won't make much difference. I have got a serious one, though. I'd like to see Penelope again and maybe find some way to make things up with her."

"You were really fond of the old girl weren't you?"

"Yes I was. I know she was cantankerous, and I'll never be able to forgive her for getting you sacked, but she had something about her. It was almost as if I could see a lot of myself in her. I don't know, I think we could have become real friends if..."

"If I hadn't arrived and spoiled things."

She pulled herself close against him.

"How many times have I got to tell you that if it hadn't been for Hawkswell, we would never have met. No, what happened was just one of those shitty packages that life throws at you every now and then. If Penelope hadn't been so paranoid about letting you guys explore, none of it would have happened. No, it was as much her fault as anyone's. I just wish none of the bad stuff had happened, that's all. And I would still like to do whatever I can to put things right."

It might have seemed like yet another half-baked New Year resolution, but Kate could have had no idea that winter's night just where that determination was to take both her and Daniel.

1980 would see all their lives changed forever.

Chapter 20

GreenGauge became the official mouthpiece of the Summerquest Institute on February 14th 1980 and pretty much every press announcement made at least some reference to either 'a marriage made in heaven' or a 'perfect match'.

For the more senior members of the magazine's staff, including Kate, becoming full time employees of the Institute brought a greatly enhanced package of benefits including a pension plan and health insurance not to mention a welcome hike in salary.

Then, one morning in mid-March, Kate was invited to join Sir Arthur for lunch at the Institute's temporary office suite overlooking Bristol's floating harbour. Although she had already learned that lunch with her new boss invariably meant an increase in her work load, the mission he handed her still came as a shock.

"I want you to find our new headquarters, Kate."

Even as she opened her mouth to give him a hundred reasons why she was the least qualified for such a role, Sir Arthur held up both hands to stop her.

"I know exactly what you're going to say and I disagree completely. I am of the belief that you understand the Institute's aims and objectives, its ethos, better than most. I also believe that you alone have the breadth of vision necessary to see what others might not, a site's potential. I'm not naïve enough to believe that we're going to find somewhere readymade that will suit all our needs right from the off, of course we won't. It might be a green field with not a single building, it might on the other hand be a derelict industrial site, an abandoned farm, a disused hospital. But whatever the starting point turns out to be, it's the final outcome I'm interested in. I've listed a few parameters."

The 'few parameters' ran to six closely typed A4 pages.

As they worked their way through the list, Kate began to understand what Sir Arthur was looking for, not so much a building or even a complex of buildings, he was looking for an entire environment, where the Institute could grow its own food, raise livestock and house its employees. It had to be sustainable, environmentally friendly and, above all, as stimulating a working environment as could be found or created.

"I want us all to be happy there, Kate. I mean everyone, including the canteen staff and the cleaners! We're going to have to deal with some unpleasant situations and some downright nasty people over the coming months and years because big business, especially multinational business is a downright cut-throat affair. When you're facing up to that kind of thing you need somewhere where you can relax and think clearly. I am certain that you know what I am looking for and that you will find the right place eventually. There's no deadline, as long as we're moved in by next Christmas." Kate was relieved to see him smile at his own little joke. "It will take as long as it takes, Kate. Above everything, it has to be right. Good luck."

Kate's first thought, as soon as she got back to her office in Bath, was Hawkswell. At first glance it was ideal. It was only when she started listing its pros and cons, with the negatives easily outnumbering the positives, that she was forced to think again.

The first and biggest of the cons was that Penelope was unlikely ever to be persuaded to sell the place, at whatever price. Next on the list was just that, the price, which would almost certainly end up well outside her budget, especially considering the colossal amount of money that would be necessary to make the place habitable. And there was more, much more.

Regrettably, she realised that the place wasn't even an outside option. One slow stroke of her pen ruled it out of the running. She spent the next few weeks contacting commercial agents throughout Somerset and Gloucestershire and then wading through the resulting piles of details. By the beginning of April she had a shortlist of more or less suitable properties.

These ranged from green field sites, some with planning consent, to empty warehouses, an old saw mill and a disused railway station complete with four hundred yards of track. Of the three that warranted an initial visit, one would take her to a complex of abandoned farm buildings only five miles beyond Hawkswell village.

The day had dawned chilly and damp, more reminiscent of winter than spring, with low cloud draping itself across a landscape sodden from overnight rain. Early hedgerow blossom had been drenched and shredded into sorry looking drifts along the sides of the lanes as Kate drove into the familiar landscape of what she had come to think of as the Hawkswell valley.

Despite reminding herself all the way from Bath that she had no intention of going anywhere near the house, when she came to a fork in the road, she turned left instead of right and soon found herself driving alongside the boundary wall to where it met the gateway to the estate.

Before she could change her mind, she plunged straight into the rhododendron tunnel, compelled by nothing more or less than a desperate desire to set things right.

Kate had no idea what to expect, except that it would probably come somewhere between a cool welcome and a door slammed in her face. She hadn't given it much thought because it was never going to happen.

Except that now it had.

She rang the bell, unsure whether to brace herself or not.

In the event, no-one answered.

Her second and third rings were equally unsuccessful.

She was almost relieved but, having made it so far she felt that she couldn't just drive away. Against all her instincts, she decided to try around the back, hopeful of finding Tom in his usual place in the walled garden.

Just a few paces along the gravel drive, out of the corner of her eye she caught a flicker of movement, a curtain being pulled back in a downstairs window. She turned her head and there, peering out through the drizzle smeared glass was an emaciated face she almost recognised... one that looked as if it had once belonged to Penelope Townshend.

A horrified fascination kept her eyes locked on the figure in the window while the curtain, instead of being dropped back into place, remained pulled back as the face turned away, its profile unmistakable. It was Penelope, but she looked like a corpse.

It seemed to Kate that she must be suffering from some terrible physical illness, surely her depression alone couldn't have brought about such a profound decline. This time she ran up the steps and slapped on the door with the palm of her hand.

"Penelope, it's me, Kate. Please come to the door. I want to know what's wrong. Please!"

She probably would have remained there for the rest of the day, calling and banging, pleading to be let in, demanding to be told something, anything that could explain Penelope's frightening deterioration. One minute, one hour, it was immaterial, as the door at last opened to her onslaught.

It was Tom.

He looked even worse than when she'd last seen him.

When he spoke, his voice was bitter and lacking in any trace of warmth.

"You are not welcome here, Miss O'Donnell. Please leave at once."

He had already started closing the door when Kate shouted through the diminishing gap.

"Tom, what's going on? What's wrong with Penelope? She looks so ill. I must know what's happening!" The door closed with the same muted clatter of locks and bolts it had taken to open it. She thought about banging and shouting some more, keeping on until Tom opened the door again, if for no other reason than to vent some of her frustration and anxiety but, after a brief agony of indecision, she realised she was wasting her time.

But giving up wasn't in her nature. Someone somewhere knew what was wrong with Penelope and what was going on at Hawkswell. All she had to do was find the right person, after which she would get the truth out of them one way or another.

She had just started the car and flicked on the windscreen wipers when, through the cleared arc of glass she spotted Tom, shoulders hunched against the drizzle, striding across the lawn towards the point where the gravel track disappeared into the rhododendrons. He glanced back in her direction, barely a flick of his head, and in that moment she knew he meant to intercept her on her way out to the road.

She started off slowly at first to give him time to get completely out of sight of the house, then drove steadily up the track and on into the shadow of the bushes. He was waiting for her a few car lengths further on. Kate stopped and reached across to open the driver's door. Tom slumped into the seat beside her, dragging with him a smell of damp earth.

"Drive on, Kate. I mustn't be seen with you. Get off the estate somewhere and then we'll talk."

She drove left out of the gates towards Hawkswell village, remembering that there was a layby about a mile beyond the end of the boundary wall. They drove in silence, although the further they got from the house, the less tense Tom appeared.

The layby was empty so Kate parked and switched off the engine. The drizzle had turned to rain by then and it drummed steadily on the car's roof, accompanied by sudden staccato rattles as heavier drops cascaded from the overhanging trees.

She turned slightly in her seat in order to see Tom's face, shocked at how haggard he looked, sitting there beside her, staring straight ahead at the rain washed windscreen.

"Why did you 'ave to come, Kate? Why couldn't you have stayed away?"

Although momentarily relieved to be called Kate and not Miss O'Donnell, she was horrified to hear Tom speaking with the tremulous voice of an old man. So Kate told him about her mission to find a new headquarters for the Institute and that, as she was passing...

He stopped her. "You don't have to explain, lass. It's the house, Hawkswell, that's what brought you back. Though it's taken longer than I thought it would." As he turned his head towards her, she saw that he was smiling. A sad, tired smile quite unlike his usual mischievous grins. She didn't know what to say, just smiled back at him.

"Oh Tom. It's so good to see you."

"And you, lass, and you."

At that, the tears that had been building behind her eyes at last escaped. "What's happening Tom? What's wrong with Penelope? Please tell me."

And so they sat side-by-side in Kate's damp Mini as the rain fell and the windows misted, and Tom painted in the weeks since she and Daniel had been forced to leave Hawkswell.

"Right after that night when – you know, she raged and raged. Never seen anything like it. Me and the missus, we couldn't do nothing right, morning to night. Then, right after you and Daniel left, that was when it got real bad. She got to sitting outside that door again, like I told you about. Now she don't hardly ever eat and never takes the doctor's pills, just flushes them down the toilet I reckon." Tom shook his head.

"She'll not last many more weeks at this rate."

"You mean she's dying?"

Maybe Tom thought it was a stupid question, maybe he found the thought unbearable. The result was that he almost shouted his reply.

"Yes, Kate. She's dying, right in front of our eyes. Fading away and I don't know why, and don't know what to do about it neither." He beat his fists on his knees is anger and frustration, his breath coming in gusts, eyes tight shut as if fighting back his own tears.

Kate reached across and touched his arm. "Oh, Tom. There must be something we can do. Maybe if I – "

He rounded on her then, his misery resounding in every word. "No Kate! You mustn't get involved. That's the very last thing you should do."

"But why, for heaven's sake? I thought she and I had become friends. We got on so well. I thought she really trusted me. I must be able to help somehow."

"I know, lass. I know. Maybe it's because she did trust you. Maybe that's the trouble. She reckons you betrayed her, see, you and Daniel."

He paused, gathering his thoughts. "I don't know how to say this without causing you more hurt, Kate, so I'll say it straight, like. You were the best thing that has happened to Penelope Townshend for many years."

Kate tried to butt in, to protest, but Tom went on. "Hear me out, lass. She didn't want to let those flats, as you know. She had always fought against letting any part of Hawkswell go, no matter what the banks or the bailiffs said. But she was in such a tight spot this time that she had no alternative but to give in to their demands. Then you and Daniel come along and, even though I know she didn't take too much to Daniel, except with his help with the *Annabella* and all that, she did take to you, my dear. And you made her very happy last summer, happier than I've seen her since I don't know when."

There was nothing more to say after that. They were both all cried out, wadded tissues strewn about the foot wells of the car. But despite everything that had been said, Kate got Tom to promise to give a message to Penelope. It was simple enough, she would do anything she could to help. And she would. Kate was at that moment prepared to go to any lengths to put right the wrongs that she and Daniel had perpetrated.

She dropped Tom at the entrance to Hawkswell and drove back to Bristol in the gathering dusk. The rain had eased to a steady drizzle and lights from oncoming cars scattered white sunbursts across the smeared windscreen.

She only remembered her intended viewing as she got back to the Clifton flat. But it didn't seem important any more, nothing did. She couldn't shake off the image of Penelope's ravaged face and Tom's words, "You made her very happy last summer, happier than I've seen her since I don't know when."

They might have made her happy then, but God knows what grief they unleashed when they opened up the well chamber.

It took Kate most of the next day and every last atom of her journalist's skills to track down the relevant health visitor and persuade her to talk, albeit guardedly and entirely off-the-record, about Penelope. What Kate heard filled her with an uncomfortable cocktail of dread and guilt.

The old lady was neither taking her medication nor eating, the growing consensus being that she was rapidly becoming a danger to herself and to those around her. When Kate asked why, she was horrified to hear a catalogue of near disasters – three instances when the fire brigade had been called out to deal with small fires caused by neglected cigarettes, two occasions when Penelope had been stopped while driving without due care and attention around Hawkswell village, on the second of which the car had been impounded. And, worst of all, a recent occasion when she had been picked up by a local GP wandering along the road outside Hawkswell in her dressing gown at four o'clock in the morning.

"There's what they call a case meeting next Monday and, unless there's a significant improvement in the meantime, we may have no alternative but to have her sectioned."

"And what will that mean, exactly?"

"She'll be removed to a secure psychiatric unit for assessment and treatment, I'm afraid. Simple as that."

"And what about Hawkswell and the Gerrards?"

"I'm afraid that I don't have anything to do with that side of things my dear. Now I've already told you much more than I should have and I'm late for an appointment. I'm sure everything will turn out for the best."

And that was that. Calming words from someone who had no doubt seen far worse and dealt with it. Kate, however, was far from convinced that any part of what was happening would turn out for the best. It sounded as if everything was leading to a terrible conclusion and, almost without knowing why, she started hunting through her address book for a particular phone number.

There was someone she could call who might be able to help.

"Mr Cowper, I don't know if you remember me. My name is Kate O'Donnell. Until recently I was renting one of the flats at Hawkswell House."

"Ah yes. Ms O'Donnell. I seem to recall there was some misunderstanding." The Townshend family solicitor sounded exactly as Kate remembered him, dusty and dried up.

"Yes, a dreadful misunderstanding, and I was asked to leave. But that's not why I am phoning. It seems that Penelope Townshend is not at all well and I – . Frankly, I just want to find out if there's any way I can help."

"Ms O'Donnell, I regret that I am not at liberty to discuss Miss Townshend's personal situation with anyone without her express permission. I would have thought that you, of all people, would realise that."

"What do you mean, of all people?"

"Because of your blatant violation of the terms of your lease, of course. You are in breach of contract with the Townshend Estate, as I am sure you are well aware and, as Miss Townshend's solicitor and executor, I represent that Estate."

Kate nearly blew it right there and then. She wanted to tell him to fuck right off and stick his legal head up his legal arse. But she didn't. Somehow she kept it together, took a deep breath and had one more try.

"Mr Cowper. I am well aware of transgressing the terms of my lease and I can't emphasise enough how much I regret doing so. Above anything I wish I could go back and put things right. But, while I lived at Hawkswell House, Penelope, er… Miss Townshend and I became friends, at least that's how it felt to me. I know the Gerrards are doing their best to look after her but they are both elderly and it can't be easy. If they section Penelope, I dread to think what might happen."

The previously quiet voice suddenly acquired a sharper edge.

"Will you please repeat what you just said about Miss Townshend being sectioned?"

"Oh, it's only something I heard."

"From whom?"

"I called Social Services and spoke to someone."

"I want that person's name, this very minute if you please. This is a gross breach of confidentiality and whoever spoke to you will – "

Then it was Kate's turn to interrupt. "Look, I don't know their name and even if I did, I wouldn't tell you. And don't think you can intimidate me either. I'm a journalist and, believe me, I know all about protecting my sources. I'm just trying to help someone that I care about, or are you completely incapable of understanding that?"

This time there was a longer pause, and when George Cowper spoke again, his voice was more controlled.

"I can see you must have gone to some trouble, Ms O'Donnell. Getting information out of the DHSS is not the easiest task in the world. I'm sorry but you have caught me at a rather inconvenient time, I have a client waiting. Perhaps we might meet. I can't promise to answer all or any of your questions, but I too am deeply concerned about the present situation with Penelope Townshend. At the same time you might also be kind enough to enlighten me about the unfortunate sequence of events that led up to all this."

Kate made the appointment and, when she arrived at Strand, Cowper & Geggs' offices the next morning, they were as gloomy and forbidding as she remembered. The welcome she received, on the other hand, was quite unexpected.

Ushered into a comfortable, well-furnished study by a dapper male secretary who looked hardly old enough to be out of school, she was offered coffee and, when it came, was astonished to be presented with a stylish cafetière with all the trimmings including an extravagant selection of biscuits. Mr Cowper arrived five minutes later and immediately insisted that Kate call him George.

Taken aback by the whole set up, she had to speak up. "Mr Cowper, I'm sorry, but this is all rather unexpected. I mean, yesterday I was public enemy number one. I had reneged on a contract with the Townshend family, been thrown ignominiously out of Hawkswell House and, to add insult to injury, there I was extracting confidential information from the DHSS. Would you care to tell me what on earth has changed so much since then?"

The elderly solicitor spread his arms wide in a quiet gesture of contrition. At the same time he edged around the huge desk to sit in a well-used leather chair.

"Nothing at all has changed, my dear Ms O'Donnell. May I call you Kate?" She smiled and nodded. "Everything happened exactly as you said and I am still extremely concerned about the releasing of privileged information regarding my client's medical condition. However, I spent a certain amount of time yesterday evening in conversation with Tom and May Gerrard."

"You actually went to Hawkswell?"

"Yes, I visited the house and what I found there disturbed me greatly." Kate started to describe what she had seen during her own visit but he silenced her with a small gesture. "The situation is precisely as you say, Kate. Penelope Townshend is in an extremely distressed condition and in my opinion, and I suspect that of her medical advisors too, is quite incapable of looking after herself. The Gerrards, as you suspected, are at their wit's end. However, Tom Gerrard did detail for me the relationship you had formed with Penelope during your tenure in her house. He also spoke of numerous acts of kindness on your behalf, Kate, of which I was quite unaware when we spoke yesterday. I therefore apologise unreservedly if my manner was, shall we say, a little brusque."

Kate smiled at his old fashioned politeness. "Apology accepted, George. Although I can't think of anything I did for Penelope that wasn't more than reciprocated. She did all sorts of things for me and I did really think we had become friends, until – "

"Ah yes, until the episode with the well. It would help greatly if you could explain precisely what happened that night, from your point of view. Naturally I have heard the other side of the story."

And so Kate told him everything – from Daniel's original approaches to Penelope regarding Howk's Well, of which he was of course aware, through the initial exploration and then the ill-fated diving expedition. George asked one or two pertinent questions, mostly about technical aspects of the actual exploration, which she did her best to answer. By the time she had finished, she needed another coffee.

After arranging for the refreshments, George Cowper sat for a while as if digesting everything Kate had told him. Eventually he sat forwards in his chair, elbows on his dark suited knees and his liver spotted hands clasped tightly in front of him. This time he spoke slowly and deliberately, his eyes never leaving her face.

"Kate, I know you feel entirely responsible for Penelope Townshend's present condition and, to a small degree of course, you are. But not in the way you think. There is some age-old trauma that links Penelope's psychological condition to Howk's Well, something that occurred when she was a young woman. She had her first breakdown back then, not long before her father's death."

Kate then explained what Tom had told her about Penelope being discovered screaming in the well chamber.

"Yes, I too thought it was grief associated with the loss of her brother that precipitated her illness, but this apparently was not so. No, something occurred during the autumn of 1915 that caused massive and, it seems, irreversible mental damage. In truth, she has never really recovered. There have been numerous breakdowns, interspersed with sometimes quite long periods of apparent recovery. But whatever shadow has followed her down the years, it is directly associated with the well. It's why she has never sold up, you know."

"I didn't know she had ever considered – "

"She hasn't. But we have, her executors and advisers. Hawkswell has been a millstone around Penelope's neck these past sixty years. You've seen the state of the place. No heating to speak of, the roof leaks like a sieve, everything needs a good coat of paint. Poor old Tom has done his best of course, and you know they haven't been paid a brass farthing since I don't know when. That house used to be full of beautiful paintings and furniture, all gone now – sold off piecemeal to pay the bills. She should have got shot of the entire estate decades ago and lived the life of Riley on the proceeds. Not Penelope. She sold odd parcels of land and rented out others. But, just like her immovable stance on the exploration, she has always been adamant that she would remain in Hawkswell until the day she died. I have to say it's quite admirable in a way. That old house has been occupied by Townshends for centuries. Heaven knows what will happen to the place now."

"Sorry, George, what do you mean, now?"

He sighed, long and deep. "From everything I have learned over the past weeks, and from my visit last evening, Penelope Townshend will almost certainly be sectioned on Monday morning and taken into care, probably that very day. Hawkswell House will, after a formal period, become the property of Somerset County Council."

Kate was astonished.

"But how, I mean why?"

"Debts my dear. Unpaid rates, overdrafts and goodness knows what else. The place is mortgaged to its chimney pots. There's a modest amount set aside in a trust to look after the Gerrards, but the house and grounds are spoken for I'm afraid. Of course, I will attend the case conference, I am after all her legal representative. But even I haven't been paid for years."

"But if that's the case, why on earth have you carried on representing her?"

Now he looked away, away from everything in that study. His rheumy old eyes became unfocused, his voice so soft she barely heard his next words.

"I'm afraid I must confess to love, my dear, no more, no less. I fell in love with Penelope Townshend when we first met. She was the most beautiful woman I have ever known, even more so because she cut such a tragic figure back then, so alone, so helpless but so determined. It would have been impossible not to have admired and, I must confess, desired her. But of course it could never be. I was nothing but a junior partner in a country solicitor's practice. She, on the other hand, was then mistress of a country estate, a local luminary you could say. No, there's never been any question of a relationship, but there was one way I could express my love, by making it my duty to look after her by taking care of her interests as best as I could. Do you see?"

Once again, Kate was astonished almost beyond words. "But does she… has she ever known?"

"Oh, good heavens no. I'm quite certain that she has never had the faintest idea, absolutely not. Even when I did my best to talk her out of marrying that dreadful RAF fellow, I am quite certain she believed my concern to be entirely professional." He smiled sadly, sat up straight in his chair as if willing himself back to the present. "But there's nothing more I can do to help her now, Kate. The end has come as I always knew it would. I don't suppose she will last long away from Hawkswell but, to be frank, I don't believe she is aware of very much now. When I visited last night, she didn't even recognise me. At least she will be warm and safe wherever they put her. And I will do my level best to ensure it is somewhere suitable for a lady of her class, if you know what I mean. It won't be easy with no money, but we'll do our best."

He looked so resigned and tragic that Kate wanted to put her arms around him and hug away some of the sadness.

Instead she asked, "Is there absolutely nothing we can do? I mean, can't we get someone to stay with her?"

"With what, Kate? Carers cost money, and Penelope needs round-the-clock nursing care now, although I doubt it would do her much good. No, I must make it my new priority to make sure that the Gerrards are looked after, my duty of responsibility to Penelope Townshend is nearing its end."

Kate gave him a hug when she left, and a kiss on the cheek which he appeared not to mind. She promised to keep in contact and asked him to let her know Penelope's address once she was moved, the Gerrards' too.

Just as she was about to walk away, the old solicitor touched her arm. "From the way you have been speaking, am I to understand that you and this Daniel Lewis are, er... seeing each other?"

Kate laughed. "Very tactfully put, George. And the answer is yes, we have become, let us say, rather good friends."

This time it was the old man's turn to smile. "In that case, will you both please accept my sincerest apologies for the dreadful way the young man was treated by both Penelope and his employer. This office was not involved in any way with that appalling chain of events, the whole thing was orchestrated by a litigation lawyer in London to whom we pass these things whenever necessary. Unfortunately, by the time I became aware of what was going on, it was too late."

Kate told him not worry and further reassured him that things had worked out very nicely for Daniel since losing his job at the university.

Returning to Bristol felt out of the question right then, so she walked down to the river, across Pulteney Bridge and up to the peace and quiet of Henrietta Gardens where she sat on a bench in the warm spring sunshine beneath the heavy pink cherry blossom. There was nothing practical anyone could do, she knew that. But it still felt like walking away, and Kate knew that she would find that desperately hard to live with.

Events turned out exactly the way George Cowper had predicted.

When all the relevant parties convened the following Monday, Penelope was declared to be: 'in such a poor state of mental and physical health as to be a danger to herself and to others'.

Two independent consultants and her GP signed the relevant papers and she was handed into the care of the North Somerset Secure Psychiatric Unit in Wells. Her situation would be reviewed in due course but apparently no-one held out much hope for any substantive improvement. Within two weeks, the

Gerrards were moved to a cottage in the village and Hawkswell House was handed over to the care of a local security company until further notice.

George Cowper and Kate visited Penelope as soon as she was 'stabilised' but it was a largely wasted journey. The poor old lady was so sedated she could barely speak and when she did it was only a meaningless muttering. The staff were disgustingly jolly and called her Penny, which was enough to make Kate want to vomit. No-one was prepared to give them any kind of prognosis, trotting out a stream of pointless platitudes along the lines of 'time would tell' and 'miracles do happen'.

Kate didn't like the sound of miracles. Any condition that required such a level of intervention was probably way beyond their curative abilities.

She visited the Gerrards a fortnight after their move and found Tom disconsolately slashing his way around a tiny weed choked garden with a billhook,

"S'no bigger than a postage stamp this, and look at it. It'll take years to get rid of these weeds and get the soil back in condition. Still . . ." he nodded in the direction of the cottage back door, "May's happy enough now. Never did like the old place much. She'll be fettling 'til next Christmas. Terrible shame about the mistress though, watching her carted off like that. We've got some of her favourite things here all boxed up safe and all. Lord knows what'll happen to the house. We've done our best but mice and birds'll be through the place in no time."

Kate stayed for a cup of tea, amazed at the difference in May Gerrard. The woman seemed to have shed years of worry and bitterness. The kitchen was small and neat, with newly sewn curtains and it looked as if those two were all set to enjoy a long overdue retirement. She felt glad for them and promised to stay in touch.

Driving away from the Gerrard's cottage, Kate felt as if the whole Hawkswell saga was drawing to a rather poignant conclusion.

As things turned out, she couldn't have been more wrong.

Chapter 21

Another month passed, during which Daniel settled into his new job along with the unfamiliar routine of working at home, while Kate was fully occupied with her increasingly difficult search for Summerquest's new headquarters.

One afternoon she received an urgent phone call.

Kate recognised George Cowper's lugubrious tones straight away and braced herself for bad news about Penelope. But her fears were short-lived since it seemed she was fine and, almost unbelievably, far more alert than the last time she had seen her. George sounded particularly chipper because Penelope had recognised him on his last visit, although only fleetingly. The reason for George's call was Hawkswell House itself.

"Things have resolved themselves in the manner I feared, Kate, The bank, as I fully expected, found itself unable to continue their support under the circumstances and I am sorry to have to inform you that they have foreclosed. What remains of the Hawkswell Estate has been passed into the hands of the local authority."

It may have been inevitable, but it still came as a shock.

"And Penelope? Surely there must be something put aside for when she comes out of hospital?"

The pause that followed was long. When at last he spoke, George's voice was soft with pain.

"Penelope won't ever come out of hospital Kate. She is 86 years old now and so very frail. To be honest my dear, I am astonished she's lasted this long. And that brings me to the real reason for my telephone call. I am convinced that the only thing keeping her going is a profound belief that she will soon be returning to her beloved Hawkswell. It seems that going home is all she ever talks about. I am very much afraid that if she ever learns that the house is no longer hers, the shock might very well be enough to kill her."

"So we make damned sure she never does find out."

"Absolutely. I have already spoken to the Gerrards as well as the staff at the hospital and they all agree that it would be in her best interests if she isn't told. You are the only other person who is likely to visit her before... well, before her time runs out."

Kate agreed of course. It also seemed that, considering the old lady's condition, it might not prove too difficult to keep the news from her. Kate promised to drop in for coffee when she was next in the area and was about to say goodbye when she thought of one final question.

"Sorry, George, but have you got any idea what the local authority are planning to do with Hawkswell?"

He cleared his throat as if he didn't want to give voice to his next words.

"Yes, I'm sorry to say that I do. They are recommending that the house be declared derelict and unsuitable for renovation. They are going to carry out a full structural survey of the house prior to making any decisions about its future. Things, I'm afraid don't exactly look bright for the old place."

Kate thought so too.

A week later, one of Kate's property viewings took her to Shepton Mallet, making it an easy diversion to Wells to visit Penelope. When she had first visited, the old lady had completely failed to recognise her and it was difficult to imagine that anything would have changed. But the difference could hardly have been more dramatic. Penelope had put on weight, her hair had grown and thickened into a wonderful silver mane and, best of all for Kate, she was recognised the moment she walked through the door of the day room.

"Kate, my dear, dear Kate. How wonderful to see you. Come, sit by me. My goodness you do look well."

Surprised would be a gross understatement. Kate was knocked sideways. It was as if the awful events that had led up to her and Daniel's departure from Hawkswell had never happened.

"First, can I just say how dreadfully sorry both Daniel and I am about everything that happened back at the House with the well and everything."

To her astonishment, Penelope actually laughed. "Oh, my dear. Surely it is I who should be apologising. I treated you both disgracefully. I should have let them do their exploration years ago. I can't think what it was that stopped me doing so, although there are a lot of things I can't really remember these days. Being here is like a holiday, you know, my first since I don't know when! I feel as if a huge load has been lifted from my shoulders. Now, tell me all your news."

Kate quickly recovered from her astonishment at the change in Penelope and started telling her all about how happy she and Daniel were in Bristol and about their plans for the future.

But then Penelope started to describe her own plans for returning to, and renovating Hawkswell. Kate nodded and said yes, what a wonderful idea, and won't the old place look so much better, knowing it all to be an impossible fantasy. She had to force herself to remember that, as far as Penelope was aware, she still owned Hawkswell, and imagined that the Gerrards had remained there to keep everything together until her return. Kate did suspect Tom and George Cowper's influence there. They would both have told Penelope almost anything to keep her happy. She also discovered that George had visited barely a week earlier and that he came regularly. Good old George, bless him. Right then she determined to give him a call the very next day. She also thought about dropping in on the Gerrards too, but that might have to wait for another time.

Kate left Penelope looking tired but happy in the benign fantasy world she'd created for herself, much relieved by the improvement in her condition and not suspecting for a moment what a pivotal part the old lady still had to play in all their lives.

George Cowper was engaged with a client when Kate phoned the following Friday and she didn't get round to calling him again until she was back in the office on Monday afternoon.

He was as gracious and polite as ever and delighted to hear that she had visited Penelope.

"I suppose she told you about all her plans for the old house. Poor old thing. To her it's only a matter of time before she returns and everything will be as before, with plenty of money and staff to work the place, just like the old days. Luckily she has no sense of time, or so they tell me. All they have to do is tell her that she'll be going home next week and she's happy. It's only that next week never quite arrives. It is all very sad."

"But she's looking so much better than last time I saw her."

"Oh, yes. They're very good in there, very caring. And they're very fond of her really. She keeps them all amused with stories from the early days at Hawkswell. It's amazing how much she can remember. There's not much wrong with her long term memory apparently, it's just that she never quite knows what's real and what isn't any more."

"So she'll never be able to leave there."

"I don't think so. No, I'm sure not. I agree she looks a lot better, but her heart's not as strong as it was." He gave a dry chuckle. "It looks as if she'll outlive dear old Hawkswell though. Ironic isn't it?"

Kate didn't quite catch what he'd said at first and asked him what he meant.

"The old house, it is going to be demolished after all."

"What! So soon?"

"I'm afraid so. The council has had the place surveyed and, even after being empty for such a short time, it has deteriorated to such an extent that it has been condemned. The years have taken a terrible toll, Kate. There's nothing much else they can do."

"So what's to become of the rest of the estate?"

"As I suspected, they've decided to parcel it up into lots for auction. It's a fantastic situation, there by the river. The lots will be snatched up for development, luxury houses for London commuters I shouldn't wonder."

Kate's immediate reaction was an overwhelming sadness. The thought of the old house being bulldozed was bad enough, but she couldn't bear the idea that such a wonderful place might be turned into a housing estate, luxury or otherwise.

She wondered if there might just be one very outside chance that Hawkswell could be saved.

Two hours later, she was in Sir Arthur's office relating to him every last detail she could remember about the house and its estate, taking particular care not to under-emphasise the scale of the investment that would be needed to put the place right.

The very next day, Sir Arthur and Mary Summers, Kate and Daniel were on their way to meet with the county land agent at Hawkswell. Luckily, they were blessed with a beautiful day for their visit, otherwise the shock of seeing what had become of Kate and Daniel's fondly remembered former home would have been far worse than it actually turned out to be.

The first noticeable difference was an ugly chain link fence topped with multiple strands of barbed wire, easily visible over the top of the boundary wall. At the entrance, a pair of similarly uncompromising gates had been installed a couple of yards beyond the two lion topped pillars. A uniformed security guard, his van parked to one side of the drive, unlocked the massive padlock on the gates and let them in.

The sight that met them as they emerged from the tunnel of greenery came as a shock to both Kate and Daniel. Whereas the view hadn't changed fundamentally, the appearance of the house was so radically altered that it seemed to affect the rest of the landscape.

In place of the three rows of mullioned windows, there were now blank slabs of chipboard with garish black, red and white warning signs. The meadows and lawns looked sadly forlorn, studded with dandelions and thistles, the fresh spring grass overgrown, rank and untended.

Greeted at the front entrance by a team from the agency, Sir Arthur waved aside offers of thermos coffee, insisting that they get straight on with the tour. Kate's spirits sank as they were forced to don safety helmets and high visibility jackets before entering. As she followed the group into the hall, the reek of damp and mould was almost as depressing as the damp chill of the place. Green tinged daylight from the lichen covered skylight exposed a scene of utter desolation. Bare walls were patterned with paler patches where pictures had once hung while the floor itself was littered with the detritus resulting from the structural survey – strips of damp wallpaper, discarded slabs of wood panelling and the dusty remains of patches of plaster all mixed in with a liberal scattering of pigeon and mouse droppings.

One of the agents handed out powerful torches and the tour began on the ground floor. As soon as she stepped into the first pitch black corridor, Kate was overwhelmed with nausea and giddiness. She turned immediately, heart hammering, and headed back towards the front door, closely followed by an anxious Daniel.

Halfway down the entrance steps, she sat down heavily, head between her knees. Daniel sat beside her and stroked her back.

"Hey Kate, what's up?"

She took Daniel's hand and gave it a reassuring squeeze while she tried to get her breathing under control.

After a while she sat up. "Jesus, I wasn't expecting that. Must have been the smell of all that damp and rat pee. I'm fine now I'm in the fresh air, but I really don't fancy going back inside again, it's all too depressing." She leaned against Daniel who gave her a reassuring hug.

"That's OK. You stay here while I go and find Sir Arthur and tell him what's happened. He'll understand, don't you worry."

As soon as Daniel had left, Kate sat and recovered for a while before getting up and walking out into the centre of the parking area. From there, the house looked even more sad than it had from a distance. She wondered if it was the contrast between the clean looking slabs of wood covering the windows and the old, lichen covered stonework? At one of the downstairs windows she checked how it had been boarded up. Knocking the panel with her fist she could tell that it was a substantial slab of timber and firmly bolted in place. There were no gaps around the edges for a crowbar to gain a purchase.

They really don't want anyone getting in here, she thought.

Maybe they're afraid of squatters, or perhaps they have to be doubly careful because of the remoteness of the place. She reckoned it would take some serious hardware to break through one of those panels. After a couple of minutes, Daniel re-joined her, suggesting they both take a look at the walled garden. Kate wasn't so sure.

"Do we have to? I'd rather remember it as it was. It'll be in a hideous state after being abandoned for the whole winter."

But Daniel insisted. "Yeah I know, but we're going to have to show the others. It's one of Hawkswell's bestselling points no matter what state it's in."

When Daniel reached the archway, Kate was two paces behind him when he stopped dead in his tracks. She stepped to one side to see why he had come to a halt so suddenly and almost wished she hadn't.

It couldn't be, it just couldn't. She had to be dreaming.

The garden was immaculate, every bed planted out, cloches in place and neat rows of runner bean canes with slim new tendrils curling up from the ground. It looked exactly as it had when she and Daniel first arrived at Hawkswell.

The only problem was that the place had been completely sealed off from the outside world for nearly four months.

Fighting down a chilling wave of superstitious awe, Kate grabbed Daniel's hand.

"How can this be Daniel?"

He gave her hand a squeeze. "Maybe there's someone squatting here."

Kate slowly shook her head and whispered, "Then they must be as good a gardener as Tom Gerrard."

They walked slowly between the beds, each one neatly labelled – carrots, spring onions, courgettes, parsnips. There were early lettuces under glass, neat squares of herbs and even a border of daffodils and narcissi for cutting. Daniel stepped into the greenhouse and called for Kate to join him.

"Look at that lot. Now tell me this is the work of a squatter."

Laid out on the benches were serried ranks of seedlings, all freshly misted, looking as if they'd only been pricked out a few hours before.

Kate looked around and grinned up at Daniel. "Someone is looking after this place and I'm pretty sure I know who."

"Hang on a minute, Kate! The place is locked up tighter than –"

"It's Tom, of course. There can't be many gardeners around here anywhere near as good as him. I reckon he's done a deal with the security firm and got himself a key. Otherwise he's found a way through the fence. We're only a half hour walk away from the village across the fields. And last time I visited him and May, he was complaining about what a tiny garden they've got. You wait and see. We'll drop in on them later and you see if I'm not right."

They caught up with the rest of the party at the front of the house as they emerged into the sunlight. Sir Arthur was the last to leave and he pulled Hawkswell's front door firmly shut behind him. As the heavy oak door thumped into its frame, something deep in the bowels of the house shifted and slipped. Anyone who heard the faint rumble of falling masonry dismissed the sound as that of a passing lorry or an aircraft high overhead. The party made their way around to the courtyard where Kate asked them to pause for a moment.

"I think there's something you ought to know before we go any further. Beyond the courtyard, there's a walled kitchen garden which used to be the pride and joy of the place. I don't know quite how to put this, but –"

As she hesitated, Daniel took over. "What Kate's trying to say is that someone, as yet unidentified, has been letting themselves in and maintaining the garden. It's immaculate and came as quite a shock when we saw it, I can tell you." Naturally, the party headed straight for the garden.

It was Mary Summers who encapsulated everyone's feelings.

"It's like a precious stone in a tired, old setting. It's quite beautiful, as if it's somehow the soul of the house. What did you say the name of the original gardener was?"

Kate answered as noncommittally as she could.

"Er, Tom Gerrard."

"He sounds like quite a character. I'd like to meet him some day."

By the time they had dragged themselves away from the walled garden and completed a full circuit of the estate, Kate was convinced that Sir Arthur would not be interested in Hawkswell as his HQ. The sheer amount of work and expense required on the house alone would surely rule it out, let alone the prodigious effort that would be needed to put the grounds back into any semblance of order. It seemed that Daniel felt the same when he spoke quietly to her while the others were talking together.

"It all looks rather forlorn doesn't it? I know it wasn't too up together when we lived here, but it looks horrendous now."

Kate agreed that the only exceptions had been the garden and the river.

"They almost had to drag Lady S away from both. But you're right, I'm not sure that even Summerquest has got the sort of money needed to put all this to rights."

While the Summers were engaged in wrapping up with the county land agents, Daniel and Kate excused themselves so that they could go down and take a look at the boathouse. It remained much as they had left it four months ago with the addition of a new pair of very solid looking doors, a serious looking padlock and a large notice stating that the building was 'Strictly Private Property' and 'Protected by Guard Dogs'.

Daniel tried to peer through a crack in the old weathered boards.

"I wonder if the *Annabella* is still up in the loft."

Their reverie was interrupted by a shout from up by the house. It was one of the agents beckoning them. When they got near enough to hear what he was saying, he told them that Sir Arthur was ready to leave.

"Oh well," said Kate, "Let's go and get it over with."

As the Bentley pulled away, Sir Arthur was the first to speak.

"That must all have been quite difficult for you two. The way you have each described the place, it sounded as if you had fond memories of your time there."

After a quick glance, Kate let Daniel answer for them both.

"Yes, it was sad seeing it as it is now. It was a lovely place to live back then, although I'm not sure I fully appreciated it at the time. I was too wrapped up in the well exploration. I don't reckon I helped Kate to enjoy it to its fullest extent either, especially as it was all down to me that we got thrown out on our ears."

At that point Kate decided to get what she was certain was going to be bad news out of the way as quickly as possible.

"So what did you think of the place?"

She addressed her question to both Sir Arthur and Mary Summers, who were seated opposite her and Daniel on the wide leather rear bench seat. After taking a moment to gather his thoughts, Sir Arthur delivered his verdict.

"The roof of the main house is in a parlous condition, likely to come down at any moment, which is of course the reason why the place has been condemned. And to be honest, the rest of the structure isn't in a much better state. The grounds would take years to get back even to how you described them. Added to that, the council is asking far too much for the place…" So that's that, Kate thought. Then Mary Summers leaned forward with a conspiratorial grin.

"But we'll get our legal team onto them straight away. They'll beat them down to a sensible price in no time." Kate must have looked as if she'd been punched in the head.

"You mean – ?"

"Of course," Mary said, widening her smile, "We love it. It's quite perfect. We have already set the wheels in motion."

Luckily, Bentleys are equipped with liquor cabinets and a little fridge. It was equally fortuitous that Sir Arthur had laid in two bottles of Bollinger just in case the trip turned out to be a success. They were able to kick start their celebrations on the way back to Bristol. It turned out that it was the setting that clinched things in the end.

Kate should have known really. You can do virtually anything with stone, bricks and mortar, turn a building into whatever you want it to be. But the setting, its position in the landscape, there was nothing you could do about that. And Hawkswell's position was, they all agreed, nothing short of magnificent.

Chapter 22

During the flurry of activity over the next few weeks, one meeting in particular would play a pivotal role in forthcoming events. It was between Sir Arthur Summers, Kate, and Simon Jenkins, the newly-appointed landscape architect who had been handed the responsibility of getting Hawkswell's grounds back into shape.

Sir Arthur's conference table was strewn with maps, plans, drawings and every reference book Kate had been able to find that made even the most passing reference to the Hawkswell estate.

The Summers' already well-voiced intentions to preserve as much of the original character of the house as possible led to Sir Arthur's opening comment.

"The formal gardens were originally laid out by Harold Peto, isn't that right Kate?"

She glanced quickly at her notes. "As far as we can tell, in 1880, yes. Although it was never considered to be one of his best."

"And there's nothing other than its archaeological footprint to tell us what it looked like?"

"Again, as far as we know. There may be photographs or even the original plans, but the only person likely to know where they might be is Penelope Townshend."

Simon made a suggestion. "What about that gardener chap you mentioned, Tom Gerrard? Might he know something?"

Kate nodded, "Yes, he's certainly worth a try. The Gerrards also have some of Penelope's personal possessions at their cottage, a fair amount from what he's told me. There could well be something amongst it all."

"Right," said Sir Arthur, "Then we need to speak to Mister Gerrard, and the sooner the better. Can you arrange it please Kate, either here or at Hawkswell, I don't mind which?"

As the meeting wound up and Kate prepared to contact Tom and May, she realised that they would have no idea that the house was being purchased by the Institute. When Kate accepted an invitation to afternoon tea at 3.15 prompt, she could hardly suppress a giggle.

The day was wet and windy, so instead of taking their tea on the little patio area, now filled with an array of potted plants that would have done credit to the Chelsea Flower Show, they sat around a coffee table in the cottage's tiny sitting room. Kate felt an unexpected pang when presented with a plate of May's freshly baked cakes.

When she outlined the Institute's plans for the renovation and conversion of Hawkswell, both Tom and May were less than enthused, their shared view that 'someone', presumably Sir Arthur, had 'more bloody money than sense'.

Tom was quite forthright. "Whole bloody place is rotten through and through. Why don't they just knock it down and start over? It isn't as if there's much worth preserving after all."

Kate tried to defend Sir Arthur's decision.

"I know it's going to take a lot to put the place right, Tom. But that's part of the Institute's ethos I suppose, to repair rather than throw away. I mean, who fixes things nowadays? As soon as something fails we just bin it and go straight out and buy a replacement." She caught Tom's look and laughed. "All right, I know neither of you do that. I reckon some of your plant pots must be over a hundred years old, and the same applies to May's jam jars. But that's my point. There's nothing wrong with them, all they need it a bit of TLC. In a way, it's the same with the house."

"That place needs a bloody sight more'n a clean," May muttered.

"Is that why this Sir Arthur of yours is so keen on renovating the place?" Tom asked.

Kate nodded. "I think so, yes. He wants to put it all back as close as possible to how it was in its heyday."

"So he'll be hiring lots of servants and gardeners and grooms and all those what kept it like that, will he. At a few shillings a week and their keep. That's the only way he'll ever get it back how it was, by exploiting people. Take that blasted formal garden what used to be out the front of the house. My old dad used to have one man working full time right through the spring and summer keeping it up to snuff. And for what? There weren't nothing to eat come from it. All it was there for was to make the blasted house look nice."

Kate's heart sank. She hadn't reckoned on such a negative response. She was working out how to respond when May pitched in.

"There's nothing to be served by going backwards. All this fashion for preserving things like they used to be years ago, it don't make no sense. Like all those folk what want to bring back steam trains. Bloody fools. They never had to wash their clothes after a journey to get out the smuts. Even then, when you hung the washing out to dry, it used to get covered in soot if you were anywhere downwind of the blasted things. I don't understand why you young people can't be happy with what you got. It's a damned sight more than we ever had."

In a rather desperate attempt to change the subject, Kate asked how they were enjoying life in the village.

"I ain't been so happy since I don't know when. I know that Tom here misses his garden and that…"

A look passed between them that immediately confirmed Kate's suspicions about the walled garden.

"But I don't miss one single thing about that Godforsaken house, I can tell you. Freezing cold most of the year and full of bugs and heaven knows what else in the summer. And that bloody Penelope, always – "

Tom had obviously heard enough. "Now I'm sure Kate's got a lot better things to do than listen to us ramblin' on, my dear."

Kate smiled nervously. "Well, I'm afraid there is something we need to talk about. But, after what you've said already, I'm not sure I dare mention it."

Tom reached across and patted her hand. "Oh, come now lass, you wouldn't have come if you was that worried."

She grinned again. "It's about that, er, formal garden that you mentioned. The one in front of the house. Well, the Summers want to recreate it and they would very much welcome your help, if you would be willing, that is."

Tom sat for a moment and Kate could see that he was struggling with a whole raft of conflicting emotions.

"She sold that garden you know, lock stock and barrel. All the plants, the shrubs, the paving, the statuettes, everything. She was forced to, I know. She hadn't got two pennies to rub together and there was all sorts of stuff needed putting right. It went to some stinking rich bloke in Hampshire I think it was. Wanted it as a present for his wife, I ask you. Back in the '60s it were. Whole load o' bodies turned up in a fleet of lorries and in less than a week it was all gone, just a sea of mud and lorry ruts left. I know I said I hated it, and in a way I did. It was a hell of a lot of work for not a lot of return if you understand me. Maybe if the place had been open to the public, it might have made sense, but it weren't. All we was trying to do was keep things running as well as we could afford to. That's always been the trouble with Hawkswell and the mistress, she never wanted to change nothin', just wanted to keep it all how it always had been.

"But when that garden went, well, nothing was ever the same after that. Changed the whole character of the place it did. It was like ripping its face off in a way. Course, once it was all levelled and laid back to grass it didn't look quite so bad, but afterwards the place always looked, kind of naked, I suppose."

With a weary sigh and a smile, he added, "Of course I'll help Kate, as much as I can. I'd like to see the place looking cared for again." Kate absorbed what Tom had said for a moment before taking another chance.

"I noticed that you haven't mentioned the walled garden, Tom. The one up at the house." Another glance flicked between the couple. Kate leaned forward and this it was her turn to reach out and pat Tom's hand.

"It's OK, Tom. Everyone knows it's you who's been looking after it. No-one minds a bit. In fact, if you hadn't, it's possible that the Summers wouldn't have been so keen on taking the place on. So what, did you come to an arrangement with the security people?"

Tom gave her one of his customary grins. "I couldn't just leave it could I? Walk away and let all those years, decades, of hard work go to waste. I've laboured in that garden since I were a lad. It's a part of me. Couldn't just let the weeds take over. Yes, I come to an arrangement with the security bloke what comes round every day. There's only one, mind, and he hardly ever sets foot inside the place. I said that I'd keep an eye on the house for him if he turned a blind eye so to speak, and let me keep the garden going. I kind of knew that if anyone wanted to buy Hawkswell, they'd like to see at least part of the place looking nice, like."

"And I don't suppose any of the produce goes to waste either."

Kate regretted her words as soon as they were out, but before she could take them back, Tom responded with a passion.

"I ain't made nothing out of those vegetables, not a penny piece. Me and the missus here, all right, we been pretty much living off what I produce. And I passes some on to Jim, the guard. Poor sod's got five kids to support on the pittance what they pay him. The rest goes to the poor folk in the village. There's nothing wrong in what I done. If I hadn't been there, there'd have been nothing produced and that's an end of it."

"Oh Tom, I'm sorry. I'm not accusing you of anything. I'm delighted you've been looking after the garden, so is everyone else. It wouldn't bother me if you'd set up a market stall to sell the produce."

"Ah, but that would've been dishonest, wouldn't it?"

"I don't see why."

"It wouldn't have been right. I been having enough sleepless nights as it is."

Kate laughed. "Well, you don't need to worry any more. You are hereby appointed Hawkswell's head gardener and you can come and go as often as you please, and do whatever you wish with the flowers and vegetables."

At that moment, the doorbell rang. Tom turned to his wife.

"That'll be young Michael about the shed. I'd better go. Excuse me, Kate. I won't be long."

As he left the room, May heaved herself out of her seat.

"Would you like another cup of tea, Kate?"

"That would be lovely, thanks. I'll come and help."

As the two women stepped into the cottage's neat but tiny kitchen, Kate asked, "Don't you sometimes miss that lovely big kitchen at Hawkswell?" Busying herself rinsing out the tea cups, May spoke with real feeling.

"Not one bit. Like I said before, place was full of damp and bugs, and I hates bugs. Couldn't get rid of the damned things – spiders, ants and woodlice, everywhere they was. No, I don't miss a single thing about that place. I was brought up in a cottage just like this one not a hundred yards from where we're standing now. I feels at home in this village, really at home."

"So whereabouts did you live, then?"

Kate was only making conversation and hardly thought about the question until the answer hit her like a bullet.

"Back Street. It's not far. Number 14. My old ma was born there, just like I was, and both my sisters too."

Kate couldn't believe what she was hearing.

"Dear God. Was your mother… were your parents called Tancock?"

May turned then, her face suddenly fixed, her eyes suspicious.

"That's my maiden name, yes. But how come you know that?"

Kate felt her mouth dry. Could the Pattie in the letters have been May's mother? If so, how much did May know about what went on?

"I, er… I think I read something somewhere, when I was researching the house. There was a lot about the village and its occupants. Most people here used to work on the estate, didn't they?"

May still looked dubious.

"Aye, they did."

"And I don't suppose your mother was called, er… Pat, or Pattie…?"

As Kate asked her question, May was midway through pouring boiling water into the teapot. She stopped so suddenly and completely that steam from the kettle's spout washed across the back of her hand. She slammed the kettle down on the work surface.

"Damn and blast!"

She turned on the cold tap and held her hand under the stream, wincing at the quick flash of pain. She spoke through gritted teeth.

"My mother's name was Elsie, Elsie May Tancock. I ain't never heard of no-one called Pattie, all right."

And that was that.

Door slammed shut, as happened every time. Kate wanted to shout at the woman, to tell her about those desperate letters from Jamie to someone he loved called Pattie who lived at Number 14, Back Street.

If it wasn't May's mother, who in God's name was it?

May knew. It was blindingly obvious.

The name had come as enough of a shock to make her scald her hand.

Dear God, what was it about Hawkswell and everyone associated with the place? You no sooner uncovered one mystery than you found another.

Tom stepped through from the passage and took in the little scene.

He glanced questioningly at Kate. "May burned her hand, steam from the kettle. Look, I'd better go. I'll call you and let you know about the meeting with Sir Arthur and Lady Summers. I think they'll probably want to include Penelope if it's at all possible."

She didn't look in May's direction as she spoke.

Tom showed Kate to the door and stepped out into the little front porch with her, half closing the front door behind him.

"Have you been at your digging again? Is that what's upset the missus?"

Kate spread her arms wide in contrition.

"I don't know what upset her, Tom, honestly I don't. It was just some old letters we found. They were addressed to her parent's house in the village."

"What letters?"

"Some letters written by Jamie when he was away in the war. They were written to someone called Pattie Tancock."

She watched his face closely as she spoke but failed to detect even a flicker of recognition.

"Well, that's not her mother's name. Her was called Elsie after her own ma."

"Was there a sister, or a cousin maybe living in the cottage?"

"Don't be daft, lass. That place ain't no bigger than this. Two little bedrooms and there was the two grownups and three little'uns. There weren't room for no-one else. Are you sure about the name?"

"Absolutely. All the letters were addressed to 'my darling Pattie'."

Tom shook his head. "Well there's a thing. I never knew that Jamie had anybody. Not the faintest clue. And I certainly never heard of no-one by that name in the village, and I reckon as how I know pretty much everyone around here except fer a couple of newcomers. But back then, no. There was no-one of that name. Leave it with me, lass. I'll see if I can get a bit more out of May soon as she's calmed down some. I'll also have a look and see if I can't find out more about that garden. I'm sure there'll something amongst some of the mistress's stuff. Sure she won't mind me looking. Do you reckon she's up to this meeting then?"

"Oh, she's much better, Tom, really. I think that as soon as she was away from all the responsibilities and worries of Hawkswell, it was as if a huge load was taken off her shoulders. Maybe being away from the well might have helped too. Anyway, she's a lot tougher than she looks."

Because of Penelope's frailty, it was decided to hold the meeting at the care home. The room put at their disposal was spacious, bright and airy. Mostly used for social gatherings and birthday parties, it had French windows opening onto a terrace and a magnificent view across a rose garden to the hills above Bath. A circle of armchairs had been arranged around a large coffee table featuring at its centre a magnificent bowl of cut flowers.

Kate had arrived an hour before the meeting to prepare Penelope and tell her about the people she was about to meet for the first time.

"I'm sure you'll like Sir Arthur and Mary, although the first thing he'll tell you to do is to drop the Sir."

"I am sure I will find them charming, my dear. The trouble is that no-one seems to want to tell me why they are coming to see me. I understand that Tom Gerrard will be coming too. Is it something to do with Hawkswell?"

Kate had hedged and havered ever since she had arrived to avoid discussing the reason for the meeting.

"Yes, it is about the house, but I really can't say any more than that."

The story that would soon be presented to Penelope was as near to the truth as was deemed safe for her state of mind. For her to discover that she no longer owned a single brick of her beloved Hawkswell would probably send her back over the edge. Even worse, the shock might be enough to kill her.

Although Penelope looked less than satisfied with Kate's answer, she was quickly distracted by Kate's suggestion that they take themselves down to the meeting room to make sure everything was ready for their guests.

The Summers arrived at precisely ten thirty in the Bentley, much to the excitement and fascination of staff and residents alike. They stepped down from the car along with Tom Gerrard, tightly buttoned into his Sunday suit. His face relaxed a little as he spotted Kate, and broke into a broad smile as soon as he caught sight of Penelope. As Kate ushered everyone into the room, Penelope made as if to get to her feet. Spotting the movement, Mary Summers hurried forward.

"Miss Townshend, please don't get up on our account. My name is Mary and this is my husband, Arthur. I think you already know Tom here."

Penelope shook hands with the Summers and grinned at Tom.

"What on earth are you wearing, Tom? I don't think we've seen that suit these last forty years."

He blushed furiously but recognised Penelope's attempt to include him.

"It seems as if we are dispensing with titles and formality today. If so, I must insist that you all address me as Penelope. You are all very welcome but I would ask one thing before the coffee is served. Will someone please tell me what this gathering is all about?"

Any ice that may have remained in the room was well and truly broken. Sir Arthur roared with laughter and slapped his knees.

"Goodness me, Penelope, I like your style. Right. No more beating about the bush. I would like to purchase Hawkswell House and its surrounding estate, if you are in agreement."

Then he sat back in his chair and beamed across at what he obviously perceived as a frail little old lady, barely capable of carrying on a conversation.

Penelope sat without moving a muscle for a moment while Kate crossed her fingers behind her back, praying that she wouldn't react badly. Eventually, she squared her shoulders and addressed Sir Arthur.

"So that's it. I thought it might be something like this. Pray, what makes you think that I am in any position to sell Hawkswell to you or anyone else for that matter?" Sir Arthur glanced across at Kate who couldn't believe what she was hearing. Before he could attempt an answer, Penelope spoke again, this time with a smile.

"I would like to know the real reason you are here, because it can't possibly be to obtain my permission about anything. My blessing maybe, but certainly not my permission. You see, I no longer own Hawkswell. I didn't own it when you and Daniel were living there."

She aimed this in Kate's direction.

"The whole place has been mortgaged up to the hilt for years. Why I haven't been turfed out on my ear long ago, I can only guess, although I believe a certain George Cowper may have had something to do with that. Now, can we please cut to the chase, as people seem to say these days, and get on with the real reason for this intriguing gathering."

Chapter 23

After they had all stopped laughing and the coffee had been poured, Sir Arthur produced a sheaf of drawings and laid them face down on the table.

"Penelope, this morning you have made us all look like the fools we undoubtedly are. I should have known that someone who could have maintained an enterprise such as Hawkswell for so long must have had her finger very firmly on the pulse. As indeed, it seems you had.

"As you have stated, you no longer own Hawkswell. As you may have already surmised, I do, or rather the Summerquest Institute does. At least we are in the final stages of negotiations to complete the purchase and I can see no good reason why those negotiations should fail at this stage. But you were only partly correct in your assumption that we are here for your blessing. Of course we are, but we are after much more – we are after your knowledge and your advice."

He paused and turned over the first piece of paper – an artist's impression of a fully renovated Hawkswell, complete with formal garden – and handed it to Penelope. After a moment or two while she found her reading glasses, she held the sheet up to the light from the French windows and scrutinised it carefully.

"I see that this bears some passing resemblance to Hawkswell."

Kate answered this time. "It's how the place could look once it's been fully renovated. What do you think?"

The old lady held the paper at arm's length before bringing it closer to her face. "Hmmm. I suppose the house might once have looked something like this. But if you are suggesting that this is how the formal garden looked, then you've got it completely wrong." And that was where the discussions really began.

The Summers' had arranged lunch in a restaurant two miles from the care home, and while Penelope travelled in the Bentley with Arthur and Mary, Tom gratefully accepted a lift from Kate.

As soon as the car door was closed, he dragged his tie away from his throat with a finger and let out a deep, heartfelt sigh.

"That were one o' the scariest things I ever bin through. I was sure the mistress would blow her top sky high when she heard about the house sale and all. Couldn't hardly believe it when she said she knew she didn't own Hawkswell no more. And there we all were trying to keep the news from her all that time. She's a sharp one and no mistake."

Kate laughed. "Sure and you can say that again. There's not much gets past her these days! So what do you think of the Summers?"

"Well he's a proper gent and no mistake, but I'd not like to cross him. That Mary though, she's something different altogether. So kind and thoughtful. I liked her a lot."

"You couldn't persuade May to come, though."

Tom shook his head.

"I tried as hard as I know, but there's something between her and the mistress like I told you before."

"So what about Sir Arthur's offer for you to oversee the garden renovation and move back into the house once it's finished?"

"Oh, I'll take the job on, don't you worry about that. But I think we'll probably stick where we are now. After all, it's not too far over the fields and I already knows the way." He even managed to look sheepish as he spoke.

Kate then asked him if he'd been able to find out any more about the Pattie mentioned in the letters, but when he told her he hadn't, Kate sensed a sore subject and let the matter go.

Lunch turned out to be a bit of a stop-go affair. The noise level in the restaurant wasn't that high, but it was still too much for Penelope's poor hearing. Determined as they were to include her in the conversation, Arthur and Mary Summers were forced to repeat not only their own comments but also those of just about everyone else around the table. Between the first and second courses, however, Penelope asked Sir Arthur to explain the Institute and its reason for taking over Hawkswell. Leaving him to bellow in Penelope's ear, Kate, Daniel, Tom and Mary Summers were left to have a much less energetic and specific discourse. Over coffee, Sir Arthur tapped his wine glass for attention.

"Friends. I believe that now is an appropriate moment to come clean on our last little surprise." He turned to face Penelope. "My dear Penelope. Now that I have explained our reasons for purchasing and renovating Hawkswell, I would like to make you an offer that I have been looking forward to making all day. I have been informed that you have lived at Hawkswell from the day you were born. In short, you are Hawkswell. And with that in mind, I do not believe that the house will function in the way we wish without your presence. And so it is with great pleasure that I formally ask you to join us as our honoured guest for as long as you wish."

Kate could see that Penelope wasn't quite sure what Sir Arthur was saying. But he went on.

"In our plans, we have incorporated a self-contained apartment with extra accommodation for staff and nursing care if necessary. It is yours my dear, rent free in perpetuity. What do you think?"

To everyone's discomfort, Penelope just sat and stared up at Sir Arthur's beaming face for a very, very long time. Kate wondered what she must be thinking, how might she react?

Then she caught a glint from one of the old lady's eyes – a single tear that formed and slid down her wrinkled cheek, swiftly followed by a second and a third.

"You mean I can come back to Hawkswell... to live?" Sir Arthur nodded. "Then of course I accept. Thank you. Thank you so very much."

Once Penelope had been mopped up and returned to the nursing home and while the rest of the party were taking their leave, Kate was asked to remain behind for a moment. A few minutes later, after being shown into Penelope's room, Kate took a seat beside the old lady who was now settled in an armchair by the window, a rug tucked around her legs and a woollen shawl around her shoulders. Her head was nodding and she was quite obviously having great difficulty in keeping her eyes open.

Kate cleared her throat quietly to let her know she was there.

"Ah, Kate. There you are. I am so sorry, but it has been a very tiring day and I've missed my nap. Goodness me, isn't it all so exciting. Just imagine, Hawkswell renovated after all these years and me living there. That's not something I ever thought would happen, I can tell you. Now, my dear. I need you to do me a favour." Kate sat forward and waited. "I need to visit the house."

"You mean Hawkswell?"

"Yes, of course. There is something I need to retrieve before any work begins." Kate frowned. What on earth could she want?

"But everything has gone, Penelope. All your furniture and belongings. There's absolutely nothing left."

"Oh, I know that. I also know about all the things that the Gerrards have stored for me. No, this is something extremely private and precious and I can assure you that it will not have been disturbed by anyone, you have my word on that."

"Is it something I can fetch for you, or even Daniel if it's at all heavy?"

"Oh no. It isn't heavy and no, it is not something anyone else can get for me. It won't take long, half an hour or so should be sufficient. Please will you arrange it?"

"And there's no way you're going to tell me what it is?"

"No Kate. Absolutely not. It is something private and precious and I am not prepared to say any more. Surely this is not too onerous a request."

"As soon as we have legal access and as long as it is safe to do so, we'll take you over."

"I have a wheelchair now you know. I didn't want to use it today, but it will make things much easier when we visit the old place."

Four months of intense, and at times bitter, legal wrangling passed agonisingly slowly, or so it seemed to those involved, before all the loose ends were finally agreed and wrapped up. During those months, Hawkswell was comprehensively surveyed and detailed architectural plans for its renovation prepared. In addition, a sizeable parcel of land a little further up the valley was purchased for the building of an entire estate of eco-friendly houses for use as either permanent or temporary accommodation for however many Institute staff wanted to take up the option.

As soon as the sale was completed and contracts exchanged, Kate raised the subject of Penelope's request with Sir Arthur. His immediate reaction was that the house wasn't safe for an elderly lady.

But when Kate told him it would only be a flying visit and that Penelope had assured her they wouldn't need to go upstairs, he agreed, albeit reluctantly. And so the visit was arranged for the following Wednesday. Daniel and Kate would collect Penelope after breakfast in Daniel's Rover and take her straight to the house. Sir Arthur had intended accompanying them, but conflicting commitments intruded at the last minute.

"Just give her my love when you see her. And make sure she takes a good look at the house at its worst, it'll make the renovation even more dramatic when it's done!"

Chapter 24

Kate helped Daniel lift Penelope's wheelchair up the short flight of steps to Hawkswell's front door. Although warned what to expect, the old lady was visibly upset by the sight of her beloved house so shut up and abandoned.

Kate unlocked and pushed the door open slowly, watching Penelope's face for signs of any further reaction, but she caught her at it and propelled herself forwards and across the threshold into the hall.

"Come along with you, dear. I knew what it was going to look like long before I asked you to bring me."

She stopped directly beneath the skylight dome, filtered light spilling around her like a soft veil. She spun herself round slowly, chuckling quietly.

"To be honest, my dear, it looks a damned sight better than it did when it was stuffed with all that horrible furniture. Never could stand the stuff, just couldn't afford anything else."

Kate and Daniel flashed each other relieved smiles.

Standing there, Kate absorbed the musty, dank smell of the place. It was exactly as it had been when she and Daniel had visited with the Summers' except for one small detail, something she couldn't quite put her finger on, a tiny difference, an addition, faint but distinct. She sniffed again, closed her eyes. It reminded her of something specific, a very clear but distant memory that...

Just as her mental fingers were about to snatch the fleeting thought from the air, Penelope propelled herself towards what had once been her living quarters.

As the wheelchair disappeared into the gloom, Daniel stepped through the doorway behind her and switched on his big, heavy torch. In the now brightly illuminated passage, Penelope stopped and turned towards him.

"Aren't the lights working?"

Daniel took two more paces towards her. "No, the mains supply was disconnected when you, er... left."

The old lady gave him a wistful half smile. "How tactfully put, young man. You know, I may come to like you more."

Kate watched as the two reached the point where the passage split, left to Penelope's old suite of rooms, right towards the wing containing the flats. To her surprise, Penelope turned right, speaking to Daniel over her shoulder as she did so.

"Why don't you try the light switch, Daniel? You never know, the old generator might still be working."

Daniel stopped as if he'd walked into a wall. "Hah! Of course. Why didn't I think of it when we were here before with the Summers?"

Even as Daniel reached for the light switch, Kate remembered what the elusive smell reminded her of – caravanning with her parents. It was the smell of LPG, liquid petroleum gas. She opened her mouth to shout just as Daniel's finger flicked the switch.

"NO-O-O-O! Gas, Daniel. There's gas!" The moment of absolute silence that followed the tiny click of the switch and Kate's shout, was broken by the distant sound of the old generator coughing and clattering into life. For another microsecond, Kate hoped she was wrong.

Hawkswell's remote location placed it far from a gas main. During the 1970s, a pair of bulk LPG tanks had been installed in an enclosure to the north of the house. Pipes were run to various locations throughout the house where the gas would be used for cooking and heating.

One pipe in particular was routed via the cellar where the fitters quickly decided that, as the cellars were unused, they would be wasting their time being unnecessarily careful in their work. Out came the lump hammers and the required holes were rudely smashed through. No-one noticed, no-one cared.

The thin copper pipe passed through a supporting wall, a double thickness of masonry with many tons of house resting on its crumbling base. Whereas bricks resist the ravages of damp quite well, mortar does not. Immediately above where the pipe penetrated the wall, a slab of bricks hung suspended like the blade of a guillotine.

The moment that Penelope was taken away to hospital and the Gerrards moved out, the heating was turned off, all ventilation ceased and Hawkswell house began to die. No-one thought to empty the LPG tanks. The damp became steadily more penetrating and that which had once been sound soon became unstable.

So it was with the slab of bricks.

When Sir Arthur Summers slammed the door behind him after his inspection, the few remaining areas of adhesion between the individual bricks failed and the whole mass slumped down with a rumbling roar onto the thin copper pipe.

It wasn't broken, only crushed enough to form a small break in the kinked copper, a break that allowed a trickle of liquid petroleum gas to seep slowly into Hawkswell's cellar.

LPG is heavier than air. It settled in the cellar, spreading and pooling across the floor until it reached the limits of the space, deepening slowly as the days passed. The diesel engine turned the generator armature one full revolution. As it did so, the tired old brushes swept across the tightly wound coils of copper wire and puffed out a tiny gust of bright blue, electrical sparks.

The mixture of gas and air that filled the cellar caught at once and, in less than a thousandth of a second, expanded to 200 times its original volume.

The blast was constrained by the same stone and earth walls of the cellar that had helped to pool and contain the gas. There was only one way for the rapidly expanding mass of incandescent gas to go, and that was straight up, taking the thick wood block floor of the hall with it. The explosion punched its way up and through the ancient glass domed skylight, soaring another hundred feet into the air above the house.

For a few seconds, the outer envelope of the fire ball reached over 500 degrees Centigrade, instantly igniting everything it touched.

Kate was hurled forwards by the shock wave and crashed into Daniel's back, knocking him to the floor and, in so doing, quite probably saving his life. The searing blast of superheated gas swept over them both, setting fire to the wallpaper and blowing doors off their hinges.

Dazed and barely conscious, Kate dragged herself to her knees and reached out for Daniel who grabbed her wrist and started dragging her further along the corridor. She had instinctively held her breath immediately after the explosion and quickly dragged her sweatshirt over her nose and mouth to try and filter out some of the heat and the smoke. The moment of ringing silence following the explosion was quickly replaced by a thunderous roar as fire took hold, the terrifying sound interspersed with the pattering and crashing of wreckage falling back to earth.

Coughing and choking, she allowed herself to be dragged around the corner to where Penelope was curled up against the wall beside her capsized wheelchair. She wasn't moving.

Without stopping to find out whether Penelope was alive or dead, Daniel grabbed one of her arms with his free hand and somehow managed to drag both women as far as the door that connected with the south wing, the wing with the flats and the well chamber.

Once through, he slammed the door on the inferno that the main part of the house had become.

With the deafening bellow of the fire reduced to a dull roar, the smoke that had followed them through the doorway began to thin out in the clean air of the corridor.

"Come on," he croaked, "we've got to get as far away from the fire as we can!"

Between them, he and Kate half carried and half dragged Penelope to the room at the far end of the corridor and the door that used to open out onto the courtyard. Daniel tried the handle before hammering at it with his shoulder. It was as firmly sealed as the windows. There was no escape that way. He slumped to the floor next to Kate who was cradling Penelope's head in her lap, feeling for a pulse in her neck.

"What the hell happened?"

Kate coughed and cleared her throat painfully. "Gas. Somehow it must have leaked from the bulk tanks into the cellar. I knew I could smell something as soon as we walked through the door. It must have been masked by the smell of damp. I only realised what it was when it was too late."

"OK, but what set it off?"

"The old generator. As soon as you flicked the switch it would have started up. All it took was one spark and 'poof!'"

He reached across and gently stroked her head, where a bruise was already showing from where she'd hit the floor.

"I think that deserves a bit more than 'poof'. How is she?"

"Still breathing, thank God. But we need to get her out of here as quickly as we can."

A loud crash from behind them brought down a rain of plaster dust and Kate shone her torch down the corridor towards the door at the far end. She could hardly believe what she saw.

The door was belching smoke from all four sides, with a rapidly expanding patch of cherry red at its centre. As they watched in horrified amazement, the fire broke through, sending a rolling wall of spark shot smoke hurtling towards them down the corridor.

"Get down!" Daniel yelled, "As close to the floor as you can get. Pull Penelope down too. There might just be enough air to get us there."

"Get us where?" Kate screamed, terrified, "There's nowhere to go. We're trapped."

Daniel grabbed her arm and pulled her towards him until she could make out his face through the smoke.

"The well chamber. It's our only chance!"

He held up the keys they had been given and Kate recognised the biggest of the bunch.

"We'll have to drag Penelope between us. Come on."

Although the door to the well chamber was only four or five yards away, to Kate that crawling, coughing, terrifying journey felt like as many miles. Penelope recovered consciousness as the smoke seared into her lungs and sounded as if she was tearing herself apart with her coughing. She started struggling, desperately trying to free herself from their saving hands.

And all the while, the air about them burned.

Kate was mesmerised as tiny points of light appeared on the sleeves of her sweatshirt, quickly spreading into brown, smoking circles before bursting into flame. She slapped at herself in desperation, whimpering, wanting to scream but trying not to breathe. Vaguely aware that Daniel was up on his knees, his head enveloped in the toxic smoke, she tried to pull him down, but he slapped her arms away.

In desperation, she kept on pulling, dragging at him, shouting, "Daniel, get down! You'll die!"

An instant later a wall of clean air washed across her face as Daniel pushed the massive well chamber door open, dragging her and Penelope through before slamming and locking it behind them.

The moment the key turned in the lock, the roar of the fire was replaced by a nerve shredding high pitched whistle.

Kate looked towards Daniel.

"That noise…?"

"I think it's air being sucked around the door frame by the updraft of the fire. We've got to try and stop it otherwise the door will burn through. There's some duct tape in one of those boxes."

He pointed his torch beam at the row of ammunition boxes abandoned after the abortive diving trip.

While Kate searched for the tape, Daniel helped Penelope across to the far side of the chamber, as far away from the door as possible. He sat her down with her back against the wall and hurried to fetch the water container the team had left there during the exploration. Thankfully it was still half full. He poured some into a plastic mug and gave it to Penelope. Several good gulps helped her relax and, in the clear air, her breathing eased a little, although when she coughed, it sounded as if her chest was being ripped apart.

When Daniel felt it was safe to leave her for a minute, he reached up to check one of the pressure lanterns. After discovering it was more than half full of fuel, he lit it, flooding the chamber with bright, white light.

Back alongside Kate, who was busily taping up the edges of the door frame, he gave her an encouraging grin and a pat on the back. Already the whistling was easing although as it diminished it became higher pitched. He packed a length of rope along the bottom of the door and taped it down. With the last length of tape pushed into place, the dreadful whistle ceased altogether.

Slightly less stressed, Kate took her first look around, astonished to see that nothing had been touched since that dreadful night when Simon had been hurt.

She shuffled across to where Daniel was giving Penelope some more water and spoke quietly.

"How long will we be safe here?"

"I don't know. And that's the truth. Hopefully long enough for the brigade to get here and get the fire under control."

"And if not?"

"If not what?"

"If they don't get here in time."

He looked at her for a moment before his eyes flicked to the well shaft. She understood but wished she hadn't.

"You're crazy!"

He leaned even closer, his voice a harsh whisper. "If the fire even looks as if it's going to break through, we'll have no choice."

Just as Kate recoiled from the dreadful possibility of descending the well shaft, they both became aware of Penelope scratching around amongst the mess of equipment. Still unsteady on her feet, Kate made her way over to where Penelope was on her knees searching and occasionally stopping to cough violently into a handkerchief.

"Penelope?" She looked up. "What are you looking for?"

The old lady stared at her for a long moment, as if considering the question and her response. When she eventually spoke, her voice was strangely calm and resigned.

"We're not going to get out of here are we, Kate? Before the fire gets through, I mean." Straight to the point, as matter-of-fact as she'd always been.

Kate tried to look confident.

"The fire brigade will get here soon," she said, thankful that her face was in shadow, hiding the lie in her eyes.

"Daniel thinks we'll be all right until then. I'm sure this place is built well enough to survive a fire."

"Kate," Penelope stated firmly, "I do not like to be patronised. It is not the fire I'm worried about, my dear. It's the roof and the gable end. If all that stonework and masonry comes down…"

Kate didn't need to imagine.

She thought for a moment about telling Penelope about Daniel's plan to escape down the well shaft and decided against it. That could wait until it was absolutely necessary.

Penelope seemed to make her mind up about something.

"There's a box here somewhere. I don't suppose…"

Kate answered immediately, "An old tin box, full of letters?"

Penelope's face froze, although whether with horror or delight, Kate couldn't tell.

"You found it?"

Kate nodded.

"When?"

"During the first exploration."

As she spoke, she realised that Penelope couldn't possibly know that there had been an earlier expedition. She tried to explain.

"The guys took a look earlier. They went down to the lake. That's when they discovered the river and... Daniel found the box."

"So where is it now?"

"Safe."

Penelope's voice crackled. "Safe where, exactly?"

"In Daniel's flat, with the rest of my things."

A thunderous crash brought down a rain of fragments as something heavy smashed into the roof of the chamber.

The sound seemed to galvanise Penelope.

"Did you read the letters?"

Kate hesitated for a moment before realising, in an awful moment of clarity, that there was no time left for any more lies.

And so she nodded.

"Yes. We read those that we could. They were from my great uncle Jamie to his girlfriend, Pattie. She lived in the village. Up to now we haven't been able to find out anything about her."

Penelope smiled then.

"It doesn't matter how hard you search, my dear, you won't ever find anything."

Kate's head was spinning. She asked the obvious question, "Why not?"

"Because, my dear, Pattie never existed."

Kate became aware of Daniel close beside her, his hand on her shoulder. Then he spoke for them both.

"Who was Pattie, Penelope?"

"A nom de plume, Daniel, or perhaps I should more accurately say, a nom de guerre." They waited for more as Penelope settled herself back against the wall.

"Might I have some more water please? I believe I have a bit of explaining to do. It's time you both knew the truth, especially as it looks as if none of us is likely to get out of here alive."

Chapter 25

They all needed the cool water desperately.

After each had drunk their fill, Daniel turned the pressure lantern down to its minimum setting to save what little fuel remained, and then he and Kate sat opposite Penelope with their backs to the well shaft.

As soon as they were settled, with the muted crashes and ever increasing roar of the fire as a background, Penelope cleared her throat.

"The time for secrets is over my dears. I'm sure I don't have to tell you that my reason for your bringing me here today was to retrieve those letters. You see, I had hoped to prevent them from ever being discovered. I've already told you that there was no actual person called Pattie. That's not strictly true. Pattie was created from my initials, Penelope Annabella Townshend, P A T. Jamie and I invented Pattie so that no-one would ever discover our secret."

Kate and Daniel both opened their mouths to speak but Penelope beat them to it.

"The plain fact is that Jamie and I were lovers. Ah! I can see from your faces that's something you never expected."

Kate broke in then, "But we, I mean everyone, thought you hated him, that you were afraid of him. So how, I mean, when...?"

Penelope held up a trembling hand. "All in good time my dears, if we have time, that is. Yes, I did find him frightening at first, and intolerably impolite and discourteous. The fact that he was living and working in the same dusty old loft that dreadful old Dan Lapways used to inhabit did not serve to endear him to me either. And there was something arrogant about his manner that set my blood boiling. So, yes, at first I did avoid him as much as possible.

"Then, after the incident with the horse on the river bank, I couldn't get him out of my mind. I kept remembering his beautiful back and his eyes as he looked up at me while he held my horse's head. They weren't mocking, as they might well have been, but were instead full of fun and laughter. To tell you the truth, right then I didn't know then whether I loved or loathed him.

"From that moment on I took every opportunity I could to pass by while he was working. I would never speak of course. But he always spoke to me, just a word or two, a good morning or good afternoon and a comment about the weather. He seemed entirely indifferent to my existence. Occasionally I would hide myself somewhere along the river bank where I could watch without being seen. Then I would marvel at his strength and the care he took over even the smallest and seemingly most insignificant component of the *Annabella*.

"Then a day came when cook caught me walking towards the boathouse and asked if I would take Jamie's lunch down to him. I objected of course, such a task was so far beneath my dignity. But then, when she showed me her heavily bandaged foot – she had bruised a toe quite badly – I relented and carried the basket down to the river bank. As I set his lunch down on one of the work benches, explaining what had led to my carrying it down to him, a heavy shower, that had been threatening all morning, broke and I had to take shelter beneath the canvas tent he'd erected over his work space.

"Suddenly the wide world that had until moments before encompassed the house, the lawns and the river bank was reduced to the space of a few square yards and it felt, dare I say, uncomfortably intimate." She gave a tight little shudder at the memory. "The downpour was so heavy that anything further than twenty feet away was obscured entirely by the rain. We might as well have been in another world. I think that Jamie must have felt it too because he invited me into the boathouse and offered to make me a cup of tea. It would have been churlish to refuse and, as it had become quite chilly with the rain I quite welcomed the idea of something warming. As he busied himself with a kettle and a primus stove, I took the opportunity to glance around our suddenly enclosed world. It was surprisingly well ordered, everything seemed to have its place and I saw for a moment how like a home it was. Just then, Jamie stood from where he had been making the tea, turned towards me and apologised for having only the one enamel mug. And, God help me, I laughed, for no other reason than because right then I was happy to share it with him.

"Unfortunately, he misunderstood my laughter and hurled the mug to the ground saying that if it wasn't good enough for me, I should go back to my bone china and porcelain and good riddance. I don't know whether it was his anger or my own reaction that shocked me most, but a moment later I had tears pouring down my face, so sad that I had made him angry.

"When I saw his look of horror at my tears, I told him that I wanted nothing more than to share his tin mug of tea, that I would rather be there with him in the pouring rain than drinking champagne out of crystal glasses up in that big, lonely house with my buttoned up old father poring over his papers, and servants who daren't say boo to a goose!

"The next thing I knew we were in each other's arms, kissing and hugging as if we were the only two people in the whole wide world." She stopped then, and the outside world might never have existed. Although the roar of the fire had eased a little, no-one noticed. After a few moments, Penelope continued. "We both knew from that moment that we had to see each other as much and as often as possible but no-one could possibly be allowed to discover what was going on between us. We used to meet at night in the boathouse loft. I would leave the house at midnight and slip down to the riverbank below the orchard and then along to the boathouse. I would return before dawn, even before the servants were about.

"During those short summer nights we often only had an hour or two each night to talk and cuddle and kiss, but it was enough. We didn't actually make love until the week before he left to join his regiment, and then I gave myself to him completely. We only had four nights and how we weren't discovered I will never know. I was so desperate for him that I used to leave my room while people were still up and about, returning in broad daylight. I didn't care anymore. Call me wanton, but it was as if I knew that was likely to be the only time we would have together. I am sure I was not the first girl to believe that, especially then.

"And so, for those few weeks that summer, we ignored the hopelessness of our situation completely. We pretended that we were just two lovers with the world at our feet and an exciting future before us. We planned to run away to Ireland where Jamie would build boats and I would produce lots of beautiful children. I can't tell you how desperately in love we were. We even took the risk of meeting right here to share a cup of Howk's Well water."

Despite their desperate situation, Kate couldn't help but laugh.

"And there was you saying the legend was all a lot of stuff and nonsense!"

"I know, I know. But you see now how very wrong I was."

"So you only had those four nights?"

"No. There was a little more time when Jamie came back from hospital to convalesce here. But things were difficult then."

"Difficult?"

"My brother Charles was dead, of course. That in itself was a terrible burden for everyone, Jamie included, for they had become friends. But the worst thing was what Jamie had seen and been through in France. It made our situation seem somehow trivial. I don't think he could understand why we couldn't tell the world about our love, why we had to keep it so secret. And I suppose with all those hundreds of thousands of young men from all walks of life dying together in that pointless war, it must have seemed absurd to have still been worried about differences between the social classes."

"But you did keep the secret."

"Yes, we did, although it was a struggle to convince Jamie of the necessity. I was sure he was going to say something to my father but then he… then something happened. I have no idea what, except that in some way it was directly responsible for Jamie's death."

Penelope coughed again and wiped her eyes before raising her head, determined to continue.

"Do you remember the chimney fire Tom told you about, when Jamie saved Hawkswell from burning down?"

Kate nodded.

"The morning after the chimney fire, as soon as I was awake, I was told that my poor Jamie had been recalled to his regiment and ordered to leave before dawn. Of course we had been expecting his recall. He'd been declared fit for service a week earlier, but I couldn't bring myself to believe that he had left without managing to find some way to say goodbye. Of course, when I thought about it a little more, I realised that he couldn't have done so because I was tucked up asleep in my room. But then I thought, a note, surely he would have left me a note. So, at the first opportunity I went down to the boathouse to check in the loft. All the signs of a hurried departure were there and none of Jamie's army clothing or equipment remained. But, search as I may, I could find no sign of a note or a letter or anything he might have left me as a farewell.

"I admit I was hurt, deeply, although I figured that if the poor boy had been in too much of a hurry to write before he left, he would surely be in touch as soon as he was able. Straightaway I took the dog cart into Hawkswell village to visit my maid and confidante Elsie Tancock – the one to whom all the letters to Pattie were addressed – to check if he had perhaps left a message or a letter there, but there was nothing. I spent the rest of the afternoon with Elsie, returning to Hawkswell in the early evening. The place was still in uproar with everyone who could be spared from other duties clearing up the mess from the fire."

"So when did you next hear from Jamie?" Kate asked.

Penelope paused then, for such a long time that Kate was about to ask if she was all right when she spoke again, this time in almost a whisper.

"I never did hear from him my dears, not by letter anyway."

"So…?" Kate started.

But Penelope carried on before she could finish. "It was four days after Jamie had supposedly left. Four long, anxious days not knowing whether he was still in England or already back at the front. There was a terrible thunderstorm that night. It had been threatening all day. They lost pails of milk in the dairy, it all curdled before their eyes. When the storm broke, so much rain fell that it seemed as if the sky itself had split in two. It overcame the gutters and poured like waterfalls off the roofs. It was without doubt the worst thunderstorm I had ever experienced at Hawkswell, and there were times when I thought we would be overwhelmed, struck dead or drowned. I hid in my room, terrified, the covers pulled over my head, praying that, wherever he was, my Jamie was safe."

Chapter 26

The woods above Hawkswell, August 1915.

As the afternoon drew on and the towering mass of storm clouds climbed higher and higher up the western sky, Jamie, far from being back with his regiment as Penelope believed, was huddled in a rough bivouac in the woods above Hawkswell. He had been alone there for four long days.

Delirious from lack of food and despair, as the storm broke, Jamie's mind let slip its tenuous grip on an unacceptable reality. The rolling grounds of Hawkswell spread out below him merged with memories of the shell blasted landscape of northern France. Both were stirred into a single stage, crammed with a cast of familiar and well-remembered faces – Jamie's long-dead parents and sisters were there, dressed in their Sunday suits, his sisters playing, blissfully unconcerned amongst the rusty, tangled wire and flayed tree stumps. There was Charlie Townshend, juggling brightly coloured hand grenades and catching them just as they exploded into streamers and stars. Many of Jamie's other comrades-in-arms also joined in the melee, all smart and bright in their new, mud free uniforms – gardeners and blacksmiths, farriers and coachmen, cooks and bottle washers, all dressed to kill. And his darling Penelope. Of course she was there, dressed all in white, laughing and radiant as she had looked on their last magical day on the river, parasol whirling in the sun.

The dead were there too, strewn about where they had fallen, carelessly, thoughtlessly, needlessly. And on marched the endless battalions, a mud-spattered, khaki tide flowing along the duckboards – whey-faced, hopeless creatures, shuffling from one kind of death to another.

There was a picnic – out in the middle of no-man's-land, on the slope of a half flooded shell crater – crisp white table cloths, bone china and crystal laid out on the stinking mud, hampers packed with imagined delicacies that turned to bully and hard-tack when touched. And there was laughter. They were all laughing. Penelope, Charlie, Jamie's parents and, standing high on the lip of the crater above them, Edward Townshend himself, laughing fit to burst.

Jamie knew there should be no laughter, not there, not in that dreadful place. 'People are dying here!' he shouted. 'This is a place of death and pain, madness and despair, not laughter!' But the more he shouted, the more they laughed, all of them. Suddenly, he realised they were all laughing at him, at newly-promoted Sergeant Jamie Kirkpatrick. The dead were laughing too, their rattling, disgusting croaks escaping from their clay packed skeletal jaws.

But before he could shout again, the guns started up, the ones along the ridge – German howitzers. He knew the shells were only a few seconds away as they looped high across the battlefield before racing down the sky towards the British lines, towards the laughing fools.

'Run, for God's sake! Take cover! Find shelter! Death is coming!' But the more he shouted, the more the picnickers ignored him.

The first shrapnel rounds burst with sharp flashes and cracks around and above their heads, releasing a lethal blizzard of red-hot splinters and acrid yellow cordite fumes. Moments later, the first of the heavy shells arrived, ploughing deep into the graveyard mud before blasting countless tons of mud, stone and bones into the already screaming sky.

Jamie could only dream on in helpless horror as the severed heads and limbs of his friends and loved ones cartwheeled into the air above his head, each fragment trailing a gushing streamer of blood and gore that spattered hot and heavy into his upturned face. He was still screaming as the blood turned to heavy rain drops, dragging him from one nightmare into another.

The wind-driven downpour punched its way through the treetops, stripping leaves and twigs before slapping through the inadequate roof of his bivouac, soaking into his clothes and battering his face and hands.

Though by then it was well past midnight, the woods were brightly lit by the almost continuous lightning, each flash overlapping the other and seeming to send the trees around him into a dancing frenzy. Thunder rolled and crashed its way from one side of the valley to the other, hunting up and along the wooded ridge before avalanching down across the pastures and meadows below.

But Jamie neither saw the lightning nor heard the thunder of an English summer storm, his poor fevered mind a world away, terrifyingly exposed on a cratered Belgian hillside in the face of yet another German barrage. Somehow he knew he was in the midst of half a million assorted combatants even though he could neither see nor hear another human being – for that is the way of nightmares. Their facts are so beyond question, their perverse reality entirely acceptable. His terror – pure and undiluted by waking – was enough to turn his bowels to water, his nerves to splintered shards.

He dragged himself to his feet, gulping at the saturated air, his hammering heart desperate for fuel to power his legs, to carry him away from this mud and blood bath! Away from the artillery, the star shells and the snipers, but above all to escape the searching eyes of the machine gunners in their sandbagged redoubts.

At last he started to run, the direction easy, downhill, down towards the valley, down towards the British trench lines and shelter, and although he couldn't have known it, towards Hawkswell. He ran blindly, cannoning from tree to tree, tripping and sprawling, rolling to his feet to run again. He ran with just one aim, one focus – to escape the guns. Even in the midst of his nightmare, his shattered mind knew of only one place where he could be completely safe.

The storm was nearing its peak as he blundered out onto the road, its surface lashed by curtains of drenching rain, slick as a river in the flickering light. Jamie ran across, bent double, too exposed, every muscle tensed against the numbing crash of the sniper round or the shredding impact of machine gun fire. He screamed as he ran, screamed out against God, the Devil, the Kaiser and King George for the vultures they surely were. He screamed at his friends for being lost and safe in death, yet mostly he screamed at himself for being such a fool as to believe fish could ever leave the seas and rivers.

But one small part of him laughed too – laughed for every step he took and stayed alive – for every breath he took to scream again – for every heartbeat that brought him nearer to his goal. The high iron gates crashed back against their metal stops as he barged through to run on down the gravel drive.

Four-square against the night, the house was soon in view, its windows as dark and empty as the shattered farmhouses of Ypres. On he ran, towards the imagined haven ahead. Once in the courtyard at the rear of the house, he found the door to the guest wing locked. He moved straight to a window and, without hesitation, plunged his elbow through the pane nearest to the catch. The sound was all but lost in the roar of the storm.

He hauled himself over the sill into the corridor, glass fragments crunching and slithering beneath his boots. Once inside, the barrage seemed amplified within the hard reflecting walls. He wasn't safe yet, not even inside the house. He knew all too well how a single artillery round could eviscerate a building and its occupants. So on he stumbled, to the door he was seeking so desperately, the heavy, iron bound door to the perfect dug-out. At first, his wet and trembling hands could find no purchase on the smooth metal of the handle, but with the strength of desperation he at last forced it open and shouldered his way into the remembered cool of the chamber.

Even in the darkness he knew his way – three paces to the parapet, up and over. Down there, in that cool, dark place lay his only chance of life and a final escape from the bullets and the shells. He grasped the winding gear above the shaft with one hand and stared down into its sanctuary. Another salvo roared overhead. The flashes of exploding shells lit the chamber. For a moment he was confused. Where were the rusty coils of barbed wire? Where were the mud washed duckboards, the sodden sandbags? Where were the mud slicked steps leading down into the dugout? And, strangest of all, where was the stench of corruption and shit, unwashed bodies and cordite fumes? Even in the depths of his dream, some part of him realised that the air was clean, fresh and chill.

A moment later, more confusion. Another voice, screaming close behind him.

He turned, saw a figure standing in the doorway behind him, silhouetted against a rippling series of flashes – a figure sheathed entirely in white. He knew immediately who it had to be – Charles Townshend. Dear old Charlie, dead and buried weeks before but back again for another go.

"Come on Charlie," he shouted, "quickly now, take cover, for heaven's sake!"

He almost grinned then.

Nearly safe and Charlie's back with us.

But then the figure shouted even louder – words this time, although they made no sense to his fevered mind.

"Jamie, my love. It's me, Penelope, your Penelope!"

Please God, no! he thought.

Not here in all this madness.

The guns roared and spat another salvo.

The Maxims too would be swinging round now, training their eager, searching sights on his unprotected back.

"Come now, Charlie. Don't play the bloody fool, for God's sake! There's no time for this!"

The figure in the doorway shrieked this time, its words slicing at last through his curtains of fear and confusion.

"This is Hawkswell, Jamie. You're back at Hawkswell. You're safe. It's only a thunderstorm. There are no guns here. Please… For God's sake, come down from there."

Home? Yes, at last. Home and safe. Charlie's dead, of course he is.

So who…?

Another flash, brighter, nearer this time.

No time, there's no time.

He gripped the cross bar, ready to heave himself over and down to safety. Then something made him take another look over his shoulder.

Penelope. It was her. He could see her face quite clearly. Jesus, why was she here, of all places? She reached out her hand, fingers stretching towards him, to draw him back.

He believed then. For one brief moment of clarity he came home. He saw the well chamber for what it was rather than the battlefield he had imagined. He heard the thunder for what it was, and saw his beloved's face clearly in the lightning's reflected glow.

Chapter 27

Hawkswell House Well Chamber, March 1980

As Penelope took another sip of water, Kate could see that she was weakening fast, but at the same time knew that she wouldn't let go until she had finished telling her story.

Sure enough, after a few more seconds she rallied enough to continue.

"Now where was I? Ah, yes, the tempest. Despite the dreadful noise, I must have fallen asleep because it was well after midnight when something woke me with a start. The storm was still battering the house but had eased a little. It must have, otherwise I couldn't possibly have heard the noise that woke me. I lay in bed and listened. Then, after a few seconds I heard it again, the banging of a door or a window downstairs. When it seemed that no-one else was going to attend to it, I plucked up all my courage, lit a lantern and went downstairs in my nightdress.

"I followed the sound to the far end of the south wing where a window was wide open, banging with every gust of wind. It was making a terrible racket. I couldn't understand why nobody else had heard it. Naturally I closed it, but as I did so, I found that my slippers were soaking wet. I looked down to see pools of water and mud strewn across the floor, along with glass from a broken pane. Someone must have broken into the house.

"Foolishly – I was probably too frightened to really think what I was doing – I followed the trail of footprints along the corridor and stopped where they did, right outside the door to this well chamber. It was unlatched and hanging open an inch or two. I must have walked right past it without noticing on my way to find the source of the banging. Without another thought I pushed it open and held the lantern up high to discover if there was anyone there. I couldn't believe what I saw."

She paused for breath before taking a long swallow from the mug that Kate held up to her lips.

"What you need to understand, my dears, is that I'd been told that Jamie had been posted back to his regiment four days before and was even then on his way back to the war. But you see, he couldn't have been, because he was right here in this chamber, standing on the parapet in full battledress, with his pack strapped to his back, and his rifle slung over his shoulder.

"I shouted of course, called out his name, but when he turned towards me I could see that something was dreadfully wrong. He was soaked from head to toe, streaming water as if he'd been swimming, his hair plastered to his forehead, and his eyes were – dear Lord, I can see them now – the blessed boy was terrified, his eyes as round as saucers and his face white as paper.

"He shouted to me then, his voice pitched high with fear, beckoning frantically, 'Come on Charlie, quickly now, take cover, for heaven's sake!' I will never forget those words as long as I live. I knew straight away it wasn't me he was seeing but my dead brother Charles. Jamie was back in the trenches, back in the war, you see. The storm. The noise of it must have sounded like artillery fire, every crash and flash slowly driving him mad. I've been convinced ever since that the well shaft must have seemed like one of the underground shelters he so often described, a refuge from the shelling, a place of safety.

"I could see what was going to happen next and so I screamed at him, desperate for him to know that it was me, and not Charles's ghost. My shouting stopped him for a moment and he shook his head as if he couldn't believe what he was hearing and seeing. So I shouted again, told him he was home at Hawkswell, that there were no guns and that he was safe.

"Then he smiled, and if I close my eyes I can still see that wonderful, weary smile. His eyes focused on mine for just a moment, 'Only a thunderstorm,' he said, 'It's only a thunderstorm. Oh Penelope, my love, I have been so foolish.' And then he laughed and began to step down from the parapet."

She paused again, reliving the moment, her eyes misting with tears. "Then his foot slipped, and took him away from this world.'

Kate gasped. "Oh dear God, you mean he fell."

"Yes Kate, he fell. The soles of his boots were sopping wet from the rain and the mud, he was exhausted, disorientated…"

She gave a tiny shrug. "He slipped and fell even as I watched. One second he was there, my beloved Jamie, alive and coming back to me, a smile of recognition and understanding on his face, and then he was gone forever.

"I didn't even hear him hit the water because I'd started screaming and screaming. I was told many months later that I didn't stop even when the ambulance took me away."

So Jamie was not buried in Belgium after all – in one of those impossibly vast military cemeteries, or even lying unmarked beneath today's lush farmland. He had died right there in Howk's Well. Suddenly so much that had been confusing and puzzling made awful sense – Penelope's neurotic behaviour while Kate and Daniel were living at Hawkswell – the Annabella, the boathouse with its dusty old bed, Jamie's letters.

Kate found herself crying, mostly for Jamie and how badly the world had treated him, but soon she found herself crying also for Penelope, for the memory of that terrible moment that she had carried unshared for so many years.

Daniel came and knelt in front of the two women, wrapping his arms around them both in silent commiseration and understanding. When Daniel pulled away, Kate found her voice again.

"So you have never told anyone what happened?"

The old lady's reply was even fainter than before.

"No. In all the confusion of the war, Jamie was posted as absent without leave. Because he was never found or apprehended, no action was ever taken against him and I suppose any file on him must have eventually been closed. That is why his name appears on no memorial even though he was as much a victim of the war as any other serving soldier."

Kate knew she could never tell her about the word 'Deserted' scrawled on his service record.

"If Jamie's body was never recovered, that means he's – "

"Oh yes, my dear. He's still here, somewhere beneath all that water."

"So that's why you had the chamber sealed."

Penelope tried to smile but her strength was fading fast, her voice nothing more than a painful whisper.

"In hindsight it seems a strange thing to have done, but in a way it was my memorial to him, as if this place had become a mausoleum, which I suppose it is. I would come and talk to Jamie when things were bad and when I felt so alone. You see the prophesy held true, I have never loved anyone except my Jamie, and I have remained faithful to his memory all these years."

Without thinking, Kate broke in.

"But your marriage to the RAF officer…"

"Ah yes, that. Never consummated my dear. Couldn't bring myself when it came to it. No, there has never been anyone else, not even poor old George Cowper, bless him, carrying a candle for me these past fifty years."

Kate smiled to herself, remembering all that George had told her about his long held love. And along with that thought came another question.

"Penelope, you said that Jamie had come down from a bivouac in the woods that night. What in heaven's name was he doing up there?"

"That, dear Kate, I cannot answer. I have struggled with that mystery ever since the night he died. At first I thought that he had started out to return to his regiment and changed his mind. I found where he had camped, up on the hill. He'd made himself a little shelter at a place where he could look down and see the house. Of course I had no idea where he'd come from that night. He just…"

Even as Penelope spoke, she was convulsed with a coughing fit that seemed as if it would never stop, each breath quickly becoming an increasingly desperate fight for air. Kate tried to help her to sip some water, but whatever she managed to get into her mouth was coughed straight out again. As the minutes passed, it seemed as if her lungs were giving up the fight, each rattling breath becoming faster and shallower.

As Kate wondered what had brought on this sudden and violent deterioration, she remembered the smoke back in the corridor. She and Daniel had both pulled their sweatshirts over their mouths and noses, which must have filtered out some of the worst of the fumes. Penelope, on the other hand, had been unconscious and must have inhaled a toxic cocktail of gases into her already weakened lungs.

Kate knew that Penelope was dying as soon as she started to expel great gouts of dark, arterial blood with every choking cough. The handkerchief that the old lady had been holding to her mouth became instantly saturated and useless as Kate watched, horrified and powerless to help.

Penelope looked up at Kate, her eyes full of knowing.

She made one last effort and managed to gasp out a request.

"Help… me up. Can't breathe… down here."

At that moment, as if in sympathy, the single pressure lantern began to stutter and dim. Daniel flicked on one of the torches.

As gently as possible, Kate began to lift Penelope to her feet, soon realising that the last of the strength had gone from those tired old legs. She found she was supporting a deadweight and, in her own exhausted state, knew she couldn't hold her for long.

"I need to sit you down somewhere. I can't hold you like this."

Penelope, her head resting heavily on Kate's shoulder, muttered, "Sit me… parapet… here."

Kate eased her down onto the stone.

No other thought crossed her mind in that moment other than that the parapet was nice and flat and made an easy seat.

Penelope settled, balanced like a new born infant, with not quite enough strength left to support her own head. She touched Kate's arm.

"Water…"

The mug still stood on the floor where Kate had left it. She held on to Penelope with one hand as she reached down with the other. But that one hand would never have been enough. As her fingers closed over the rim of the mug, she felt the fabric of Penelope's sleeve snatched from her fingers even as Daniel screamed, "Penelope, NO!"

Kate lurched to her feet to find him staring wide eyed and open mouthed at the empty space where Penelope had been sitting. At that moment, the deep, booming sound of an impact gushed from the mouth of the well shaft.

Kate could only stare, quite unable to make sense of what she had just seen and heard. But the moment the realisation hit home, she screamed, "Penelope!" and fell to her knees, unable to tear her eyes away from the sight of the single shoe that rested up against the well shaft's retaining wall.

Daniel grabbed her, held her, cradling her head against his shoulder to try and hug away the grief.

"It was deliberate, Kate. She pulled herself away from you and leant back. It wasn't your fault."

But as Kate tried to make sense of what Daniel had just said, a thunderous impact shook the chamber, sending a cascade of stones and rubble clattering amongst the equipment strewn in front of the door. A cloud of dust mixed with acrid smoke filled the air.

Daniel yelled above the suddenly increased roar of the fire.

"Kate, the whole place is going. We've got to get out of here right now. Come on!"

But Kate didn't seem able to move and stayed there on the floor, slowly shaking her head.

"What about Penelope?" she screamed, "She might have survived. We've got to do something!"

Daniel grabbed her shoulders and shook her violently.

"Penelope is dead Kate. There's no way she could have survived that fall. She won't have felt a thing. Now get a grip! We've got to move."

"But she'll still be down there, won't she?"

Daniel could hear the horror in her voice and fought to control his own revulsion at the prospect of coming across Penelope's shattered body floating below the shaft.

"There'll be nothing there. She'll have plunged so deep that the current will have taken her. She's gone, Kate, believe me."

Even as he spoke, he prayed to all the gods he knew that he was right.

Chapter 28

For Kate, the moment of Penelope's death signalled the absolute end of Hawkswell and all her plans and hopes for the old house. She also knew that it meant the end for her and Daniel. Nothing on earth would persuade her to descend the well shaft, she was certain of that. And even if she did, what then? She would rather die right there and then in the chamber than linger on in the cavern below the house to suffer starvation and eventual madness.

She felt herself dragged to her feet.

Daniel was buckling something around her waist and between her legs, shouting all the time. The smoke was becoming thicker, the air by then unbearably hot, making it almost impossible to breathe.

She felt something slipped onto her head and buckled under her chin – a helmet. Daniel was showing her how to work the lamp clipped to the front. It meant nothing, his words just noise amongst noise. She coughed, smoke and fumes searing her throat and lungs.

I don't want to die.

Maybe it was a prayer.

If there is a God, He'll make the nightmare end.

Her legs gave way and she slumped to her knees and began to crumple onto her side.

But Daniel held her up.

He dragged her up onto the parapet.

"Come on! We have to go now. Help me Kate!"

Stone cracked, mortar tumbled and the air was filled with dust and fumes. Cracks were opening all around them in the fabric of the chamber. But neither of them saw any of it. After an awkward slide and a sudden drop, Kate was hanging over that awful chasm, suspended on a thin piece of nylon webbing attached to her harness.

She screamed against the roar of the fire and the disintegration of the house, a thin, shrill sound not recognisable as her own.

Daniel's body thumped against hers, his hip against her face. She saw the wall of the shaft close by, reached out to touch its cool, damp surface. She wanted to press her smoke scorched face against the stone but it started moving slowly upwards.

No, no, that isn't right, she told herself, it's us, we must be descending. She screamed again, and this time the sound bounced straight off the shaft wall, to hammer straight back at her, clear and sharp.

As they slid lower and lower, the mortared stonework gave way to smooth, natural rock. Sounds from the chamber gradually receded and the air became clean and fresh, with not a trace of smoke or dust.

Her first long breath seemed to clear her head for a moment and she realised that she was dangling beneath Daniel, who was controlling their descent.

She looked up, the lamp on her helmet shining full in his face.

This was a Daniel she had never seen before – tight jawed with concentration, his attention utterly focused on the task in hand. His reassuring grin helped steady her even as he turned his eyes away from the glare.

"Not far to go now. We'll be safe soon. You're doing really well."

She tried to grin back, but her face didn't behave quite how she'd intended and she knew it was screwed into a terrified mask. I'm halfway down Howk's Well. I'm underground, beneath Hawkswell, and the house is collapsing on top of us.

She felt her reason slipping away but knew that if she let go, she would become useless to Daniel and to herself.

That way lay madness and death.

Do something! Hold on! Be positive!

So, instead of allowing herself to be overwhelmed, she caught hold of Daniel's leg and pressed her face against his thigh, absorbing his warmth, his strength, his smell. She felt his hand touch her cheek.

At that moment the wall of the shaft disappeared and they stopped for a few moments while Daniel did something with the ropes. She couldn't know it, but he was transferring them onto the ropes that hung from the belay at the bottom of the shaft. A few seconds later, they dropped out into the vast emptiness of the cavern. Instead of the closeness of stone, Kate looked out along an endless roof of tiny white stalactites. The overwhelming beauty of the sight washed away her terror for a brief moment.

Daniel heard her gasp.

"Magnificent isn't it."

If it wasn't the most beautiful thing Kate had ever seen, it was certainly the strangest. As they dropped steadily towards the almost supernatural stillness of the lake, the cavern opened out around them. The reach of their lamps was so limited that the sense of space was amplified almost beyond bearing.

They were suspended from an infinite black sky above an infinite glass ocean. Kate, forgetting herself for a moment, found she was searching for any sign of Penelope's body, catching only hazy reflections from the lake which looked as black and empty as a starless sky.

They spun slowly as Daniel lowered them towards the water.

Occasional small stones and debris from the disintegrating chamber whirred past them or smacked against their helmets and shoulders, Kate flinching every time one hit.

Daniel stopped them a foot or so above the surface, his voice sounding strangely loud in the silence.

"The dinghy's still here, but it's pretty much deflated. Pray there's enough gas left in the bottle to re-inflate it." As he struggled with the mass of black rubber and canvas, Kate twisted herself round and grabbed a handful to help. As they tugged, the rope stretched and her legs were dropped into the shockingly cold water.

Eventually Daniel found the CO2 bottle and cracked the valve. The inflatable writhed and twisted until it began to look more like a boat. As soon as he judged it capable of taking their weight, Daniel lowered them down into its water filled interior. Once more the cold grabbed Kate's legs and thighs like claws.

"There's a bailer somewhere. It's on a yellow lanyard." After searching around Kate found the plastic bucket and started to chuck water over the side. All the while, bits and pieces of debris issued from the mouth of the shaft above them, mostly pattering or splashing into the water to one side of the boat, but some thumping off the taut rubber to bounce away into the darkness.

And there was another sound, like the snap, crackle and pop of breakfast cereal, except magnified and distorted by the shaft – the fire.

As Kate tired, Daniel took the bucket from her to clear the remaining water from around their feet.

"Kate, see those pipes?" He pointed out the two iron pipes that descended from the shaft. "Try and swing us round to the other side of them, there's likely to be some big stuff coming down soon and we'd better get out of the line of fire."

She followed Daniel's instructions without question, relieved as soon as they were clear of the rain of fragments. Once the boat was stable enough to move, Daniel grabbed hold of a thick orange rope that stretched away across the surface of the lake.

"This is the line we left attached to the beach. I fixed it myself so it won't have come adrift." He pulled it taught. It held. He turned back to Kate and gave her a relieved grin.

"This'll take us all the way to the camp on the beach. There's everything we need there, tent, lights, sleeping bags, food and cooking gear. We'll be fine then."

Kate helped him pull their way along. But even as they slid forwards, Kate felt the buoyancy of the boat shift beneath her.

It soon became harder and harder to pull their weight through the water.

"Daniel, the boat's going down again. It must be punctured."

"Shit! It must have been some of the debris from the chamber." He found the gas bottle and turned the valve. It hissed loudly before fading away to nothing. They looked at each other and Daniel said, "I hope you can swim."

Kate tried to grin, her skin tightening at the prospect of that freezing black water.

"Like a fish."

"Come on then. We're wasting our energy trying to drag this old thing." With that, he rolled over the side, gasping at the cold, careful to keep his helmet and lamp above the surface. Kate did the same and, although she was prepared, felt her entire body recoil from the water's bitter embrace.

Then, hand over hand, one behind the other, they dragged and kicked their way along the rope towards the beach still hidden in the darkness, way beyond the reach of the lamps.

Once, Kate turned to look back the way she had come, catching a glimpse of a faint rain of glowing fragments drifting down from the mouth of the shaft.

Fifteen seemingly endless minutes brought them to the beach. By the time they had dragged themselves out onto the muddy slope, both were numb from head to foot and shivering so hard they could hardly speak. Daniel pulled Kate towards the little tent that sat, absurdly, on a patch of level ground a few yards further on.

He told Kate to strip off her wet clothes and, as soon as she was down to her underwear, dried her off as well as he could with the one towel that had been left in the tent, before helping her into one of the down filled sleeping bags. Then, working as quickly as he knew how, he lit one of the big pressure lanterns and placed it inside the tent door.

Only then did he struggle out of his own clothes, rub himself down with the already damp towel, and pull the other sleeping bag around his shoulders.

Squatting there beside Kate, who was still shivering violently, he fired up the camping gas stove and unclipped one of the ammunition boxes full of supplies. All the while, Kate's big, frightened eyes followed his every move.

"You... you're in your el... element down here, are... aren't you, Daniel?"

He shook his head and grinned lopsidedly at her.

"No. Not really. Not under these circumstances anyway. I'm normally well prepared, well equipped and wearing a wet suit. I don't think I've ever been so fucking cold." He soon had a pan of water boiling and made them both a mug of hot chocolate, liberally laced with whisky from the bottle that he'd placed in the ammo box all those months ago in anticipation of the celebration of a successful exploration. He couldn't possibly have imagined back then how useful it would turn out to be.

He handed a mug to Kate. "There you go. That should put some colour back in your cheeks." As he sipped his own drink he noticed that Kate didn't seem interested in hers.

When he asked her if there was a problem, she mumbled, "Too cold. Can't... hold the... mug."

There were bright tears in her unfocused eyes and something else that he recognised and that filled him with dread. She had stopped shivering, and that could only mean one thing, hypothermia. Without another thought, he crawled out of his sleeping bag and unzipped it fully. Then he undid Kate's own bag and crawled in close beside her, pulling the other sleeping bag over both of them. He unclipped and pulled off her wet bra and threw it out of the bag. Then he hugged her hard, rubbing her back and shoulders roughly to get her circulation going. And as he did so, he talked to her, slowly and calmly.

"Kate, you mustn't give up. Breathe in the steam from the mug. That's it. Keep breathing. Now wriggle your legs and arms. Come on, really hard. Wriggle as much as you can. That's it. Good girl. Brave girl. That's my Kate. If I haven't told you today, it's about time I did. Kate O'Donnell I love you so much. You're the best thing that's ever happened to me. Breathe the steam, come on. Now try to drink, just a sip. Good, good. We're going to get out of here, babe, you wait and see. And then we're going to get married and live in a lovely cottage out in the country by a river so that you can row whenever you want. And I'll come too. You can teach me. Come on, see if you can drink some more. Well done."

And as he spoke, monotonously encouraging and cajoling, he rubbed and chafed Kate's arms, legs and back until he started to feel that dreadful chill begin to fade. It was nearly half an hour before he felt able to relax a little. Fifteen minutes later she was recovered enough to sit up, still wrapped in her sleeping bag, and drink another mug of chocolate. A while later, she reached across and gave Daniel a tired hug.

"Thank you. You've saved my life twice today. I couldn't feel any warmth anywhere, not even deep inside. I felt as if I was drifting away and I didn't want to go."

Daniel brushed away a tear from her cheek. "You're fine now and everything's going to be OK. Trust me."

She grinned back at him and sniffled. "While you were warming me up, you mentioned something about... getting married?"

"Ah. I did, didn't I? Must have come as a bit of a surprise, I guess."

"A bit. I assume you were only saying it to try and shock me back to life."

He looked deep into her eyes. "No. I wasn't just saying it. I meant every word. I know this is hardly the time or the place for a proposal, but now we're on the subject..."

As soon as Daniel knew that Kate was over the worst, he took a look out of the door of the tent. He called to Kate.

"Quickly, come here. You've got to see this."

Still in her sleeping bag, she shuffled her way to the doorway and lay beside him staring open mouthed at the awesome spectacle taking place a hundred yards away in the centre of the cavern.

From the mouth of the well shaft high in the roof, blazing timbers and glowing blocks of stone were cascading towards the black water below, trailing streamers of sparks and flames as they plunged. The stream of fire was reflected in the rippled black water to give the impression of twin volcanic streams, one from above and another from below, merging in a cataclysmic burst of spray and steam as the blazing debris slammed into the surface of the lake.

As the brightest pieces burst into view, their light caught the myriad water droplets on the tiny straw-like stalactites, sending wave after wave of sparkling light across the roof of the cavern towards the tiny beach. Likewise, as each piece splashed into the lake, a set of concentric wavelets washed outwards, slowly diminishing until they were lost in the terrible blackness. The spectacle was at once immensely beautiful and utterly terrifying.

Kate pulled herself close to Daniel and he hugged her to him.

"It's like watching something dying," she whispered, "I can hardly bear to look."

Even as she spoke, a final cascade of blocks crashed into the lake's surface sending up a massive bloom of steam that vanished as the last flames were extinguished. Something, a partially intact section of roof maybe, must have fallen across the upper end of the shaft, cutting off the flow of debris.

A few distant thumps and crashes still echoed down the shaft, growing fainter with each passing moment. Eventually, there was only the occasional tiny splash like that made by feeding fish. Soon even those small sounds ceased, leaving a silence broken only by the sound of the last of the wavelets lapping on the beach a few yards from the door of the tent.

Kate asked quietly, "I know all that you said earlier, but please tell me the truth now. What exactly are our chances of getting out of here alive, Daniel?"

He kissed the top of her head. "Excellent. We've got enough food to last at least a week and more than enough of the best water in Somerset to drink."

He swept his arm to encompass the lake.

"And hopefully enough fuel to keep the lights going for a few days. Even when the batteries and the petrol run out, I'm sure we've got enough emergency candles to see us through."

Kate's head reeled.

The thought of being there in total darkness was so far beyond terrifying that she daren't even go there.

Daniel continued.

"The fire brigade may not have been able to control the fire, but there are enough people who know we were visiting the house, and my car is still parked out front. They'll start searching soon and I'm sure they'll find the well shaft quickly enough. They're bound to put two and two together and take a look down here."

Kate wished she could believe him, although she couldn't quite shake off the gut clenching fear that the shaft might be totally and irreversibly blocked. After a while, Daniel lit one of the stand-by candles outside the tent door before turning off the pressure lamp to conserve fuel. Their world immediately shrank to the range of the candle flame, a mere two or three yards. He suggested they get some sleep.

"We'll feel much better after a kip. We'll have something to eat when we wake up."

And so they settled down in each other's arms and, despite their terrifying circumstances, Kate quickly fell into an exhausted, dreamless sleep. Daniel, on the other hand, lay awake in the darkness, certain that no-one in their right mind would think to look for them down the well shaft and wondering how long it would take before the rescuers gave up searching.

Chapter 29

It felt to Kate as if she was climbing out of a deep, dark pit, desperately trying to escape the hand that was shaking her violently and the voice shouting, "Wake up! Quickly, wake up. Come on!"

Daniel's head torch was shining full in her face, blinding her, and she pushed it away.

"God, Daniel," she croaked, "What's happening?"

Even as she spoke, the crashing realisation of where she was swamped her sleepy brain. Then, as she became more aware, she realised that both feet and the bottom of her sleeping bag were soaking wet. She sat up quickly then, and as she put a hand down for leverage, was horrified to find the tent ground sheet swimming in three or four inches of icy water.

"Daniel... what...?"

Daniel's breathless answer came before she could complete the question.

"Those stone blocks from the chamber, the ones that came down the shaft. They must have blocked the continuation tunnel – remember, the one Simon got caught in – it's directly below the well."

"You mean – ?"

"Yes, the river's backing up."

There was nothing more to say.

Either Daniel had a plan to save them or they would either drown or freeze to death, whichever took them first.

Blindly following Daniel's terse instructions, Kate pulled on her soaking wet and hideously cold clothes before having her climbing harness buckled back tightly around her waist.

He spoke as he worked, dreadfully aware that their time was running out fast.

"I know all the abseil and safety ropes leading up to the well chamber will have come down with the debris, but let's pray there's at least one rope still attached to the belay station at the bottom of the shaft. Some of the pegs were placed deeply enough not to have been wiped by all that stuff that came down. Even if there is only one rope, we'll at least be able to haul ourselves out of the water."

As he was talking he was shoving one of the sleeping bags into a waterproof dry bag along with some ration packs and a short crow bar, normally used for clearing jammed boulders from underground passages.

With helmets and head torches in place, they each grabbed one of the foam sleeping mats to act as a buoyancy aid and slipped back into the bitter water. Miraculously, the polypropylene rope was still attached and they were able to pull themselves rapidly out into the middle of the pitch black lake.

Scraps and larger pieces of charred timber marked the area where the debris had struck the surface. Only one of the two iron pipes remained and Daniel prayed that it was intact all the way to the surface. If his plan worked, it might still save their lives.

Quickly attaching a pair of ascenders to one of the two climbing ropes that still hung from the roof of the cave he gradually applied his full weight. It held. While Kate trod water, he attached her harness to his waist.

"I'm going to work my way up the rope until we're both out of the water, OK?"

Kate had no idea how he was going to do it, just answered, "Yes."

Daniel gave her the big yellow dry bag and told her to clip it onto her harness with a karabiner. "That's our life saver, don't lose it." Then he started to inch his way up out of the water. By using the two ascenders – clamps that slid up the rope but gripped when downward pressure was applied to them – he was able to heave himself and Kate out of the killing chill of the water, raising them, twelve inches at a time, away from the lake's surface.

As soon as Kate's feet were ten feet or so above the surface of the lake, he slumped back into his harness, exhausted and fighting for breath.

"Well, at least that's warmed me up a little," he gasped.

"Now it's your turn to do some work. Get your top off if you can, wring it out and try and dry yourself off as much as possible. Then pull that sleeping bag out of the dry sack and wrap it around you. It's not perfect but it's better than nothing."

"But what about you?" Kate asked.

The strangely muted echo of their voices caused her to shiver even more.

Daniel's answer didn't make sense at first.

"I'm going to be busy summoning help."

With that, he swung himself over until he was hanging almost horizontally from the rope and reached across to grab the remaining pipe hanging in space to his right. He attached a nylon sling and carefully clipped it onto the rope they were suspended from.

"Kate. Can you find the crowbar at the bottom of the bag?"

"I think so… yes, got it."

"And the piece of yellow tape tied to it?"

"Yes."

"There's a karabiner on the end of the tape. Very carefully, can you clip that karabiner onto the rope above you before you hand me the crowbar."

As soon as the heavy length of steel was handed over, Daniel told Kate to brace herself for some noise and commenced hammering on the iron pipe.

Clang, clang, clang… clang… clang… clang…, clang, clang, clang. Three close together, three spaced out, three close together.

Morse code for SOS, the international distress signal. As he hammered, he tried to reassure Kate, shivering below him despite being cocooned in the sleeping bag.

"It must be morning up there. There are bound to be people searching by now. This pipe is connected to others on the surface, it'll take the sound and spread it around. Someone's bound to hear, you wait and see."

After another few minutes pounding, he felt Kate tugging on his trouser leg.

"Daniel, the water's up to my knees."

And so it went on. Every time the water level reached Kate, Daniel heaved them up as far as his dwindling strength allowed before re-commencing his banging on the pipe.

Each time he did so, the distance they managed to climb was shorter and his recovery took longer. Soon the crowbar was slipping from his grip after only a few hits, to dangle from its tape. Eventually Kate took it from him.

"Let me take over the signalling, Daniel. I need to do something."

As soon as she had a firm hold on the metal bar, she started hammering out the monotonous rhythm, pausing every thirty seconds or so to listen for any response. Meanwhile Daniel slumped against the rope, too exhausted even to shiver.

Minutes slid by and Kate felt the water lapping at her feet again. By then, they were only ten or twelve feet below the bottom of the well shaft and she didn't dare to think what would happen when they ran out of rope. She tugged again at Daniel's trouser leg.

"The water, Daniel."

But this time there was no response. She tugged a little harder and tried to shout.

"Daniel. We must get higher!"

Nothing. Kate twisted round and, as she did so, her fading head lamp shone fully in Daniel's face, hanging above her. He didn't squint or move his head away from the light.

Dear God, he's dead, she thought.

There was no emotion attached to the realisation, no sense of loss, just acceptance of an unfortunate fact. Her shivering had stopped too and, deep down inside, she knew that her end also wasn't far away.

Better keep on hammering though.

But as she reached out towards the pipe, the crowbar slipped from her numbed fingers for the last time. She knew she hadn't got the strength to haul it back up from between her legs and so she beat her fists against the cold hard metal again and again and again. There was no pattern anymore, merely a hopeless pounding of flesh on metal that barely made a sound.

All too soon, her arms lost their strength and fell to her side.

She leaned her face against Daniel's thigh, as she had done while they were descending from the well chamber. Only this time, there was just stillness and a deep, deep chill. At least he'd still got a pulse, she could hear it faintly even though it was strangely irregular. As Kate slipped into welcome unconsciousness, the last thing she heard was what she thought was Daniel's heart-beat in her ear – three long, a pause, one long, one short, one long. A puzzling rhythm she was incapable of understanding.

Three long, a pause, one long, one short, one long.

Morse code for OK.

Chapter 30

Apocalyptic. No other word could come close to describing the scene confronting the fire and rescue services that March evening when they first arrived at Hawkswell.

The old house, already catastrophically damaged by the initial explosion, had burned like a torch, the towering column of flame and smoke visible from twenty miles away. Although the alarm had been raised almost immediately by a passing motorist, the fire had taken hold so swiftly that, by the time the first appliances arrived, it was way beyond any sort of control. Daniel's Rover that had been parked at the foot of the entrance steps was nothing but a white hot skeleton, barely discernible against the glare of the inferno.

The senior Fire Officer at the scene ordered his crews to remain well clear until they could be certain that there was no danger of any further explosions. The many fire engines, ladder units, water bowsers, ambulances, police cars and support vehicles were ranged across the lawns to either side of the approach road, impotent for the moment but ready for the signal to swing into action.

It wasn't until nearly midnight that they were able to start the damping down process, by which time the house was nothing but a smouldering shell. Only the right hand gable end of the main part of the house still stood, the two wings reduced to piles of debris no more than ten or twelve feet high.

By six in the morning, and certain that no-one could possibly have survived such an inferno, the Chief ordered the remaining gable to be pulled down straight away, primarily concerned for the safety of the men under his command.

As the smoke lessened and the dust from the demolition settled, the full scale of the disaster became clear. With dawn's revealing light slowly spreading across the scene, the crowd of onlookers gradually realised that they were looking at the remains of a funeral pyre. Kate, Daniel and Penelope were dead, their ashes mingled with those of the house that had once been their home. There would be little left to find, but all who stood before Hawkswell that morning knew that a search had to be made, no matter how futile.

Sir Arthur Summers and a few members of his staff had arrived during the night, having been contacted by the police. He stood, bleak faced, gazing out across the ruins of a dream.

So much hope lay buried there, so much promise. And he wasn't thinking about the house.

The tens of thousands of gallons of water that were being sprayed in high, ostrich feather arcs across the remains of the house eventually reduced the temperature under foot enough to enable the first heavily protected search teams to move in. Led by hose-men blasting a shield of cooling water ahead of them, they inched their way with infinite caution across the piles of rubble and smouldering timber. By that time, a watery sun had climbed above the wooded ridge to cast its bleak light across the scene. A seemingly endless tangle of hoses wound and writhed their way across the lawns from a pair of centrifugal pumps that had been installed beside the river.

Sir Arthur was sipping a mug of coffee from a mobile canteen when a spreading wave of shouting reached the crowd gathered on the muddy grass.

The Chief Fire Officer used a megaphone to ask for absolute quiet. Quickly, all the hoses were turned off along with the pumps and anything else that was making a sound. An extraordinary silence spread out from the centre until it covered the entire area.

A moment or two later, a shout went up from one of the teams that had been clambering over the remains of the south wing.

An arm waved and the figure shouted again.

This time Sir Arthur and everyone else gathered around the command vehicle were able to make out the words.

"There's someone alive under here!"

It didn't make sense.

How could anyone have survived the fire, let alone being buried beneath that enormous pile of wreckage? But as people hurried forward, the man shouted again.

"Someone's tapping on a pipe or something, it sounds like an SOS."

What had a moment earlier been nothing more than a grisly search for human remains, suddenly became a full scale rescue effort, and a race against time. Whoever was knocking was growing weaker, the sound becoming less precise, more sporadic. Only minutes later it stopped altogether. One of the firemen had found the end of a piece of iron pipe protruding from the rubble and began pounding on it with a brick, more in hope than anything. Three long, a pause, one long, one short, one long. Morse code for OK.

As soon as the well shaft was identified as the only possible source of the tapping, the Chief Fire Officer called together his team leaders and anyone else with any knowledge of the house for a hurried conference to discuss the safest and swiftest way of proceeding. Sir Arthur insisted on being included. After long minutes of discussion, he broke in with a chilling statement.

"The longer we stand here talking, the less chance those poor souls have of surviving. But remember one thing, the only pipes that run down that shaft are the two that originally supplied the pumps. Anyone tapping on them can only be in one place, directly below the mouth of the well. Anything that we let fall will hit whoever is down there. Utmost speed and utmost care gentlemen, if you please."

Working from outside the estimated footprint of the well chamber, four teams cleared a wide, level area to enable lifting equipment to be positioned around the site of the well itself. Then, with infinite caution, they began to remove the debris piled immediately on top of the shaft. One stone and one piece of timber at a time, they worked their way steadily downwards, as if playing a giant game of spillikins.

Every now and then, something would slip and work would stop while they re-appraised the loosely balanced heap before proceeding. Each time they stopped for more than a few seconds, someone would shout and bang on the single exposed piece of pipe. There was never any reply but, far from giving up hope, the rescuers merely redoubled their efforts.

After an hour of concentrated effort, all that remained were two overlapping sections of the roof structure balanced precariously on top of the well shaft parapet which looked to be pretty much intact. After probing and inspecting for any further heavy debris, the decision was taken to lift the two pieces in a single operation.

Once everything was lashed together securely with ropes and nylon straps, the crane gradually took up the strain, its driver carefully repositioning the tip of the jib every now and then to prevent the unstable structure from slipping sideways.

At last, to a collective sigh of admiration and relief, the ungainly mass of timber was clear and able to be swung sideways away from the mouth of the shaft. Such was the skill of the crane driver, nothing but a fine trickle of ash and a few small stones ended up falling down the shaft.

A fireman, already harnessed and clipped into a safety line, approached the gaping mouth of the well and, after carefully sweeping any loose debris from the top of the parapet, leaned over and shone a powerful torch down into the darkness.

"I can see something. There's definitely someone there, right at the bottom. Hello! Can you hear me?"

There was no answer and no movement.

Instead of wasting time rigging a scaffolding framework, the Fire Chief entrusted his man into the hands of the crane driver. Webbed with safety lines and with a spare rescue harness clipped to his own waist, the fireman was lowered slowly into the shaft.

After what seemed an impossibly long descent, his voice came clearly up the shaft.

"There's two of them, a man and a woman. The woman's definitely alive but unconscious, but I can't be sure about the man. He's too cold and I can't feel a pulse. No, hang on."

His next words were shouted.

"He's still breathing! He's still breathing! I'm going to put him in the harness first and I'll wait here with the girl while you bring him out."

And so, first Daniel and then Kate were lifted into the daylight almost exactly 24 hours after they had first arrived at Hawkswell.

Both profoundly unconscious and severely hypothermic, they were rushed by helicopter straight to the Royal United Hospital in Bath.

The prognosis for each was grim.

The search for Penelope Townshend continued until the daylight failed and heavy rain set in before being called off.

Chapter 31

Silence. There was nothing else, only an astonishing, numbing silence. She was neither hot nor cold, wet nor dry. No pain, no feeling at all.

The well chamber had changed, its stones now free of algae, crisp and sharp as if freshly chiselled.

Daniel. Not there. No sign. Did that matter? Not sure.

She couldn't think. He must either be safe or dead. Maybe those two were the same. Perhaps there was no difference.

She hovered, weightless in that silent, comfortable void. Waiting yet not waiting, unaware of the passage of time until, without warning, the chamber, her world, was flooded with intense, white light.

She tried to raise a hand to shield her eyes, but there was no hand, no wrist, no arm. The surrounding walls melted away, but instead of the smoking ruins she might have expected, she found herself sitting on a grassy slope, bathed in warm spring sunshine under a bright blue, cloudless sky.

She was almost overwhelmed with the intoxicating scent of apple blossom and freshly mown grass, while a magical chorus of birdsong rang about her head.

She did not question, did not wonder why or how.

Someone brushed past her in a billowing white summer frock.

Penelope Townshend, but not the dying woman last seen moments before plunging down Howk's Well. Here was a young, vital Penelope, a beautiful creature, her face alight with love and laughter. The rejuvenated Penelope paused to look down before speaking for the very last time.

"Fish and birds may find it difficult to exist together in the world, Kate, but with enough faith and love they should at least be able to swim and fly side-by-side for a while."

Then, she turned and ran as nimbly as a gazelle down the slope towards the nearest margin of a vast apple orchard that stretched away into a hazy distance. In the shade beneath the blossom heavy branches, where the trees met the grassy slope, stood the figure of a young man.

Penelope threw herself into her lover's arms to be twirled around, hugged and kissed before, hand-in-hand and with only a brief backward glance, the two figures strolled away into the dappled shade of the trees to merge with the rolling cloud of pink blossom. Kate lay back on the sun-warmed grass and cried and laughed until her eyelids fluttered closed, and the warmth and delight of the moment carried her back into a deep and dreamless sleep.

Pain. A bone deep ache in Kate's leg lunged up into her groin in waves that matched her heartbeat.

Thirst. Her mouth was like a summer sandpit. When she tried to swallow it felt as if her throat would close up altogether.

Noise. A series of low, asynchronous hums interspersed with high pitched beeps.

Light. Too bright. She kept her eyes closed as she explored the rest of her surroundings. She was in bed, warm but not hot, and when she tried to lift her head it felt like a block of concrete. There was something in her nose, in each nostril. She sniffed and the air was cool and slightly metallic.

Sleep. Maybe that was the best thing to do. Drift back to the warm, dark place from which she had just surfaced. She let her head sink back into the pillow.

But something in her head nagged her into opening her eyes and trying to sit up.

A hand eased her gently back down onto the pillows as a disembodied voice came out of the brightness.

"It's all right, Kate. You're safe and in hospital. Just rest for a moment and you'll feel better."

Hospital. Why was she in hospital?

She tried to speak but all she could manage was a croak.

The unseen person lifted her head a little and she felt a straw being placed between her lips. She sucked and drew the coolest, most welcome trickle of water into her mouth. She drank until the straw sucked dry and lay back exhausted.

She tried her voice again.

"My leg…?"

"Ah, yes. Is it hurting?"

Kate tried to nod, thought better of it and said, "A lot."

"It's nothing to worry about. We'll give you some more pain relief and that will make it easier."

Kate opened her eyes a little and, squinting against the glare from the overhead lights, made out a nurse beside her making adjustments to some equipment. A second or two later, the fierce ache in her leg faded to something more gentle, something she could almost ignore. And with that relief, the gentle darkness returned and she slipped back to sleep.

She woke again two hours later and, within minutes of opening her eyes, her bed was surrounded by doctors, nurses and technicians. Once they were satisfied that she wasn't going to slip away from them again, they started the process of decoupling Kate from most of the technology before moving her onto a ward.

When she asked about the pain, she was told that the straps of her harness had severely restricted the blood supply to her already damaged leg, so much so that large areas of muscle had effectively shut down. It was the gradual restoration of circulation that was hurting so much. The doctor went on to assure her that the leg would recover fully although she would require physiotherapy to, as he put it, 'ease out the kinks'.

Once installed in a private room organised by the Institute, she was given a thorough check up and an equally rigorous bed bath. Her hair was washed and dried, her gown changed and, within an hour, she was propped up on a mountain of pillows, half asleep but more hungry and thirsty than she would have believed possible.

She asked for more water which arrived, chilled in a large glass jug. Although it worked wonders for her thirst and her sore throat, something about its temperature troubled her. After a second long swallow, the events that had been so mercifully forgotten crashed down on her like an avalanche. The water glass slipped from her fingers onto the bed as image after image flashed across her consciousness – arriving at the house with Penelope in her wheelchair, the explosion, the fire, Penelope's revelations about herself and Jamie, her death and their frantic battle to escape the fire.

The cold that had nearly killed her washed through her head, leaving her shivering and blue lipped. A nurse pressed the emergency bell push and moments later a gaggle of doctors and nurses were huddled at her bedside. But by then Kate's problems were neither physical nor mental, they were purely emotional as she sobbed uncontrollably for Penelope and for Daniel, refusing to believe that he was alive, convinced that he had died back in the well shaft and that everyone was keeping the truth from her.

In the end, they had to wheel her into the Intensive Care Unit to peer through the window at Daniel's sleeping form, barely visible amongst its web of wires and tubes, the tell-tale blips and wandering lines on the monitors the only signs of life. Calming and reassuring words from doctors removed the worst of Kate's panic, a small sedative did the rest. By the time she woke the next morning, Daniel too was back in the land of the living.

Although unable to share a room – heaven forbid, private or not, no respectable hospital could dream of allowing such a thing – as soon as she was allowed out of bed, Kate would hobble along to Daniel's room and collapse into the armchair beside his bed. And there they would spend most of the day, holding hands and talking, dozing off together and making plans.

They laid Penelope and Jamie to rest in their own way, wiping away the horror of those two separate but inextricably linked events, replacing them with wonder and gratitude at their own survival.

On the afternoon before they were both to be discharged, Kate received a completely unexpected visitor, May Gerrard. Tom had dropped by once before on his own, quite obviously very uncomfortable with the hospital environment.

"At my age, if they ever get you in a place like this, they never let you go. I seen it happen to too many good people. They go in for something straightforward and come out in a box. Sooner you're out of here the better, is what I say."

Kate had laughed but even so, hers and Daniel's close encounter with eternity was still a bit too fresh to ignore entirely.

May carefully closed the door behind her before depositing a heavy bag of grapes on Kate's side table and settling herself in the bedside armchair.

"Tom said as how you was feeling a lot better and you certainly look it."

Kate managed a smile, unsure of how to react. Not that she needed to because May had obviously arrived with a carefully rehearsed speech.

"I know you and I haven't always seen eye to eye and I know I've been rude to you in the past, specially about your prying… sorry, your looking into the history of Hawkswell. Well I ain't come here to apologise, that's not in me nature. I come to explain. Now that Penelope's gone, it only seems right that you should know the truth."

Kate reached out and put a hand on May's arm.

"May, I know all about Jamie and Penelope, about Pattie and everything. Penelope told me just before she… she died."

May looked at her long and hard. "Well, that's stolen my thunder right and proper, ain't it?" She looked so put out that Kate couldn't stop herself laughing. Luckily, May joined in the laughter until it was spent.

"I don't know, Kate. What a time you've had. I'm sorry she's gone, especially like that. We used to get on each other's' nerves something chronic, but I worked for her for must be forty years or more. I can't quite remember when I started it was so long ago. And she wasn't a bad old thing really, keeping the house going all that time and her on her own and all."

"How did you find out about Jamie, May? I thought no-one knew, at least that's what Penelope told me. She didn't reckon anyone had the faintest idea."

"No-one else did except me and my old ma, God rest her. We was the only ones and she made me swear on our old family bible never to tell a soul while the mistress lived and breathed."

"But…?" Kate's mind whirled, "Surely…?"

May stopped her. "Did Penelope tell you about how she and Jamie used to meet up down in that there boathouse loft?" Kate nodded. "Well, they used to do a lot more than just meet up in my opinion, but that's by the by. My ma was Penelope's lady's maid at that time and, because she never wanted to live in, she used to walk across from the village every day. One morning she arrived especially early for some reason and she was looking out of one of the windows when – "

"Oh, my God, she saw her coming back."

"No Kate, she didn't. What she saw was two lines of footprints in the grass leading down to the boathouse and back again. It was the dew you see, that's what give them away. Of course, soon as the sun come up, they disappeared. No-one else in the house got up early enough to notice, it being the summer and all."

"But how did she know they were Penelope's footprints?"

"A while later, she went down one night and waited, hiding by the river bank. What a thing to do! I've never quite forgiven her for that. Anyway, what she saw and heard left no doubt. It was Penelope all right and her was ever so in love with your Jamie, that much she did tell me."

"So did she ever let on, to Penelope, I mean?"

"Lord no. O'course, the irony was that, when Penelope wanted someone to act as a post box for Jamie's letters, who should she choose but my ma. She was never told about Jamie, mind. She got presented with some cock and bull story about Penelope having met an officer in Bath and wanting to correspond without her father knowing, but Ma knew all along. How she kept it to herself I'll never know, but she knew what it would have done to them both if it had ever got out, and she liked them, especially Jamie I reckon."

"So he was a bit tasty then?"

"A bit what?"

"Attractive, Jamie."

"Oh, he was attractive all right. A real looker by all accounts, once you realised he wasn't well, you know… a gypsy and all. And nice with it. Shy, of course, but he must have been a lovely lad. And to die like that, so far away from home."

Kate took a small breath. "He died in the war, then. In the trenches."

"Of course."

There was something about the way that May said 'of course' that didn't ring true.

"You don't sound too sure. I thought he got recalled to his unit and left without saying goodbye."

At that, May blushed, and Kate knew there was still more to uncover. She held her breath and waited.

"That might not have been quite what happened."

"What do you mean?"

"I know that's what everyone believes, but there was something that happened around then that kind of suggests that something else might have occurred."

"Like what?"

"I don't know, and that's the truth of it. All I know was what old Brian Gerrard told me not long afore he died. And don't you go whispering a word of this to no-one, promise, because even my Tom don't know none of this."

Kate agreed, wondering what could possibly be coming next.

"Remember when he told you about that chimney fire and how young Jamie helped to put it out?" Kate nodded. "Well, as I heard it, he was asked to go and take a drink with Edward

Townshend as soon as he was cleaned up, so the master could thank him, I suppose. Well, it was Brian Gerrard as was sent to fetch him and, instead of returning straight to his quarters, he took a moment to collect up some of the canvas that had been used to put out the fire. The door hadn't been closed properly and, because he was right outside, he couldn't help but overhear everything what happened."

Chapter 32

Hawkswell House, August 1915

Edward Townshend raised his glass to Jamie.

"I am in your debt, Sergeant. That was a magnificent thing you did this evening. You took control, led the effort, something I am sure my son Charles would have done had he been here. You saved the day and, in so doing, you have helped me reach a decision I have been struggling with these last few difficult weeks."

Jamie sipped his own brandy, the fumes stinging his nose and making his eyes water. He waited patiently for whatever was coming his way, increasingly certain that the moment had at last arrived to ask the question that was burning in his breast.

"I need someone to help me here, a manager, someone I can trust. This damned war will be over soon and with Charles gone there is only me and my daughter to run this entire estate. I am not getting any younger and I have no other close relatives or associates who would be up to the task." He paused momentarily, swilled the brandy around before taking another sip. "I wonder, Sergeant, if you would consider taking the post when you return? I will of course provide you with accommodation, your keep, and a realistic salary. The work will be hard and my expectations are high, but it will be a good living and I am sure you will make a go of it. What do you say?"

Although astonished and delighted by the offer, Jamie was also exhausted and suffering from the combined effects of the evening's exertions, his burns and the brandy. Maybe if his judgement had been more settled or his head a little less in thrall to his heart, he might have taken the opportunity presented to him at face value and left the main prize for a later date.

But right then, in Edward Townshend's panelled study, all he could see in front of him that night was a previously unimaginable future laid out before him on a plate, ready for the taking.

"I am flattered greatly by your confidence in me, sir, and of course I accept your generous offer. I expect to be sent back to the war soon, so, as you have already stated, I will not be able to take up the post yet awhile. There is one thing however, that I may be able to secure before I leave, one very important request that you may feel more able to grant after this night's events."

Edward Townshend's smile eased a little at Jamie's words and he took another mouthful of brandy, inhaling the fumes deep into his lungs.

"Well, come on man, spit it out."

"Mr Townshend sir, your daughter Penelope and I... you see, we love each other very much. We have done so for some while now and I humbly ask if you would consider granting me her hand in marriage. I know we cannot possibly be wed until I return from the war, but we would beg your blessing on our betrothal."

At that moment, the only sound to be heard in that room was the slow and steady tick of a grandfather clock.

Jamie waited, hoping and praying.

But when Edward spoke at last, his voice was entirely devoid of warmth.

"Ah. I knew there was something. I have been watching my daughter closely these last months and I have seen changes in her, distractions, a more care worn nature than one would expect from someone her age. May I ask how long this, er, liaison has been going on?"

"Since last summer, sir, while I was putting the finishing touches to the Annabella... the boat."

After another long silence, Edward spoke again, his voice lowered this time as if to prevent his being overheard.

"Good God, man. Have you no shame to confess such a thing as if it were no more than a trifle, an exchange of gifts!?"

Jamie smiled wistfully. "No sir, I have no shame, nor I am certain has Penelope. And, now you come to mention it, an exchange of gifts is a remarkably good way of describing what we have."

"Enough!" The shout was loud enough to rattle glasses in the drinks cabinet. "I will not hear another word on the subject. I would remind you that this is my daughter you are referring to, my daughter, do you understand?" He gripped the arms of his chair, fighting to remain calm.

"Sergeant Kirkpatrick. You are a brave and resourceful young man. These past months I have developed a high regard for your commitment to your work and, until this evening, your integrity." He tossed back the remains of his brandy and poured himself another generous measure from the decanter at his side. No such refill was offered to Jamie.

"These are strange and terrible times and, under such circumstances, I am prepared to make allowances. But there are things I am not prepared to overlook. You and my daughter are both young and inexperienced in the ways of this world, despite her extensive education and your own recent experiences in the war. You have seen little and know even less. Your life in particular has, until recently, been conducted in two places only, your home and here at Hawkswell. Penelope, on the other hand, has already travelled extensively both in this country and in Europe. For heaven's sake man, you are different creatures with entirely dissimilar histories and even more diverse futures. Penelope's ancestors fought at Agincourt, against Cromwell, and at Wellington's side at Waterloo. You and she are made of different clay, can't you see that? To marry my daughter would be to ruin her. I have no other heir. When I die, she will inherit all this." He swept his arm in an arc to encompass the room, the house and the rest of the estate.

"Would you ask her to throw all this away, her very birth right?"

Jamie pushed himself up from his chair and stood with his fists tightly clenched at his sides.

"Sir," he said, striving to remain civil, "We are in love. Can you not understand that? Were you not also in love once yourself? History makes no difference to that. I know we speak differently, that we wear different clothes, but we are all just flesh and blood. We eat, breathe and sleep the same. I have been fighting alongside men from all walks of life these past terrible weeks. Bank clerks, painters, poets, train drivers, farm labourers as well as all those from far more privileged backgrounds than mine. We all smell the same after a while."

He knew his words were running away with him, but what needed to be said had to be said. "Soon there will be no more classes. All that is ending right now, over there in those bloody trenches. Things are changing, and if you can't see it, if you can't accept it, it will destroy you. You must see that!"

His last words hung in the air like cordite smoke, and when Edward Townshend spoke, his voice was hard and cold again.

"That's enough of this Bolshevik nonsense. I refuse to hear another word. I am prepared to forget what you have told me about your relationship with my daughter and, considering what you have been through, I won't have you thrashed for your impertinence. But if I hear one more mention of this radical madness, I will see that you receive the severest punishment the law will allow, do you understand?"

But he was too late. His words fell on deaf ears. Jamie was far beyond the reach of threats or intimidation, the ice cold calm of battle having steeled his nerve.

"I fought alongside your son, Charles. He was killed by a bullet that made no class distinction. I have seen piles of corpses, German and British, officers and enlisted men all tangled together, their blood, sweat, shit and vomit stirred together in the mud. How come your son and I can fight and die side-by-side and yet your daughter and I have no chance of living out our lives together? Can you answer me that?"

He saw the blood drain from Edward Townshend's face as he hauled himself to his feet.

"How dare you bring my son into this? How dare you! You are not fit to speak his name. You are insane, I say, quite insane! The shelling has done for your senses. You no longer belong in this house or on my land. Get out and never let me set eyes on you again! Get out!"

After standing his ground for a moment, Jamie realised the sheer futility of his situation and he stumbled from the room, tears of impotent rage blinding his eyes. He ran out of the house, across the lawns and down to the river, to the one place he hoped he might find the peace and time to figure out how everything had gone so terribly wrong.

Later that evening, shaved despite the burns on his face and dressed in his uniform, Jamie presented himself at the front door of Hawkswell, determined to see Penelope even though he knew there was no chance of resolving his differences with her father.

He was met at the door by a stony faced Brian Gerrard who told him that Edward Townshend refused to see him and that Mistress Penelope had been sent away earlier that afternoon to stay with relatives. When Jamie pleaded with him for understanding and help, he was told that he must leave the house and grounds immediately or the police would be called and he would be treated as a trespasser. Brian whispered that he was sorry but had no choice.

Despite being desperate to speak to Penelope, Jamie was aware that if he was arrested he would be turned straight over to the military police. So he collected his pack from his room together with a blanket and some scraps from the kitchen and took himself off the estate and up into the woods above the river.

There he built himself a rough bivouac and sat, staring down through a gap in the trees at the lights of Hawkswell House far below wondering what his precious girl was doing right then. Was she curled up asleep in her bed or lying awake and thinking of him? What he prayed for above anything else was that she hadn't gone down to the boathouse that night, because then she would be desperate to know where he was.

What he couldn't possibly have known was that Penelope had already been told that he had been ordered to return to his unit without delay and that he had left without saying goodbye or even leaving a note. Returning from Hawkswell village confused and grief-stricken, she had refused to join her father for dinner and locked herself in her room. Even as Jamie sat, huddled in his greatcoat on the hill, she too was staring out into the darkness waiting for dawn and an end to her nightmare.

After a sleepless night, Jamie made his way back down to the house, believing that he could hardly be arrested for marching up to the front door in full daylight. He left his rifle and equipment in the woods, not wishing to provoke more than absolutely necessary.

He got no further than Hawkswell's gates.

There he was confronted by three large men he didn't recognise, who had obviously been told to look out for him and to deny him access to the estate. When he steadfastly refused to leave without speaking to either Penelope or her father, one of the men ran back to the house. Fifteen minutes later he returned with Edward Townshend, who was carrying a shotgun. He told the men to wait further down the drive and positioned himself at the midpoint of the gateway, his feet wide apart and the shotgun levelled at Jamie's belt buckle.

"You will leave this place immediately Sergeant, or I will treat you to a dose of buckshot!"

Despite the threat, Jamie stood his ground. "I wish to speak to your daughter, sir. Just that, no more. I give you my word that I will leave then with no trouble."

The old man paused for a moment before delivering his carefully constructed lie, the devastating consequences of which he could not have envisaged even in his worst nightmares. It was the lie that would lead directly to Jamie's death in Howk's well and Penelope, so precious to both men, being overwhelmed by a madness and despair from which she would never fully recover.

"That is something you will never do again, Mister Kirkpatrick. My daughter is beyond your reach now. She was dispatched on this morning's train to Liverpool where she is booked passage on a ship bound for Canada. I have relatives there who will be glad to receive her and keep her as long as I wish. She was happy to go and left me no message for you, sir. I have also sent a message to the military police barracks in Salisbury informing them that you have deserted, and so I suggest that you find them before they find you. Now be gone from here and may you rot in hell."

With that, the man closed the big iron gates and dropped the latching bar in place before summoning the three men who stood facing Jamie through the bars. Edward left them with a single instruction before marching back towards the house.

"If he tries to get past you, break his legs. You won't have to stay here long, the military police should arrive within the hour and they'll deal with him."

It was over.

As the realisation dawned on Jamie that he would never again walk the paths and lawns of Hawkswell, he glanced up at each of the guardian lions atop their tall brick columns, then at the gates that had so recently defined paradise but were now barred against him.

His eyes glazed with exhaustion and anguish as he stood, rooted to the ground, unable to take the first step away from all his dreams, his fists clenching and unclenching at his sides, silent tears coursing down his face.

What a fool he had been to have even dreamt that he could cross the yawning gulf between his world and Penelope's.

His father's words echoed in his head from a market day in Killarney when he had caught a glimpse of a beautiful woman stepping down from an immaculate carriage. He had stood stock still and stared in wide mouthed wonder until his father pulled him away.

"Fishes and birds, Jamie. All God's creatures under His heaven, but from such different worlds, they can never be one and one together."

He had been left in no doubt as to who was the fish.

The air was hot and heavy as he dragged his broken heart back up the hill towards his bivouac. He would never see Hawkswell in daylight again.

Chapter 33

Hawkswell House, June 1983

Three years on, Hawkswell's gateposts still stand tall, their rain and wind softened guardians staring out across a landscape barely changed since they were first carved. A brand new pair of gates, perfect facsimiles of the originals, stand open and welcoming. The small sign discouraging tradesmen and vagrants has gone, replaced by a much bolder, carefully crafted slab of local stone etched with the words 'Hawkswell House – The Summerquest Institute'.

So much has happened since those entrance pillars were first raised. Two world wars and countless other conflicts across a troubled world. So much traffic has passed through, from horse drawn traps and carriages to modern cars and lorries. And the people – so many individuals, some merely to visit for a few hours or days, others to remain for a lifetime – all of them touched in some way by their time spent at Hawkswell.

The drive now curves between banks of carefully tended rhododendrons. The potholes are gone, replaced with a clean sweep of smooth black tarmac. But any familiarity fades as you round the final bend.

The ornamental lake, now cleaned and restored to its former glory, forms a backdrop to the faithfully recreated Peto garden, its symmetrical beds alive with Gertrude Jekyll inspired swathes of colour.

As for the house, it will cause you to stop and look again. At first glance, it is Hawkswell as it might have looked when it was first built. But, you remind yourself, that is impossible, the original house having been continuously altered and modified over generations.

Next you will most likely notice the windows. They are larger than before, the whole frontage more open, somehow lighter, more confident. It is only then that you will realise that this is a brand new building. From the elegant sweep of steps leading up to the wide and welcoming entrance, to the clusters of false chimneys outlined against the summer blue sky, the entire building is a modern evocation of all the elegance that had once been. It stands as a tangible link between past and present.

And there is life here too, a buzz, a vibrancy. People from all corners of the world walk amongst the trees and richly planted borders, men and women from all sectors of society, deep in conversation while others gather around a circular conference table beneath by a wide canvas pavilion.

You will hear laughter, voices raised in debate, music from another part of the house. There are no divisions here, neither of class or culture, race or belief. The changes in the structure of society that Jamie foretold have come to pass, not least here at Hawkswell.

The beautifully tended lawns beyond the house sweep down to a river now cleared of weeds, its banks buttressed and restored, its willows freshly pollarded and bright with new growth against the sparkling water. The boathouse too has changed, although at first glance less so than the house. Its roof line is straighter, the whole leaning a little less towards the water. And there is a boat, drawn up on the little beach on the far side of the island – a rowing skiff, the sun sparkling on its varnished gunwales.

And there, well beyond sight or sound of the house, hidden behind a high grassed bank, there lies an indentation in the ground. No more than four metres across, its proportions echo those of a cupped hand, its depth barely enough to screen it from the outside world. An echo maybe of the hollow where

Thomas Howk first discovered his well, although this time without a hole at its centre, nor any livestock to mar its charm.

This is Kate and Daniel's special place, their personal sanctuary. Daniel's rowing, under Kate's tutelage, is improving steadily. They race as a coxless pair whenever they can, although Kate has been finding it a little more difficult to get in and out of a boat lately.

Being six months pregnant doesn't exactly help.

She and Daniel were married exactly two years after they first met, the wedding attended by the combined staff of both GreenGauge and the Summerquest Institute. Even Daniel's parents made the effort although Daniel reckoned that their attendance had a lot more to do with the prospect of meeting Sir Arthur and Lady Summers than in seeing their son happily married. Kate told him he was being cynical but secretly admitted to a very similar opinion.

Although long past any reasonable retiring age, Tom Gerrard has thrown himself into the work of restoring and re-planning the estate with twice the energy of a man half his age while May, as resolute as ever, keeps the home fires burning back in the village.

The atmosphere at Hawkswell was predetermined from the moment the first workmen commenced clearing the rubble of the old house, a task undertaken with infinite care under Daniel's watchful eye, each stone stacked for cleaning ready to be incorporated into the new building. Somehow, everyone involved felt compelled to make the place special right from the start.

Given an empty canvas, the Institute, through its combined board of Trustees and Governors, could have built a brand new, purpose designed centre on the ashes of Hawkswell. They could have built on another part of the estate, further from, or nearer to the river, built larger, smaller, in steel and glass or concrete and plastic. But if they for one moment believed they had a free hand to do as they wished, they reckoned without Kate and Daniel Lewis.

During the months after the fire, while they both slowly recovered from their ordeal and the insurance claims and inquests and investigations were convened, conducted and concluded, they planned the resurrection of Hawkswell together.

Centred around the well shaft and based soundly on the original footprint, their combined vision of the new house quickly won over the few sceptics.

Environmentally and aesthetically sound throughout, the new house proved a perfect marriage of the very best architectural advances of the last hundred years with the accumulated style and elegance of the last five centuries.

The main part of the building provides the broad, impressive frontage and contains conference facilities, administrative offices and a ball room that doubles as a plenary chamber. The north wing features kitchens and a dining hall with guest accommodation on the first floor. However, it is the South wing that has undergone the most fundamental change. The ground and first floors, together with the re-built well chamber, have become the Institute's reference library, while the top floor has become a spacious apartment for Kate and Daniel – a light and airy dwelling, with picture windows that overlook the lawns and the river, and enough room for their expanding family. There are no servants quarters at the new Hawkswell, today's staff share the same accommodation as the people they serve.

And what of Howk's Well itself?

After the falling rubble had blocked the continuation shaft, the river had continued rising until it punched an untidy hole in a downstream farmer's meadow and carved itself a new channel to reach the river.

As soon as it was safe to do so, teams of divers removed the debris that was blocking the shaft and the lake quickly regained its original level while the newly formed tributary dried up as if it had never been. The farmer's meadow was repaired and the new hole filled in.

Cave diving teams were allowed access to the system right up until rebuilding work was scheduled to commence and, during that period, the entirety of the accessible system was mapped and surveyed along with the course of the underground river. Many long standing questions were answered although no trace was ever found of either Jamie or Penelope. Their bodies lie somewhere deep underground, hopefully, as Kate expressed, together.

A number of submersible pumps have been installed below the well shaft to supply that specially reliable water to the new house and its residents and guests. No mention has ever been made of the legend.

There are no plans to install a turbine, although it remains a possibility for some time in the future. The mouth of the shaft is now protected by a heavy iron grille, only ever unlocked to provide maintenance access to the water pumps.

At Kate's insistence, a substantial steel ladder has also been installed to reach all the way down to the water's surface.

The sump beside Hawkswell's main gate was filled in and the pipe from the spring in the woods removed. Further exploration carried out at the time, proved that Daniel had been correct in his supposition that the spring was directly linked to the underground river.

The main conference area at Hawkswell was named for Penelope and her family – The Townshend Hall – while a second, smaller arena on the first floor was named for Jamie – The Kirkpatrick Suite – although, as Kate pointed out, the entire estate was, in some ways, a memorial to both. If they had not met and fallen in love, and Jamie not met his tragic end in Howk's Well, Penelope would not have felt so compelled to keep Hawkswell unchanged. She would have sold up and moved away, leaving the house to its fate.

Despite their historical significance, Jamie's letters to Penelope have never been, nor will they ever be, published. Carefully restored, they now reside within the secure conservation area of the Institute's library.

Occasionally, when Kate's unborn baby is restless or the night is too warm or too windy to sleep, she will sit by her bedroom window and gaze out at the night blanketed landscape, down towards the river, to where the boathouse nestles within its line of willows.

And if, as sometimes happens, she is still awake when the dawn light slips through the trees on the ridge above the house to lift gentle shapes from the solid black of night, she will watch the dew silvered grass appear like a slowly developing photograph.

Then, if she is very lucky, for a few fleeting moments, she may glimpse two faint lines of footprints curving down across the grass slope between the house and the river bank before disappearing like a long forgotten memory.

She has never mentioned these sightings to Daniel, preferring to keep them to herself as a gentle reminder of Hawkswell's secretive past and the tragically short love story that was Penelope and Jamie.

The End
© David Hermelin, 2015

ACKNOWLEDGEMENTS

Firstly, an apology to the residents of Newport, Rhode Island, and anyone else who has ever visited the place – I know there is no breakwater at the southern end of Goat Island, especially not a high one. I am afraid that my invention of such a thing is part and parcel of the wonderful world of fiction. If it ain't there, just make it up. Anyway, I'm sorry if I have caused any offence.

Now to the inevitable thanks. Along with the dedication, I must thank my wife, Sam, for her enduring patience and encouragement. Being married to a writer can't be easy, especially when you can never quite be sure what world he is inhabiting at any particular moment! Further thanks are due to Andy Morton for his invaluable nautical advice, Cheryl Meddeman for her editing skills, and Sam Llewellyn – one of my all time favourite novelists – for his forensic dissection of an earlier manuscript, and for his resulting advice and encouragement. Finally, thanks to all the friends who have read and commented on earlier versions of the story. Don't worry folks, this is it, no more re-writes!

Printed in Great Britain
by Amazon